FORBIDDEN BOSS

A MANHATTAN BILLIONAIRES NOVEL
BOOK 6

LILIAN MONROE

ONE

NIKKI

ON THE SEVENTH day of my employment at the Blakely Advertising Agency, I found myself locked in a room with a giant dildo. That was unfair; it wasn't really a dildo—at least, not in the sense that I was familiar with them—but it *was* distinctly phallic. And huge.

As the minutes bled into one hour, and then two, I stared at the giant bottle of perfume that was to be the star of an advertising campaign for an emerging luxury fashion house, and I saw dick.

"I think it's the slight curvature," I told my friend Penny, who was busy wrangling her toddler. "And there's a texture to the bottle that if you squint, looks almost...vascular. And the shape of the bottle itself doesn't help. Like an elongated bullet with a bit of a flared tip to accommodate the spray nozzle. They've put it on a little trolley with some fake clouds clumped around the base that are very testicular."

The phone ruffled and a child squealed in the background. Penny huffed into the microphone and said, "Why the clouds?"

"The theme of the shoot is celestial sensuality. Models wearing gauzy dresses and shimmer all over their bodies reclining in the clouds while they hug this thing."

"So it's intentional."

"You'd think so, but no one has mentioned it."

That seemed to get Penny's attention. "You mean you've been working on this shoot for a couple of days, and no one has mentioned that the bottle is a giant cock?"

"They keep talking about the freshness of the scent and the aspirational nature of the campaign. Taking people to heaven."

"Let me guess. A man came up with this concept?"

I barked out a laugh, leaning against one of the wire shelves behind me. "Yep. They say Mr. Blakely himself was the brain behind this one."

"The guy who owns the company?"

"Yeah. Apparently the client loved the idea, and they've run with it ever since. Yesterday they shot with smoke and glitter, hence me having to wash and polish this thing."

Penny giggled. "So you've been stuck in a room for two hours rubbing down a giant—"

"Yep."

"And no one's mentioned it."

"Nope."

"How long did it take for you to figure out you were locked in?"

"About twenty minutes."

"What's taking so long? Why aren't they getting you out of there?"

"Took forever to find the keys, then they figured out the lock was broken, then their usual locksmith was on vacation, so they had to call around to get someone over here quickly. Now the longer I look at this thing, the more it looks like a huge dildo."

"Maybe it's all in your head. Maybe you need to get laid," she suggested.

I considered Penny's words. After all, it had been a while since I'd been with a man. I let my gaze trace the six-foot perfume bottle and said, "No. It's definitely a huge cock."

Penny giggled, then gasped and told me, "Nikki, I need to go. Timmy just spilled juice all over our kitchen floor." Her four-year-old was cute as a button and also happened to be an absolute terror with more energy in his little toe than I had in my entire body. That she'd been able to chat as long as she had was a surprise.

"All right. Thanks for entertaining me for a while."

"I wish I could talk longer. Any word on when you're getting out of there?"

"The locksmith should be here any minute."

"Text me when you're out."

"Will do," I replied, staring at the giant penis. It had to be intentional. There was just no way dozens of people could design and approve this bottle without knowing they were mass-producing perfume-filled phalluses. Just no way.

"Nikki?" a voice called out through the metal door. "How are you doing?"

It was Eleanor, the prop stylist for the shoot. She was a few years younger than me, in her mid-twenties, and she'd been the only person to befriend me on set so far. Over the whole of the studio was a thick sense of urgency, a palpable fear of messing up. Thankfully for them, I was here to take the fall for everyone as the daily screwup.

"I'm okay," I answered.

My prison wasn't the worst place to be. The storage room had light and air, and I'd been able to sit on one of the tables on the back wall. One side of the room was covered in shelving that held various props and cleaning supplies. I'd been tasked with polishing the penis before its big moment on stage. It wasn't until I was done rubbing it down with a microfiber cloth that I realized the door behind me wouldn't open. I had to call Eleanor before anyone even noticed something was wrong. That had been nearly two hours ago.

"The locksmith was stuck in traffic but he's down with security as we speak, so it won't be long."

"Thank you. Is everyone freaking out about the shoot being delayed?"

There was a pause. "It's not too bad."

I snorted. "Be honest."

Through the door, I heard Eleanor's soft huff. "Ophelia's losing her mind. She's rushing around trying to get everyone to get back to work, but there's nothing to do until we can get the perfume bottle out. The last shot we need is with the big one."

I eyed the proverbial big one through slanted eyes. "Right. Why is she so worried all of a sudden?" And where was this urgency two hours ago, when the lock on that stupid door first jammed? It took them nearly forty minutes of messing around with keys before they even contacted a locksmith.

"Well..." Eleanor dropped her voice so I had to press my ear to the door. "I heard someone say Rome Blakely is on the way down."

"Ah," I answered. "That explains it."

"Ophelia's worried he'll fire her on the spot. It's costing them a hundred thousand dollars an hour to hold the talent here for this project." They'd hired famous models for the shoot, but the number still staggered me.

"That's a lot more than I get paid in a year," I noted.

"You and me both, girl."

Cringing, I tried the door handle again, just in case. It rotated into nothing, not engaging the latch to open the door.

"Would he really fire her for something that isn't her fault?"

"Well...he's been known to fire people for less."

I heard the subtext of her words and swallowed thickly. "So my new job might be over a lot faster than I expected, is what you're saying."

"This wasn't your fault," she protested, but her voice lacked conviction.

"Right."

"Ophelia's calling me. The locksmith will be here soon."

I grunted halfheartedly. The minute that door opened, my employment at this advertising agency would be over.

New York is an at-will employment state, so if Mr. Blakely did see fit to pin this disaster on me, it wouldn't be the first time I was let go for less-than-scrupulous reasons. The whole reason I was working this crappy job in the first place was because my previous boss decided he didn't want to follow through on his promises to promote me. When I finally worked up the nerve to ask him about it, he fired me instead. That was *after* I'd paid for a business management certificate out of pocket after he'd told me he'd reimburse me once I got promoted.

Like an idiot, I'd bought his bullshit. Had the debt to prove it.

A consultant had informed my former boss it'd be cheaper to replace me than to pay me what I was worth, and that was the end of that.

Life hadn't exactly been going according to plan lately. The loss of my job seemed to be the first domino in a long line of increasingly alarming events. First, the promotion turned into a firing, leaving me high and dry with a useless certificate and a lot of debt. Then the landlord for the rent-controlled apartment I'd been living in for years told me he wouldn't be renewing my lease, so I had three months to find somewhere halfway afford-able if I didn't want to end up on the street. That was just over two months ago, so time was ticking.

Then, the cherry on top of the crap sundae, the guy I'd been half-seeing told me he met someone else.

It nearly broke me, which hadn't made sense to me at the time. I didn't love the guy, and he didn't love me, but his rejec-tion stung. It was so patently clear that I'd been a placeholder for him while he looked for a woman he wanted to keep. And maybe I'd been a placeholder for my landlord, so he could make some money off his place while he lived his life elsewhere. And, hell, maybe I was a placeholder for my old boss, who let go of me without so much as a reference.

And now I was stuck in a room with a giant glass cock filled with pink perfume.

One of many dicks that had done me wrong lately.

Grimacing at the pink phallus, I admitted the truth: It was the loss of my job that had really hurt. I'd been working for a vintage clothing store as a manager and buyer. I'd go out and purchase all kinds of treasures, then care for them and put them for sale in our store. Looking back on it in the weeks of unemployment that followed, I realized that the owner had taken advantage of me for a long time.

I had started as a sales associate and quickly started taking on tasks outside of my job description. Much of the time I spent trawling through online consignment shops and thrift stores was unpaid. I told myself I enjoyed the activity—and didn't I want the shop to be as good as it could be?

But the truth was, I should have been paid for that time. I should have *demanded* to be paid for that time. Instead, I drank in the empty promises of a promotion that included health insurance, dental, and a 401k match that would see me through my golden years, and the reimbursement of the school fees I'd incurred for upskilling.

What a bunch of bull.

I'd been a placeholder. A convenient person who went above and beyond because she thought she was appreciated, but really, she was a chump. Maybe that's what I should've put on my resume to get people to hire me. Nikita Jordan: Will go above and beyond for free because she was, in fact, born yesterday.

A knock at the door drew my attention.

"Hello?" I called out.

"Locksmith," an older man's voice proclaimed. "Give me a few minutes and I'll get you out."

My shoulders dropped in relief. "Thank you." I moved toward the table and crossed my arms to wait for the locksmith to do his thing.

But instead of the door opening and sweet relief flooding my veins, I stared at the dull gray metal of the door and listened to the old man's frustrated grunts.

I moved closer. "Is everything okay?"

"Lock won't budge. Have to take it apart."

I jumped back when there was a bang on the door.

"Stupid thing," the old man grumbled.

Then, another voice. This one younger and more commanding. "Why isn't this door open? What's the holdup?"

"Buddy, I'm trying here," the locksmith protested.

"Try harder," the other man said, danger laced through his words.

"Sir, he only just arrived," I heard Ophelia simper from a little farther away.

And I understood. The second man was Rome Blakely, billionaire, entrepreneur, and dick-loving advertising mogul. My gaze narrowed on the steel door, then shifted to the pink penis.

I'm not sure what came over me then. It was some kind of deep, seismic shift in the very core of me. I'd been tossed aside by so many people so many times recently—and not so recently —and I was sick of it. Facing down the end of my employment, I discovered that this arrogant man being rude to a poor locksmith was pushing me closer and closer to the edge.

Blakely said, derision dripping from his voice, "How hard could it be to get a simple lock open?"

The locksmith said nothing, and the silence on the other side of the door turned oppressive.

My boss's boss's boss said, "Well?"

And I couldn't take it anymore. Who was he, to treat this nice, grumpy, old locksmith like he was dirt under his shoe? I didn't see Rome Blakely picking up the tools to get me out of here. And besides, I was about to get fired anyway! It was just another injustice in a long line of injustices delivered by men who were far wealthier and more privileged than me.

And I was sick of it. "Back off, Blakely," I snapped. "He's just trying to do his job."

The silence thickened, but I was filled with too much righteous fury to let it bother me. I crossed my arms and glared at the door. "Well?" I said, echoing his rudeness.

"And who do we have hiding on the other side of this door?" he finally said, voice slithering through the gaps around the door toward me.

"Like you care," I responded. "Just let this guy do his job and get out of the way."

"I'm finding that I do care," the billionaire on the other side of the steel barrier responded. "After all, you know my name. Shouldn't I know yours?"

"Sir, it's Nikki Jordan. A new hire. Don't worry about her. She'll be gone before the end of the day."

I heard the man hum. "And how did Nikki Jordan get herself locked in the room with the single most important asset for this campaign?"

Somehow, I knew that despite the way he'd phrased the question, it was directed at me. So I responded accordingly. "Nikki Jordan did what she was told and buffed the giant perfume-filled dildo to a high shine"—the gasps on the other side of the door should have been a warning that I'd gone too far by mentioning the unmentionable, i.e., the fact that we were advertising male genitalia instead of fragrance, but outrage had buoyed me, and the man was just a faceless entity on the other side of a locked door. At that moment, he couldn't hurt me. Nothing could hurt me. So I continued—"only to discover that Rome Blakely failed to maintain the operation of the locks in the building that bears his name, and she found herself locked in a small, windowless room for"—I checked the time on my phone—"two hours and seventeen minutes."

The only sound I heard was the rushing heartbeat in my ears and my heavy breaths filling the small space.

But hey—I'd already lost my job. What did I care if I made an enemy along the way?

"Got it!" the locksmith exclaimed, and something metallic clattered on the other side of the door. "But—" He grunted, and there was a muffled thump on the other side of the door.

"What seems to be the problem?" Mr. Blakely asked in a slow drawl.

"It's jammed somehow. Hey, lady, is the hinge on the door okay in there?"

I took a step to the side and inspected the hardware. "One of them seems wonky. When I first opened the door to get in here, it was a bit sticky."

"I think the hinge failed," the locksmith explained, "and it put pressure on the locking mechanism, snapping this piece here. You really should go for higher-quality locks, especially somewhere that's getting this much traffic. I would never recommend a hook lock like this for this type of door."

"Fascinating," the jerk who owned the building replied. "Now get it open."

"That might require a pry bar of some sort."

"I'll get maintenance up here," Ophelia said, then called out, "Ben! Get maintenance up here."

I pursed my lips and moved away from the door to lean against the table on the back wall again. In a strange way, I didn't want the door to open. Once it opened, my job would be over. And I'd have to face the man I'd just sassed. The man who would fire me on sight. The man who would make me start all over again, because once again, they hadn't hired me for me. They'd hired me to be a placeholder until they found someone better.

As my temper cooled, I began to dread the prospect.

The paycheck wasn't much, but it was keeping the loan sharks at bay.

The sound of voices on the other side of the door faded and then increased again. I heard the sound of metal on metal, and the locksmith called out, "Stand back, lady!"

"I'm clear," I replied, straightening.

There was a bit of grunting, the sound of a tool scraping against the door, then a horrible squeaking sound. After a moment, all was quiet except for the locksmith's panting.

"Give me that thing," Mr. Blakely ordered.

"Sir, we'll get one of the grips—"

"Give me the pry bar," he snapped.

My mouth went dry. I gripped the edge of the table with both hands, waiting for the noise of the tool being propped between the door and its frame. There was a scrape, then a beat of silence before the door was flung open with far more force than I expected.

I jumped, letting out a yelp, as the door swung open and flew toward the metal shelving.

And here's where I might have messed up. The giant perfume bottle was on a wheeled dolly since it weighed a few hundred pounds. But as I'd vigorously buffed it, I'd found it hard to get some of the scuff marks out while the caster wheels let it move around. I'd tried hugging it with one arm while my free hand buffed, as unpleasant as that had been, but I kept leaving marks on it with my supportive arm. They didn't have any locks on the dolly's wheels, so I'd jammed it into the bottom of the metal shelves.

So the door flew open, and I caught a glimpse of Rome Blakely's silhouette. He was in his shirtsleeves and tie, with a big metal bar grasped in strong hands. A dark lock of hair had fallen over his forehead, and his eyes were filled with a violent sort of victory.

Then the door hit the dick. The giant phallus, with its base jammed into the bottom of the shelving, was forced to bear the brunt of all of Rome Blakely's considerable strength. The door slammed into the perfume bottle with enough force to make it rebound toward its frame.

Then a few things happened at once.

Mr. Blakely put his foot in the opening and stopped the door from closing again. I didn't have time to be grateful, though, because the giant perfume bottle, being tall and slender, began to wobble.

Had the testicle-clouds been made of something solid, they might have been strong enough to hold the penis-bottle upright. Being made of fluffy cloud-like material, however, they failed to stop the bottle from wobbling.

In retrospect, I should have let the thing smash on the ground. Maybe the bottle wouldn't have broken. Maybe all the drama that followed could have been avoided, if I'd just sat back and let things happen the way they would.

But I was a good girl. I was a little worker bee who always jumped in to help when I was needed. That's how I'd ended up doing the job of four people for my old boss, and why every romantic interest seemed to slowly learn to take advantage of me. Why I always had been, and always would be, a stepping stone that people used while they were waiting for something better.

So, when the six-foot-tall cock began to tip toward me, I leaped forward to catch it. It, however, had the advantage of being taller and heavier than I was, and already on the way down.

I felt a sharp pain in my finger as it jabbed against the glass phallus. Then I tried to divert the thing's descent but only managed to slam it against the shelving and nick the edge of it.

I heard a roared, "Get away from it!" and finally had the good sense to listen.

Cool glass kissed my leg as I stumbled and fell back, and then several hundred pounds of cock-shaped perfume fell to the concrete floor and shattered. A glass shard embedded itself below my knee while another slashed across my calf. Blood gushed.

A gasp slipped through my lips as I watched my clothes become soaked with the pink perfume flooding the room. A patch of dark-red blood diffused into the puddle of pink as I stared, not quite understanding. My hand throbbed.

The smell was horrendous. The bottle had actually been filled with perfume, and not some colored water. Why, I had no idea. I didn't know why anyone thought that was a good idea. It was like a scented bomb went off, and suddenly I was dizzy and bleeding and the pain in my finger was unbearable.

It all must have happened within a couple of seconds. Distantly, I heard the clatter of the metal pry bar on the concrete floor, and then strong arms clad in a crisp white shirt were siding beneath my knees and around my back, and my boss's boss's boss was picking me up.

"I'm bleeding on your shirt," I noted.

"Quiet," he barked.

"It's white. It looks expensive."

"I don't care about the shirt. You! Call an ambulance. You, Ophelia. Get a towel. Bring that table over, we need to set her down. And open a damn window."

The edges of my vision were going fuzzy. The fingers of my uninjured hand felt clumsy as I reached up to feel the fabric of his shirt between my fingers. "Good-quality cotton. The fil-a-fil is a nice touch. Subtle blue tinge." I glanced up, then my head lolled when I couldn't keep it up. "Like your eyes."

He had beautiful, startlingly blue eyes. His eyelashes were thick and very black, almost making it look like he wore eyeliner. Some people had all the luck.

Those remarkable eyes met mine. He was angry for some reason. "Will you stop talking?"

"Why?" I asked, surprised to find my voice was slurring.

I was jarred when he kicked something, and a chair went flying. Then, more gently than I would think him possible, he set me down on a hard surface. Glaring, he said, "I told you to be quiet. You're bleeding."

"Sorry about your shirt," I said, pouting at the red stain on his arm. "But I already know you're going to fire me, so it's okay."

"Just—don't die, all right?"

"Firing me will be your loss," I told him. I was a star employee, after all. They'd only had me for a week, and they'd put me on dick-polishing duty. "Big mistake for *sure*."

The last thing I saw before everything went black were the dark slashes of his eyebrows drawing together, his full lips pursed in displeasure.

TWO

ROME

THE IMAGE of Nikki Jordan unconscious on the table stayed with me all day. Her mouth had fallen open slightly, her pillowy lips painted a dark, vampy red. Her hair had been arranged in careful waves that had become mussed in the chaos. She wore dramatic eyeliner that had survived without smudging.

She had the face of a difficult, high-maintenance woman, which was no surprise. It had taken me about ten seconds to figure out she was a difficult, high-maintenance woman before I'd ever laid eyes on her.

I hadn't expected her to look the way she did, though. Taller than I'd expected. Curvier, with dramatic features. More striking. Just...more. She'd been wearing a dress that could only be called modest, with a square neckline that didn't show much more than her collarbones and hit well below her knee. But there was something about the way it traced her curves that made it look indecent.

And her shoes. Her shoes had been entirely impractical. No one needed to wear those types of heels to work as a runner in a studio. No wonder she'd been injured. What a ridiculous, difficult, irritating woman. I was glad I didn't need to interact with her any longer. Once had been enough.

Gritting my teeth, I tore off my glasses and tossed them on the desk before rubbing the bridge of my nose. Leaning back in my chair, I cast my gaze over the multitude of lights in the Manhattan skyline. My domain. Today had been chaotic. The past six months had been chaotic, actually. Sales were down and companies were cutting their advertising budgets. People were outsourcing to smaller companies and freelancers. I'd had to halve my copywriting division, and I knew the remaining few were overworked. I was having to work harder to secure new clients, and a lot of our long-term relationships were beginning to feel strained.

"How did the call with Garcia go?" asked my chief operating officer, Cole Christianson, naming the designer behind the perfume bottle that had been destroyed earlier today. He reclined in the seating area across from my desk, one arm thrown across the back of the black leather couch.

I grimaced. "He wasn't happy. It'll take two months to get a replacement bottle of that size. We'll try to use CGI to get the campaign over the line, but he's old school. I think he'll want us to reshoot it, which will push back the launch."

"Old school," Cole repeated with a snort. "I'm guessing that's why they filled the thing with actual perfume instead of dyed water?"

A sigh slipped through my lips. "We talked about water

when we initially pitched the idea, but he said the light refracts through perfume differently. He insisted on the real thing."

"So CGI is definitely not going to work, but we're going to have to spend the money to try."

"Basically, yeah."

"I'm guessing the chick who caused this has been fired?"

I'd met Cole about a decade earlier. He'd been working on Wall Street making more money than he knew what to do with, but he was bored. My company, at the time, was going through its first big growth spurt. I considered it a coup to convince him to work for me at the time, and that sentiment hadn't changed. He was detail-oriented in work and in his personal life, all the way down to the way he matched his socks to his outfit and made sure his beard and hair were trimmed twice a week.

As I watched him lean back, crossing his legs at the ankle, I wondered how long it would take for him to move on from this company. He wasn't a sentimental man, and I was sure he could see the sharks circling around us.

"She's been let go," I confirmed. "Ophelia made it happen this afternoon."

"At least you were able to tell Garcia that."

"He doesn't care," I answered, shaking my head. "All he cares about is art."

"Is that what we're calling the giant glass dick we've been advertising?"

I huffed, unable to stop myself from thinking of the dark-haired beauty we'd just fired—the only other person who'd called a spade a spade—and done it to my face.

Well. She'd been behind the protection of a steel door at the time, but she still said what no one else had.

But she was gone now, and I couldn't afford to give her one more moment of my time, even in my thoughts.

This perfume campaign was crucial. I couldn't afford to mess up. Making sure Garcia was happy with our performance would help us get one step nearer to closing the deal with the other whale in the cosmetics industry: Wilbur Monk. The billionaire owner had been flirting with us for eighteen months about taking over their advertising work for half a dozen of his subsidiary companies. The contract would be worth nine figures. It would lift us out of shark-infested waters and see us through the next few years. I needed that contract—badly.

Which meant I needed the distraction of a woman with red-painted lips and ebony hair like a hole in the head. But she was gone now. Away from this building and away from me. I wouldn't have to worry about feeling her weight in my arms again or having any more of my shirts ruined with bleeding gashes caused by stray shards of glass.

That was a good thing. Everything would be okay.

After a deep breath, I felt calmer.

A chime sounded. Cole checked his phone and let out a soft grunt. "Monk confirmed he's attending the children's hospital fundraiser next week."

I groaned, and Cole laughed.

"Guess I have to go now," I said, grimacing as I jiggled my mouse to wake my computer up. I checked my calendar, only to see that my assistant, Clara, had already scheduled the event in. I scanned the screen and saw more events—dinners, galas, garden parties—sprinkled into every available slot. Monk would be at most of them, and winning his business would mean my attendance would be mandatory.

Sometimes I really hated my job.

"Got a plus-one?" Cole asked with a broad grin.

I gave him a dark look. "You know I haven't."

Cole hummed. "Monk won't like that."

"What I do in my personal life has nothing to do with him. We'll win the contract because we're the best advertising agency in the city. Not because I have a hot date to every social event he attends with his wife."

Cole put his palms up, backing off. "Fine. I was just saying."

Gritting my teeth, I glared at the calendar. The worst of it was, Cole was right. Wilbur Monk had just celebrated his fiftieth wedding anniversary. His wife was his muse and had been since before he'd started working in cosmetics. He credited Roseanne with all his success.

Being single was a mark against me, and I knew it.

"I'm not bringing a plus-one," I repeated in the silence of my office, a little petulantly. "I can't do a relationship, and a revolving door of casual dates to all these events we've got coming up will play worse than if I went alone."

"Heard," Cole replied, but his eyes were on me. "Although..."

I narrowed my eyes. "Although what?"

"I heard through the grapevine that your being on your own is one of the main hang-ups he has about signing on with us."

"That's the stupidest thing I've ever heard."

"He thinks you're untrustworthy."

"Because I'm not married?" I clenched my fists. "I've built this company—this *empire*—and not having a ring on my finger hasn't stopped me once."

"Monk is old school, Rome. We've known this since we first pitched him."

A deep sigh left my lips. One of the things that made Cole so valuable as a COO wasn't just his attention to detail and his ability to know exactly what was happening in every corner of the company, it was the fact that he could read people like an open book. Once, I'd watched him conduct an interview and walk out of the room saying that we could hire the candidate, but we'd regret it. The candidate had been perfect on paper for our accounts department and had interviewed beautifully. Cole hadn't been able to explain his intuition, but he was certain we were making the wrong choice. That employee ended up trying to steal from us within a year and had to be let go. Despite the warning, the employee's attempted theft had blindsided me.

If Cole told me that Wilbur Monk wouldn't hire me if went to these social events on my own, I had to believe him. Pinching the bridge of my nose, I racked my brain to think of something.

"I could call Heather."

"Heather is married to European royalty."

My head snapped up. "What? Since when?"

"A year or so ago."

"A year..." I did a bit of mental math, then leaned back in my chair. "It's been four years since I had a girlfriend. That's longer than I thought."

"Girlfriend is a little generous for what you and Heather had, don't you think?"

At the look I gave him, Cole began to laugh. The worst of it was, he was right. But how could I have a girlfriend when I'd learned a long time ago that when you needed people, they abandoned you? I hated being reliant on anyone. I hated feeling like they could pull the rug out from under me. I hated being vulnerable.

So most of the time, I was alone. Just the way I liked it.

Cole slipped his phone into his pocket as he stood, then said, "What if you hired someone?"

"What, like an escort?" I arched my brows. "That'll go over well with the most famous monogamist in the city."

"Not an escort," Cole mused, his eyes on the city skyline. "A...companion."

"A companion," I deadpanned. "What does that even mean?"

"She would be hired and paid to accompany you to social events as needed."

"And the minute anyone caught wind of it, my reputation would be trashed."

"We'd get her to sign an NDA."

"And how would I introduce her? I don't think my clients would respond well to me lying to their faces at every social event I attend."

"You could just introduce her by her name. Don't give her a title. If someone asks where you met, you say you interviewed her for the position and laugh like it's a joke."

"Monk would go for that?" I was skeptical. It didn't seem like a man who cherished his marriage would approve of a hired companion. If I went for it and Monk found out, I could kiss those nine figures goodbye.

Cole stood by the windows with his arms folded. He glanced at me over his shoulders, tilting his head. "I think Monk believes that we, as men, need a partner's influence to reach our full potential. He might think you're hiding something, but he'd be glad there was someone at your side."

I sighed. "I don't know. I'll see how the children's hospital dinner goes first."

There was a pause, and I knew my second-in-command was considering pressing the issue. Finally, Cole nodded. "All right." He inhaled like he was about to say something but was interrupted by a soft knock on the glass door leading out of my office.

I arched my brows at my assistant, Clara. "Yes?"

"Arthur Knox is here," she told me. "He wants to go over what happened this morning."

I nodded. "Send him in." Glancing at Cole, I asked, "You want to stick around for a few minutes?"

He pursed his lips. "It's never good when Arthur stops by after hours."

I grunted in assent and moved to the small fridge concealed behind wood paneling in the corner of my office. I tossed Cole a bottle of water and grabbed one for myself.

Hearing the shuffling footsteps of my chief legal counsel entering my office, I turned and lifted a bottle to offer it to him.

He waved it away, then tossed his leather-bound portfolio on the coffee table in the office's seating area. "Gentlemen," he greeted. "We have a problem."

Of course we did. I sipped the water, letting it ease my parched throat. "Oh?"

Arthur, having a flair for the dramatic, paused for several long seconds. His face was beginning to show the signs of age, with a network of lines around his mouth and eyes, but he looked younger than his sixty-two years. Dark eyes rested on me, then on Cole, who bore the theatrical pause with the patience of a man who knew that interrupting it would only prolong the pain.

Arthur turned and watched me from beneath thick brows and said, "The production assistant."

I frowned. "The production assistant?"

"The production assistant," Arthur intoned, "is a problem."

"What production assistant?" Cole asked.

"Nikita Jordan," Arthur told him. "Goes by Nikki. Total employment at Blakely was six and a half days."

I blinked. "What about her?"

My lawyer grimaced. "I've spoken to all the witnesses, and it's my professional opinion that she might have a case against the company."

Condensation beaded on my bottle and wetted the tips of my fingers as I tried to make sense of the lawyer's words.

Cole was the first to speak, leaning his hands on the back of the sofa across from where Arthur sat. His gaze was intent. "A case for what? Her injuries? We'll handle the workers' comp claim. She survived, yes?"

Arthur waved a hand. "She's in the hospital as we speak. A few stitches and a broken finger. She's fine."

I set my bottle down and wiped my hands on a towel hanging on the rail of my bar cart. "So what's the problem?"

"She was hired as an independent contractor. This injury won't be covered under workers' comp."

A gust of breath left me. I scrubbed my face with both hands. "Fine. We'll pay her off. What's the damage?"

"I'm not sure it'll be that simple," Arthur said darkly.

There was another long silence. I watched Cole's fingers

curl into the back of the sofa until his knuckles turned white as he physically stopped himself from leaping over and shaking the older man until he explained himself.

Arthur finally inhaled, straightened his tie, his cufflinks, and his hair. Then he said, "Between the injury, the hours of confinement, not to mention the dismissal that could be constituted as retaliation for the shattering of the perfume bottle..." Arthur pinched his lips. When he spoke, there was nothing theatrical in his face. That's how I knew Arthur wasn't just being dramatic. "It's not good, Rome. And if she were to go to the press about her experience, the optics would be very, very bad."

Cole met my gaze, grimacing. "A lawsuit right now will lose us the Monk contract. And probably half a dozen others. We're on thin ice as it is."

My bottle crunched in my hand. That *woman*. That woman would ruin me, and she'd probably laugh the whole time.

I couldn't let it happen. This company was all I had. Sure, I'd had casual relationships. I had friends and acquaintances and people like Cole, who were somewhere between trusted friends and loyal employees. But the company was the one thing I could point to in my life and say, "I did this."

I wasn't going to let some lipstick-wearing, black-haired viper take it away from me.

I grabbed my suit jacket from the coat hanger where it hung in the corner of my office. "I'll handle it," I told the two other men, then threw open my office door. "Clara!" I called out. "Bring the car around to the front and find out which hospital is treating Nikita Jordan. I have to have a conversation with her."

"Sure thing," she said, pressing a button on her phone to organize things while I headed for the elevator.

This woman had wormed her way into my business and my brain, but I wasn't going to let her destroy everything I'd built. If she was feeling litigious, I'd make sure she knew exactly who she was going up against.

And I wasn't going to go easy on her.

THREE
NIKKI

MY RIGHT RING finger was sprained. The X-ray showed me an unbroken bone, but the thing hurt so much I wondered how it could still be whole. Besides the sprain, I'd needed three stitches on my leg. All in all, things could have been worse. I could have been crushed. The glass could have cut an artery. I could have died in the Blakely Advertising Agency studio, killed by a six-foot penis.

What a way to go.

By the time I got my discharge paperwork, it was just after eight o'clock. I'd been in the hospital for nearly ten hours, most of it spent waiting. My injuries were minor, but I was ready to collapse in bed.

Tomorrow, I'd deal with the fallout. The job search. The rebuild.

The hospital bill.

I'd had a lovely conversation with the hospital's insurance representative when I was lying in a bed waiting to get stitched up. And by "lovely," of course, I mean "short," because I didn't have insurance, and I'd made too much money at my old job to qualify for Medicaid.

Now, falling between the cracks of two jobs, I was screwed.

I didn't know how much the bill would be, but I knew I couldn't afford it. Hell, I couldn't even afford to *live*. And how would I find a new apartment if I couldn't show proof of employment or old paystubs? How could I pay off my stupid, idiotic loan without an income?

Three stitches and a cheap plastic splint on my finger were going to put me in more debt than I'd been in my entire life.

Stupid Rome Blakely and his stupid perfume penis. Buff and polish the giant glass dildo, they said. Do it out of the way so we can keep shooting, they told me.

I'd worked for less than seven full days at that place, and it would cost me all my financial stability. I'd been a placeholder and a fool.

The glass doors whirred as they opened for me, a tired-looking doctor brushing past me as I stepped outside. Cool, damp air surrounded me, but I couldn't take a deep breath. I couldn't seem to think straight.

Apparently, this would be the thing that sent me over the edge. I sank onto a bench under the hospital's high awning, white, fluorescent lights spilling onto the pavement around and in front of me. The emergency department wasn't far away, just on the other side of the parking lot, and I watched an ambulance come in with lights and sirens blazing.

I saw the shape of a person on a stretcher, and I hoped for their own sake they had insurance.

I tried to pull myself back from the brink. It was just a bill, and I didn't even know how much it would be. For all I knew, by the time I got it, I'd have a new job and a new apartment. At worst, it would be a debt that would take me a few years to pay off. I could handle that. Logically, I knew.

But my eyes stung, and, horribly, humiliatingly, I felt myself begin to cry.

It was getting fired from the vintage clothing store, and then getting the notice to vacate my home, and then getting broken up with, and then the stupid giant dildo-that-wasn't-a-dildo, and then getting fired again. And now this.

How could I ever get ahead? I didn't even know what that meant! Getting ahead? Ahead of who? I didn't want to be ahead of anyone. All I wanted was a bit of stability. As I leaned back against the cool metal of the bench, watching the paramedics close up their ambulance to make space for the next arrival, I wondered how everything had become so bleak.

The logical thing to do would be to ask one of my friends for money. Penny had married a man who made a fortune in tech, and she ran a successful small business of her own making dog clothes. They could probably pay my hospital bill with the loose change from their couch cushions.

Besides, Penny would understand. We'd reconnected a few years ago, and she hadn't been much better off than I was now.

There was Dani and Layla, but I wasn't that close with them, and I hated asking them for money. Then there was Bonnie, but Bonnie was in just as much of a bind as I was. She'd had to take a job as a nanny for a man she'd slept with years ago at a business conference. The only silver lining for her was that he hadn't remembered her.

She wouldn't have the means to help me. The logical choice

was to call Penny for help. I'd known her since college, and we were close.

But I stared at the blank screen of my phone, and it wasn't the hour that stopped me from messaging her.

It was the fact that I was the placeholder.

What if I was a placeholder for her too? What if this friendship had blossomed again after we'd lost touch after college, but if I asked her for this favor, she pulled away? What if we'd reconnected but she didn't *really* care about me, not enough to mix money with friendship?

Then I'd lose her. And I'd lose my friendship with Bonnie and Dani and Layla by association. Sure, we didn't spend as much time together as we did a few years ago, since most of my girlfriends had their children and husbands now. But maybe the gulf between us would just be a little bit too wide to bridge if I pointed out how broke I really was.

It would kill me to realize I was a placeholder for them too.

So I couldn't ask them for money. I couldn't even ask to crash on one of their couches—and by one of their couches, of course, I mean one of the multitudes of luxurious guest rooms they owned in various buildings dotted around Manhattan and beyond.

Asking for help would be tantamount to plastering a big neon sign on my forehead that said, I DON'T BELONG HERE.

A hot tear rolled down my cheek, and I brushed it angrily away, jarring the edge of my splint on my face. Pain lanced through my sprained finger, and I let out a whimper.

Panic and heartbreak and despair whirled around me like I was the eye of the hurricane, and my emotions were the wind and rain wreaking destruction on the life I'd carefully built. I sat in the eye of the storm, dead inside, waiting for the hurricane to flatten me.

That's why I didn't hear his approach until I saw a pair of shiny black shoes come to a stop in front of me.

My gaze traveled up, up, up. Up the perfectly tailored pants with the quarter-break and crisp center pleat. Up the bespoke shirt—white again—that was now without a tie and open at the collar. Up the strong jaw and the hard male lips, until my gaze came to a stop on glittering blue eyes.

We stared at each other for a moment.

"You're crying," Rome Blakely told me with a frown.

"No, I'm not," I replied, stupidly, because I definitely was.

"Did they not give you enough pain meds?" He shifted to look at the sliding glass doors behind me, like he had half a mind to march in there and demand I be treated again.

Maybe I'd hit my head, and I was hallucinating. Why else would the billionaire in charge of the company that had just fired me be standing there?

His jaw clenched, and he returned those thick-lashed eyes to me. "Why are you sitting here on your own?" he demanded.

I reared back. "Why are you here at all?"

He blinked slowly, ignoring my question. I arched a brow, but I was fragile. I didn't have it in me to resist, so I answered his question first. "I was just enjoying the evening air before I head home," I told him, not mentioning the pit of despair I'd accidentally fallen into. "Now it's your turn. Why are you here?"

He nodded to the black sedan idling behind him. "I'm here to take you home."

"What?" I asked his back because he'd already turned to

head to the car. His driver jumped to open the back door for him, and he didn't even deign to give me a glance before disappearing into the dark interior.

The hospital's sliding glass door whirred behind me, and two women walked out, gossiping. They called out a greeting to a third person, and I just sat there staring at Rome Blakely's car like the useless lump I was.

His driver cleared his throat. "Miss?"

"How did you find me?" I asked him.

"The paramedics told us which hospital they were taking you to this morning. Mr. Blakely wanted to make sure you made it home okay."

"I don't believe you," I told him, frowning.

The man's face was impassive. He held the door open and blinked at me, unmoving.

The stubborn part of me considered walking away and getting a cab. But I couldn't afford that. I could take the subway...

But there was a car right there. If a rich, overbearing asshole wanted to drive me right to my door, who was I to refuse? I mean, I enjoyed a bit of true crime now and then and this was definitely how people got themselves murdered, but still. I was tired and brittle, and my finger throbbed.

I stood, meeting the driver's gaze. Then I asked the most important question: "Does he have snacks in there?"

The driver's eyes sparkled. "Yes, miss," he told me.

My own gaze narrowed. "Good snacks?"

"I can't answer that. I don't know what kind of snacks you like. The mini fridge is fully stocked, though."

My shoulders dropped, and I relented. "Fine."

Shuffling to the open car door, I shoved the discharge paperwork in my purse and ducked inside. It was surprisingly roomy, not quite a limo but bigger than a sedan. Blakely was seated beside me, his long legs spread and his arm resting on the window frame.

When the driver closed the door, Blakely leaned forward and pressed a button, and a mini fridge slid open in front of us where the front seats' center console should have been. I saw small bottles of alcohol, a variety of sodas, and a good selection of snacks. I grabbed a chocolate bar that promised to be studded with almonds and a bottle of water.

"Thank you," I told him primly.

Blakely pressed the button again, and the mini fridge disappeared. The car was whisper-quiet as the driver put it in gear. We went around the circular drive and back out toward the hospital's exit. The only noise in the back seat was the crinkling of my chocolate bar wrapper.

"I've never heard of this brand," I noted, inspecting it.

"I get them flown in from Belgium."

"Well, la-di-dah," I said quietly, and took a bite.

At that brilliant riposte of mine, the billionaire in the seat beside me turned to stare at me, the passing streetlights casting his face in alternating light and shadow.

Decadent chocolate exploded over my tongue. I let out a surprised noise, letting the rich flavor melt in my mouth for a moment before crunching through the perfect amount of almonds. I closed my eyes and leaned back, enjoying one more bite before shaking my head. "Wow," I said.

"I'd like you to explain your comments to me," Blakely said, voice harsher than I thought was really warranted.

I frowned over at him, only to find him glaring at my chocolate bar. Maybe it was really expensive, and he'd missed the day in preschool where he was supposed to learn to share?

"What comments?"

His gaze traveled over my now rumpled dress, lingering on my collarbones before rising to my eyes. "You said firing you would be a mistake."

"Well, duh," I said, and took another bite.

That was the thing about being in an expensive car with a very rich man the day that you got fired for getting injured, ruined a multiple-hundred-thousand-dollar photo shoot, and then discovered that not only would you be homeless soon, but you'd also be in a mountain of debt. It tended to put things in perspective.

In other words, I didn't give a rat's ass what this arrogant, privileged man thought of me. I eyed the space where the mini fridge hid, wondering if I could snag another chocolate bar before he dropped me off. They were flown in from Belgium, after all.

"Explain."

I turned to look at him. "Explain what?"

"What kind of mistake are we talking?"

I blinked. "The kind of mistake that you regret, obviously." I frowned at him. Firing me was his loss! I might have been a peon in his company, but I was a hard worker, and I always went above and beyond. I knew I was a valuable employee, even if my previous boss hadn't appreciated me. That was *his* loss too! My old boss would have to hire three people to replace me, and he could stick that in his fancy consultant's pipe and then take the pipe and shove it up his hole.

But Blakely's reaction was strange. His eyes got intense, and his jaw went hard. A muscle feathered in his cheek until he faced forward and took a deep breath, like he needed to gather himself.

I finished the chocolate bar and eyed the mini fridge again before scanning the door on my side. Maybe one of these buttons would open it up. Belgian chocolate was worth looking like a glutton in front of a man I'd never see again.

"The company will cover your medical bill," he finally said in the silence.

I started. "What? Why?" Then, because this was a gift horse and I'd just told it to go *ahh*, I added, "I mean, thank you. That's the least you could do, really."

He hummed, and I watched his hand curl into a fist before stretching out again. All they'd given me at the hospital were a couple of ibuprofen, but maybe they were stronger than what I was used to. I was having trouble following his reactions.

He seemed...stressed? Angry? At me? But why? I hadn't asked him to find me and personally escort me home. That had been his prerogative.

My gaze dropped to the chocolate bar wrapper on my lap. Was he *actually* mad about the chocolate? How much could one chocolate bar cost? Wasn't this guy a bazillionaire?

My eyes were beginning to feel sore, and tiredness was seeping into my bones. All I wanted to do was get away from this guy, curl up in my bed, and feel sorry for myself in peace.

I breathed a sigh of relief as we turned onto my street in Brooklyn. When we came to a smooth stop outside my building, I began to gather myself to leave the strangest car ride in automotive history. Not knowing what to do with the chocolate bar wrapper, I stuffed it into my purse.

"I'd like you to take the rest of the week off," Blakely finally said as his driver circled toward my side of the car to open the door for me. My ex-boss's voice was utterly calm. "Come into the office on Monday and we'll discuss options. My assistant will be in touch to organize it."

I pulled my gaze from the driver's movements outside to look at him again. "Other options for what?"

"I'm sure we can come to a mutually beneficial solution here, Ms. Jordan," he said, his voice dark and silky. The light from outside cast half his face in shadow, carving out the space below his cheekbones and under his bottom lip. "My assistant will be in touch, and we'll go from there."

The door beside me opened. "Okay," I answered, and I got out. The car didn't pull away until I was inside my building, watching its taillights disappear around a corner from the lobby.

I trudged up to my first-floor apartment, locked myself inside, and collapsed on the couch. I had no idea what had just happened, but at least I'd gotten good chocolate for my trouble.

The meeting on Monday was another story.

FOUR

ROME

"SHE'S PLAYING HARDBALL." I bit off the words, meeting Arthur's troubled gaze across my desk. Cole swore and spun around, shoving his hand through his hair. I pushed away from my desk and crossed the few feet to stand by the floor-to-ceiling windows in my office.

Dozens of stories below us, Manhattan squirmed with life. Pedestrians jostled on the streets and cars sped past in a frantic flow of life and energy.

I loved the city. Loved the chaos of it, loved how there was always something to see or do. I'd grown up feeling like a cast-off, like I belonged nowhere. Now, surrounded by the life and turmoil of the millions of residents of Manhattan, I felt like I was part of something bigger than myself.

I'd *built* something bigger than myself. The one thing I was proud of.

And she was going to take it from me.

From all the way up here, the mayhem on the streets was

quiet. All I could hear was the quiet hum of the air conditioning, my computer's fan, and the movements of the two men behind me.

"Explain to me again," I said, watching a cab swerve around a bike messenger and speed around a corner, "why she was hired as an independent contractor."

The tense silence that followed my request prompted me to turn. I met Cole's gaze as he pinched his lips.

"Cost savings," he finally answered.

I swung my gaze to the lawyer rubbing his forehead as he stared at the wood grain of my desk. "Arthur," I asked, "how exposed are we, company wide?"

He grimaced. "You currently have a hundred and seven employees hired as independent contractors. From my preliminary review, at least ninety-three of them could potentially have a case for misclassification."

"Which is—"

"A violation of state and federal employment laws. An independent contractor would have their own office, insurance, logos, letterheads. They maintain their own schedules and have specific deadlines and tasks outlined in their contracts... They're not production assistants running around in a company-owned studio doing tasks set out by their boss."

"Like buffing a perfume bottle for a shoot."

He nodded. "Exactly."

I met the older man's gaze for a long moment, then looked at my second-in-command. "I want a thorough review of every employee in this company. Anyone who's been hired as an independent contractor should either be let go if the terms of their contract have been satisfied, or they should be offered full employment with benefits."

I'd never seen Cole look contrite. He exhaled, then dipped his chin. "Heard. But, Rome, the labor costs alone of—"

"Arthur," I interrupted, heat crawling up my neck. "What's our exposure here? Give me a number."

The old lawyer cleared his throat and adjusted his tie with careful movements. "Well, that depends on if each of them files independently or if we're looking at a class-action suit. And then there's the bad press and the cost of any lost contracts..."

"Give me a number," I repeated, my voice hard.

There was a beat of silence before Arthur said, "We're talking eight figures. And for someone like Ms. Jordan, who also has a case for retaliation since she was let go as a result of a workplace accident... Well, that alone could be disastrous. Even if she settled, if the press got even a whiff of this... It's not a good look, gentlemen. Not a good look at all."

Exhaling, I leaned my palms on my desk. Blood rushed in my ears. I could feel my pulse in my fingertips as I tried to pull myself back together.

I could see it: the end. The end of everything I'd built. The one thing I was proud of, gone. Destroyed by a vengeful woman in red lipstick.

Anger pulsed through me. Anger and something deeper, an itch I couldn't scratch. She thought she could threaten *me*? She thought she could turn around and throw the book at my face because she felt like she'd been slighted?

She didn't have the first idea what hardship was.

I held myself apart from people because this was how I thrived, and I refused to be brought low by the likes of her.

Lifting my head, I met Cole's gaze. "Fix this," I told him. "Immediately."

He nodded, then ducked out of my office. Arthur, grim-faced, waited for me to speak.

It took me another two breaths to get my temper under control to the point that I could say her name. Finally, I gritted out, "Ms. Jordan is coming in on Monday. I want you to sit in on the meeting."

"What's your game plan?" Arthur asked, braiding his fingers over the paunch of his stomach as he leaned back. He frowned his bushy brows, considering me. "If you say she's ready to play hardball, how much are you willing to pay to make this go away?"

I pulled my chair closer and sat down, then woke my computer up with a press of the space bar. Calm descended over me like a weighted blanket. I hadn't built this business without knowing how to react quickly to avert disaster.

Ever since I'd been a small child, I'd had to rely on no one but myself. I'd been born to stand on my own. This was where I thrived.

It was why I didn't have a wife at my side the way Wilbur Monk wanted. It's why relationships never lasted. It was why I was able to take the privileges I *had* been afforded in the form of seed money from my wealthy family and turn it into something much, much bigger.

Nikita Jordan was an existential threat to me, and I had to face that head-on.

This was exactly the type of situation I was made to manage. No one could break me. No one could drag me down.

Weakness had been wrung out of me by the time I was twelve years old, and that wasn't going to change now.

Jordan might have thought she was clever, but I knew the truth: She was a grifter. She'd seen an opportunity, and she was going to squeeze me for everything I had.

Ha. She'd try.

But the woman didn't know what happened to people who threatened me. I hadn't gotten to where I was by rolling over at the first sign of a fight. If she wanted to get a dime out of me, she'd have to earn it. And I wouldn't make it easy on her.

Last night, I'd seen something. She'd been crying when I arrived at the hospital. I watched her pull herself together and hide that vulnerability behind the lash of that sharp tongue of hers.

But it was too late. I knew just how close to the edge she really was.

The woman was desperate.

She was also beautiful, clever, and not afraid to speak her mind. I could use that.

If I played my cards right, I might just be able to wriggle my way out of this mess with no lawsuits at all—and snare Wilbur Monk in the process.

"I'm not going to offer her a pot of gold," I told Arthur. "I'm going to do exactly what we're doing with the other hundred-odd employees who were hired as independent contractors."

He watched me, silent. It was my turn to indulge in a dramatic pause.

I gave him a shark's smile. "I'm going to offer her a job."

FIVE

NIKKI

MY FRIEND PENNY LITTLETON lived in a cool refurbished factory in Soho. Her husband, Marcus, had been living there when he hired Penny as his dog walker. Seeing my bright, smiley friend end up with such a dour man had been a surprise, but I'd seen glimmers of Marcus's personality since then.

Like how whenever he liked one of Penny's outfits, he'd ask her if it was from the Littleton Collection, which I learned was an inside joke between them from Penny blurting out that particular lie to a snooty sales associate at a designer department store.

She'd upcycled the dress herself, using her amazing sewing skills.

Marcus thought it was hilarious and reminded her of it at every opportunity.

These days, Penny didn't spend much time in thrift stores.

She had a child and a dog and had been absorbed by Marcus's vibrant family—but she still made time for me.

A couple of days after my strange car ride with my billion-aire ex-boss, I sat on one of the bar stools next to her kitchen island and enjoyed a margarita with a perfect salt rim. Holding it in my good hand, I let the tart, fresh drink lift my mood.

"So, wait," Penny said, arranging a few dried apricots on the charcuterie board she was putting together. "The perfume bottle fell on you, shattered, injured you, and then they fired you?"

I nodded. "Yep. And then, weirdly, my boss picked me up from the hospital."

"That Ophelia woman?"

I shook my head. "No. The big boss. Rome Blakely. The guy whose name is on the building."

Marcus had been frowning at his phone until then, his dog's head resting in his lap. At my words, he looked up. "Rome Blakely picked you up from the hospital?"

"Weird, right? He told me he wanted me to come in on Monday to discuss things."

Penny checked the baby monitor to make sure her toddler was still sleeping soundly, then shifted her gaze to me. "What does he want to talk about?"

"I don't know. I mean, I was exhausted and kind of woozy, so I wasn't exactly on my game. But it kind of seemed like he was probing for information somehow."

"Hmm," Penny replied, frowning.

"There was one good thing, though."

"What's that?"

I smiled. "He had really good chocolate, said he flew it in from Belgium. So I got to eat that on the way home, at least."

"I can make you a T-shirt: 'I got fired from the Blakely Advertising Agency and all I got was a delicious Belgian chocolate bar (and this T-shirt).'"

Snorting, I grabbed a grape. "Seems a bit wordy."

"Let me brainstorm something better. 'I met Rome Blakely and all I got was a gash on my arm and a ride in his limo.'"

"'I got fired from Blakely and all I got was an hour with a giant dildo.'"

Penny laughed, and I crunched down on my snack, grinning.

Across the room, Marcus stood and drifted closer. Bear, the dog, jumped off the couch and followed at his side before trotting over to Penny to demand scratches. Penny obliged, her smile still pointed at me. While she scratched, the red-and-white polka-dot dog collar around Bear's neck wiggled back and forth. It was one of Penny's creations, and it was adorable.

Marcus leaned a hip on the kitchen island and crossed his arms. His scowl was pointed in my direction. "Was Blakely trying to intimidate you?"

I cut off a chunk of smoked gouda and put it on a fancy multigrain cracker that had definitely come from a specialty grocery store that was too expensive for the likes of me. Glancing at Marcus before taking a bite, I said, "I don't think so. He did give me a chocolate bar." The gouda was creamy and delicious, with the perfect amount of smoke flavor. The cracker had a bit of sweetness, and the whole thing was like tasting nirvana. I groaned. "Penny. This cheese is divine."

"Isn't it? Try the Brie."

"Don't mind if I do," I said, spinning the board around so I could get at the good stuff.

"And he gave you no sign about what he wanted to talk about at this meeting?" Marcus asked, still frowning.

I tore my gaze away from the cheese and shrugged. "He said he wanted to discuss options, and that he was sure we could come to a mutually beneficial solution."

"Hot," Penny said.

I rolled my eyes, laughing.

Marcus pulled his phone out. "Do you have representation?"

Cheese knife in hand and busy strategizing about the Brie, all I responded was, "Huh?"

"Are you bringing a lawyer?" he clarified.

I paused, a hunk of cheese stuck to the knife. My eyes were wide as I stared at Marcus. "Do you think that's necessary?"

"Absolutely."

Suddenly, the Brie didn't seem so appetizing. I swallowed thickly, staring at the soft white cheese, my heart thumping a little bit harder. "You think they're trying to sue me?"

"I think you need to make sure you have support," Marcus said, then put his phone to his ear. "Phil, thanks for taking my call. I need a favor."

Penny let out a besotted sigh. "I just love him," she said, smiling at her husband.

Meanwhile, the image of my quickly dwindling bank account flashed across my mind. I cleared my throat. "Listen, guys, I really appreciate this, but..."

Marcus finished his call and hung up the phone. He arched a brow. "But?"

"But I'm not... I don't think... It just seems a bit much, is all. I don't think I need a big-shot lawyer with me for a simple meeting."

"Phil Phillips is one of the best lawyers—"

"His name is Phil Phillips?" Penny interrupted. "Did his parents hate him?"

Marcus's gaze fell on his wife, and some sort of silent communication happened between them. For a moment, I felt like I was intruding on a charged, intimate moment. After a while, when Penny's cheeks had flushed red, Marcus let his hand drift to her lower back and shifted his gaze back to me. "Phil Phillips is one of the best lawyers in the city. He's happy to give you an hour of his time."

"See, the thing is"—I cleared my throat—"I'm not sure I can exactly afford an hour of his time."

"Don't worry about it," Marcus said, gaze dropping to the charcuterie. He picked up a little bundle of prosciutto cut so thin it was nearly transparent. "Monday's meeting is covered. If you need his advice beyond that, we can talk about it then. I have work to do." He ate the meat, planted a kiss on his wife's temple, then disappeared down the hall.

Bear, torn, took a few steps to follow then reconsidered and stayed close to Penny—and the charcuterie board.

Penny smiled at the hallway. "Isn't he just a sweetheart?"

He was gruff and grumpy and didn't seem to like many people besides Penny, his kid, his nieces and nephews, and his mom, but sure. He was a sweetheart. I arched my brows at my friend. "Are you sure it's okay for this Phil Phillips guy to come with me?"

"Of course!" Penny beamed at me, flicking her red hair over

her shoulder. "Marcus is right, you know. You shouldn't be going in there on your own."

"Right," I answered, grateful and uncomfortable all at once. Penny and I had known each other before she married into wealth, and it was still strange to see her circumstances changed so dramatically. I was grateful for her help, of course, and I loved her company. She was a great friend.

I just couldn't shake the feeling that I was a placeholder. I slotted in conveniently to the place in her life that required easy friendship. I was someone she could call over for a simple char-cuterie board, and she knew she didn't have to dress up or try to impress me.

I hated having those thoughts. I knew Penny had a big heart. But there had been so many things in my life lately that shook my confidence and my self-esteem a little too violently. I wasn't sure where I belonged anymore. I wasn't sure if I'd squandered one too many chances to make something of myself.

"Have you seen Bonnie lately?" Penny asked.

I nodded. "We went shopping together last weekend. I haven't talked to her about this, though." I lifted the splint on my finger.

"Hmm," said Penny.

"I'm catching up with her next week. Why?"

"I think she's screening my calls."

"Really?"

"Yeah. Weird, right?"

It was weird, and I wondered if Bonnie was like me—unsure of exactly where she stood in the world and in our friend group.

"I'll see if anything is up when I see her," I said, then looked down as Bear came over to my side of the island to inspect whether I'd dropped any tasty morsels on the ground for him to enjoy. Finding nothing, he sat down and panted at me, hopeful.

I rubbed his head and smiled. "If everyone were as simple to understand as you are, Bear, life would be a lot easier."

He tilted his head, one of his gigantic ears prickling. Then he licked his chops and put his paw on my leg, and I laughed.

If only Rome Blakely were motivated by the promise of food, I'd know how to deal with him. As it was, I had to prepare for a Monday meeting with no idea what I'd be facing.

SIX

NIKKI

THE ENTIRETY of my employment at the Blakely Advertising Agency had been spent in the studios located on the bottom two floors of the skyscraper, with the exception of a visit to HR on the fifth floor to do some paperwork on my first day.

As I entered the glossy, luxurious lobby on a brisk autumn morning, it already felt like a strange place in which I didn't belong. My heels echoed on the marble floors as my gaze snagged on a few palm fronds fluttering in an artificial breeze in the corner.

The security desk was to my right, with the elevators directly in front, behind a row of electronic gates. I took a deep breath.

"Everything will be fine," Phil Phillips told me reassuringly. "Let's just hear them out. I'll cut in if I think they're trying to do something that isn't in your best interest."

He was a tall, wiry man in his early sixties, with kind brown eyes and a full head of hair. His suit looked expensive—bespoke, probably—and he wore a designer watch. He moved easily, like he knew he belonged in spaces exactly like this one.

I was glad to have him beside me. "Okay. Thank you for coming," I told him.

The older man inclined his head, then strode to the security desk to check in.

I scurried after him, stopping at the chest-high piece of marble. The man behind the counter had dark-brown skin and close-cut hair. His beard was trimmed to millimeter-precision. He looked as glossy and attractive as the rest of the people who worked in this building, and I wondered how I'd snuck past that particular filter to get a job in the first place.

But I was here, and there was an expensive lawyer beside me, so I might as well see why Blakely had set this meeting in the first place.

"Nikita Jordan here to see Rome Blakely," I told him, my voice wobbling a tiny bit. "I have an appointment."

The man nodded and tapped on his computer. "He's expecting you," he said, then shifted his gaze to the lawyer beside me. "And you are?"

"Phil Phillips. I'm representing Ms. Jordan."

"Of course. Please fill out the tablet in front of you to sign in, and I'll issue your visitor passes." He gestured to the device bolted to the check-in desk, then waited patiently for us to finish the sign-in process. Once we were done, he gave me an encouraging smile as he handed me my visitor pass. "Take the elevator to the forty-second floor. Someone will be there to greet you."

"Thank you," I said, then took a deep breath and passed through the gates that granted us access to the elevator bank.

"Nikki?"

I turned to see Eleanor struggling through one of the doors leading to the ground-floor studio at the back of the building. She had an unwieldy cardboard box in her hands, and I hurried over to help her with the door.

"What are you doing here?"

"I have a meeting with Rome Blakely," I explained.

She looked at me like I'd started speaking another language. "What?"

I laughed. "I know."

Her dark hair was pulled back in a sleek ballerina bun. She blew out a breath and shook her head. "Good luck. You want to grab a drink or something this week? How's the hand? Have you heard about them offering everyone full benefits this week?" She glanced behind me and shook her head. "The elevator's here. Call me when you're done! We'll go out tonight and you can tell me everything."

Smiling, I nodded and hustled over to where Phil held open the elevator door. One of the security guards swiped his pass and pressed the button for the forty-second floor for us before stepping out to let the doors close. I noticed it was as high as the numbers went. We were headed to the top of the building.

"What was she saying?" Phil asked. "The woman you were speaking to."

"Who, Eleanor? She just wanted to grab a drink with me later."

"No. The other thing."

"Oh. Apparently they've offered everyone full benefits, or something? I didn't have time to get the full story."

A slow, victorious smile stretched over Phil's lips. "They're covering their asses."

The screen above the door flashed with increasing numbers as the elevator shot up through the core of the building. "What do you mean?"

"Everything is going to be fine. They're scrambling, Nikki. We have the upper hand. Now look sharp," was all he said.

The elevator slowed so smoothly I barely felt it, and then the doors opened to reveal a bright white lobby and a woman of about forty, staring at us from behind thick-rimmed glasses. She wore a dark-green dress with an asymmetrical neckline and a perfectly tailored waist. I wanted to ask her where she got it, but I doubted I'd be able to afford it even if I knew. Her brown hair had golden highlights that had obviously been done by someone who was an expert colorist.

Her gaze was sharp as she took in my appearance. I'd chosen a black tweed dress that fit close to the body. It was piped in white and had big, white, fabric-covered buttons. It was fabulous, even if I'd bought it for less than twenty dollars in a bargain bin and had to do some major repairs to the aged fabric. Whether or not the woman agreed was hard to tell.

All she did was nod and say, "Ms. Jordan. Mr. Phillips. My name is Clara. Mr. Blakely will be with you in just a moment. Please follow me."

I was impressed she knew our names—especially Phil's. Then again, she'd probably been notified of us signing in, which meant she—and Rome, and whoever else would be attending this meeting—now knew I had brought legal representation.

My heart thumped as we crossed the white space. Two white leather armchairs were clustered around a heavy-looking wooden coffee table. The walls had a few large pieces of art to break up the blank color scheme so that the overall effect of the lobby was one of money, prestige, and—to me—intimidation.

I took a deep breath and trotted after Clara, my heels clacking in time with hers. Beside me, Phil stalked, utterly calm —almost serene. A small smile teased the corners of his lips.

If only I could have an ounce of that confidence. As it was, I felt like I was walking deeper into the dragon's lair. Danger lurked just beyond my sight, but I could sense it.

I didn't belong here.

"Please," Clara said, gesturing to an open door. We entered a medium-sized conference room with a great view of Manhattan.

I drifted to the windows to glance down at the world spread out below my feet, then turned when Clara cleared her throat.

"Can I get you coffee or tea? Water?"

"Water's fine," I said.

Phil chose a seat with his back to the windows, midway down the long table. "I'd love a coffee, if you don't mind," he said. "Dash of cream if you have it."

Clara inclined her head, then clip-clopped down the hard floors until the sound of her shoes faded. I sat beside Phil who rocked slightly back and forth in his chair, his fingers drumming on its arms. He looked like he was out for a day at the beach instead of a boardroom in a billionaire's building.

I, on the other hand, was full of nervous energy. I unclasped my purse and pulled out my compact mirror and my bullet lipstick. My hands trembled slightly, but the familiar motion of uncapping the lipstick and twisting it up settled my nerves enough that I could reapply it without worrying about looking like a five-year-old who'd raided her mother's makeup drawer.

I was halfway through swiping my favorite rust-red onto my top lip when I heard the sound of many footsteps. I would look stupid if I stopped now, since the pigment on my bottom lip had worn off slightly, so all I could do was keep going. That meant that when Rome Blakely strode through the conference room door followed by half a dozen men and women wearing severe suits and scowling faces, I was in the process of painting my bottom lip.

Lifting my gaze, I saw Rome's thunderous expression as he watched me. Long fingers grabbed the back of the leather chair across from mine as a network of tiny lines tightened in the corners of his eyes. He wore another one of his expensive white shirts under a perfectly tailored suit. His tie today was black silk. He looked powerful and in control of his domain.

I felt like a trembling little mouse with a bullet of red lipstick in her paws.

Beside me, Phil stood. "Mr. Blakely," he greeted politely. "Very nice to meet you."

I snapped my compact mirror closed and slipped it into its designated slot in my purse. Then I worked the lipstick bullet back into its tube and slipped the lid back where it belonged. My movements were slow and deliberate, because otherwise I'd betray the fact that my heart was fluttering, and my fingers felt swollen and uncoordinated. The last thing I wanted to do was drop something and make a fool of myself.

It wasn't until I put the lipstick away and stood beside my lawyer that Rome Blakely tore his gaze away from me to bare his teeth at the man to my left. "I wasn't aware Ms. Jordan had engaged your services," he said.

Phil shrugged, unconcerned. "I'm sure we can all come to a resolution today. That's why we're here."

The man to Blakely's right snorted. "Give me a break, Phillips. You've never wanted to resolve anything amicably in your life."

Phil met the other man's snarling face and gave him a genial smile. "Arthur. Long time. How're Trudy and the kids?"

Arthur's face went bright red. He opened his mouth to retort, but Blakely put his arm up.

"Gentlemen," he said, voice low. "Please."

Clara entered a moment later, defusing the last of the tension. She pushed a trolley into the room, then grabbed a pitcher of water off it and set it in the middle of the table, followed by glasses for everyone. Then she walked around and gave Phil his coffee. He thanked her politely and she gave him a curt nod.

The final item she moved from the trolley to the table was a carved crystal bowl full of foil-wrapped somethings. I peered at them, recognizing the brand of imported Belgian chocolate.

As I glanced up, I caught him watching me intently. His jaw was tight and his eyes slightly narrowed, like he was holding himself back from showing his anger.

But why was he angry?

And why the chocolates? A bribe? Something to throw me off?

Well—joke was on him because I'd been thrown off for days.

I leaned back in my seat and shifted uncomfortably, waiting for someone to speak.

Blakely arched a brow, faint amusement twinkling in his eyes. He reached a long arm across his side of the table and plucked one of the chocolates from the bowl. The only noise in the room was the crinkling of the foil paper. He held my gaze as he inspected the truffle, then popped it in his mouth.

My mouth watered despite myself. I didn't know if it was the sight of Rome Blakely staring at me like he wished he was eating me instead of the chocolate, or if my poor nerves had finally decided to lay down their arms after a long and arduous war.

I just wanted to get this over with.

Phil spoke into the heavy silence. "My client mentioned that you wanted to speak to her about options. Might we know what options you had in mind?"

Blakely patted his lips with a small square cocktail napkin, then nodded at the lawyer to his right. Arthur pushed a packet of papers across the table to me, then another set across to Phil.

When I read the words CONTRACT OF EMPLOY-MENT at the top of the page, I frowned.

"When it came to my attention that Ms. Jordan had been let go after the unfortunate incident with the Garcia campaign last week, I felt compelled to look into her background," Blakely started, talking to Phil. He shifted his gaze to me. "You've worked in fashion for the better part of a decade, and you've completed a certificate in business management."

My palms were clammy. I nodded. "That's right. I was the primary buyer for a vintage clothing store."

"We can use someone with your expertise," he replied, which was crazy. What expertise was that? Vintage brands? Old manufacturing techniques? Textile quality?

Maybe. But it didn't seem likely. None of this made sense.

Phil was busy reading through the contract beside me. He made a strange noise, like a mix between a grunt and a choking gurgle. "Companion? What exactly does that mean?" His frown was severe as he lifted his gaze to glare at Blakely.

Rome Blakely leaned back, smiling slightly. "Exactly what the contract says." His glittering blue eyes shifted to me. "Your job duties would include accompanying me to social functions and events to act as my on-call plus-one. You'd have to know my clients' details and be ready to make appropriate conversation. You'd represent me, and the company, to various stakeholders."

It took a few seconds for the words to sink in, then I was on my feet. My chair shot back and crashed into the windows behind me. "I am not an escort. What is this? What are you trying to do? Did you bring me here to humiliate me in front of your legal team?"

My cheeks stung, and I knew they were stained red. My broken finger throbbed. I wanted to grab the pitcher of water in the middle of the table and smash it over Rome Blakely's head. Then I'd take a handful of those fancy chocolates and shove them down his gob.

"Please, Ms. Jordan," the other side's lawyer said, placating. He'd calmed down after his confrontation with Phil, and his face was back to its normal beige color. "Turn your attention to section 7.2.1 of the contract. 'No physical or sexual contact is to occur between Employer and Companion, beyond what could be considered normal professional conduct. Refer to the Blakely Advertising Agency Code of Conduct,'" he read, then added, "Which we've included in Appendix B."

I realized I was breathing heavily. Halfway through the

older man's speech, I'd stopped glaring at Blakely and started glaring at him. I dropped my eyes to the page, which Phil was helpfully pointing out. It read exactly like he said.

Slowly, I sat down.

"It wasn't my intention to offend you," Rome said, his voice warm and low. "My apologies for the clumsy delivery. What I'm looking for is someone who can attend any and all events as my companion, hold her own in conversation, and represent the company appropriately."

A refusal hung on the tip of my tongue. The last thing I wanted to do was spend more time with this man. He was arrogant and rude, and his behavior made no sense. Carrying me from the supply room in his arms while telling me to be quiet? Picking me up from the hospital after firing me? Calling me here just to intimidate me and then offer me this crazy job?

This was nothing but trouble. My life might have been on the way to the gutter, but I knew accepting this would be a terrible decision.

It was basically signing up to be a paid placeholder. It was humiliating.

The back of my throat burned, but I kept my back straight.

"If you'll turn to pages six and seven," Arthur continued, in his element now, "you can review the compensation for the position. I trust you'll agree it's more than generous."

Eyes prickling, I tried to look at page numbers while my fingers trembled and struggled to grip the sheets. When I flipped to page six, my brain just—shut down.

The number written beside "Total Compensation" was five times what I'd been making at the vintage clothing store. Listed under "Benefits" was health insurance, dental, and a fat 401k match. I read the page three times, just to make sure the letters hadn't magically rearranged themselves to show something that wasn't there.

My breathing was shallow, my voice completely gone.

Then I flipped the page, and it took all my self-control to keep my face blank. The final benefit that Blakely was offering me was a clothing and beauty budget of one thousand dollars... *per month*!

My voice finally returned, and I pointed to the number. "Is this..." I cleared the croak from my voice and tried again. "Is this the correct number of zeroes? Per month?"

There was a tense silence. I looked up to see Rome Blakely's eyes full of darkness as they glared at me from across the table. The muscles in his neck were stark. His hands fisted then relaxed, and he held my gaze while he angled his head toward Arthur and gave him an infinitesimal nod.

Arthur let out a huff before nodding to one of the younger women sitting at the end of the table. She tapped on the laptop in front of her, then pressed a button. No one spoke while she stepped out of the room. I focused on remembering how to breathe and hoped my heart would survive this encounter.

I had no idea what the hell was going on.

Why was he offering me a job? Why was he offering me *this* job?

A thousand dollars a month on clothes and beauty! But— that had obviously been a mistake. They were reviewing the contract, and a more reasonable amount would be offered. Still, a hundred bucks a month would cover nails, at least! Or I could get a blowout or makeup done before events. It would make it possible to look presentable, at least. I had a closet full of vintage clothes that could hold their own at a variety of events. I only had a handful of designer pieces, but I could do this.

If I wanted to. Which I didn't.

The young lawyer reappeared in the doorway. She handed both me and Phil a fresh Page Seven, still warm from the printer.

And I almost keeled over.

They hadn't taken a zero away. They'd added another one.

Ten thousand dollars per month to spend on beauty and clothes stared up at me from the warm sheet of paper, right there in black and white.

In that moment, I considered whether the giant perfume penis had in fact hit me in the head and I was now lying in a hospital bed in a coma. Maybe none of this was real. I'd wake up any minute with an even bigger hospital bill than the one coming to me, still jobless, still nearly homeless. There would be no handsome, wealthy weirdo picking me up from the hospital parking lot. There'd be no fancy lawyer, and no job offer.

I shifted my uninjured hand under the table and pinched the side of my leg. The dart of pain assured me what was happening was real.

Which meant that the stuffy suits across from me were now offering me a hundred and twenty grand per year to spend on *clothing*. And hair. And beauty.

I would get laser hair removal *everywhere*. The pesky hairs that had started sprouting on my chin when the clock struck thirty would be the first to get the zap. I would buy so many bags I could stitch them all together and live in them, and I wouldn't need to find a new home. I would go on a shopping spree to end all shopping sprees, and I would buy every fabulous dress I'd ever salivated over.

This couldn't be real. It just couldn't.

I realized I'd been sitting there, completely still, fantasizing about raiding every designer store I could find while a room full of rich people and their minions stared at me.

I looked up. Rome Blakely looked like he was carved from stone, his expression hard as he watched me like he could read every thought written on my face. He was the one to break the silence. "Is that more to your liking, Ms. Jordan?" He bit off my name like it was an insult.

Heart hammering, I clenched my uninjured hand in my lap to hide the tremors in my finger. I lifted my other hand and pointed at the number with the end of the splint still holding my broken finger immobile. "This number...is higher than the one that was written before," I pointed out, because I felt the need to clarify things, and my brain wasn't exactly operating at full capacity.

It had to be a mistake. I was an honest person; I didn't want to sign the contract under false pretenses.

And, actually, I wasn't even sure I wanted to sign the contract at all.

But—purses! Clothing! Hair! Nails!

While my inner Julia Roberts basked in her very own *Pretty Woman* moment, Rome Blakely gritted his teeth at me. His eyes darkened as he watched me, then he let out a violent gust of breath and jerked his chin down at his team of lawyers again, his jaw clenched so hard the muscles at the side bulged.

The same little dance happened once more. The old man

lawyer nodded at the younger woman. She tapped on her laptop, scurried out, and scurried back in.

The tension was unbearable. I felt like a huge weight was sitting on my chest, and all I wanted to do was run away from here, but I was stuck.

This would all be figured out soon. She'd come back, and they'd realize they were offering me something that was completely bananas.

The fresh sheet of paper was once again warm.

Before I could even utter a gasp, Phil cleared his throat. "I'd like a moment alone with my client," he said, strangely solemn. The usual playful note in his voice was gone.

My mind, meanwhile, was going on a drunken rampage on Fifth Avenue, cackling evilly at the sky while dozens of bags hung off both of my arms.

The stiff, stern, scowling lawyers filed out. Blakely remained seated for a long moment, watching me. His eyes shot daggers. Withstanding the force of his stare was an effort I wasn't sure I could muster, so I dropped my gaze to the bowl of chocolates, grabbed one, unwrapped it, and popped it in my mouth.

He watched me chew for a second, glowering.

I let out a little noise as the soft center of the truffle hit my tongue. I had to give him one thing—the man knew good chocolate.

"Don't push me too far, Ms. Jordan," he warned, then stood and prowled out the door. It closed with a soft snick behind him, the pack of people in suits moving down the hallway and out of earshot.

"Phil," I whispered. "Does your Page Seven say the same thing mine does?"

He pushed his sheet over so I could read. And right there in black and white, just like mine, was a number that broke my brain.

Twenty-five thousand dollars. Per month. For fashion and beauty. Plus the huge salary. Plus the benefits.

I dragged my gaze from the paper to Phil's face, flabbergasted. Nothing made sense. I didn't understand. What had just happened? What was going on?

All this just to go to a few fancy events on Rome Blakely's arm? How—why—what?

It had to be too good to be true. There had to be a catch.

"Phil," I whispered again.

"Yes, Nikki?"

"What the heck is going on?"

His eyes glittered, and the corners of his lips twitched. "We'll go through the contract with a fine-toothed comb," he told me. "But from what I've read so far, they're offering you this in exchange for indemnity against any lawsuit you might have been planning to bring against the company."

"What?"

His eyes twinkled. "Like I said before, this right here?" He tapped a finger on the contract pages on the table. "This is a group of people trying to cover their asses after a major fuck-up."

Suddenly, I understood. They were buying me off. Blakely picking me up from the hospital was him probing me for information, and whatever I'd said had spooked him. Meanwhile, I'd been eating chocolate and dreaming of my bed.

I'd tripped and fallen into a swimming pool full of gold. Or maybe he'd pushed me into it.

I huffed, amazed. "What do I do?" My voice was hoarse. Imaginary me had cackled a bit too much.

The older man hummed, tilting his head. "You want to know what I would do?"

I nodded.

A smile broke over his lips. "I'd bite their hand off. Any settlement I negotiate for you will be far less than this, and it won't include any of these benefits. Take it, Nikki, milk it for all it's worth, and don't look back."

SEVEN

ROME

I PACED the length of my office, my steps heavy on the carpeted floor. Blood rushed in my ears. My hands clenched and unclenched.

That little minx was squeezing me for all I was worth, and I did *not* appreciate it.

I gritted my teeth and turned, pacing in the opposite direction. Cole watched me from the corner of the room where he leaned on the wall, his arms crossed.

"You think she'll go for it?" he finally asked.

"She will if she knows what's good for her," I fumed. The cheeky little thing. Painting her lips like she didn't have a care in the world. Demanding more and more and more from me, even though we'd offered her a great deal to begin with. Munching on my truffles like they were her due.

Her dark-brown eyes had flashed across the table from me, that little black-and-white outfit taunting me with every movement of her body. She thought she could waltz in here and make a fool of *me*? She thought she could get one over on *me*?

Ha!

"To be fair," Cole said, interrupting my inner rage, "if she's attending a full schedule of events, a grand wouldn't be enough to cover what she needs. Twenty-five k is generous, sure, but at least she'll be able to dress the part."

"That's not the point," I snapped.

Cole arched a brow. "Oh? What is, then?"

"The point is, she thinks she can tighten the screw on me. She thinks she can play a tune and my feet will start dancing. I don't appreciate it, and I don't appreciate her."

"So pull the offer. Especially if you don't think you can stand to have her on your arm four or five times a week. Maybe more with the holidays coming up. You need to at least pretend you get along, or else this whole thing falls apart."

I bared my teeth at him, then whirled around and stalked to my bar. I poured myself a tall drink, letting the alcohol burn my throat.

"I can't pull the offer," I finally said when my glass was empty. "You were right about Monk. He won't hire me unless he knows I can take criticism, and in his geriatric, wife-obsessed mind, the only way to show that is to have a softening influence in my life. I need a companion."

"I wonder how he deals with same-sex couples."

Setting my glass down, I shook my head. "He's fine with it. It's the partnership he wants. He thinks a committed relationship changes someone and makes them worthy of trust."

"So you need her."

"I don't need *her*," I shot back petulantly, glaring at him. "I need *someone*. She just happens to be the convenient option."

Cole tilted his head, considering me. "I see," he said, and it sounded like he saw a lot more than I wanted him to. Like he might be able to see just how easily Nikita Jordan had gotten under my skin. And how badly I wanted to march back in there and demand she stop playing around and sign the damned contract already.

"I can't afford a lawsuit right now. Especially not a public one," I told him, even though that wasn't the only reason I wanted her to work for me.

It galled me that she was winning. It boiled my blood to know she'd gotten one over on me. It wasn't right.

I wanted to teach her a lesson.

But most frustrating of all was that I couldn't think of a single person I'd met who would be better suited for the job. She had personality, a vibrancy, that was rare. People warmed to her—I'd seen it in the way her coworkers had worried when she was injured. There had even been a few muffled protests when Ophelia announced she'd fire her for the perfume stunt.

The woman was likable, damn her. And I needed that more desperately than I was willing to admit.

Cole hummed, and we both turned when the door opened. Tabitha, the junior lawyer who'd amended the contract, poked her head in. "They're ready for us," she said, then held the door open for Cole, Arthur, and me to step through. The hallway leading to the conference room narrowed and stretched before me. Every step felt like it jarred my body, and it was all I could do to keep my breathing steady and my movements smooth.

She sat on the other side of the conference table like a

queen. Back straight, chin lifted, eyes steady. Her lips drew my gaze, red and lush. I wondered what they'd look like mussed, with that red lipstick smeared by my thumb. Wrapped around my—

Blinking, I sat in front of her and braided my fingers together. "Well?"

Phil Phillips cleared his throat. "We'll need the rest of the week to review the contract," he said.

"No chance." I leaned back, holding Nikki's gaze. "You walk out of here today without signing that contract, and your decision is made."

Her eyes narrowed, and I could tell she was biting that sharp tongue of hers. I wanted to goad her into speaking.

Her lawyer inserted himself smoothly by saying, "This is highly unusual."

I slid my gaze across to meet his. "I'll give you as long as you'd like to review the contract in this room. Once you leave this floor, though, there won't be going back. So decide now if you want to sign those pages or not, because I won't be jerked around by you any longer."

"I resent that," Nikki said softly, her words laced with venom.

I smiled at her but felt no humor. "Good for you. We'll give you the room, and Clara will organize whatever you need. You have until five o'clock this evening. Sign the contract and the NDA or don't. But that's all the time you'll have."

I pushed back and left the room, feeling her gaze on my back the whole way. I made a beeline for my office, locked the door, and ducked into my private bathroom. Splashing some water over my face, I leaned over the sink and gulped down ragged breaths.

As my temper cooled and water dripped from my nose and chin into the white porcelain sink, I realized I was making a mistake. She was infuriating. Spending more time with her could only bring disaster.

But the alternative was paying her off and letting her win. Never seeing her again. Knowing that she was out there, with her red lips and her flashing eyes, laughing at me.

And that was worse.

I knew one thing: If she signed that contract, I would make her life hell.

And sign it she did. Four hours later, with a few minor revisions to the verbiage, Nikita Jordan inked her name on the contract and officially became an employee of the Blakely Advertising Agency. Clara dropped the paperwork on my desk and met my gaze.

"Are you sure this is a good idea?" she asked quietly.

Clara was a genius executive assistant. She'd been with me for twelve years, and she, along with the half-dozen administrative staff she managed, was the one who made my life run as smoothly as she did. She had severe features framed with thick-rimmed glasses, but in moments like these, her eyes were softer. Concerned.

In a flash, I understood what Wilbur Monk meant. Clara's approach was gentler, even though she was echoing what Cole had said earlier. But when she stood in front of my desk, I didn't want to snap back in the face of her kindness. I wanted to be honest with her. I wanted to reassure her.

What would it be like to have someone in my life with

whom I could have these kinds of conversations? Or deeper ones? My relationship with Clara was based on professional respect. She knew me, knew how I worked, so she knew when to be concerned and when to push.

But what if someone liked me just for me? What if they saw me, all the way down to my core? How would it feel to open up the part of me that had to stay locked in an iron box? Would I still be able to be the ruthless executive if I cared for someone else?

And, most importantly, what if I opened up, let them in, and then they tossed me aside when I needed them most?

The thought shut me down. Cold sluiced through my veins as I leaned back in my chair. I met my assistant's gaze and dipped my chin. "She'll toe the company line, or she'll lose the cushy job she just earned herself and will have no recourse to sue. This is the best possible outcome."

Clara didn't seem convinced, but she nodded. "When would you like her to start?"

A sense of calm settled over me. I pushed back from my desk and stood, smiling. "Immediately."

EIGHT
NIKKI

I STUDIED one of the abstract paintings in the lobby next to the elevator, wondering if I'd just made a big mistake. But how could it be a mistake when I had health and dental insurance? How could it be a mistake when as soon as the sign-on bonus hit my account, I'd be able to secure a new apartment, pay my hospital bill, and maybe even clear my loan for the business management certificate?

Most of my problems had been solved with one swoop of the pen. I could afford to live, I could pay off my debts, and I would no longer be homeless.

Sure, I was still a placeholder in my job and my personal life, and my love life was in shambles, but at least I had a bit of stability. That was progress.

The artwork before me consisted of a gigantic canvas covered in dramatic dashes of color. Teal and sage green and navy and orange shouldn't have looked good together but did.

Something like this would look good above my velvet couch in whatever apartment I ended up moving to.

I smiled to myself. I'd have money to decorate! I might even be able to save up to buy somewhere. Probably not in Manhattan, but Connecticut, maybe? I could commute if I needed to, if it meant I could live a decent kind of life.

A different kind of existence stretched out before me. One where I wasn't scrambling whenever a surprise bill showed up in my mailbox, or where I didn't scrutinize prices at the grocery store.

Then I heard footsteps. Before I even turned, I knew they were his.

Rome Blakely strode across the marble floor, eyes boring into me. He'd ditched his jacket and was in a crisp white shirt with the sleeves rolled up. His tie had disappeared at some point in the past few hours. It hit me, then, how attractive he was.

He walked with a prowling kind of grace, commanding, in control. His forearms were dusted with hair and as he came to a stop in front of me, he folded his arms and drummed long fingers on his opposite biceps. His eyes, under the white light in the lobby, looked cold. I had to tilt my chin up to meet his steady gaze, noticing the shadow of hair on his jaw that would darken until he shaved it again in the morning.

He smelled delicious. I was woozy.

"Going somewhere?" he drawled, arching a dark brow.

I straightened my shoulders and narrowed my eyes. "As soon as Clara confirms my start date, I'll be going home."

"No."

I reared back. "No?"

"No, you won't be going home. You have work to do tonight."

I huffed. "Since when?"

"Since you signed your name on that piece of paper, Ms. Jordan. You're my companion. You will accompany me." He turned his head toward Clara, who was standing silent a few steps away. "Joanne is expecting me for dinner tonight. Find something appropriate for Ms. Jordan to wear."

"Of course," Clara said, then gestured to the elevators. "Ms. Jordan, please."

"Now, hold on a minute," Phil interjected, standing at my shoulder.

Blakely's dark gaze shifted to meet the lawyer's. "Is there a problem?"

Phil ignored him and turned to me. "Are you okay with this? I can—"

I put my hand on his arm. "It's fine, Phil."

Because Blakely was right. I'd signed that piece of paper, which meant I had a boss. If he wanted to take me to dinner with Joanne—whoever she was—then that's what I would do. This job was unexpected, and it might be the thing to lift me out of perpetual brokehood into something better.

Sure, my boss was an overbearing ass with a perma-scowl. But I could deal with that. That was the decision I'd made in that conference room, with my pen poised over that contract. I'd accompany him to every social event, and I would dazzle and charm like my life depended on it.

For all intents and purposes, it did.

I needed this job, and being a high achiever was part of my

DNA. If this was the decision I'd made, I would do my best. Starting right now.

I nodded at the lawyer. "Thank you so much for today."

He scowled at me, then sighed as his shoulders softened. Under Rome Blakely's watchful gaze, I got in the elevator with Clara and Phil. Once the doors closed, the lawyer pulled out his card and gave it to me. "You need anything, you call."

I nodded, "Thank you."

Clara said nothing. She pressed the button for the twelfth floor, where she and I disembarked, and I waved goodbye to Phil Phillips. I was on my own.

Greeting a few curious faces as we strode past, Clara led me to a room secured with a touchpad lock. Her fingerprint granted us access, and I was greeted with a temperature- and moisture-controlled piece of heaven. Garment racks lined the walls, filled with thousands of pieces of clothing. I sucked in a hard breath.

"The costume archive," she said. "We've downsized some, now that we're outsourcing a lot of the shoots, but there should be something in here we can use."

I touched a beautiful silk dress in mustard yellow. It would look terrible on me, but the fabric fell over my fingers like liquid. I sighed. Boss notwithstanding, so far, this was the best job *ever*.

"Who's this Joanne lady?" I asked while Clara flicked through various garment-bag-covered outfits.

She frowned at one of them, then glanced over her shoulder. "What size are you? I think this could work."

My heart sank when I saw her pull out a beige suit. It was beautifully crafted, but it was just so...boring.

"Why can't I just wear what I have on?" A business dress

with chic piping and a perfect cut would be better than a beige pantsuit.

Clara took in my blue-and-white outfit that hit my knees, down to the black hose-covered legs and fabulous pumps. "Absolutely not."

"What's wrong with this dress?" I asked, then pointed to the suit she held. "That looks like I'm going to be an extra in a courthouse movie."

Clara snorted, her eyes sparkling. "Extra in a courthouse movie is exactly the vibe we're going for. The nonspeaking, fade-into-the-background kind of role."

"You're sure I can't wear something like this?" I asked hopefully, pulling a black dress from the rack. It had a square neckline with halter straps, and the skirt flared out in an A-line. Conservative, simple, but at least it wasn't beige.

Clara shook her head. "Definitely not. Try these pants on. We'll call a tailor if they need to be adjusted."

I ducked behind a curtain and pulled the pants on. A pale cream silk blouse appeared on the rail above my head. It had a slight sheen and little pearl buttons, so by default it was my favorite piece out of the three. I walked out from behind the curtain and slipped on the blazer Clara held up, then turned to look in a floor-length mirror leaning on the wall.

"Perfect," Clara said. At my grimace, she shook her head. "Trust me, Ms. Jordan. It's perfect."

"You can call me Nikki," I told her. "Although in this suit I feel like more of a Ms. Jordan."

"It's a good suit, Nikki."

I smoothed my hand down the fabric of the pants on my thighs, feeling the weight and softness of the weave. "I know," I told her. "It's just not me. I like something a bit more...unique." Something with at least one element of flair.

Clara snorted. "You don't want to stand out where you're going."

My black stilettos and black shoulder bag worked just fine with the outfit, so I carefully folded my dress and shoved it in my bag. "Right," I said, trotting after her as she headed for the door. "About that. Where am I going, again?"

She eyed me critically. "Your hair is fine. I'd recommend wiping the lipstick off."

"Why are you evading my questions? Where am I going? Who's Joanne?"

"Nikki, I've got a job to do, and that job is to get you ready. We've succeeded."

"Ready for *what*?"

We got back in the elevator and headed up. I frowned at the numbers above the door, wondering what I'd gotten myself into. I didn't feel like myself. My armor had been stripped away, and now I was wearing someone else's clothes and living someone else's life.

But—*deep breaths*—it was just a job. It was the best job I could hope for right now, and I might as well make the most of it. I counted to ten and steadied my nerves.

It was one dinner. How bad could this Joanne lady be?

The elevator doors opened, and Clara led me to an office in the opposite corner of the floor to the location of the conference room. She knocked on the frosted glass door, and I heard the deep rumble of Rome Blakely's voice on the other side. Clara opened the door and strode in, gesturing for me to follow.

Blakely was wearing glasses. They were rectangular with

slightly rounded edges, the frame a deep blue that brought out the color of his eyes. He frowned at me and took his glasses off, pressing the end of the glasses' arms on his bottom lip.

I looked at that depression on his firm mouth, and heat swept through my middle.

His gaze traveled from my shoes, up my beige pants, and over the silk blouse, finally coming to rest on my lips. He frowned slightly, and a vein of stubbornness split open inside me.

"I'm not taking the lipstick off," I told him.

His gaze slid the final distance to my eyes, and he blinked slowly. The heat in my abdomen got a smidge warmer. Anger—and something else. It made me uncomfortable to be studied so blatantly, but it also made me feel alive.

He set his glasses down and stood. "Fine," he told me.

"Who's Joanne?" I blurted.

It didn't surprise me when he flicked his eyes toward me then glanced at Clara. "Is the bird ready?"

"Whenever you are," she confirmed.

He nodded, then without so much as a glance at me, walked out of his office behind Clara. I had no choice but to follow, with no idea where we were going, who we were meeting, or why everyone refused to answer my questions.

There was a moment, then—just a second, really—when I considered throwing in the towel. I could quit, walk out of here, and never come back. Sure, I'd lose the benefits and the perks and the salary, but at least I wouldn't be ignored and treated like a prop. At least I could be my own person and be proud of my own integrity.

Then Rome paused on the threshold and looked at me. His

eyes were dark. They sent that same heated shiver coursing through my veins, and I discovered that that flame of stubbornness hadn't yet been extinguished.

I was a professional. When I set my mind to something, I followed through. I'd signed up to be this man's companion, so I'd accompany him to his social events, and I would be good at it—no! I'd be *great* at it. I would be the best damn companion he'd ever had. He'd have no choice but to keep filling my bank account (and my closet) to the brim.

It didn't matter that he was a billionaire with all the power, and I was pretty sure he was toying with me. He was just as bound by that contract as I was. After all, *he* was the one who'd thought I was trying to sue him. He thought I'd been negotiating before, when I'd just been confused.

I had the upper hand in that negotiation, and I hadn't even known. So he wasn't the all-important god he thought he was.

Phil was right. The best thing for me to do was milk this for all it was worth, even if I had to wear a boring beige suit while I did it.

I lifted my chin and arched my brows at him. "Regretting your decision to hire me?" I challenged.

His lips curled into a mirthless smile. "Not even a little bit, Jordan. Now keep up. We haven't got much time."

NINE
ROME

NIKKI'S shiny black shoes poked out from under the tan fabric of her pants. She leaned against the side of the elevator as we traveled up toward the roof, watching the numbers on the little black screen above the door.

She looked...not *better*, but definitely more appropriate for where we were going. Still, I found myself missing the figure-hugging dresses that echoed a faint pinup style that I'd seen her in before. She didn't look uncomfortable, but other than the red lipstick, the shoes, and the glossy black waves, she didn't look like herself.

I turned away, gritting my teeth.

It was better that way. Better to be inconspicuous and blend in so we could get in and get this dinner over with.

As we reached the top floor, a staff member nodded and opened the door to the roof. Beyond it, helicopter blades sliced through the air in a steady staccato. I strode to the door and turned when Nikki didn't immediately follow.

Her eyes were huge. "We're taking a helicopter?"

"Why else would we go to the roof?"

"Right," she said, then followed after me.

Waving to the pilot, we made our way into the bird and strapped ourselves in. I watched as Nikki frowned at the headset, flipping it in her hands before sliding it over her ears. She shot me a quick glance, then turned those wide brown eyes out the window.

The crew did their final checks, and then we took off. Nikki's knuckles turned white as she gripped the edge of her seat, her face so close to the window that I expected her nose to leave a smudge on the glass when she finally tore herself away.

The helicopter turned at a sharp angle, and Nikki's chest moved with a sharp inhalation.

A softness entered my chest at the sight of her like that, so enthralled by what we were doing. I found myself fascinated by watching her. Traveling to Long Island by helicopter had become a normal part of my routine. It was more convenient than taking a car.

But now, as I watched Nikki, I realized that the view from the helicopter was spectacular. The setting sun painted the sky in a wash of pastels at our backs. Spread below us, the city was alive with lights and motion. The East River, lit with the setting sun, cut a path of golden fire between the landmasses, quickly disappearing behind us.

Ahead, a few stars dotted the darkening sky. The moon hung low over the horizon, a pale crescent barely visible in the sky.

"Wow," Nikki breathed, peering down as we passed over the lives of millions of people.

"Ever seen the view from up here?" I asked through the headset.

"No." She turned to me, her lips spread in a broad smile. "It's incredible."

I nodded, following her gaze as she looked out the window once more. My eyes were drawn back to her, though. To the slope of her neck and the way her fingers relaxed their grip on the edge of her seat. How she shifted and stretched a leg out so I could catch a glimpse of her ankle. Her lips parted, eyes shining, and I felt an uncomfortable tightness in my chest.

Rubbing the spot to ease the ache, I pulled out my phone and flicked through the dozens of emails that had landed in my inbox since I'd last had a look. Nikki shifted when the helicopter slowed above the familiar sprawling grounds of an estate, her curious eyes roaming over the contours of the tree-lined drive and the stately stone home at the end of it.

The bird flew to the back of the house, and we alighted on the helipad set back from the main house. Grass flattened itself at our landing, ripples flowing through it and across the surface of the nearby pond. A duck made a hurried escape to a clump of rushes on the far side of the water.

I unclipped my seatbelt and removed my headset. Nikki did the same, then followed me out of the helicopter and onto the grounds of the lavish estate.

The house was just the same as it had always been: big, imposing, and cold.

The blades above us slowed as we made our way toward the house; the pilot would wait there for us to return.

Nikki's heels clacked on the stone pathway beside me as she finger-combed her hair with hasty movements. "Hold up," she said, then dug through her purse to pull out a tiny hairbrush that unfolded to full size. She ran it through her hair a few times then fluffed it, looking at me. "Better?"

"Your hair's fine." I checked my watch. We were a few minutes late, which wouldn't go unnoticed.

"Oh, great. 'Fine.' Just what I love to hear."

Arching a brow, I met her sparkling eyes once more. "Are you done? We need to get in there."

"And do I get to find out what 'in there' actually is, or am I to be presented to this Joanne lady without any warning about what's coming?"

"Let's go."

"I see you choose Option B," she grumbled, but her heels clacked beside me and the scent of her teased my nose. We rounded perfectly groomed topiaries—one in the shape of a swan, the other a bunny—and crossed a square containing a dramatic fountain. The lights were on, so the water danced through the air as colors shifted through it, to a dazzling effect.

Or it would be dazzling, if I didn't hate this place.

"Wow. That's so cool!" Nikki slowed beside me. "And listen! There's music! They've timed the fountain to the music!"

"They had it designed after a trip to Dubai. It's a miniature version of the fountain outside the Burj Khalifa." I kept walking.

"You're not impressed by this?"

I shot her a sideways glance. "The novelty wears off," I said. I'd gotten used to noticing all the changes that occurred to this place while I was away. And all the things that stayed the same.

We passed two more topiary sentinels—perfect spheres—and the vastness of the house came into view.

Half a dozen stone steps lined with chunky carved banisters

led to a huge back patio dotted with soft, buttery lamps. The music of the fountain mingled slightly with the sound of harp music coming from the other side of the French doors.

The home was almost a palace, all gray stone and severe lines. It had eight bedrooms and nine and a half bathrooms, a kitchen big enough to run a catering company, and at least half a dozen living spaces. It was decorated sumptuously, with antiques collected from trips all around the world—most of which should probably have been in a museum instead of a private collection.

It was a beautiful home. Nikki gasped.

And I crashed to a stop. She stumbled and bumped into my back, catching herself on my arms. The weight of her fingers against my biceps sent warmth arcing through my veins. I turned, and she took a hurried step back.

"This was a mistake," I told her. "Go back to the chopper."

Dark brows drew together as her lips tightened slightly. "What?"

My heart thundered. She stood here, gawping at fountains and staring at topiaries, and we'd go in there and she'd be eaten alive. And I would be the one who'd have to save her or watch her suffer. And then I'd be the one who'd get the criticism for bringing her here in the first place.

"This was a mistake," I repeated through gritted teeth. "Turn around and go—"

"Rome," a voice called out from the top of the steps. "You finally made it." There was a short pause. A pause that said as much as any words, because the woman at the top of the steps was a master at using silence like a weapon. In the stillness of the evening, with crickets chirping around us, delicate music dancing around us from two directions, and the last sounds of the helicopter engine fading, the silence said, *You're late, and I'm unhappy.*

I turned to see a woman in her early sixties, dressed in black pants and a cream top with a cashmere sweater draped over her shoulders. Her throat was adorned with a necklace of huge freshwater pearls, the ones in her ears completing the matching set. She had dark hair and few wrinkles, and eyes of dark, judgmental blue.

Her thin lips curled into a predator's smile as her gaze slid from me to the woman behind me. "And you brought a friend."

Yes, I had, and I regretted it, but it was too late to do anything about it now. Resigned, I stood straighter, and said, "Hello, Mother."

TEN
NIKKI

MY BODY WENT STILL, all the way down to my little toes. I stood in front of the most gigantic house I'd ever seen, surrounded by beautiful, manicured gardens, and all the color leached out of the world before my eyes.

The woman at the top of the steps looked down at us, haughty and unimpressed.

Beside me, Rome shifted, putting his hand on my lower back. "Mother, this is Nikita Jordan. Ms. Jordan, my mother, Joanne Blakely."

I realized the smile plastered to my face had slipped, so I did my best to stretch it a little wider. "The famous Joanne!" I said, and immediately realized that was the wrong thing to say when her cold gaze narrowed on me. And I remembered—I was a courtroom extra. Bland and beige, with no speaking lines.

And I'd already put my foot in it.

Clearing my throat, I used every bit of willpower to keep that stupid smile in place as I changed tack, trying to appear demure and uninteresting. "It's a pleasure to meet you, Mrs. Blakely."

The woman just blinked and slid her gaze to my boss. No words were spoken, but they seemed to communicate just fine. The woman whirled and strode toward the open French doors.

And by "the woman," of course, I meant Rome Blakely's *mother*. Which meant this was his home. And he'd brought me here with zero warning or preparation.

Suddenly, the horror faded, and I was angry. He'd done this on purpose! This whole thing—the outfit change, the helicopter, the introduction—was just a way to get me off-balance.

It was his way of saying, *You thought you had the upper hand? Think again, Jordan.*

And that pissed me right off.

Rome tipped his head to indicate that we should follow. I walked beside him and hissed, "You don't think you could have warned me?"

"About what?"

About what? *About what?* Apparently, billionaires could suffer from extreme obtuseness.

Glaring, I spoke through clenched teeth. "About the fact that tonight's engagement was a dinner with your mother, you dimwit."

"I don't see how that's relevant." He seemed unruffled, cold, even. When I paused, he stopped and gestured impatiently toward the doors. "Please."

"Not until you tell me exactly what's going on."

"We're having dinner with my family. It's a monthly affair. My mother insists."

"Right. And you didn't think it would be a good idea to mention that to me at any point during the past hour or so?"

"Again, Ms. Jordan, I don't see how that would change anything."

"I could mentally prepare myself! I could google her and see if I could find at least one safe topic of conversation. I could google *you* so I can pretend like we actually know something about each other. Other than the obvious."

His brow twitched. "Which is?"

"That you're a colossal jerk, Blakely."

His jaw clenched, and his gaze bore into mine. "There's nothing to prepare. Your job is to accompany me to social functions. This is a social function. You're here in a professional capacity. Now please, let's go inside and get this over with."

Without waiting for an answer, Blakely turned and stalked toward the open doors. The set of his shoulders was rigid, and there had been a hardness in his eyes that hadn't been there before.

Even when he'd been furious with me, when he thought I was litigious and vindictive against his precious company, he hadn't looked like that.

It only took me a second to take stock of the situation and decide to trot after him and make the most of it, but in that second, I realized a few things.

First, Rome Blakely didn't have a good relationship with his parents. He hated this monthly engagement, and he was doing his best not to show it. Second, him not telling me about it might not have been a way to get back at me for anything. It was possible, I realized, that Rome hadn't mentioned it because he hadn't wanted to talk about it at all. Maybe what he needed was support. He'd dragged me along here because, on some level, whether he knew it or not, he wanted someone in his corner.

And, hell, the man was giving me twenty-five grand a month to spend on clothing and beauty. The least I could do was make pleasant conversation with his uptight family, right?

That's how I justified it to myself as I followed, noticing his mother beyond him speaking to an employee in an all-black uniform. The employee nodded, glanced at me, then ducked into a room. Through the crack he left open in the door, I saw him hastily set another place at the dining table.

Mrs. Blakely turned toward us, her gaze flicking to my suit, down to my shoes, to my purse, and finally up to my lips. There was a minute tightening of her features, and I understood why the lipstick had been discouraged. This was one hell of a judgmental woman, and apparently, she liked dinner guests to display precisely zero personality.

This would be fun.

But I wasn't part of this world, and thus, couldn't be judged by its standards. I wasn't going to make myself a bland, blank canvas just because some rude woman didn't like the look of a bit of lipstick.

It's not like I was marrying her son; I was working for him. And when I'd read the contract earlier, it hadn't mentioned anything about lip color.

"Your brother got here earlier. He and Natasha wanted to go over a few details for their wedding."

"I was working, Mother," Rome replied. "I came as soon as I could."

It struck me that he was answering a comment she hadn't voiced out loud. I could sense the strain in his voice, and I noticed the way he tapped his index finger against his thumb in a rhythmic, unconscious motion.

Despite myself, a bit more sympathy was wrung out of the dry husk of my heart for him. He was an ass, but maybe in this particular situation, I could be sympathetic. I knew what it was like to ride the undercurrents of parental relationships.

"The hotel at Lake Como has confirmed they can accommodate three hundred and fifty guests," his mother continued, not acknowledging what her son had said. "Your father is pleased."

I arched a brow. I wondered if Rome's father cared at all, or if it was Joanne herself who was satisfied by the venue choice. I had the distinct sense I was walking into a booby-trapped room. Words had no meaning and conversations happened on multiple levels simultaneously. I had to tread carefully.

Rome's fingers kept tapping against each other as his mother led us deeper into the home. The ceilings were high, with gorgeous chandeliers throwing glittering light over every surface. The rugs under our feet were thick and richly patterned. Artwork hung in nooks that we passed at regular intervals.

We came to a stop outside a door, and another black-clad staff member nodded to Mrs. Blakely before opening the door.

I stole a glance at my boss. His fingers had stilled, but his breathing was heavy and his frown deep. I touched his elbow and arched my brows. *Are you okay?* my look asked.

His shoulders eased and he dipped his chin.

Then we walked into a sumptuously decorated sitting room.

"Rome brought a friend. Nicola, was it?" Mrs. Blakely asked, her piercing gaze coming to rest on me.

"Nikita, but you can call me Nikki," I said, nodding to the

people in the room. There were three staff members trying to be inconspicuous at the edges of the room, along with an older man, a younger man, and a young woman. I used my vast powers of deduction to figure out that they were Rome's father, brother, and soon-to-be sister-in-law. Rome grunted out a greeting and dropped into a sofa to our left. I perched on the edge of the cushion next to him.

Mrs. Blakely waved a hand at staff members, who jumped to offer us a drink. Rome asked for wine, and I decided I wanted my wits about me, so I asked for sparkling water.

"Have you knocked her up already?" the young man called out, chortling, from the sofa across from ours. He had his arm around a gorgeous blonde dressed almost identically to me, except her pantsuit was a deep navy blue, and she'd skipped the lipstick.

"Fuck off, Will."

"Don't speak to your brother that way."

The sharp rebuke from his mother made Rome's arm stiffen next to me. I cleared my throat and gave the other man my best smile. "Congratulations on the wedding," I interjected.

The woman—Natasha, Mrs. Blakely had named her— smiled, but it didn't reach her eyes. "We're thrilled," she said, sounding anything but.

"It sounds lovely. Have you been to Lake Como before?"

The blonde laughed. "Of course. I summer there every year. My uncle helped us secure the venue. He knows the owners of the hotel. Haven't you been?"

My smile felt a little forced, but I gave it my best. My cheeks would be sore by the end of the night. I shook my head. "Not yet. It's on my list."

"On your list," Natasha replied, baring her teeth at me. "That's cute."

"Natasha, be nice," Will said, glancing at his wife-to-be with a look that wasn't exactly loving.

"Your uncle is a gem," Mrs. Blakely interjected, giving her son a quick, significant look.

Undercurrents abounded. I shifted uncomfortably in my seat; my pants were itchy. I cleared my throat and smiled at the waiter who presented me with a glass of cut crystal full of delicately bubbling water. A perfect, juicy crescent of lemon perched on the impossibly thin edge of the glass. "Thank you," I said as he placed a coaster and a little cocktail napkin down on the side table.

The man nodded and drifted away.

"So how did you two meet?" This came from Will, who flicked his fingers at one of the staff and pointed to his near-empty glass. The waitress jumped to obey him, and Will's eyes came back to rest on me.

"Well, funny story," I started, thinking just the thing this party needed was a story about a giant perfume-filled penis and a trip to the emergency room, but Rome just said, "We met through colleagues."

"Colleagues!" Will repeated, delighted. "Dipping your pen into company ink." He gave me a lascivious grin before leering at Rome again. "Naughty boy."

"I am not," Rome replied tersely. He cleared his throat, then awkwardly shifted so his arm rested on the sofa behind me. "Nikki and I are together. She will be accompanying me to events for the foreseeable future. I thought this would be a good start."

"Really, Rome," his mother chided, "do you think that's appropriate?"

"Which part?" Will cut in with a laugh. "And what, exactly, did you mean when you met through colleagues? Yours, or hers?"

"It all makes sense now," Natasha said, her lips smiling but her eyes telling a different story as she looked me up and down.

I sat there stiffly, knowing they were insinuating exactly what I had when I first saw the contract, and visualized the beautiful quilted black Chanel flap bag I'd buy myself as a reward after this ordeal.

These people couldn't hurt me. They looked down on me, but they didn't realize they were the ones who had nothing. No compassion, no grace, no love.

Throughout it all, the father remained silent. He stared at his phone, seeming completely checked out. A deep sense of sadness filled me. I should have been feeling discomfort, or embarrassment, or something that made sense. But all I could see were people who threw barbs at each other and lacked the ability to connect.

Maybe Rome's father had the right idea. It was easier to disengage completely.

My gaze drifted around the room. There was a family portrait above the fireplace, but it only had the two parents and Will, looking like a young teenager. On the opposite wall, I saw another photo of Will in a cap and gown, holding a diploma.

This must have been an intimate room because the rest of the spaces we'd walked through had very few personal touches.

But—

"Where are the pictures of you?" I asked, glancing at my boss.

A heavy silence met my words. Rome, holding the stem of his wine glass in his left hand, cleared his throat. "There aren't many of them," he replied. "I spent most of my youth away at boarding school before I left for college."

"Rome was so bright," his mother explained, and it was the first nice thing I'd heard her say about him. "We knew it would be best for him to get an education at a good school."

I nodded. "But wouldn't there have been summers...holidays...vacations?" I pointed to a photo of young Will on a sailboat, laughing at the camera.

"He was a very studious boy." This gruff rebuke came from Rome's father, who watched me through deep-set eyes from across the room. The first thing he'd said since I walked in.

"My parents were in the midst of a big business transition when I was small," Rome explained, turning his head toward me but not meeting my eye. His face was oddly blank, his eyes flat as they stared at nothing. "Massachusetts was a good place to grow up. I made lots of friends."

"Well *that's* the most surprising thing of all," I said, because apparently when faced with uncomfortable situations, my internal filter malfunctioned.

I clamped my lips shut.

Finally, Rome lifted his gaze to meet mine, disbelief written in his eyes and the line of his mouth. "Excuse me?"

It was funny—there was one part of my brain screaming at me to pipe down and back off. But there was another part that had hated seeing him shut down the way he had before, and I loved the fact that I'd brought that spark back to his eyes.

Sure, the spark was fury, and it was aimed at me. But I liked it better than blankness.

I had to spend time with the guy, after all. If I was going to milk this opportunity for all it was worth—and get the fabulous wardrobe to match—it was better to be myself the whole while. That's what I told myself, anyway. I ignored the part of me that wanted to make Rome feel better.

He scowled at me. "I have friends."

I nodded. "Okay."

"I *do*."

"I believe you."

"Jordan," he snarled. "I have friends."

A wicked smile curled my lips. "Name one."

"Cole."

"Doesn't count. He's your employee."

"Arlo Noble."

I blinked. That was Bonnie's new boss. Not wanting to go down that route, I blew a raspberry and said, "You think billionaire buddies impress me? My best friend is married to Marcus Walsh."

He stared into my eyes, and I felt a bit dizzy at the intensity of it. "Bullshit."

My grin couldn't be stopped. "How else do you think I got Phil Phillips to come negotiate for me this morning?"

His mouth dropped, then pursed. Victorious, I leaned back and reached for my sparkling water.

That's when I noticed the curious gazes from the rest of our audience. Mr. and Mrs. Blakely were watching us, looking faintly horrified. Natasha was confused. Will, for some reason, was glaring at me.

I sipped my water and set it back down on its coaster and looked at Will. "You didn't go to boarding school?"

The other man was still frowning at me, but he nodded. "By the time they had me, Mom and Dad had more time. I wanted to stay at home."

As any child would, I thought to myself. I wondered if being shipped off to another state was the reason Rome seemed to hold himself apart from everyone. I hadn't seen him interact with his so-called friends, but every interaction I'd seen people have with him—or the way people had talked about him when I was working in the studio—was vague fear and awe.

"Will got the fun childhood, but at least I got a good education," Rome said, drawing my gaze.

I nodded, somber. "Don't forget all the friends you made along the way."

Rome shot me a glare, to which I replied with an angelic smile.

"I think it's time for dinner," Joanne announced loudly, then stood. Her arms were stiff at her sides as she marched across the room to the door. The rest of us followed her lead and headed into the dining room. Rome pulled my chair out to help me sit, then took the spot next to mine.

While the others took their seats, Rome leaned toward me. "Thank you," he said, so quietly I nearly missed it.

I nudged him with my shoulder, and he nudged me back.

Deep in my heart, a shard of ice melted. Maybe this job wouldn't be so bad.

Not wanting to dwell on that thought, I turned to Natasha and asked her a thousand questions about her wedding plans, which she was more than happy to discuss. Dinner was three courses of delicious food, including a melt-in-your-mouth-tender steak and the creamiest mashed potatoes I'd ever tasted. I caved and had a glass of red with dinner, which was divine.

The wine, plus the food, plus the forced company meant that by the time we headed out the back door and rounded the corner that would lead us to the helicopter, I let out a long breath.

"Was it that bad?" Rome asked as the helicopter blades began to whir. He met my gaze and I saw none of the anger and none of the arrogance that had been there before. He looked tired.

"Now the fat paycheck makes sense," I answered, and he gave me a ghost of a glare. Better than nothing. We took our seats in the helicopter, and I spent the ride looking out the window at the glittering lights spread out like a carpet below us.

ELEVEN

ROME

THREE DAYS PASSED in the normal rhythm, but I was restless. Work was as hectic as usual, but it failed to keep my mind occupied the way it normally did. I had a phone meeting with Wilbur Monk, and he gave me the runaround about signing on with my company. I had a feeling tonight's charity gala would be a pivotal moment.

Which reminded me—

I picked up my phone and dialed. It rang three times before a bright, cheerful voice replied, "Hello?"

"Have you found a dress for tonight?"

There was a pause. Then—"Who is this?"

I leaned back in my chair, glancing out the floor-to-ceiling window in my office as a smile tried its hardest to curl my lips. "Don't play with me, Jordan."

"Your number is unlisted," she noted. "You could be one of the many men who call and demand to know what I'm wearing."

"Is that what you heard from my question just now?" I frowned. "And how many men, exactly?"

She laughed, and the sound made the middle of my chest feel heavy. "I have a dress," she teased, "and it's fabulous."

"The car will pick you up at seven."

"See you then!"

I hung up the phone and tossed it aside. I'd seen her the day after the dinner at my parents' place, when she came in to do some paperwork at the office. But I'd only nodded at her and watched as she chatted with Clara then sat down at a computer. Other than that, I'd seen some expense reports come in this morning for hair, nails, makeup, and clothing with her name on them. Instead of making me angry about how much she'd squeezed out of me, the expense claims made me want to laugh. The woman wasn't wasting any time spending her monthly beauty budget.

Cole burst through my door. He skidded to a stop and frowned at me. "You're smiling," he accused. "Why are you smiling?"

"I'm not smiling."

"You are. Well, you were. You had a big dopey grin on your face just now."

"Why are you here?"

His eyes narrowed, but he shook his head and said, "The last independent contractor signed a full-time contract today. We're clear."

I blew out a breath. "Good. Thank you."

Cole nodded. "You ready for tonight?"

"Ready as I'll ever be."

"And the girl?"

I shrugged. "Clara prepared a packet for her. She was told to study it so she knows what to expect."

"Hopefully Monk will take to her, and we can close on this deal."

"Hopefully," I agreed.

The rest of the day dragged. Finally, I headed home to shower and dress in my tux, then called the car and headed to Nikki's place in Brooklyn. I could have fetched her to meet me here to avoid going out of my way, but I wanted to use the drive to make sure she'd reviewed the packet and knew what she was doing. Tonight was important, and we needed time to make sure we were on the same page.

The car pulled up outside her place, and my driver informed me that she'd been notified of our arrival. I waited a minute or two, then glanced at my phone in frustration.

"You're sure she knows we're here?" I asked.

"She said she'd be down right away."

Drumming my fingers against the door, I watched the front of her building and frowned. Where was she? I checked my watch, as if it would tell me something different from my phone screen, then glared at the door. Finally, unable to wait another minute, I got out of the car and took a step toward her building's front door, intending to press her buzzer until she had no choice but to come down here and do her job.

Then I saw her.

She floated down the steps, a vision in blue.

Her dress had long sleeves and a plunging neckline. The fabric looked sheer but was embroidered with fine, glittering blue fabric that curled and swooped in strategic areas. It looked like she wore almost nothing, but she was fully covered. Her shoes were simple silver heels with a small strap across the toes and one across the ankles. It was just like her usual style: not exactly revealing, but intensely arousing. She moved like a goddess, elegant, graceful, sensual.

My mouth went dry.

She opened the building door and stood there, two steps above me, looking down. She'd put something on her skin so it glowed faintly, highlighting the sharp angle of her collarbone and the space between her breasts.

That was the moment I realized she was beautiful. I'd known it before, of course. It would've been impossible not to notice from the moment I pried open that supply room door. But she wore a dramatic blue gown like she belonged in a classic old movie, her hair glossy and dark, her lips painted red, her eyes watching me through hooded lids.

In her hands was clutched a ridiculous purse shaped like a bow, covered entirely in dark-blue crystals. I stared at it, and at her, speechless. Even the splint on her finger didn't detract from the look.

Then she did a slow turn, showing me the embellished back of the dress that hugged her shape to perfection. The dress was a tease. I could see so much—and so little—of her body all at once. She spun around again and struck a pose, touching the length of her arm with her opposite index finger, the crystals of her bow purse glittering in the streetlights as she held it extended to the side.

Then she grinned. "See? Fabulous. I told you."

I wanted her. It hit me all at once. I wanted this woman like I'd never wanted anyone before.

I wanted to spread those long legs and bury myself between

them. I wanted her to turn back around so I could pull the zipper all the way down to the base of her spine and run my tongue back up the bared expanse of flesh. I wanted to feel the weight of her breasts in my palms. I wanted to kiss her until she gave herself to me fully, completely.

Blinking, I cleared my throat. She was my employee. I'd specifically chosen her to be my companion to these events so I wouldn't have to date anyone. So I wouldn't have to complicate these networking opportunities by dating someone who wanted sex—or worse, affection.

"We're going to be late," I told her.

She straightened, grasping that tiny, inconvenient-looking purse in both hands. "Right." A smile lifted her lips, but I could tell it was forced. "Lead the way."

I held the car door open for her, my hungry gaze on the way her body moved as she entered the car. Angry at myself for feeling out of sorts about a woman who didn't mean anything to me—a woman that *worked* for me—I slid into the seat and nodded at my driver, who'd gotten out to close the door behind me.

But she was just there beside me, and now, in the confines of the car, her delicate perfume teased me and tormented me. The shape of her breast against the embroidered fabric drew my gaze, along with the nip of her waist, and her long, long legs. Heart pounding, I sat there, sick with wanting.

"Wilbur Monk is a potential client we've been courting for months," I said, dragging my gaze away from the bare flesh exposed by her plunging neckline and toward the front of the vehicle. I popped open the small fridge and grabbed one of the chocolate bars Nikki liked. "He'll likely be there with his wife."

She looked at the chocolate bar I handed her, brow raised. Clearly, the promise of good-quality chocolate and almonds wasn't worth the power struggle, because she took it after only a moment's hesitation. As she opened the wrapper, she said, "Roseanne Monk. A patron of the arts and regular attendee of the New York City Ballet. She attended three shows at New York Fashion Week last year and made complimentary comments about Rodarte specifically."

I clamped my lips shut, glancing at Nikki, who shot me an impish grin.

"You did your homework," I noted.

She took a bite of the bar, made the same maddening little moaning noise she'd made the first time she'd eaten one, swallowed, and said, "These are so good. And I did more than my homework. After I read the dossier that Clara sent through, I did extra research." She swept her arm down her side, tracing the edge of the lace. "You're looking at a Zuhair Murad dress from the most recent ready-to-wear collection. Mrs. Monk viewed the most recent haute couture show when it was presented in Rome. She was photographed in the front row. And this"—she patted the bow-shaped crystallized purse—"is a Judith Leiber clutch that was *very* hard to procure on time. But when I was scouring the internet for photos of the happy couple, I saw her wearing a lot of unique bags, at least three of which were Judith Leibers. So I took a chance."

"Right. She likes fashion."

Nikki let out a long-suffering sigh, then shook her head. "Blakely, how do I explain this? The woman is a fashion girlie. I am a fashion girlie. I'm wearing head-to-toe icebreakers. You want me to stand at your side, look the part, and help you land this contract? This is what it looks like." She gestured to herself, arching dark brows.

I grunted, my gaze touching the neckline of her dress, the embroidered, embellished fabric, the crystal clutch. "At least you're making use of the clothing budget."

Her lush lips curled into a wicked smile. "I haven't even gotten started, honey."

The words sounded like a promise. Despite myself, I found my lips twitching. I wanted to find out what she had in store. Wanted to see how good she'd look on my arm at every event. Wanted to hear the things that came out of her mouth and see the flash in her eyes when I made her angry.

But that was beside the point. She was here to facilitate a relationship with a client. Nothing more.

"Good. Let's go over the other people who will be there."

Nikki settled into her seat, shifting so her knees pointed toward me. I kept my gaze away from the slit in her dress and focused on what was important: work.

TWELVE

NIKKI

THE FUNDRAISER WAS HELD at the New-York Historical Society, a gorgeous building made of white stone with a dramatic colonnade at the front. As I stepped out of the car, my gaze was drawn up the wide steps, past the dramatic entrance, and up to the row of windows on the second floor. It was a gorgeous building, and I was in a gorgeous dress, and I couldn't quite believe this was my life.

Rome's hand brushed my lower back, and we walked up the steps together. There was something thrilling about being at a beautiful venue, dressed to the nines, with an attractive man as my date. Logically, I knew it was simply my job. I was able to take his arm around my back and explain it away as Rome simply acting the part.

But there was another part of me that took the warmth of his hand on my back and made it mean something more. My cheeks flushed and my heart thumped a little bit harder. I found myself leaning into his touch the slightest bit, my shoulder brushing his, catching a hint of his warm scent whenever he moved.

His face was granite-hard, as if he dreaded walking into the event but knew he had to. It was the same hardness that had sat across from me at the negotiation table earlier in the week. It would be easy to think of him as a heartless, hard man who would do anything to close a deal. But then I thought of that little boy whose parents shipped him off to boarding school, and I wondered...

What if he pursued his business goals so ruthlessly because it was the only thing he had? He'd needed to hire me to be his date to this event, and all the others on the calendar. So he had no significant other, few friends, and a fraught relationship with his family. He was all alone.

I knew how hard that was. I had friends, but even so, I never quite felt like I was understood. Like I belonged.

We were greeted by an usher in a crisp white shirt and black vest who directed us to the event space. Soft music filtered through between the noise of many conversations.

We were accosted within moments of entering. An older woman kissed Rome on both cheeks, then turned to me with a smile.

"And who do we have here? It's not every day Rome Blakely brings a plus-one."

"I'm only here for the canapés," I quipped.

The woman laughed, the jewels dangling from her ears glittering in the warm light of the room. She wore a dark-purple dress that fit her like a glove.

"This is Nikita Jordan," Rome said. "Nikita, meet Gloria Beck. We worked together on a successful campaign a couple of years ago for her company's fantastic athleisure division. Gloria is also one of the best poker players you'll ever meet."

"Oh, stop it," the older woman said, swatting at Rome. "Is he always this charming?"

"No," I replied. "Mostly he scowls."

She laughed again, shaking her head, then excused herself and floated to another acquaintance. Feeling Rome's gaze on the side of my face, I turned to meet his gaze.

"Mostly I scowl?"

"You're doing it right now."

"No, I'm not."

I popped open my bow-shaped clutch and pulled out my mirror, flicked it open, and held it up in front of him. Rome didn't even blink. He didn't look at the mirror. He just held my gaze for a long moment, until I had to bite my lips to hide my smile.

"I'm regretting this arrangement," he told me, fingers curling around my elbow.

"You love this arrangement."

"You're a pest," he said softly, but his hand tightened on my elbow, and he pulled me ever so slightly closer.

"I handled that exactly right. She was eating it up."

"I should never have brought you here."

I was hard up against him then, my chest brushing his, chin tilted up. Breathless, I said, "I don't know why you insist on lying to yourself, Blakely."

He opened his mouth to answer, but another voice interrupted us. Another former client stopped by, watching me curiously, and Rome shifted his hand from my elbow to my lower back. I felt unsteady on my heels during that interaction, all my attention focused on the fingers that traced the embroidery on my dress just above the curve of my ass.

I wasn't sure this was exactly outlined in the company's code of conduct, and I found that I didn't care.

A waiter stopped by with a tray full of champagne, and I was glad to have something to do with my hands. I met lots of people that had been in Clara's briefing document, and many more that weren't.

Most of them oozed wealth. I felt like I wore a big neon sign proclaiming me an outsider, but all I could do was pretend it didn't exist and fake it until they thought I belonged. I watched Rome navigate conversations like a shark slicing through water. He closed two business deals almost casually, and I wasn't sure the other person even realized what had happened.

Then I felt pressure on my back a mere moment before he straightened beside me. "Wilbur," he intoned, reaching out to shake the older man's hand.

Wilbur Monk was a tall, broad man who clearly enjoyed the finer things in life, as evidenced by the large paunch hanging over his belt buckle and the wide, genial grin. In one hand, he expertly carried a glass of champagne and a little plate laden with canapés, leaving his other hand free to shake Rome's. His skin was tan and slightly leathery, as if he enjoyed the sun and didn't believe in sunblock. He had a wide smile and shrewd eyes that slid over to me the moment he dropped Rome's hand.

"This is a surprise," he said. "I've never seen Rome with such a beauty on his arm."

"Or one so fabulously dressed," his wife added. She walked up to our group, smiling, then put her hand around Monk's elbow. She wore a simple black sequined dress, cut close to her body, that I suspected was custom. Her neck was adorned with a gigantic diamond pendant, her matching earrings completing the set. Not a hair was out of place, and her makeup was expertly applied. She would have been a beauty in her youth because she was still looking fantastic.

"You must be Roseanne," I said, smiling. "I'm under strict instructions to make a good impression."

Beside me, Rome stiffened, but Wilbur and his wife both threw their heads back and laughed.

"Sounds like Rome knows who's really in charge here," Wilbur said, winking at me.

"How did you two meet? I can't believe Rome convinced someone to put up with him." Roseanne's lips stretched into a wide smile.

"I'm still on the fence about it, to be honest," I said, grinning.

More laughter, and Rome relaxed next to me.

"Nikki was a contractor for the company," Rome explained. "We met just before her contract finished up."

"Rome is being modest," I said, patting him on the chest with my free hand. His arm slipped around my back to tug me closer. "What really happened was that I got myself locked in a supply closet, and he pried the door open with brute force. The rest, as they say, is history." And a very specific contract including an NDA. I wiggled my finger splint. "I've got the scars to prove it."

The older couple laughed, delighted. Rome's fingers tightened on my waist.

"I'm glad to see it. I've always said you needed someone to stand beside you, Blakely."

"I think he needed someone to keep him from fumbling his way through these things," I said, waving a hand at the event at large.

"Fumbling," Rome repeated, glancing at me with arched brows. "How would you know I've fumbled?"

"Please," I said. "It's obvious."

"I take offense to that."

"But am I wrong?"

"That's not the point." Rome scowled at me, which made my smile widen. He caught himself and cleared his expression, then reflexively scowled again.

I laughed. He was cute when he wasn't trying so hard to be an intimidating jerk.

Roseanne let out a chuckle and shook her head. "Well, seems like you've found the right woman for the job." She turned to me. "I just adore your purse."

"Thank you! It's so silly. I love it." I held up the bedazzled blue bow, stroking it softly with my fingers.

"I have a small collection of Judith Leiber bags myself," Roseanne said. "Sometimes they're just the right thing for a bit of fun."

I smiled. I liked this woman. Too many people took themselves too seriously, but fashion and style was one area that was best when there was an element of fun, or campiness, or the unexpected. I'd bought this bag for this event because I thought it would be a good icebreaker, but I also bought it because I loved it, and it wasn't something I'd be able to afford on a regular salary.

We fell into an easy conversation. I asked her about her

gown, and she told me it was a custom design. When she found out I used to work in vintage fashion, her eyes lit up.

"You *have* to come see my personal collection. I've got so many wonderful vintage pieces. Mostly they're stored away in a climate-controlled room, and to be honest with you, most of them don't fit anymore. But I'd love to share that with you. Wouldn't that be wonderful, honey?" she asked her husband.

Wilbur, who had been deep in conversation with Rome beside us, glanced over. His gaze softened as he met his wife's, his hand curling around her lower back. "What's that, sweetheart?"

"Nikki used to work as a buyer for a vintage fashion store. I said she should come see my collection sometime. I'd love to show it off to someone who gets it."

"If I were a suspicious man, I'd think Blakely here planned this."

Rome cleared his throat. "What if I did?"

Wilbur chortled and clapped Rome on the back so hard he rocked on his toes. The older man shook his head. "I guess that would mean you really want our business. When are you free to come down? We'll be there for the holidays."

Where was "there?" He was asking me, so I shrugged. "Whenever suits you," I said. I glanced at Rome questioningly. This seemed a bit extracurricular. Would he be mad if I went over to Roseanne's place to look at clothes?

"It would give us time to iron out the last details to finally put some ink to this deal, hey, Blakely?" Wilbur's eyes glimmered as he glanced at my boss.

Rome nodded. "I'll have to check my schedule, but I should

be able to clear a few days to take the jet down before the end of the year."

"Great!" Wilbur exclaimed, and Roseanne beamed.

I, on the other hand, frowned. "A few days? The jet?"

"My clothing archive is at our primary residence in Grenada," Roseanne explained. "We've got a gorgeous little island there. You'll love it."

"Oh," I said, nodding. "Of course."

Had I just agreed to go see this woman's vintage designer clothes on her private island in Grenada? It sounded like it! I hoped Rome wasn't mad about an impromptu trip to the Caribbean.

But it also sounded like it had helped my boss take one step nearer to closing the deal with Wilbur Monk. So that had to be a win-win.

We chatted with the older couple for a few more minutes before an announcement informed us it was almost time for dinner to start.

We all shook hands. When Wilbur grasped mine, he held my palm with one hand and patted it with the other. Glancing at Rome, Wilbur said, "I'm glad to see you embracing the influence of others, Blakely. I wasn't sure you'd be able to. But Nikki here is proof you've got hidden depth."

Rome inclined his head, then put his hand on my lower back and guided me into the dining room. We found our table and settled into our seats, and then Rome leaned toward me. His breath warmed my ear as he said, "Good work, Jordan."

I gave him a little grin as I turned to look at him, not realizing just how close his face had been to mine. Our lips nearly brushed, and neither of us moved back.

For one long, breathless moment, I could feel the heat of his skin so close to mine. He'd leaned one hand against my chair and his other elbow on the table, so I was surrounded by him. I met his gaze, heart thundering, wondering if I was imagining things.

Like the heat sparking deep in my core, and its twin burning in his gaze. Or the way his eyes dropped to my lips and darkened. Or the electricity crackling in the scant space between us.

Then, as quickly as it happened, the moment was over. He pulled away and I, flustered, reached for my glass of champagne with a trembling hand. The bubbles danced on my tongue, but the drink tasted more bitter than it had before.

I took a shaky breath, then focused on buttering the piece of bread that a waiter dropped on my side plate with gold-plated tongs. When I glanced over at him, Rome looked entirely unaffected. He'd already turned to talk to someone who stopped at our table, deep in conversation about an upcoming campaign.

And dread crept through my guts—because he wasn't just my infuriating, arrogant boss anymore. Now he was the man who had made my thighs clench with nothing more than a look. The man who made me want to throw out the rule book, burn my contract, and destroy this once-in-a-lifetime opportunity just for the chance to taste him.

Which made me a grade-A idiot in a beautiful dress.

I was in so much trouble.

THIRTEEN
NIKKI

THE NEXT MORNING, bright and early, I woke up to the sound of my phone ringing. Pawing at my nightstand, I squinted at the screen.

An unlisted number, which meant one thing.

"Hello, Blakely," I said, flopping onto my back.

"It sounds like I woke you up."

I rubbed my eyes and huffed. "That's because you did."

"It's nearly nine o'clock in the morning, Jordan. What are you still doing in bed?"

"You had me at that charity gala until after midnight. I didn't fall asleep until two. I was wired." Now, the reason I was wired was because my heart pounded every time my boss's hand touched my elbow or my back, and when I got home, I was so full of nervous energy I ended up scrubbing my kitchen for an hour after stripping my dress and makeup off. But he didn't have to know that.

When he answered, his voice was gruff. "Well, get up and

get ready. I have a lunch meeting with an old client, and I want you there."

"Dress code?"

"Business casual. The car will pick you up at eleven."

"Anything I need to know about who we're meeting?"

"Clara's sending a dossier through now. Read it and get ready."

The phone clicked off. I pulled it away from my face to stare at the screen, then stuck my tongue out at it. He didn't get to wake me up after keeping me out all night, boss me around, then hang up on me.

Although, I guess that was my job now, so he could do whatever he wanted. Groaning, I rolled to the edge of my bed and threw the blankets off. My feet hit the floor, aching from their time in those fabulous heels last night. I stood and stretched my back out, then shuffled to the bathroom to do as I was told.

Now, I'd never been a lazy person. It wasn't that I didn't want to work—in fact, in the short amount of time I'd been in the position, I spent many hours educating myself on the people in Rome Blakely's social and professional circles, then made sure I was prepared for every event coming up on the schedule.

This included attending briefings at the Blakely offices with Clara and other members of the team, as well as going back through the company's archives to make sure I knew about brand relationships and campaigns that had been significant, depending on who would be attending each event.

So it wasn't that I wanted a free ride. I was working more than I ever had before—although a lot of the work was enjoyable. For example, when I spent four hours getting my hair and nails done before last night's gala and deciding on the exact perfect dress to purchase.

By the time I'd fixed my hair into an updo—it still had a lot of product in it from last night's event, so I did the best I could—and slipped on some vintage cigarette pants and a button-down top, my phone buzzed to let me know the car was downstairs.

"Hi, Keith," I said to the usual driver who held the door open. Peeking inside, I asked, "No boss today?"

"We'll pick him up on the way."

"Got it."

My knee bounced as I clipped my seatbelt on, and I pulled out my compact to check my makeup once again. When we pulled out to start heading toward Manhattan, a flutter went through my belly.

I channeled my nervous energy into studying the document Clara had sent through. It didn't take me long to become engrossed in it. We were meeting three men who were planning a Super Bowl commercial for the following year's event, which our company was hoping to produce.

I jumped when the door next to me opened. Suddenly, the car was full of Rome. He sat next to me as Keith closed the door, his eyes coasting over my hair, makeup, and outfit.

"You made it," he noted. "I wasn't sure if you would."

"Hello to you too, Mr. Blakely," I answered with a heavy dose of snark. "Of course I made it. I take my job seriously."

His eyes were dark in the dimness of the back seat. He blinked slowly, nodding once. "You sounded exceptionally groggy, is all." He paused. "Did something keep you up last night?"

Keith drove smoothly, but my heart still hammered. This

was ridiculous. I wouldn't be able to accompany my boss to all these events if I got tongue-tied every time he looked at me. Was he tall, attractive, and commanding? Yes. Did he make me wonder what it would feel like to be his, even for just a moment? Sure. I was human, after all.

But was I a complete idiot and about to give in to those urges? Absolutely not.

So, I covered my nerves with a snort. "As a matter of fact, something did," I told him. "Or rather, some*one*."

His body went still. "Oh?"

"A man, specifically."

"A man." He gritted out the words. The focus of his attention felt almost heavy. His eyes narrowed ever so slightly, and then he relaxed, as if by force of effort. "I wasn't aware you were seeing anyone. That might get complicated. You remember that you signed an NDA?"

"The man that kept me up insisted on parading me around this charity event long after most of his clients had left, and then instead of letting me go home and go to bed, he drove there with me and insisted on debriefing me when it was well past midnight."

The air in the limo, which had become stifling, lightened considerably. I met Keith's inscrutable gaze in the rearview mirror, then turned to Blakely and popped a brow.

He gave me a stony glare. "Get used to it, princess. We'll debrief after every event."

I hummed, and the car stopped. We'd arrived at the restaurant.

The lunch went well. I discovered that one of the men was an avid scuba diver and spent most of the meal talking to him about his various dives. I had just been reviewing one of the underwater campaigns that the Blakely Advertising Agency had done for yet another perfume launch, and I'd gone down a research rabbit hole about diving. So I was able to pretend like I knew what I was talking about—at least enough to carry my side of the conversation.

Being a companion to Rome Blakely, it turned out, was easy. People loved talking about themselves—and the powerful people who ran companies and signed deals with the likes of Rome Blakely *really* loved talking about themselves—so all I had to do was persuade them that I hung on their every word. It was like dating, except I didn't care about the outcome so there was no pressure.

The scuba diver, Dean Garrett, was about a decade older than me, in his mid-forties, but he looked fit and healthy. A strong hairline framed his handsome face, and he smiled at me with straight, white teeth. He looked like a man who threw his money around and was used to getting what he wanted.

I'd gotten the impression Dean liked feeling like a big, important man, so I was really hamming it up. "I don't think I could ever do a night dive," I told him, shivering dramatically. "So scary!"

"I could take you," he told me, grinning. "Keep you safe from all the things that bite down there."

And there it was—the fine line between being an entertaining companion and crossing over into murky flirtation. I'd misjudged it, apparently.

Before I could come up with an appropriately soft refusal that wouldn't offend the other man and ruin my boss's business chances, Rome's hand slid across the back of my chair. "She's not going diving with you, Dean."

The heat of his arm seared across the top of my shoulders. I felt every inch of his nearness: the arm across my back, the hand he curled around my shoulder, the press of his knee against my thigh as he leaned closer. He smelled divine, and he was too close. I leaned forward and grabbed my glass of water to take a sip in the hopes of cooling myself down.

Dean grinned. "I think the lady should speak for herself."

I painted a grin on my lips and said, "The boss has spoken."

"Is he always this possessive of you?"

"Only when deep-sea creatures are involved," I said, laughing as I gave Blakely a side-eye. He met my gaze steadily and said nothing. Heat curled low in my stomach, and my thighs clenched. There was something about this man's attention that made me want to melt. When he focused on me, it made me feel almost giddy and breathless. Special.

And wasn't that just the silliest thing in the world?

He shifted his gaze to his potential client, and I let out a breath. The moment passed, but Rome's arm stayed on the back of my chair for a while longer. By the end of the meal, it sounded like a deal had been struck.

But Rome didn't seem happy about it.

As we exited the swanky restaurant, I nudged him with my elbow. "You okay?"

He arched a brow at me. "Yes. Why?"

"You're doing that scowl-till-I-scare-small-children-away thing again."

"I do not scare small children."

"What about that little girl just outside the restaurant

before we walked in? When you got out of the car, she stumbled back and clawed at her mother."

"That was the pigeon's fault."

I laughed. "Seriously, Blakely. Why the face?"

He faced me fully, standing in front of his waiting car. "Did you want to go scuba diving with Dean?"

Startled by the question, all I could do was blink. "What?"

"Did you," he asked slowly, "want to go scuba diving with Dean?"

"No," I answered.

"It sounded like you did. You talked to him for the better part of an hour."

"Yes, because that's my *job*."

"You were batting your eyelashes and *giggling*, Jordan."

"Excuse me?"

"You heard what I said," he gritted out.

Okay, that pissed me off. I planted my hands on my hips and glared. "Have you forgotten that you hired me to sit beside you and make pleasant conversation?"

"That's right. I didn't hire you to flirt with other men right in front of me. You're there to be with *me*."

"I was not *flirting*. I was showing interest in his hobbies. What else was I supposed to do?"

"Talk about—I don't know—the weather."

"The *weather*."

"Men look at you laughing at their jokes and they think they've got a chance."

I let out a snort. "Right. Isn't that the point of having me at your side?"

His jaw clenched. "I didn't like it, Jordan. Don't do it again."

"You got the contract, didn't you? Would you rather I sit there like a wet sock and drag the mood down?"

Eyes flashing, he stared me down.

But I wasn't intimidated. I took a step closer, so we were nearly nose to nose. "I made him laugh and stroked his ego so you could come in and close the deal. That's the whole reason I'm here. And, in case you haven't noticed, I'm really, *really* good at it."

I poked him in the chest for emphasis with every word until he snatched it before I could finish the last poke. His fingers dwarfed mine as he clasped my hand, clutching it between us. I could feel the calluses on his palm, the heat of his skin against mine. My breath caught.

He stared into my eyes, then dropped his gaze to my lips. I felt like a doe who'd just realized she was in the hunter's crosshairs, trembling and ready to bolt.

Rome clearly wasn't as affected as I was. He dropped my hand and took a step back as he straightened his tie. "Let's debrief on our way back to the office."

On trembling legs, I followed him into the car. He didn't look at me as we went over the lunch, then talked about what would be required for the rest of the week. There was only one more event for me to attend, and I'd have Sunday off.

I barely heard him. The more I sat there in his car, listening to him order me around, the angrier I got. By the time we got to the office building, my jaw was clenched and my fists balled. I stomped after him to the elevator, resenting the fact that I had to trot after him like a little lapdog and that I was the one who'd signed up for this in the first place.

The elevator doors closed, and we leaned against opposite walls, glaring at each other.

He arched a brow. "Why do you look like that?"

"Like what?"

His lips twitched at my barked response. "Like you want to bite my head off."

"I just think you're taking a lot of liberties with my job description," I said. "You want me to parade everywhere on your arm and make pleasant conversation, and then you get mad when I do. You think you have a right to tell me whether or not I can date just because I signed a contract with your company."

He pushed off the wall and prowled closer. We traveled up toward the top floor, and I suddenly realized I was trapped here with him. It only took him two large steps to stand toe-to-toe with me, his broad chest pressing against mine. Both of his hands came to rest on the wall on either side of my head.

"You seem to have forgotten one thing, Ms. Jordan," he enunciated, eyes flashing. His head dipped slightly so I could feel his breath against my cheek.

"What's that?" I asked, trying to sound tough. My fingers curled into the handrail behind me, and my breath stuttered. He was so close. So overwhelmingly male. So...angry.

"While you work for this company," he said in a low, dangerous voice, "you belong to *me*."

His face dipped, but his lips remained just out of reach. His eyes bored into mine, pinning me in place. I could feel the warmth of his body all down my front, feel his breath against my lips. My world narrowed to the spaces between us. The fraction of an inch between my mouth and his. The brush of his suit jacket against my breasts. The touch of his knee between mine.

The elevator came to a stop, and Rome pushed off the wall, straightened his tie, and faced the doors a moment before they opened. He stepped out like he didn't have a care in the world while I tried to catch my breath, clinging to the handrail, watching his retreating back.

He paused just on the other side of the elevator doors to glance back at me. "From now on, your presence is required for daily dinner briefings with me. My office. Five o'clock. Until then, talk to Clara about the next few events you'll need to attend."

Without waiting for a response, he disappeared around the corner and left me panting in the elevator. The door began to close before I shot my arm out to stop it. Wobbling, I clutched my purse to my stomach and made my way to Clara's office, eyes darting to the frosted glass door across from hers. The one that belonged to Rome.

I gritted my teeth.

He'd done that on purpose just to knock me off-balance. The jerk. Straightening my shoulders, I strode to Clara's door and knocked on the jamb. She looked up and waved me in.

I gave her my best smile. If Rome thought that little stunt was all it took to get me to take off running, he was dead wrong. I was here to stay, and I wasn't going to be stupid enough to fall for an arrogant billionaire who thought he could boss me around.

FOURTEEN
ROME

I LOCKED myself in the bathroom attached to my office and leaned against the vanity. My pulse pounded. I could feel the blood thrumming in my fingertips, my toes, my cock.

The woman drove me nuts.

Tugging at my tie, I tossed it aside and stripped off my jacket. It was too warm in here. Too stifling.

I hadn't been able to think straight since Nikki had told me she'd been kept up by another man. Before I realized she was teasing me, I'd wanted to turn the car around, tear through her apartment, and find whoever it was that had shared her bed— and end him.

It was an itch under my skin. An urge I could scarcely resist.

But that was crazy.

It was just because I was worried about this stupid scheme in the first place. I didn't actually care if she slept with another man. It wasn't like we were together. Not for real. I was just paranoid about this whole thing blowing up in my face. I'd made headway with Wilbur Monk for the first time in months, and I was antsy about anything that could make it fall apart.

Yeah. That was it.

Except when she'd laughed at that prick Dean Garrett's jokes one too many times, I'd wanted to throttle him too. His eyes had lingered on her lips, her breasts, her mile-long legs, and I could see what he was thinking by the look in his eyes. Then he'd had the gall to actually ask her out in front of me.

I should have gotten up and left right then and there.

But.

Nikki was right. The whole reason I'd hired her was for this exact reason. She softened my potential clients so I could come in for the kill. She made it easy to cut the tension. She made me look good.

And though she'd only been in the position since the beginning of the week, I already knew that she was better at her job than I could have ever expected. She charmed men and women alike. She found topics of conversation and navigated them with ease. She laughed easily and made people feel good about themselves.

Last night, at the gala, I'd found myself actually falling for her charms. She made me feel good about myself just by leaning into me slightly when we walked, or giving me that little side-eyed glare whenever I said something she didn't like.

And I almost went and ruined it by kissing her in the elevator.

Except I didn't just want to kiss her. I wanted to tear her clothing to shreds and take her against the wall. I wanted her to understand that she belonged to *me*. That she was mine, and I wouldn't tolerate anything less.

A knock on my office door brought me back to the present. I washed my hands and walked out to the main room in time to see Cole poke his head in.

"How'd it go?" He was asking about the lunch meeting.

"They're in," I said.

Cole whistled. "Between that and the Monks inviting you down to Grenada, seems like your little investment is already paying off."

I grimaced. "Yeah."

Cole frowned. "You don't think so?"

"I'm just not sure how long I can keep this up," I told him, and it was the truth. There was a reason I kept myself to myself. I'd learned from a very young age that I was on my own, and that was how I'd made myself into a success.

Now, a week into having this woman at my side, I was panting after her like never before.

This wasn't me.

Besides, I didn't like lying to my clients. I hadn't said anything directly untrue, but I knew Monk and Garett and all the others inferred something more about my relationship with Nikki.

This had to end before it got too complicated.

"After we sign the deal with Monk, I'm terminating her contract," I told Cole.

He rubbed his jaw with his forefinger, nodding. "You might want to wait a little while so it doesn't look like you pulled a bait and switch on him."

"I'll come up with some excuse. We grew in different directions. Went our separate ways. It was amicable. Something that makes us both look good and doesn't raise any red flags."

"If that's what you think," Cole said.

"You don't?"

He shrugged. "Seems pretty effective so far. Who knew all you needed was a beautiful, charming woman at your side to start closing all these deals so effortlessly?"

My shoulders stiffened. "Beautiful and charming, huh."

Cole laughed at the look on my face. "Tell me again why you don't think you can keep this companion thing up?"

"It's a lie, and it's not right."

"Uh-huh. It's got nothing to do with the fact that you're having to spend so much time with the woman, does it?"

"No."

"Right. So if I called her up the day you terminate her contract and asked her out, you'd be okay with that?"

"If you do that, I'll take it as an immediate resignation on your part."

Glee shone in Cole's expression, and I knew I'd said the wrong thing. "Well *that* is interesting."

"How would we explain that to our clients?" I tried to rationalize, but Cole's grin just widened. Not one to be deterred even though I knew it would be best to clamp my mouth shut, I continued, "What if the Monks get wind of my second-in-command dating the woman I've just tossed aside? How do you think that would play?"

"Tossed aside," he repeated, brows arched. "Is that how it would go down?"

"She would never be interested in you anyway."

At that, Cole straightened. "What's that supposed to mean?"

"You know what I mean."

"No, I want you to explain. Why wouldn't she be interested in me? I'm just as successful as you. Better looking, too."

I snorted. "On what planet?"

"You're so full of shit, Blakely. You want her and even the thought of me taking her out for a drink is driving you crazy."

"Why are you here? Why are we even talking about this? We'll get the contract with Monk, and then we'll go our separate ways. This has nothing to do with you." The skin under my collar felt warm. I tugged at the fabric, glaring at my friend.

He crossed his arms and widened his stance, watching me curiously. "I've never seen you like this. You've barely known her for two weeks."

"Get out of here," I bit off. "I've got work to do."

He put his hands up, relenting, then walked to the door without a word. I waited for the door to close behind him before sinking into my chair. Pinching the bridge of my nose, I groaned.

This whole thing had been a terrible idea. The smart thing to do would be to pull the plug and snare Monk some other way.

But the only progress we'd made in closing the deal was with Nikki by my side. I needed her for this. Needed her to save my company.

So I'd do exactly what I told Cole: I'd close the deal with Monk, then terminate her contract and go back to the way things were before. Then everything would be fine, and normal, and great.

All I had to do was survive the few months that she had to be by my side. I'd grit my teeth and bear it.

But a few hours later, when she walked into my office at five o'clock sharp, giving me a little sideways look that was designed to get a reaction out of me, I forgot all about terminating her contract. I became very busy watching the way she moved when she unpacked takeout containers, or how her hair shimmered when she bent her head over the schedule I gave her.

Until she walked out again and my brain came back online, I forgot everything in the world except how much I wanted to have her.

FIFTEEN

NIKKI

MY FRIEND BONNIE looked at me curiously on Sunday, as we reclined on my velvet couch and talked about our weeks.

"You're attracted to him," she said when I finished complaining about all the running around my boss had made me do this week.

Of course, I couldn't tell her about the specifics. If I told her about the companion job, who knew who she'd tell? I trusted her, but this was the kind of gossip that could not be contained. If I started telling my friends that I'd been hired to be my boss's plus-one, I knew it would eventually blow up in my face.

Plus, I was a little embarrassed. The niggling feeling that I was just a placeholder in their lives, the same way I'd been with my ex-boyfriend—if you could call him that—and my landlord, and my old boss. Even with my mother, I think I'd just filled a daughter-shaped hole in her life, but I never actually lived up to who she wanted me to be. Maybe that's why our relationship had never been strong. I was a placeholder to her, but there was no one else that would come to relieve me of the position. No one more successful, or more understanding, or more supportive. There was only me, and I wasn't enough.

So I said nothing. I did what I always do, and I went on the attack. "Projecting, much?"

"Stop trying to deflect. You have the hots for your boss."

Her eyes were sparkling, and all I could do was throw my hands up and give in. "Fine! Yes. He's attractive." That was obvious. With the wide shoulders that couldn't quite be hidden by the well-tailored suit, the blue eyes, the thick eyelashes, lush lips, strong jaw... "But he's seriously not my type. He's so..."

"He's so..."

I glared at her. "Just not my type."

She must have seen something in my face, because she let me off the hook and said, "I can't judge."

Seeing my opening, I prodded her about her own situation. Bonnie had started seeing her own boss, and she told me it felt like it was the real deal.

Maybe it was my own situation that made me skeptical. Or my own secrets. But I tried to understand how Bonnie could fall for a man like...well, like Rome, really, without worrying about what it all meant. If it could really last, when we came from such different worlds.

I'd been admitted to another universe in the past week. And it wasn't just the designer clothes and the fabulous bags. It wasn't just the good food and the amazing service. It was the *ease*. A car appeared when it was needed. A helicopter could land on the roof at the snap of the fingers. Doors were opened, literally and figuratively, that had previously been locked and barred.

I wondered if Bonnie might have been dazzled by it all. Maybe she wasn't thinking straight, and her Prince Charming would turn out to be nothing more than a frog in a glitzy penthouse.

She didn't take it well. We left off feeling vaguely angry at each other, and I didn't know if I'd been wrong to challenge her. Maybe I was projecting.

After all, I wasn't faring much better than she was. And if she could find happiness with a man, who was I to begrudge it of her?

But after she'd gone, I sank down on my old couch, staring at the cracks in the walls and the peeling linoleum in the tiny kitchen to my left, and I wondered if this was just another ending. Another person realizing that they didn't actually want me for me. They'd enjoyed the idea of me, or the vague shape of me in their life, but they didn't actually want *me*. The placeholder. The one you called when there was nothing better around.

The companion.

ON MONDAY, there were no planned events but I had a few meetings to attend at the office. I wanted to do some research about a few upcoming events. There were a number of people I'd met that I hadn't really been able to converse with, and I knew I could do better.

Unsettled by my day with Bonnie—and with the itch I felt anytime I heard my boss's voice down the hall—I threw myself into my work.

The day flew by, and before I knew it, it was five o'clock and time to walk across to the other end of the floor for my nightly debriefing.

I found Rome in his office frowning at his computer. He glanced up when he saw me, then waved a hand at the seating area, where takeout had already been placed. I took a seat and inspected the Styrofoam containers. Thai food. Delicious.

"We're going down to Grenada the week before the holidays, which means we have seven weeks to keep the Monks interested," Blakely said, standing up to join me in the seating area. He sat on the couch across from me. "It's very important that I close this deal, so I want to go over some expectations."

I nodded and started serving myself from the various dishes. "Expectations. Got it."

"We'll be there for three days. They'll probably take us out on their boat to go fishing and snorkeling. They might want to go hiking, since there's a path around the island. And I hear they care very much about preservation, so anything you can learn about that would be a bonus."

I nodded. "No problem."

"I want you to use the time we have to prepare as well as you can for this. It's very important."

"You've mentioned that," I told him calmly, "and I understand."

He met my gaze for a beat, then nodded. "Good."

I straightened. I hadn't expected that from him—for him to treat me like a competent member of his team. It felt good to be trusted with something so important. Maybe he saw the type of person I was beneath the lipstick and the great clothes—saw my work ethic, my intelligence, my competence.

It made me like him a little bit more. I still thought he was arrogant and annoying, but at least he didn't treat me like a dolt.

We ate for a few minutes as I glanced around his office. Last week, we'd had one of these office debrief dinners on the Friday of the luncheon, but I'd been so focused on not spilling food on myself that I hadn't really looked around. He had his degrees up on the wall, and a large piece of abstract art behind his desk. Everything looked expensive. The view was great.

The whole room was extremely impersonal—except for one thing. When I got up to toss my takeout container, I paused beside Rome's desk to look at the only photo in the entire room. It was a young Rome with a beaming smile on his face, a basketball under one arm while the other was hooked around an older man's waist, who was busy ruffling his hair. The man wasn't his father.

"Who's this?" I asked.

Rome glanced up from his food, then looked away. "Coach Reggie. Basketball. Reg coached the team through high school."

I set the frame down carefully. "I hadn't realized you played."

"Stopped when I graduated, but I kept in touch with Reg until he died."

"Oh, I'm sorry."

He set his empty plate down and leaned back. "It's fine."

"You were close?"

"Closer than I was with my own father," he admitted. "He's the one who told me I could build companies if I wanted to. He told me the only thing that would hold me back was my own mind."

"And was he right?"

"About most things, yeah."

"What was he wrong about?" I sat down across from him, crossing my legs as I leaned back. A deep, unquenchable curiosity opened a pit inside me. I'd spent hours with this man at various events over the past week, but I knew precious little about him, other than the fact that he was great at closing business deals and his family sucked.

But there'd been a mentor. Someone who had cared about Rome Blakely, the boy, and not just Rome Blakely, the business mogul.

"He told me if I didn't let people in, things would crumble in the end. No man could stand on his own, he said. But I'm here, and I'm standing."

"On your own."

"Precisely."

"On the other hand, my dad once told me that lighthouses don't run around looking for boats to save. They just stand there and shine." I grinned at the memory. My dad was a cheeseball.

"Maybe I missed the shining memo." A hint of a grin twitched over his lips in response.

Encouraged, my smile widened. "You just stand there and wait for unsuspecting boats to crash at your feet."

That coaxed a chuckle out of him, and he asked, "What about you? Close with your dad?"

"I was," I said. "He passed when I was fifteen."

Rome nodded. "Sorry."

There was no pity in his voice. No discomfort that usually came with people hearing about loss. He seemed to understand me without me having to say a word. We sat across from each other, separated by several feet and a food-laden coffee table, but I felt closer to him than I ever had before. "Thanks. Stomach cancer. It was horrible."

"I can imagine. Reg was a smoker. Got his esophagus in the end, and then spread. But it's funny; after he died is when this really took off." He waved a hand around his office. "Sometimes I think it was his final gift to me. The last push I needed to make something of myself."

Or maybe, I thought, he channeled his grief into work, because the alternative was standing on a windblown coastline watching ships shatter on the rocks.

My phone buzzed, interrupting our conversation. I glanced at the notification and let out a frustrated huff.

"Everything okay?"

Glancing up, I saw the frown on Rome's face. I shook my head. "It's fine. I've just been applying for rentals for weeks and I keep getting rejected. I don't get it. My new salary should be more than enough to satisfy these people. But they don't just want an employment contract, they want months of pay slips. They want deposits. They want my firstborn child. It's never-ending."

His frown deepened. "A rental for what?"

"Um. To...live?" I laughed. "An apartment. I have to move out of mine by the end of the month."

"How come?"

"The owners are moving back in. It's a real shame because it was a rent-controlled place, and my living costs are going to skyrocket now." I grimaced. "Not that that's your problem."

"I'll talk to Clara. She'll sort something out."

Warmth spread through me, but still, this job had fallen into my lap. I didn't want to tie my living situation to it as well. Then if things went wrong, I'd be in *really* bad shape. "No, that's okay—"

"It was inconvenient for us to pick you up in Brooklyn. We'll get somewhere on this side of the bridge so we don't have to drive so much." He stood and stalked to the office door then poked his head out. "Clara. Find somewhere for Jordan to live. Somewhere we don't have to cross half the city to get her to an event on time."

I scowled at his back. He sure had a way of making a favor from him sound like it was my problem.

When Clara called out an answer, he crossed back to the couch in front of me. "Next weekend is the anniversary party at Garcia's place in the Hamptons. We're going to have to address the perfume bottle incident."

"Right," I said, trying to follow the subject change. We were done talking about personal issues, it seemed. Back to work. "I'm guessing he was angry about the damage?"

"We've been working on a CGI version of the commercial, but the man is obsessed with authenticity. We need to wait for a new bottle, and I know he's getting antsy. He'll have to delay his launch because of the mistake."

Because of my mistake, he meant. Guilt squirmed through me, and I shifted uncomfortably. "I'm sorry."

"Don't be. It was an accident."

I straightened. "You mean that?"

His gaze settled on mine, and he arched a brow. "Off the record, I do."

A smile twitched at the corners of my lips. "What's that supposed to mean?"

"It means I won't say it in your lawyer's presence."

My smile widened. "You think he's that much of a shark?"

"I think I'm done being squeezed for all I'm worth by opportunistic women in red lipstick."

"Opportunistic!" I protested, even though it was true.

"Don't play the innocent doe. It doesn't suit you."

"I think you're mad you didn't intimidate me."

He scoffed. "Hardly."

"Would you believe me if I told you I wasn't trying to squeeze you for all you were worth?"

The flat look he gave me was answer enough. I shrugged, not wanting to protest too much. If he wanted to think the worst of me, that was his problem. Wanting to escape his incisive gaze, I rooted through my purse and pulled out a little plastic packet containing two chocolate chip cookies.

"What are those?" Rome asked, frowning.

I lifted the packet. "These are my emergency cookies."

He blinked. "Emergency cookies?"

I nodded. They were the hard kind you got at the grocery store with the chocolate chips that tasted kind of bland and waxy, so not ideal, but that was why they were emergency cookies. "For when I need a snack," I explained. Or something to do with my hands when faced with a large predator sitting on the other sofa. A predator who was shifting and leaning forward.

Before I could open it, the package was plucked from my fingers. "What the hell is this?"

"Hey! Give those back!"

He held them between his thumb and forefinger like they were some disgusting biohazardous waste, his lips curled. "You eat this shit?"

"Blakely. Give me my emergency cookies."

"These aren't cookies. These are garbage." He stalked to the trash can next to his desk and dropped them in.

I stood, aghast. "You can't just throw my cookies away!"

"Again, Jordan. They aren't cookies. They're sugary cardboard circles."

"But they're *my* sugary cardboard circles."

"If you want chocolate chip cookies, I'll get you chocolate chip cookies."

"That's not the point!"

"Grab your things," he said, and he walked out of his office.

I stared at the takeout containers on the coffee table and then slid my gaze to the trash can. They were individually wrapped, and his trash was mostly paper, so I could retrieve them if I really wanted to be stubborn about it. But before I could decide whether I was part-raccoon or not, Clara poked her head in and said, "I'll handle the cleanup. He's waiting at the elevator for you."

"I don't know how you deal with him every day. I've got whiplash after one conversation."

She flashed me a smile and shrugged. "He hasn't been so bad lately."

"Jordan!" my boss's voice boomed from the other end of the floor. "Get over here!"

"Not so bad?" I asked, slinging my purse onto my shoulder.

Clara laughed and waved me off. I made a point to walk at my normal pace, because I wasn't scurrying for a man who trashed my sugary cardboard circles without even consulting me. He glared at me from the elevator, his arm across the opening as the doors tried unsuccessfully to close.

"Where are we going in such a hurry all of a sudden?" I

stepped into the elevator and felt the same thrill as I did whenever I was in an enclosed space with the man—all of a sudden, there wasn't enough air in the place, and there was altogether too much him.

"We're continuing your education," he said, shooting me a sideways glance. "Clearly, you need it."

"You are insufferably rude. Did you know that?"

He turned to face me as the elevator shot downward, closing the distance between us. I backed up until I hit the wall, giving him my best glare.

He didn't seem intimidated by it. A broad palm landed on the wall above my head, and then my boss was only inches away from me, his dark gaze roaming over my features.

This was familiar. And just like last time, my breath hitched and my body went on high alert.

"I think you like it when I boss you around," he said softly, the toes of his glossy black shoes touching the toes of my cherry-red pumps.

"I think you're delusional," I said, trying to sound tough and failing. My voice came out breathy, because he was so close I couldn't breathe properly, and his eyes seemed to be devouring me, and his scent was everywhere, and I wanted to know if his lips were as soft as they looked.

Because I did like it when he bossed me around. I liked it a whole lot more than I should've.

I was once again saved by the elevator coming to a smooth stop. An electronic voice announced that we were not on the ground floor, but one of the basement parking levels. Blakely pushed himself off the wall and strode out. Heart clattering in my chest, I followed.

Now, I had never been a car person—still wasn't, to be honest—but when Blakely stopped in front of a hot little two-seater coupe with a Ferrari logo on the hood, my middle gave a tiny, undeniable thrill.

He watched me from across the roof as the doors unlocked as if by magic. "Get in, Jordan. We're getting cookies."

SIXTEEN
ROME

THE ENGINE PURRED BENEATH ME, and Nikki let out a little puff of breath. I glanced over, brows arched. "You good?"

"Uh-huh," she said, fingers tracing the perfect stitching on her leather seat. "Nice wheels."

I grinned and put the car in gear. It handled like a dream as we exited the underground parking garage and headed out into the streets. Nikki settled into her seat beside me, her gaze avid as she glanced around the car and finally over at me. "This really isn't necessary, Blakely."

"Judging by that garbage you were carrying around in your purse, it's absolutely necessary," I said, taking the next left.

I didn't turn to look at her, but I sensed Nikki's smile. Having her this close to me was the sweetest form of torture. I felt like I had in the helicopter; I wanted to give her a taste of my world. Show her things she couldn't have dreamed of before. Watch her reaction and relive all these experiences through her.

She made life sweeter. Even driving this car was more fun, and I enjoyed it on a good day.

Nikki reached for the volume knob on the center console, and I arched a brow. "What are you doing?"

"I'm turning the stereo on," she said, as if I were dense.

"You don't touch the stereo when someone else is driving."

Her laugh informed me just how intimidated she was by my rules. A song from two decades ago came on, and Nikki grinned. "I love this song."

"You've got some nerve, putting that on in my car," I grumbled, but I didn't change the music. I liked seeing that smile on Nikki's face.

"Have you any idea how uptight you are? It's staggering, actually."

"Hiring you was a mistake," I said darkly.

Her laugh was bright as a midsummer's day. "Probably, yeah."

We drove a while longer, and some of the tension in my shoulders relaxed. I hadn't even known I was tense. But having her here beside me, bobbing her head to the music, filling my favorite car with her sweet perfume, made everything just a little bit better.

Besides, she was my companion, wasn't she? Coming along with me wherever I chose was the entirety of her job description. Even if I'd originally conceived the plus-one duties around galas and networking events, and not impromptu trips to my favorite bakery.

When we turned down a darkened alley, Nikki shifted in her seat. I navigated around a dumpster and pulled to a stop outside a nondescript steel door, painted rust-red.

"Uh, Rome...?"

"Scared, princess?" I gave her a wolf's smile.

She rolled her eyes, glancing over when the red door swung open. A gigantic man blotted out the light that spilled through the opening, his massive shoulders silhouetted by the buttery yellow glow beyond. He kicked something with his foot to keep the door propped open, then shifted into the light so I caught sight of his scowl.

He trundled up the two steps that brought him to street level and walked around to my side of the car. In his hands, he clasped a white bakery box.

I rolled down the window. "Evening, Sal."

"Next time you want something, give me more than twenty minutes' notice, all right?" He thrust the box through the window, barely giving me enough time to grab it before he let go and walked back to the bakery door.

"Cheerful sort of guy," Nikki noted.

I laughed, handing her the box. "Hold these," I said as I rolled up my window. When she had the box in her lap, I drove out of the alleyway and onto the street. I pulled into the first open spot where I could park on the street and flicked the overhead lights on.

Nikki's face was aglow with a mischievous grin. "This is unexpected, Blakely. I haven't seen this side of you."

"What side is that?"

"The side that has a hook-up for emergency cookies, and that pulls onto the side of the road to eat them."

"Open the box, Jordan."

She laughed, and the noise made my own lips twitch. Turning the box toward me, she presented me with its contents.

Sal had come through with a dozen warm, gooey, perfectly baked cookies the size of side plates. I took one and then nodded for Nikki to do the same. She set the box down on her lap and studied the selection, choosing a cookie near the edge of the pile with lots of chocolate studded through it.

Holding it in her hands, with her shiny red nail polish providing a strong contrast to the brown-and-beige cookie, she inspected the treat like the fate of the world depended on her verdict. One dark brow arched, and Nikki shifted her gaze to me. "Not bad," she conceded.

"Be quiet and eat the cookie, Jordan."

"You are unspeakably rude," she replied, then took a huge bite. When her eyes rolled back and a noise of pure pleasure came from her throat, a grin stole over my lips. She chewed slowly, another of those delightful sounds escaping her closed lips, and I felt a twitch below my belt.

Tearing my gaze away from Nikki's chocolate-chip cookie-induced ecstasy, I took a bite of my own. Delicious. I couldn't help the groan that slipped out of me, and Nikki grunted in agreement.

We ate in silence, savoring the deliciousness as Manhattan life buzzed just outside the car. Traffic flew past, cars honked, and people hurried along the sidewalk. I saw none of it. All that existed was buttery, crispy-chewy perfection, chocolate, and Nikki.

"Wow," she finally said, popping a finger in her mouth to lick the tip. That nearly made me groan again, but I pulled some napkins out of the center console instead. She thanked me as I offered her one, and we cleaned up the evidence of our gluttony.

"I gotta hand it to you, Blakely," Nikki finally said when our cleanup was done. "That was one amazing cookie."

I grinned. "Glad you've come to the correct conclusion," I said. "I was worried I'd have to fire you when you pulled those crimes against cookies out of your purse."

When I looked up to catch Nikki's gaze, I noticed a little spot of chocolate on the corner of her lip. Before I could stop myself, my hand rose, and I caught the smudge with my thumb. Nikki's eyes widened, but she didn't pull back. If anything, she leaned into me, mouth dropping slightly open as her tongue darted out to swipe across her bottom lip.

It caught the edge of my thumb, and I found myself leaning into her, gaze caught by her perfectly formed mouth. I needed to taste it. Needed to feel it against mine. Needed to know if kissing her would make this ache inside me go away.

I was hard as rock behind the placket of my pants. I wished we were in my apartment instead of in this tiny car. Wished I had her propped up on my dining room table so I could smear chocolate over her skin to lick it off. Wished I could take my time kissing her until I knew I'd had enough.

Nikki's breath coasted across my wrist, her lashes fluttering as she tilted her head—

A honk right outside my door made us both jump. My hand dropped from her face, and Nikki backed away like she'd been burned. The box of cookies slid from her legs, and she scrambled to catch them before they landed on the floor.

"I—uh—" She gulped. "I don't know—"

"I should take you home," I said, putting the car in gear and keeping my eyes pointed firmly forward.

"Just drop me off at the subway," she said, and we both

knew I'd ignore that particular request. By the time I pulled up outside her apartment, the temperature in the car had cooled.

When Nikki handed the box to me, I shook my head. "Keep them," I said.

Her fingers curled around the edges of the box, and she nodded. "Okay. Thanks."

We didn't mention the... What was it that had happened earlier? An almost kiss? A moment of insanity? A narrow miss?

Whatever it was, it remained unspoken. Nikki opened her door and put her foot on the pavement outside, as if to assure herself that she was still on solid ground. "I'll see you tomorrow. Thanks for the cookies."

"Tomorrow," I managed to grunt, then waited until she was safely inside before driving away.

That couldn't happen again. No matter how much I wanted it to, I couldn't let my control slip like that in the future. She was my employee, and we were already navigating a precarious relationship. If it got complicated—and if anyone found out—I could lose everything.

I'd hired her to stand at my side and make me look good. That's all she would be to me, no matter how much I wanted more.

THE COOKIES LASTED all of two days. Loath as I was to admit it, they were the best I'd ever had. Not that I'd ever tell Rome that particular fact. Whatever had happened in the car got buried under a thick layer of professionalism, and for the next week, neither of us edged anywhere near the line of impropriety. I did research and prepared for all the upcoming events on our calendar. I didn't want to mess this up—especially not by kissing my boss.

The last event before our jaunt to the Hamptons for Raphael Garcia's anniversary party was a gala honoring Rome's parents for their work with the Society of Gout Sufferers of New York, for which the Blakelys were apparently major donors.

I could tell Rome was dreading the evening the minute I slipped into the back seat of the car. I'd chosen a simple black velvet dress with matching black gloves for the night, trying to keep it elegant and understated. I tucked the bottom of my dress inside the car and nodded at Keith, who closed the door beside me.

Clasping my black clutch on my lap, I glanced over at my boss. His jaw was tight and his eyes glued to the window, where rain splattered the car and the city beyond it. The privacy screen was up, which meant he hadn't even wanted Keith's subtle attention on him. My presence was probably an irritant, but if I was to do my job properly, I had to lift his mood before we got to the event.

The car pulled away from the curb, and Rome still hadn't said a word.

"It's getting cold out these days," I said to fill the silence.

Rome shifted, glancing over at me with cold blue eyes. "Yes," he replied.

There was a gulf between us, one that hadn't been there in the week since he took me out for chocolate chip cookies. I could still feel the pressure of his thumb against my lip, could still remember the heat in his eyes when he'd met my gaze.

No one had ever looked at me like that—like they *ached* for me. Like holding back from kissing me was pure torture.

As a lifetime placeholder, being seen—being wanted—by a man like Rome Blakely was a particularly strong drug. Especially when he'd shown me glimpses of the man beneath the arrogance and the scowls.

I'd seen below the surface, and now I wanted more.

He was a complicated man who liked to distance himself from anything that might hurt him. I could understand that. Hadn't I been doing the same with my romantic relationships for the past decade? Hadn't I been doing the same with my friends?

I'd seen Bonnie again this week to help her choose a dress for an event she was attending while Rome and I would be in the Hamptons—a gala for her boss's charity. Even though it would have been the perfect opening to share the secrets of my new job, I told her nothing about my situation. It wasn't because of the NDA. I kept myself apart because I was afraid of her judgment. Afraid of her rejection.

Beside me, Rome was doing the exact same thing. I knew because it was familiar to me. I could tell he was putting a wall up between himself and the rest of the world in preparation for tonight, when he'd have to smile and clap and pretend to be happy that his parents were being honored by the upper echelons of the city.

Meanwhile, he'd be remembering all the ways they let him down.

I couldn't stand the distance between us, so I reached over and slipped my hand into his. He glanced down at my velvet glove, then slowly curled his fingers around my hand. A tightness eased in my chest.

"We don't have to stay the whole night," I said quietly.

His hand tightened slightly, then softened. "Yes, we do."

"I'll be right beside you," I said.

He glanced over at me, the tilt of his eyebrow slightly sardonic. "To protect me from the big, bad wolf?"

I met his gaze levelly. "If that's what it takes."

He huffed and looked away, but he didn't remove his hand from mine. We sat like that as we snaked through the streets toward Midtown. All too soon, we arrived at our destination. In the few moments between the car stopping and Keith opening the door for us, I watched Rome don his armor. His face became remote. His hand slipped out of mine, and he straightened his tie and cufflinks. By the time the door beside me opened, there was no hint of the man whose gaze sparkled with amusement when I said something he didn't expect, or the man whose gaze burned through me whenever we were alone. The man who had a surly baker at his beck and call, who had a photo of a high school basketball coach in the place of honor in his office.

This was Rome Blakely, business mogul, giant of the industry, and perfect son to the guests of honor.

I hated it. I wanted the real him. The man he kept hidden behind the remote exterior. But I had a job to do, so I donned my own mask. The pleasant smile and open expression that made it easy for people to approach us. I became his companion, his plus-one, and nothing more.

The dinner was held at a huge, airy space in Midtown that had been decorated in silver, blue, and ice-white. Delicate music floated through the space, exactly the same way it did at every one of these events. The far end of the huge room had a big stage with a clear podium and a fluttery curtain as a backdrop, with large round tables filling two-thirds of the floor space.

Where we stood, by the door, was a bar and a clear area for people to mill around and network. We were immediately accosted by an older couple who complimented our clothes, then commented on the space, then inquired about our attendance at the Garcia event this weekend.

"We'll be there," Rome said, sliding his hand down my spine. A shiver followed his touch. Even through the heavy fabric of my gown, I could feel the heat of his touch.

The woman smiled. "Marvelous. Garcia's place is just magical out there."

"We heard your work with him included some challenges," the man said. "Delays in the planned launch schedule."

Rome smiled. "Nothing out of the ordinary," he said. "I'm confident we'll be able to deliver on our promises."

"You always do," the woman said, smiling, but her eyes were sharp. She patted Rome's arm, then led her husband away to speak to another couple. I was learning the language of these people—the subtle jabs, the taunts, the probing questions. Just as much could be said with the twitch of an eyebrow or a significant silence as could with words.

Rome was a master at it. With Joanne Blakely as a mother, I was sure he'd gotten a rigorous education in that particular style of communication.

The evening continued like that for the next twenty minutes or so. I did my best to be the charming companion who added color to conversations when I could, and stayed quiet when I thought it was called for. Rome stood a little further away than he usually did. Tension ran through him, evident in the set of his shoulders and the stiffness of his movements.

I wanted to fix it. I hated this distant, cold man who responded exactly as he should and showed no hint of personality. As we flitted from conversation to conversation, I wondered if anyone else noticed. They didn't seem to; men joked with him and took his polite, wooden smiles as if Rome had guffawed along with them. Women flirted and charmed, not put off by my presence or Rome's distance.

The longer things dragged on, the more uncomfortable I became. This wasn't right. This wasn't him. I didn't like it.

Then a booming male voice called Rome's name, and he put his fingers on my elbow to turn me toward the noise. His mother and father glided toward us, waving and nodding politely to the people who greeted them along the way.

They came to a stop in front of us, and Joanne inspected Rome's tux, then my dress, her lips pursing ever so slightly.

"You brought the girl," she said, not looking at me.

"Hello, Mother. Father," Rome replied, inclining his head. "Congratulations. You must be happy about all this."

"I really would have preferred you came alone," his mother said, "or brought someone more appropriate."

An elongated pause. "The food leaves a bit to be desired," Rome noted.

They were doing that thing again—talking past each other. Having two separate conversations where the things that weren't said were as meaningful as the things that were.

It reminded me of my teenage years with my mother. After my father died, she was consumed with grief—we both were— but she forgot that I needed her. I didn't exist to be her shoulder to cry on. Didn't exist to ease her pain. She forgot that I was hurting just as much as she was. So we talked exactly like Joanne spoke to Rome. At each other, instead of with. Never connecting, and never even attempting to.

I inhaled slowly, trying to tamp down the heat that crawled up my neck.

"The Gerbers have a daughter, you know," Joanne said, her gaze flicking to me for the briefest moment. I gathered I was supposed to wonder who the Gerbers' daughter was, and how she stacked up against me.

Too bad for Joanne, I had the benefit of a contract and a healthy paycheck to keep me right here, smiling politely at her hidden barbs.

"I don't know the Gerbers or their daughter," Rome finally replied directly. "Nikita has accompanied me to every event for the past three weeks. It would be noticed if she weren't here tonight."

"Still," Joanne said, her lips curling as she glanced down my gown. "It amazes me how you manage to make things about yourself."

Rome stiffened next to me.

"Your mother's right," his dad said, leaning in as he lowered his voice. "Attending these events solo never seemed to bother you before, and now the spotlight is on you and your date instead of on your mother where it rightfully should be. Why couldn't you just come alone? You couldn't do that for your mother, just this once?"

Outrage filled me and moved my tongue before I could clamp my mouth shut. "You'd like that, wouldn't you?"

For the first time, Rome's parents met my gaze, their expressions startled, as if they'd forgotten I was able to speak.

I sneered at them. "Why do you want your son to be alone? Do you enjoy the thought of isolating him from people? Is that why you sent him away when he was just a boy and rubbed his face in it when you had a second child?"

"You have no idea what you're talking about," Joanne whispered at me, the apples of her cheeks growing bright red.

"I know damn well what it feels like to be the family punching bag," I replied in the same harsh whisper.

"You shut your mouth, you little—"

"Mother." The word whipped out from Rome's mouth, sharp.

Her eyes widened, and Rome's father cut in. "Get a handle on your woman, boy."

Rome's hand appeared on my lower back. Suddenly, my blood ran cold. What had I done? What had I *said*? I was supposed to be the perfect, charming companion who took all the off-color jokes and the boring conversation and pretended to love it.

I wasn't supposed to talk back to my boss's mother, of all people. Especially not on a night when she was the guest of honor.

Her face was tight, and, judging by the fury and triumph flashing in her eyes, she knew I'd just realized I'd messed up.

Slight pressure on my back drew my attention to Rome, whose other hand wrapped around my elbow. He guided me around his parents and led me toward the front of the room, where the exit was located. He murmured greetings to people as we sliced through the crowd, not slowing down as he marched me out of there.

My chest collapsed. I'd messed up. I'd messed up *bad*.

With every step we took, dread grew claws that sank into my chest. In the far corner of the room, a corridor led off toward the bathrooms. Rome walked me down the hallway, past the bathrooms, all the way to a stairwell. The sound of our footsteps echoed as we walked up the steps, and all I could do was focus on keeping my steps steady as my mind whirled.

I shouldn't have said anything. I'd forgotten myself. I was reading into our relationship when all it should have been was professional. My attraction to the man blinded me and made me mess up, and now I'd be jobless and homeless, and—

And I'd never see Rome again. That shouldn't have been the thought that made me want to burst into tears, but it was.

"In here." Rome pushed open a door at the top of the stairs. To our left, the sound of conversation filtered through. There were a few tables on the mezzanine level overlooking the main event space, but he led me to the right, into what looked like a smaller, private dining space that hadn't been set up for the event. Chairs were stacked around the edges of the room, with a few boxes full of miscellaneous supplies strewn here and there. A long table dominated the space, with light from the big dormer windows illuminating the room.

The door latched shut, and I turned to face him. My heart thumped as my throat constricted, but I had to get the words out —had to explain. "I'm sorry," I said, staring at his bowtie. He'd shaved, but I could see the shadow of his beard on his jaw and throat. "I shouldn't have said anything. She was just being so horrible to you, and I couldn't take it."

"To...me?"

I blinked, lifting my gaze. "What?"

"You're upset because she was being horrible to me?" His brows tugged together.

I gulped and nodded. "Well...yeah. All that crap about you coming alone. It's like they *want* you to be miserable. Not that I'm the one to make you happy, but *someone* will. And you deserve that! But the way they talk, it's like they want you to just stand there and absorb all their criticism because it's your job. It's not right, Rome. It just isn't."

My eyes stung, and I blinked a few times to clear them. When I finally looked up again, Rome's expression had changed. His eyes were focused on me with an intensity that made me suddenly go still.

"You weren't upset about what they were saying about you? Talking like you weren't even there?"

I shrugged. "Sure, but I mean, whatever. No offense, but they kind of suck. So their opinion doesn't really matter to me." I took a deep breath, dropping my gaze to his bowtie again. I knew what I needed to say, and I didn't think I could do it while looking at his face. "I understand if you need to fire me. I know I was out of line down there, and I completely failed at my job. I should never have talked back, especially not to your family and *especially* not when they're the point of this whole event. So, it's okay. I understand—"

He hummed, then lifted his hand and slid it over my jaw to curl around the side of my neck. The movement startled me so much I stopped talking and looked up at him.

"I'm not going to fire you, Jordan," he said, his voice warm and faintly amused.

"You're not?"

"Why would I fire the only person who's ever ridden to my defense?"

At my startled blink, he let out a low chuckle—then he dipped his head and before I knew what was happening, my billionaire boss pressed his lips to mine and kissed me.

It wasn't a gentle kiss. It was a kiss that said, *I've been waiting for this moment.* He curled his fingers around my neck and banded his other arm around my back, pulling me flush to his body. I clutched his shoulders and kissed him back, heat burning away every thought that might have crowded my mind and stopped me.

His lips demanded so much of me. He kissed to possess. To own. The arm around my back shifted and his hand slid down to my ass, squeezing. He groaned against my mouth then moved to kiss my jaw, my neck, and back up again. His hand clutched my hair as he bent me backward, and all I could do was pant and cling on for dear life.

"You make me want things no man has any business wanting," he said, voice like gravel. He pulled away to look in my eyes, his hands still holding me exactly where he wanted me.

"Like what?" My chest heaved. My mind reeled. I didn't know what was happening, but it felt so good I couldn't stop. He walked me backward until my shoulder blades hit the wall, then pinned me there with the bulk of his body. His hands slipped down my arms to my wrists, which he circled with his fingers and brought up above my head, pinning them there with one hand.

"Like this," he said darkly. "You, breathless." His free hand moved to my face, and he traced the outline of my bottom lip. "Your lipstick smudged."

"Some of it ended up on you," I noted, glancing at the red smeared on his lips.

He grinned. "Good," he said, then kissed me again.

Rome was no gentler the second time around. He pinned me to the wall with his hips against mine and his hand shackling my wrists, his free hand tilting my head so he could kiss the breath out of me. His tongue slid against mine as he groaned, and then his teeth nipped at my lip. I laughed, leaning my head against the wall, loving the way he was watching me, like he'd forgotten where and who we were.

In that moment, I'd forgotten too.

All that existed was the dark heat in his eyes, the press of his body against mine, the heat burning through me. I'd never felt so consumed by a man before. I'd never had my mind go so quiet, where all that mattered was the feel of his body, the rhythm of his breath, the sin in his gaze.

We kissed until our movements became frantic. He dropped my wrists and I clung to his lapels, my hips bucking against him. I could feel him pressed against me, hard, needy. His hands cupped my breasts, fingers digging into the flesh above the sweetheart neckline, and then he grabbed my thighs and spread them, holding me pinned to the wall in that darkened room where we had no business being.

I moaned, muffling the sound against his neck. My core pulsed. I wanted him inside me.

A dish clattered outside the door, and reality intruded. We flew apart. I ended up clutching the wall, gasping for breath. Rome stood with his back to me, his hands leaning on the table in the middle of the room, head bowed. Silence pressed in.

Gulping, I took a deep breath and bent down to pick up the clutch I'd dropped at some point in our little encounter. Thoughts came to me in fits and starts. My hands trembled. I unclasped the kiss lock at the top of my clutch and pulled out my compact mirror and the travel-sized makeup wipes I always brought with me.

Rome glanced my way, his eyes dark. "That shouldn't have happened."

His mouth was smeared with lipstick. My heart thumped. "It certainly went against the code of conduct from Appendix B," I noted, then pulled out a makeup wipe and handed it to him before pointing to my own lips.

He scrubbed his lips with the wipe as I did the same, albeit with slightly more precise movements using my mirror. When I looked up, he was frowning at the smears of red on the makeup wipe.

"You missed a spot," I said, then took the wipe and dabbed at the corner of his lip. He stood very still, his gaze steady on mine.

When I was done, I threw out both wipes and touched up my makeup, then went to work fixing my hair and dress. It wasn't perfect, but it was the best I could do. Rome straightened himself, frowning at one of the wrinkles in his jacket from where I'd gripped it in a tight fist.

As I set myself to rights and watched him do the same, the full consequence of what we'd done settled over my shoulders.

I couldn't fall into a relationship with this man—for a multitude of reasons.

First, he was my boss. It was written out in black and white in my contract that this kind of thing was unacceptable. That should have been enough to guide my actions. If I wanted to gain some sort of financial stability, I needed to work this job longer than three measly weeks. At least until I found somewhere to live and saved up a bit of an emergency fund.

Secondly, he was wealthy. Men like him just didn't end up with women like me. He'd use me and then toss me aside. That was pretty much written in my contact too. I was the official placeholder. I'd agreed to it. Letting myself get wrapped up in him would be disastrous not just for my stability, but for my sanity too.

I wasn't able to separate sex from emotion. I was already feeling the pull of his charm. If we did something like this again,

I already knew I wouldn't be able to keep myself from developing feelings for him. That absolutely couldn't happen.

Kissing him had lit a fire in my gut. It had made me want to submit to him, to give him my body and my heart and my soul. He'd made me feel alive, and I wanted more.

But I wasn't stupid. The first thing he'd said was that it shouldn't have happened, and I agreed.

He met my gaze. "Jordan—"

I held up my hand. "Let's not. That was... That happened. We agree it shouldn't have. We can just move on and go back to the way things were before."

"Can we?" His question was slightly cynical, his eyes shadowed as the light from the windows silhouetted him against them.

I straightened, adjusting the fall of my dress. "Yes. We can. You've hired me to do a job, and that's what we need to remember."

Standing my ground while he stalked toward me, I ignored the fluttering in my chest. I tilted my head to meet his gaze as his eyes bore into mine. Having him this close to me challenged my resolve. His energy pressed against me, weakening my defenses.

If he told me he wanted me in that moment, I'm not sure I would've refused. Despite all the logical reasons to stick to what was outlined in my contract, a big part of me wanted to rip those papers to shreds, wrap my arms around him, and deal with the consequences later.

But he just slid his hand across my back and guided me back out the door and into the glittering blue and silver of the event.

By the time we got back downstairs, the interlude in that room felt like a distant memory.

EIGHTEEN

ROME

MY FATHER GAVE a charming speech that earned him raucous cheers and thunderous applause, and I didn't hear a word of it. I sat next to Nikki obsessing about the taste of her lips.

I ran over the events of the last hour, cursing myself.

I shouldn't have touched her. I was courting trouble. She was an employee, first of all. Touching her at all went against the explicit bounds of our contract. Not to mention the fact that we'd have to be spending time together for the next few months, and now I knew how her body felt pressed against mine.

But she'd flown to my defense when my parents trotted out their tired old criticisms, and something had snapped inside me. Suddenly, Nikki wasn't the plus-one that made me look good. Now, she was a strong woman who wasn't afraid to stand up to the guests of honor in order to defend me.

Not even Coach Reggie had been able to do that—not when my parents donated buckets of money to my boarding school and dangled that over the administrators' heads at every opportunity. He'd supported me in private and deferred to them in public.

But Nikki hadn't been afraid. She'd straightened her shoulders and stood there like I needed a champion, and she was the perfect person for the job.

For the first time in my life, I had someone in my corner.

I leaned my arm on the back of her chair, my fingers drifting over her shoulder. She angled her head toward me, slowly lifting her gaze to meet mine. Her cheeks grew pink, and I grew hard. My eyes traced a strand of hair that had fallen out of place, the only evidence remaining of our interlude upstairs.

Dinner was served and I'm sure I made pleasant conversation with the other guests seated at our table, but I wouldn't be able to remember anything I said. Every cell in my body was focused on her. On the graceful movement of her fingers as she tucked a strand of hair behind her ear. The way she smiled at the old man seated to her left. The curve of her neck as she leaned over, laughing.

That night, in my mind, was a series of vivid snapshots. The sight of Nikki pressed against the wall, flushed with desire, lipstick smudged onto her cheek. Her graceful descent down the stairs. The smell of her skin. The way she glanced at me from the corner of her eye when dessert was served, our shared secret plain in her gaze.

I was a man discovering the depth of a new addiction. A man on the way down.

In the car, when the evening was over, I watched the play of the streetlights over her face, her dress, her folded hands. I glanced down at the heels on her feet, wishing they were propped on my shoulders. We didn't say a word to each other until we stopped outside her apartment.

Keith got out, and Nikki met my gaze.

"The car will pick you up tomorrow at noon. We'll take the bird over to Garcia's place."

Her eyes were dark and liquid. She dipped her chin. "Sure."

Keith's shadow moved outside her door, and I knew I only had a moment longer with her. "Thank you," I blurted.

"For what?"

"For tonight."

She held my gaze for a long moment, then gave me a little half-smile. Keith opened the door, and then she was gone. I waited until she disappeared from view, then gave my driver a nod. By the time I got home, I was cold and alone and empty.

NINETEEN
NIKKI

TWENTY-FIVE GRAND WENT QUICK when you bought a designer dress and purse for your first event in the calendar. I'd rented the gowns for future events, but the money had still disappeared in a flash, which was as ridiculous as it was true.

As I packed for a weekend in the Hamptons, I found myself grimacing at my first few purchases. I had to look the part for an entire weekend, and garbing myself in head-to-toe designer gear would cost several months of my clothing and beauty budget.

But I was resourceful. I scoured consignment stores and chose a few key pieces. I raided my own closet and decided that style mattered just as much as labels. We'd be rubbing elbows with people in the fashion world, so leaving a good impression mattered.

My apartment was mostly packed up. When we got back from the weekend, I'd be moving into a place that Clara had found for me on the Lower East Side. It wasn't company-owned, and when I expressed that I wasn't entirely comfortable tying my living situation to my work, she assured me all she'd done was get my rental application in front of the right people. It was a hell of a lot better than homelessness.

Zipping my suitcase, I smoothed my hand down the blue tweed of a vintage Balmain suit dress I'd bought years ago when I sourced clothing for my old store. It had two rows of buttons down the front with a subtle peplum effect at the hips. The dress went all the way down to mid-shin, and it made me look like I had curves for days. I'd had it tailored to fit me, and it made me feel powerful and put-together.

To me, clothing was more than just fabric that covered my nakedness. It was a way of expressing myself. Sometimes I was able to lift my mood simply by putting a favorite outfit on. Combined with makeup and hair, I'd used clothing and beauty as a way to lift myself out of funks since I'd been a teenager.

Today, my clothing was meant to say, *I belong here.*

The company car picked me up, and I was carted across the bridge and to the Blakely offices. We drove straight to the underground garage, where I bundled myself and my suitcase into a private elevator and shot up to the top floor.

My heart rattled. As I rose through the building, I tried to stay composed. I was calm. I was professional. I was here to do my job.

But it was also the first time I'd see Rome since the gout fundraiser the night before. Since the kiss.

The elevator slowed to a stop. The doors opened. I took a deep breath and stepped out.

I wore patent leather black pumps that clacked on the hard flooring, the wheels of my little suitcase clattering behind me.

Clara looked up as I rounded the corner, then gestured to the frosted glass door separating us from Rome's office.

"He's waiting for you," she said, then got up to help me with my suitcase. "I'll get this loaded up."

"Thank you."

Not a woman to waste any time, Clara was on the phone and dealing with my suitcase within seconds. I, on the other hand, wanted to waste all the time I could scrounge instead of facing the man who had kissed me like it meant something to him before telling me it could never happen again.

With a deep breath, I lifted my fist and rapped my knuckles on the glass.

"Come in," Rome's deep voice said from the other side.

I inhaled. Straightened my shoulders. Exhaled.

And entered.

He stood with his back to me, his gaze on the skyline spread out beyond his floor-to-ceiling windows. The cut of his navy suit perfectly highlighted the breadth of his shoulders and the taper of his waist. He turned, and his gaze drilled into me.

I said the first thing that came to mind, running my hands over the lapels of my suit dress. "We match."

His gaze traveled down the length of my body and back up again. It felt like a physical touch. When he swept his gaze over the curve of my hips, I remembered what it felt like to have his hands grab me there and pin me to the wall. When his eyes lingered on my chest, I thought about the feel of his fingers sinking into my flesh. He made me feel naked and exposed, and I wasn't sure how I felt about it.

"You wear clothing like it's a weapon," he finally said, and I blinked. His steps closed the distance between us until I had to crane my head up to keep meeting his gaze. "I find myself wondering if you're planning on using it against me."

I arched a brow. "That's a bit presumptuous, don't you think? Maybe I dress for myself."

Rome's finger traced the white piping on my lapel, across my chest, and down. I felt the barest brush of his touch against my breast and fought to keep my breathing steady.

Something had changed between us, and the ground was unsteady beneath my feet. We'd flown apart after the kiss and decided it was a mistake, but now...

"Do you?"

I blinked. "Do I what?"

"Do you dress for yourself?"

I took a small step back. Anything to put a bit more space between us. "Of course."

He hummed. "I think there's more to it than that. You always seem to know exactly the right balance to strike no matter where we go."

It surprised me that he could read me so easily. Most people —men especially—thought my interest in fashion and beauty to be frivolous. It was girly. It was silly. But of all people, Rome saw what was beneath the surface. I liked that about him. I liked that he didn't dismiss me just because I liked to wear vampy lipstick.

But liking him and kissing him again were two different issues entirely. I had to work for the man for the foreseeable future. I didn't want to get involved with him.

I clasped my hands in front of me, arching a brow. "I'm guessing this outfit is a winner?"

He grinned. "You think it isn't? Garcia's going to take one look at you and call you his new muse."

I flushed, unable to keep the smile from my face. "We'll see."

Rome's hand slipped down my arm to my elbow, the touch sending heat skittering through my veins. He guided me out the door, nodding to Clara before heading for the elevators. Once inside, he let go of my arm, and I could breathe.

"Have you always liked clothing?" He watched me from where he leaned against the wall of the elevator. We traveled up toward the roof, a short ride up to the very top of the building.

The doors opened as I nodded. "Mostly, yes, but my interest really started in my late teens." I paused, my throat suddenly tight.

Rome stopped at the exterior door leading to the roof. "What is it?"

I looked up to see his brows drawn, his gaze intent. There he went again, seeing me. The real me. I shook my head. "We're going to be late."

He leaned against the metal door and crossed his arms. "Something's on your mind. Tell me."

"Ordering me around isn't going to work, Rome."

He grinned at me. "But you used my first name, so you must be warming up to me."

"Marginally."

He laughed, and the sound made my own lips twitch. When he quieted down, his gaze was warm. "Tell me what you were thinking about."

"It's nothing, really." I shook my head. "It's just old memories. They're hard to explain."

"Try me."

"Why do you care?"

"We need to pretend to be a real couple for the entire weekend. Maybe I think knowing a bit about the real you will help."

My heart wilted the tiniest bit. He didn't actually want to know about me; he was just doing this because he thought it would help his cause. But I could tell by the set of his shoulders that he wouldn't open the door at his back until I spoke.

"My mom grieved my dad's death for a long time. She's still in the thick of it, and it's been two decades. The way she grieved was by letting everything around her collapse. Our house was a mess unless I cleaned it up. She lost her job. She did the bare minimum to feed and wash herself." I stared at Rome's tie, not wanting to see his face. "So when I started putting more effort into my appearance, she took it as a personal insult. She thought it meant I didn't care about my dad."

"Because you wore nice clothes?"

I lifted my gaze to his, smiling sadly. "My dad's passing really messed her up. Messed both of us up. I think she became incapable of seeing me as my own person. Everything I did was interpreted through the lens of her experience and her opinion. My clothing choices had nothing to do with her, but she still had something to say. That made me rebel. Our relationship deteriorated from there."

Rome held my gaze for a long moment, then dipped his chin. "I'm sorry."

I shrugged. "It is what it is."

He huffed, and for a few moments, I felt a connection with him that I hadn't felt with anyone else. He also knew what it meant to be alone in his family. He had fraught relationships with parents who were supposed to take care of him but hadn't.

My dad's death broke my mother. I no longer blamed her, but the truth was that she had failed me. I'd been alone from the moment he passed until now.

Rome knew how that felt. I believed that to my core.

He pushed the door open to reveal the helipad and helicopter beyond. "Ready?" he asked.

I took a deep breath and straightened. "Let's do this."

TWENTY

NIKKI

I'D NEVER BEEN to the Hamptons, so I didn't know what to expect. When the helicopter landed on a lawn at the back of a five-acre estate, it took me a minute to realize that the mansion and both other small guest houses were all part of the same property. A tennis court took up the entire backyard of one of the guest houses, lined with perfectly trimmed bushes and trees that had lost most of their leaves. The main mansion was right on the white sand beach, with the water and sky the same color of overcast gray.

This place would be spectacular in the summer and early fall.

As it was, there were tons of staff milling around to greet us, lots of guests already lounging on a covered porch with heat lamps, and more people inside the home. One of the lawns next to the mansion was set up with tables and fairy lights, and I guessed we'd be out there for a cocktail hour tonight.

"Raphael Garcia has exploded in the last few years. He just

showed his fourth haute couture collection and is expanding into cosmetics."

I nodded at Rome's quiet words. "Hence the importance of the perfume launch."

"We need to salvage the relationship this weekend. His feathers are ruffled, and by Monday I want him to feel confident we can deliver."

"Roger," I said, nodding.

A staff member led us to the grand entrance at the end of the drive, then swept open the front door just as Raphael Garcia came floating down the wide hallway toward us. He was a bald man with a perfectly trimmed beard and round glasses.

"Blakely!" he exclaimed, spreading his arms, gaze shifting to me. "And guest!"

I painted a smile on my lips, even though I felt a twinge in my chest. It was a good reminder of where exactly I stood, though. I was the placeholder, the plus-one. I was, "and guest." Rome might ask me personal questions, and he might even kiss me in a dark room at the back of an event, but I didn't belong here. I wasn't one of these people, even in my vintage Balmain dress.

"Raph, this is Nikita," Rome said, his hand sliding down my spine. Despite my mental reminder, the touch sent warmth spiraling through my core.

Raphael studied me. He was a tall man with sharp blue eyes that watched me from behind his round glasses. He wore a perfectly tailored button-down with a subtle embroidered pattern which was half-tucked at the front of his relaxed slacks. The look could have been sloppy but for the clear luxury of the fabrics and their perfect cut. He looked easy and relaxed and rich.

I felt like an impostor. Which wasn't a great surprise since that's exactly what I was. "Thank you for having us," I said, widening my smile. "Your property is gorgeous."

"Oh, this old place?" he said lightly, then he frowned at me. Well, more specifically, he frowned at my dress. I gulped and tried not to fidget. Had I misjudged? Should I have gone for easy and breezy? I went through the mental catalog of the clothing I'd brought and began frantically planning my outfits for the weekend.

Then Raphael rubbed his chin. "You," he said, "have a point of view."

His eyes rose to meet mine. I blinked. "Don't we all?"

His expression turned wry. "Darling. Don't be ridiculous." Whirling, he called out, "Come! Let me give you a tour. Marcia! Where are the welcome drinks!"

Rome let out a slight breath, shooting me a quick glance. I thought I read approval there—or maybe it was relief. A lady appeared from a side room bearing a silver tray with three flutes of champagne. Raphael plucked two of them from her tray to give to us, then thanked her as he took the third.

"The cocktail hour will be at five o'clock tonight through that door," he said, flicking his hand at a huge carved timber door to the left. "The library. The small salon. Dining room is through there. We're doing casual breakfasts between seven and nine. Come down and serve yourself. Through there to the beach. Water's a bit too rough to take the kayaks out, but it's still nice to take in the fresh air once in a while. Sunroom. Billiards room. Upstairs!" He swept his arms out and guided us toward the dramatic staircase covered in rich red carpet.

The decor was a mix of mid-century modern pieces and a few timeless classics. It felt like they'd been here for ages, but the few modern art pieces told me that this place had been curated. I loved it. It was edgy and cool without verging into stiff and uncomfortable.

Compared to the overdone event spaces we'd seen and the stuffy estate owned by the Blakelys, this place was homey and wonderful. I found myself enjoying the glimpses I got, and I readjusted my opinion of Raphael Garcia from penis-perfume-bottle designer to someone who actually had great taste.

"Here we are," he proclaimed, throwing open a set of double doors. "Your room."

The three of us stepped into the space, and my stomach dropped. Raphael turned with a smile, sweeping his arm dramatically. I did my best to curl my lips and hide the dismay creeping through my chest.

It was a gorgeous room with high ceilings and ornate crown molding. Even from across the room, I could tell the view from the big bay window would be fantastic. I could see a slice of beach and the expanse of the ocean beyond. The furniture was timber and solid-looking, probably antique. The door to an attached bathroom gave me a view of the corner of a claw-foot tub and cute mint-green tiles.

That was all fantastic.

But there was a problem.

A big, fluffy, king-sized problem.

"I'll leave you to it!" Raphael announced. "I think I just heard someone else arrive."

He walked out again, and a member of staff nodded to us as she closed the doors. Our bags had already been carried up and unpacked in the walk-in closet, which I noticed in the quick glance I sent that way. Then my eyes returned to the main piece of furniture which was causing me significant distress.

Namely, the bed.

The one bed. That I'd have to share. With my boss. Whom I'd kissed just yesterday.

Rome cleared his throat. "I'll sleep on the floor."

I blinked and glanced at him. "Do you think that's necessary?"

He gave me a flat stare. "Judging by the look on your face, yes, it is."

I reared back. "What look on my face?"

"The horror and dread."

"Horror and dread!"

His lips twitched as he said, "It's right there."

"I'll have you know I feel no horror or dread."

"Do you not?" He turned to face me, and I made the mistake of retreating. Rome advanced, and then he was crowding me against the wall.

My breath quickened. "We shouldn't be doing this."

"Doing what?"

"Whatever this is."

He paused, then stepped back and shook his head like he needed to clear it. "You're right."

"Maybe we should talk about last night."

"What is there to talk about?"

I moved to peek into the closet, noting the plush seat and big vanity. It was an honest-to-goodness dressing room. This place was a dream. "We got carried away," I said, running my fingers over the velvet hangers where my clothing already hung. Garcia's staff moved *fast*. "We can pretend it didn't happen and go back to being Rome Blakely and guest."

He hummed. "Or...maybe we shouldn't fight it."

I glanced over my shoulder to see Rome leaning against the dressing room doorjamb, watching me. I arched a brow. "We shouldn't fight it?"

"We obviously have chemistry. Maybe this is something we should indulge."

"Rome, you're my boss. We have a contract. I'm here to make you look good. Adding sex to the equation is a terrible idea."

Even though it was tempting. As he dangled the forbidden fruit before me, I considered it. Ever since we'd kissed, I'd felt off-kilter. I couldn't think straight. I'd dreamed of him last night, looking at me with those dark-blue eyes while my fingers curled into his shoulders.

But it was a terrible idea.

He tilted his head in agreement. "Probably."

I turned my back to him to explore the space. On top of the big, tufted ottoman in the center of the space was a tray with two bottles of water and some fancy snacks. When I glanced up, I met Rome's eyes in the vanity mirror.

He hadn't moved, but I felt his presence everywhere. My resolve was being chipped away, and the man was doing nothing but watching me.

As if he could read my mind, Rome pushed off the wall and approached. I stood in front of the vanity, watching him come nearer as my heart took off at a gallop.

"I've been thinking," he said in a low voice.

"Uh-oh," I replied. "Don't hurt yourself."

Giving me a flat look, he came to stand directly behind me. His palms landed on the vanity on either side of me, the heat of him a bonfire at my back. "I've been thinking about what happened at the gala yesterday."

His lips moved close to my neck, and it took all my self-control not to lean into him, to feel the press of his chest against my back. "What about the gala yesterday?"

"It's been a long time since I felt that kind of spark with someone."

My heart tripped over itself.

"Do you disagree?" His eyes met mine in the mirror.

My face gave me away. The wanting that coursed through my veins right now was unlike anything I'd ever felt before. One look caused my blood to heat. Now his nearness made it hard to focus on logic and reason.

But I clung to it anyway and said, "Just because we have a spark doesn't mean it's a good idea to get involved."

His hands moved from the vanity to my hips, right above the flare of the peplum. "What if it's a great idea? We're supposed to be convincing everyone we're together anyway." His smile was wicked.

"I think you're horny," I said, slightly breathless at his closeness, "and that has made your brain malfunction."

"Give me one good reason we shouldn't fuck." His hands moved up to my stomach, tracing the two rows of buttons on the front of my dress.

My pulse pounded, and I stopped resisting his pull. Leaning against him, I let my head fall against his shoulder. "We work together. Our contract explicitly states that no physical contact will occur between us."

"Our contract states that no physical contact is required for you to complete your job duties." His hands moved higher, tracing the undersides of my breasts. "It doesn't say we can't touch each other."

My nipples tightened, but Rome kept his touch just beneath my breasts. I could feel his hardness against my ass, could read the desire in his gaze in the mirror. "You're my boss," I protested weakly.

"Last night," Rome replied, his lips near my ear, "last night I was so hard I couldn't think straight. The moment I got home I had my hand around my cock because of you."

I closed my eyes. It was hard to think about anything except the feel of his broad hands on my body and the image of him losing control because of me.

I was nearly losing control myself. His hands stroked upward, over my breasts, and a shudder went through my body.

"You want me," he cajoled. "Let me have you."

Angling my face against his neck, I inhaled the scent of him. My whole body trembled. I'd never been seduced like this. It should have been a turn-off, but there was something addictive about being wanted by someone so badly he was ready to break all the rules for me.

In some far-off corner of my mind, I knew it was a very bad idea. He could fire me at any minute, and I'd be left with nothing but a few nice clothes and my banged-up pride. This wasn't true love or even affection. This was convenience. I'd been hired as a placeholder, and he was treating me exactly like one.

I turned my head away, and the movement of his hands on my body stilled.

"I don't know," I said. "I don't know."

His palms slid down my sides to my hips. "Okay," he said softly, then took his hands away. I was left in that beautiful dressing room surrounded by fantastic clothes and expensive furniture, breathing heavily, wondering how the hell I'd gotten myself in this position.

TWENTY-ONE
ROME

I'D GOTTEN CARRIED AWAY. I knew that. Nikki knew that. But I couldn't bring myself to regret it.

She fit against me like she was made for me. I could sense her fighting herself, fighting the desire inside her that had to rival my own.

I'd seen her charm clients and fit in at every event. But she was more than a beautiful woman in nice clothes. She understood how it felt to be alone, and she'd been at my side when I needed her.

As I got ready for the cocktail hour outside, I should have been thinking about how I'd get Raphael Garcia back onside. I should have been going over my notes about how to approach him about the perfume campaign and smooth-talk him back into the fold.

But I dressed in a fresh shirt and listened to Nikita's movements in the dressing room. The whisper of fabric against skin, the clack of coat hangers against each other. After I'd finished with my own clothes, I glanced over to see her sitting at the vanity, applying makeup.

I became entranced. All her little pots and potions were laid out in front of her, and she used them with such precision. I watched her transform herself into an ethereal, glowing goddess.

And I was sick with wanting her.

It wasn't like me, but it was how I felt. I'd gone through the past years—longer—having casual flings with women whenever the fancy struck. This was different. This was a woman who intrigued me, who might even understand me if I let her in.

She didn't pretend to be bored with the trappings of wealth around us. She unabashedly admired beautiful things—and I found that refreshing. I'd watched her walk through Raphael's home, her gaze lingering on artwork and rugs and beautiful furniture, and I'd been able to appreciate his home with a new perspective. I noticed the splashes of red in a room and the way the carpet on the stairs complemented the artwork on the way up. I saw the view from our bedroom with new eyes.

Nikki did that for me. She made life feel new. She made me take stock of what I had, where I was, what I'd accomplished, and *feel* something. I wasn't just the head of a corporation, trying to amass wealth with no purpose. I was living a charmed life that had started with a bedrock of privilege and grown from there.

I realized, for the first time, what Reggie had meant when he told me to let someone in. I understood why Wilbur Monk believed in working with people who had long-term relationships. Sharing a life with someone was more than just having them in your bed. It was a transformation of all that was familiar into something different.

"Ready?"

I turned, and my heart stumbled. Nikki stood on the other side of the room wearing a floral cocktail dress that cut down in a square neckline, flared out at the waist, and hit her just below the knee. The fabric was ivory with a slight sheen, and the embroidered flowers were purple, indigo, and blue. Her makeup was flawless. Her hair fell down in silky waves.

She was a woman who knew how to put herself together, and I liked that. I liked that she was unapologetically feminine. I appreciated the efforts she went to to adorn herself in beautiful things.

And I liked that it was my arm she'd be clinging to. Possession swept through me as I stood and extended my hand, because this woman was mine. Her beauty, her charm, her intelligence, her cheeky little side-smiles and flat looks—all mine.

At that moment, I didn't think about the fact that she wasn't mine in truth. I didn't acknowledge that our relationship was a sham, and it was based on a crazy contract that would kill my business if it ever got out. As Nikki slipped her hand into mine and let me lead her out of our suite, I knew that I had to have her.

"You look beautiful," I told her as we stepped into the hallway.

She smiled at me. "Thank you. I love this dress."

I hadn't been talking about the dress, but I nodded in response. We made our way downstairs and out to the side patio, where soft music filled the silences between the guests' conversations. Lights were strung up outside, and heat lamps warmed the space.

"Rome!"

I turned to greet the older woman smiling at me and Nikki, and I put on my best Blakely Advertising CEO persona. Nikki did the same, and we wound our way through the tables, chatting, laughing, and complimenting the host.

Raphael appeared not long after with his partner, walking up to a small dais near the door. "Thank you all for coming to our little celebration," he announced. "This year has been a dream, and I'm so pleased to be here to celebrate it with you all. Being married to the love of my life has made everything even sweeter."

Raphael's husband, Matt, smiled and blew a kiss at him. The crowd applauded, and Nikki even leaned her head against my shoulder.

"They're sweet," she said, smiling softly.

I watched the play of the lights over her hair, her skin, her shoulders. "You think you'll ever have what they have?"

Her eyes were dark and liquid. She glanced at the happy couple as Raphael continued his speech, then looked at me again. "I think it's rare to find someone who's your perfect match," she admitted, "but I'm holding out hope. You?"

I huffed. "I don't think that's in the cards for me."

"Maybe the best thing to do is take scraps of happiness wherever you can find them."

Holding Nikki's gaze, I wondered if I was reading things there that didn't exist. There was a scrap of happiness here between us. Something alive and hot and real, if only we let ourselves indulge.

If we forgot that she worked for me. If we pretended I didn't hold all the advantages. If we promised each other it was temporary.

Applause jarred me out of my thoughts, and I joined in. A little while later, while waiters drifted through the small crowd with drinks and canapés, Raphael approached. He held his arms out to Nikki and air-kissed both her cheeks, then introduced us to his husband.

"Congratulations," she told them, smiling. "Your speech was beautiful. I can see the love you have for each other so clearly, and it's just wonderful."

"Now how did a sweet woman like you end up shackled to Mr. Dry and Dusty, over here." Raphael nodded to me.

Nikki gave him a grin. "I can't tell you that. I signed an NDA."

The two of them cackled, clearly having no idea she was telling the honest truth. I slipped my hand down Nikki's back and pinched her side. She responded by bumping me with her hip and giving me that sexy side-eye I loved so much.

"Rome was telling me about his ideas for your launch campaign," Nikki said. "Have you seen any of the updated concepts?"

Garcia let out a dramatic sigh and gave me a disappointed look. "I just—I just can't. It needs to be the real thing, but the glass manufacturers can't get us a new four-hundred-gallon bottle for another three months. We'll have to delay."

Nikki nodded sympathetically. "I see."

"It has to be perfect."

"I understand," she responded, and there was a stiffness in

her shoulders. I wondered if she was blaming herself for what happened.

"Especially now," Garcia added.

I frowned. "What do you mean?"

"Well, after the story about the accident leaked. Everyone knows that our campaign is delayed because of it. I couldn't possibly put something out that isn't absolutely real."

Which meant he was determined to reject anything that used CGI—and our contingency plans were out the window. I tried to rein in my frustration while my mind spun. I needed to salvage this. If we failed with Garcia, it would be a black mark against us when it came to closing the Monk deal.

"What if you leaned into it?" Nikki said.

Raphael frowned at her. "What do you mean?"

"Take the campaign in a new direction. Less ethereal angels wearing very little clothes while they, uh, stroke the perfume bottles, and more...strength."

Garcia glanced at his husband, then at me, and finally frowned at Nikki. "I'm not sure I follow."

I cleared my throat, intending to save this ship before it went down, when Nikki said, "I was there when it happened. The glass smashing, the perfume sloshing, the screams—it was very dramatic. Very captivating."

The other man tilted his head. "Go on."

"Line those bottles up and smash them with a baseball bat," Nikki said, smiling fiercely. "The perfume is supposed to represent divine feminine energy, correct?"

Garcia nodded. "Yes."

"Well, part of being a woman is unshakeable strength. Have

the models wear fabulous clothes while they show exactly how powerful they are.”

I held my breath. It was the opposite of what we’d pitched, but I could tell Garcia was considering it. He stared at her for a beat, then let out a bark of laughter. He pointed at Nikki and said, “You are a genius. Genius!” He pointed at me. “Can you get it done in our original timeline?”

I dipped my chin. “No problem.”

“Do it. Send me new storyboards by the time we’re back in the city.” He snapped his fingers and turned to his husband. “The clothing. We can leak the new collection in some of the shots.”

“Build momentum on your next ready-to-wear collection,” the other man said, eyes sparkling.

Garcia laughed again, then grabbed Nikki by the shoulders and planted a kiss on her cheek. He turned to me and said, “Never let her go.”

Then he was away, and I curled my fingers through Nikki’s. She glanced up at me through her lashes, trying to gauge my reaction.

I squeezed her hand. “Maybe we need to expand your job description,” I told her quietly.

Her lips split into a smile. “I don’t come cheap,” she warned.

I laughed. “I’m aware, Jordan.”

Eyes sparkling, she grinned at me like a mischievous sprite, all dark hair and dark eyes and dangerous enchantments. And she’d already snared me.

TWENTY-TWO
NIKKI

AFTER THE COCKTAIL HOUR, we were led to a dining room where a delicious four-course meal was served. There were twenty-two guests invited to Garcia's home for the weekend, and all of them were there to have a good time. I laughed more during that meal than I had in all the other events combined.

By the time we got back to our room, I'd had two glasses of champagne and a glass of red, way too much food, and I was still riding the high from blurting out my idea for the perfume campaign.

Which reminded me—I wanted to double-check that Rome was okay with me doing that. He'd seemed to respond positively when we were downstairs, but he could just as easily think I overstepped my job description.

I tended to get overambitious when I had ideas. I liked working, I liked doing a good job, and I loved collaborative projects. But I knew that sometimes, people in positions of power responded badly to my enthusiasm.

It had happened before. When I worked at the vintage clothing store, I started scouring thrift stores and estate sales to buy for it and then eventually went to my boss with ideas for ways to change the store itself. I'd mocked up a design for an online store and pitched him the idea of expanding into country-wide sales. He told me he'd consider my idea but fired me a month later. Sometimes, when I was particularly bitter about it, I thought he goaded me into spending money on that business degree just to spite me.

So now, as I unhooked my earrings and dropped them onto a mirrored tray on the vanity, I peeked sideways to see if I could broach the topic with Rome.

But he had his back to me and his phone to his ear. I finished removing my jewelry and crept closer, my thoughts beginning to whirl. I'd tell him that it was a one-time thing. I'd explain that the idea just popped into my head, and I had to get it out. I would cross my fingers and toes and hope he understood.

Then I heard what he was saying to the person on the other side of the phone call.

"Yeah, new direction. I want a full new storyboard by Monday. We're smashing the bottles. Divine feminine energy, but make it angry. Take it to the design department and see if they can link up with Garcia's people. Good."

He hung up the phone and turned, freezing when he saw me staring at him wide-eyed. "Everything okay?"

"You're not mad?"

Rome frowned. "About what?"

"About me blurting out my idea like that."

His lips tilted into a wry smile. "Babe, anytime you get an idea that saves me millions of dollars in delays and missed launch deadlines, you blurt it out whenever you like."

I bit my lip as my lungs crowded out my chest. "Okay," I whispered.

He held my gaze until I looked away and angled for the bathroom. When I closed the door behind me, I let out a long breath.

Maybe I could carve a role for myself that wasn't just a placeholder. Maybe I could find someone who valued me for my ideas, for my thoughts, for myself.

By the time I re-emerged from the bathroom, my emotions had subsided, and I felt calmer. Until I saw Rome reclining on the bed, one arm curled behind his head, the other holding his phone as he read something on the screen. He wore black-framed glasses, and the sight of him slightly undone on a bed made heat twist in the pit of my stomach.

He lifted his eyes, then let his gaze roam over my nightie and down to my bare legs. When I'd packed for the trip, I mistakenly assumed I'd have my own room. In retrospect, that was a silly mistake—but it meant that I was now standing in a luxurious bedroom wearing a pale pink satin nightie trimmed in white lace. The alternative was sleeping in regular clothes—none of which would be comfortable or appropriate for bed.

"I thought you claimed the floor," I blurted.

Dark-blue eyes lifted to meet my own. His brow arched. "I changed my mind."

Suddenly, this whole situation felt perilous. I wasn't sure I could resist his pull any longer—wasn't even sure I wanted to.

Sure, he was my boss. But this whole situation was unusual. We kept having to pretend to be a couple at all these public events. Was it any wonder that closeness had muddled the boundaries a bit? All the touches of his hand on my lower back, my waist, my shoulders, the shared looks between client meetings, the way his thumb stroked the outside of my elbow when he wanted to guide me into the next room.

It had been weeks, and I was tired of resisting.

Rome set his phone on the nightstand, then slipped his glasses off. He glanced at the space on the bed next to him, then looked at me. "Do I terrify you that much?"

"I wouldn't call it terror."

His lips kicked, and I started moving. I fluffed the pillows—they were divine—then threw back the plush comforter and got under the blankets. My heart thumped and my movements felt jerky. The mattress was soft beneath me, but I couldn't relax.

Rome was right there, wearing loose pants and a T-shirt. He got under the blankets on his side, and I could feel the heat of his body just inches away from mine. The mattress dipped as he rolled over to turn off his light, and the room was plunged in darkness. After a few seconds, my eyes adjusted to the silvery light of the moon.

The only sounds were our breathing and the rustle of fabric against fabric. I rolled over so my back was to Rome, but my eyes remained open. Sleep was far away. With my gaze, I traced the shape of the lampshade and followed the corner of the wall up to the crown molding. From this angle, I could see a slice of the dressing room, including the tufted ottoman in the center of the room. I noticed the way the moonlight cut shadows across the walls, how it reflected off the ocean outside to throw shimmering light across the walls and ceiling.

But my awareness was all on Rome. On the weight of him behind me. His breathing. His stillness.

My body felt alive, and we hadn't said a word. We hadn't touched. But I felt heaviness in my breasts and pressure in my core. I curled my knees up and clenched my thighs as my heart thumped.

His breathing was deep and even, and I wondered if he'd fallen asleep. Wouldn't that be funny? I'd lie there, tortured by unrequited lust, and he'd snooze away, unaffected? It would be typical of my life. Always the placeholder, never the chosen one.

Then he shifted. I heard the rustle of fabric and felt the comforter tug as he moved. His fingers curled around my hair, gently moving it away from my neck. My breath quickened. His fingertip was warm as it traced the shell of my ear, moving down my neck and across my shoulder. He slipped it under the thin strap of my nightgown, following the fabric down to the lace trim near my shoulder blade. His touch feathered over my skin, but it still felt intense. My focus narrowed to the scant few inches where our bodies connected.

"Do you wear this kind of thing to bed every night?"

"What do you mean?"

"Silky, lacy things." His fingers moved back up along the strap, sliding it toward my shoulder. "I need to know if I should edit the fantasies I've been having of you."

I rolled onto my back and arched my brow at him. He was leaning on his elbow, his head propped on his hand. His smile was dangerous.

"I like wearing nice things, and that includes bedtime," I told him.

He made a rough noise at the back of his throat, his fingers moving to trace the neckline of my nightclothes. "All this time, I thought you dressed up to convey a message. But you don't, do you? You do it for yourself. Just like you told me."

I hummed in agreement, and he shifted his hand so his palm rested on my breast. He stroked the silky fabric of my nightgown with his thumb, watching the movement of the fabric under his touch.

It was unbearable. It was delicious. I wanted the moment to last forever, and I wanted him to wrench my thighs apart and bury himself inside me. It no longer mattered who he was or who I was. We were in a cocoon of stillness and moonlight, where the real world wouldn't intrude. It was a weekend away from reality.

When he plumped my breast and pinched my nipple, I arched into the touch—and that was all the invitation Rome needed. He leaned over me, taking my breast—fabric and all—in his mouth. My fingers twined into his hair as my breaths panted, lightning darting through my veins at the feel of his breath through the satin, the heat of his palm as it moved over my ribs.

"Rome," I panted, curling my hand into his hair.

He kissed my neck and jaw. "You want me to stop?"

"God, no."

He let out a harsh laugh—little more than a huff of breath—and kissed me. I wrapped my arms around his neck and pulled him closer. My knees bent and my thighs spread to cradle him between them, the nightgown pooling at my hips.

Rome's movements were hurried. He swept his hand down my side and over my thigh, pushing it wider to palm my core. He groaned as his hand met with the heat of me, his fingers dipping beneath the gusset of my panties.

"I've wanted you for weeks," he growled.

I gasped at the feel of his fingers sliding through my wetness. My hips bucked; I needed more. When he buried a finger inside me, I let out a low moan.

"So wet and hot for me," he said, his cheek creasing as he grinned. "Greedy for my cock."

I glared at him, even though it was true. Laughing, Rome fell onto his back and took me with him so I was straddling his hips. I leaned my palms on his chest and tried to catch my breath.

His fingers dug into my hips as he pulled me down against him. My eyes flew open at the feel of him there, just a few flimsy layers of fabric separating us.

"It's not just you," he admitted, eyes half-lidded. "Feel what you do to me." He used his grip to grind me against him, bucking up to meet my movements.

My eyes rolled back. "That feels so good."

His answering groan was harsh. As I rode him, he lifted his hand and wrenched my nightgown down to expose my breasts. I lifted my arms out of the straps and let it pool around my waist, my hips rocking against his hardened shaft.

The way he looked at me intoxicated me. Eyes half-lidded, mouth slightly open, he watched the movement of my body like he'd never seen anything so good in his life. One hand guided the movement of my hips while the other swept down my chest, over my breast, down to my waist and back up.

I let out a whimper. I was so close. Heat wound in the pit of my stomach as my movements became jerkier. He met my thrusts with his own—but it wasn't enough. My core clenched on nothing as I rode him, but my frustration mounted.

Finally, I lifted myself off him and shoved my hand in my underwear.

Rome let out a harsh breath and pushed his own pants down far enough that he could take himself in hand. I knelt there, holding my nightgown out of the way, rubbing my own slickness over my clit while he fisted himself beneath me.

"This is the hottest thing I've ever seen," he said, his eyes glued on the movement of my hand. "Show me. Show me what you're doing."

I pushed my panties out of the way and let my head fall back. It felt dirty and wrong and so fucking good to be doing this with him. I could feel his movements get more frantic beneath me. Little flutters went through me, and a sort of desperation took hold. Tears gathered in the corners of my eyes. I was so turned on, so out of control, so needy.

I yelped as Rome curled his fingers around my panties and tugged. They came apart, and he tossed the ripped scrap of fabric aside. His control was slipping the leash as much as mine was.

"Do you have a condom?" I shoved my own fingers inside myself, bucking as my hair fell down over my shoulders.

Rome swore. "No."

"Shit," I said between breaths. "Okay."

"Are you on the pill?"

I shook my head. "No." Hormonal birth control made me a

crazy person, and I hadn't seen the point in taking it when I didn't have regular sex. I was regretting that now.

He closed his eyes for a beat, then moved his hands to my hips once more. I ground myself against him like before, but without the layers of fabric separating us. We groaned in unison. My breaths became harsh as I rode against his cock, desperate for an orgasm.

He was right there. I could shift the angle of my hips, use my hand to angle him ever so slightly, and I'd feel him where I wanted him most. I wanted to. I was desperate to. But I didn't.

Rome used his hands to guide my hips, pressing me down against his hard shaft as my desire made our movements slick. His neck muscles were stark, his biceps straining at the fabric of his sleeves.

"I want you so fucking much," he rasped, his eyes wild.

"I know," I panted.

He groaned, shoving my hips back and forth as I twisted my hands into his tee for purchase. The mattress groaned.

And I couldn't take it anymore. Lust had addled my brain to the point where all I could think about was how badly I wanted to come. All I knew was how good he looked and how much I wanted him. I reached between us and angled him upward—then impaled myself. I fell forward, moaning.

His eyes widened as one hand flew to the back of my head, twisting into my hair. "Nikki—" He bit my name off with a groan, his hips bucking beneath me.

I gasped, clinging to him for dear life. Then I was on my back and Rome was holding my knees in the crook of his elbow, driving himself inside me so deep I could think of nothing else.

"Touch yourself," he commanded, eyes wild as he pistoned into me.

I bunched the fabric of my nightgown out of the way and did as he ordered. I felt him entering me, felt the taut skin of his shaft against my fingers, my wetness coating him. Within seconds of my fingers making contact with my clit, my orgasm finally—*finally*—detonated.

Every muscle in my body clenched as I arched off the bed. I let out a cry through clenched teeth, riding the intensity of my pleasure until it felt like I'd fly apart. Distantly, I heard Rome swearing. I felt his movements become jerky and uncoordinated. I squeezed my thighs against his arms as he held my knees up, his hands finding my ass to lift me up for a deeper angle.

I couldn't breathe. I couldn't think. All I knew was the most intense orgasm of my life was blinding me to everything but pleasure.

"Nikki—"

I opened my eyes to see Rome clench his teeth. A second later, he pulled out of me and spilled his seed all over my stomach and thighs and sex. All over the hand that was still busy wringing the last notes of pleasure from my orgasm. I trembled, gasping for breath, feeling the heat of his orgasm on my skin. My fingers dragged through it as another, smaller wave of pleasure washed over me.

Finally done, I collapsed onto the pillows as Rome's gaze took in the mess of my midsection. His thumbs stroked the inside of my thighs, spreading the evidence of his own pleasure over my skin. His breaths were heavy, his cheeks red.

"What the fuck just happened?" he asked, dazed.

The sight of my usually surly, confident, competent boss so out of sorts wrung a laugh out of my exhausted body. I squeezed him with my knees in response.

He let out a long breath, then extricated his limbs from mine and padded to the bathroom. The sink ran for a few seconds, and he came back with his pants on properly and a wet washcloth in his hands. When he ran it over my skin in gentle strokes, the washcloth was warm and damp. I melted onto the bed and let him care for me, still too dazed and pleasantly numb to think about the consequences of what we'd just done.

TWENTY-THREE
ROME

NIKKI LOOKED like a slumbering angel on the bed, her lids heavy, body relaxed. I took my time washing her, enjoying the sight of her mussed hair and crumpled nightgown. She'd made no move to cover herself, so I found myself admiring the curve of her breasts, the shape of her nipples, the way her stomach dipped at the navel.

And lower, the way the petals of her sex glistened in the moonlight.

I found myself liking her like this. Undone. Sated. Mine.

She shivered as I ran my fingers over the side of her breast, a small plaintive noise coming from her throat. I huffed a laugh, letting my hands run down her hips, where I noticed red marks that my fingers must have left. I'd been rough with her. Rougher than I'd intended to be.

Leaning over, I kissed the marred skin. She shifted, her fingers sliding through my hair in a tender caress. I wasn't ready to let this moment end. Her skin was warm and soft, and she was more relaxed than I'd ever seen her. Hell, *I* was more relaxed than I'd been in a long time.

In this room, with the curtains open to reveal the expanse of ocean, the big bed with fluffy duvet and feather pillows, we were in a cocoon. Nothing else existed.

I ran my lips along the crook of her hip and kissed the edge of her core, my lips tracing her softness there. With my fingers, I spread her open.

"You're insatiable," she complained.

I glanced up to see her watching me, one arm curled behind her head while the other pushed the crumpled nightgown out of the way.

I grinned and curled my hands around her thighs to spread her open for me. And I tasted her. She let out a harsh breath, her hand clenching into the silky fabric of her pajamas. I smiled against her skin and took my time. The taste of her drove me crazy. The smell of her made me hard. I lost myself for a few minutes, feeling the way her hips rolled in response to my ministrations.

This wasn't like me. Later, I would look back and wonder how I'd gotten so caught up in this woman. When did it start? Why did it happen?

But in that moment, there were no thoughts other than pure, unadulterated need. A need to claim her. To possess her. To explore every inch of her body and uncover all its secrets.

Like the way she gasped when I slid a finger inside her as my tongue worked her clit. Or how she made a special kind of noise when I slipped that finger lower, teasing the rim of her ass. Or how her chest became flushed when she came, and how she said my name like a prayer in the throes of it.

I was drunk with the sight of her, with a deeper kind of lust than what I'd experienced before. She wasn't just a pretty accessory I wore on my arm; she was clever and funny and sensual. She made me feel like there was a whole new side of life that I hadn't even known existed. I wanted to see the world through her eyes. I wanted her to tease me with her half-grin and poke me in the ribs with her elbow.

Everything was better with her. *Everything.* Sex was no exception.

I rose up above her and wiped my lips, meeting her gaze in the dimness of the room. She gave me a little smile and shook her head. "This is so bad."

"I think the word you're looking for is 'fantastic.'"

Her laugh was a balm. I lay down next to her and put my hand on her stomach because I couldn't bear the thought of not touching her for a minute. We'd had little more than a taste of each other, and I was already addicted.

I lifted my hand to run my thumb over her flushed cheek. She smiled and turned her head to place a kiss on my palm, and a stirring occurred in my chest. Content, satisfied, and maybe even happy, I curled my arm around Nikki and pulled her toward me. She stripped her crumpled garment and draped her naked body over me and was asleep in an instant.

It took me longer. I watched the reflections of the moonlight on the ceiling and let my fingers trail over her skin. I pressed kisses on her hairline and tucked the dark strands behind her ear. I thought very little in those moments, consumed by the feel of this woman at my side. She let out a little mewl and bent her leg to cover mine, her hand stretching out onto my chest. I wished I was as naked as she so I could feel the silken, warm length of her against all of me.

After a while, I curled my arms around her, inhaled her scent, and slept.

By the time we woke, we'd moved. I found myself spooning her, my left arm angled up near the headboard beneath my head and my right arm curled around her. Sometime during the night, my hand had found a comfortable perch on Nikki's breast.

I moved my thumb over that soft flesh, and Nikki stirred. Her movements were sensuous, languid. There was a sort of haze over us, something that made our movements slow and heavy. Her ass wiggled against me, and it was the only invitation I needed. My hand ran down her stomach to dip between her legs.

The sun was barely up above the horizon, its buttery rays bathing the room in gold. Nikki's skin shone with the light of it as she arched against me, grinding her perfect curves against my body. My cock nestled itself between the globes of her ass as she arched into me, and I wrapped both arms around her to pull her closer.

She came on my fingers with a soft, throaty cry and the sexiest panting I'd ever heard, and a moment later I was making a mess of my sleep pants just from the feel of her in my arms. Her hand landed on my arm, and she gave me a few soft pats, like she was congratulating me on a job well done.

I huffed and placed a kiss on her shoulder. I loved the smell of her. Loved the feel of her in my arms, loved the way she glanced over her shoulder with sleep still in her eyes.

"Morning."

"Morning," I responded.

"I see we haven't learned our lesson in the light of day."

I grinned. "No? I happen to think we've learned something momentous."

"And what's that?"

"How good we are together. How hot you are for me."

She rolled her eyes and smacked me with the back of her hand. I caught her palm and brought it to my lips, pressing a kiss against it as I chuckled.

"Arrogant men aren't my type," she proclaimed, but her argument was somewhat diminished by the fact that she was naked and postcoital beside me.

I swept my hand up her stomach and cupped her breast. "You sure about that?"

"This is an anomaly," she insisted, but she was smiling. Then she wriggled out of my hold and put her feet on the ground. "I need a shower."

I watched the jiggle of her ass as she crossed the room, then followed a moment later. Nikki's eyes were slightly amused as she watched me in the mirror, and her cheeks got red when I stripped off my clothes. She'd turned on the shower and now she stepped under the spray, glancing at me over her shoulder.

It felt like there was a rope tied around my middle tugging me toward her. After last night, I couldn't even bear being in the other room. I needed to feel her body in my hands, pressed against mine, her arms wrapped around me. I followed her into the shower cubicle and gave in to my urges, my hands sliding around her hips to pull her back to my front.

It didn't surprise me that I was half-hard, even after all we'd done. All those weeks of pretending I didn't want her had built up inside me, and now I couldn't resist the slightest touch. I wet a washcloth and lathered up some soap, and I took my time running it over her body. Water drenched us both. Her skin was slippery with suds as I ran my hands over it, memorizing the shape of her.

"My body feels out of control," she said, arching her back as I spent some time worshipping her breasts with my hands. "I've never felt this horny for this long before."

"That makes two of us," I admitted.

She turned in my arms, and my hands slid down to shape her ass. Her arms circled around my neck as the water beat down on her back. "Do you think we're making a mistake?"

I squeezed her curves. Her body was perfectly propor-tioned. "A mistake about what?"

"This." Her hand stroked my neck, her thumb tracing my jaw. "Sleeping with each other. Not sticking to the rules. It could blow up in our faces."

I hummed, and one corner of my mind began functioning for the first time in twelve hours. I said, "I'm not looking for anything serious," which was true, but tasted like ash on my tongue.

She nodded. "I know."

"Are you?"

She stared at my jaw for a moment, then shrugged. "I don't even know anymore. I don't know if it's possible for me to have a real relationship."

I frowned. "What do you mean?"

"Well, do you? Truly? Do you think you can have what Wilbur and Roseanne have?"

I nipped at her bottom lip. "No. But that's beside the point."

My hands shifted closer to her cleft, pulling her tight to me. "*This* is the point."

She huffed a laugh. "That's what I'm saying. Maybe it's better to enjoy this—whatever this is—because it's as good as it gets."

I pulled away to meet her gaze. I wasn't sure exactly what she meant, and I wasn't sure I liked the sound of it. Nikki was beautiful and funny and smart and perceptive. Of course she'd find someone to make her happy. She wasn't like me. She didn't thrive on her own the way I did. She hadn't been put through a crucible as a young kid, abandoned, and tossed away because it was supposed to be what was best for her. That's what happened to me, and that's why I would always be alone.

But she'd find her Wilbur. How could she not, being all that she was?

Still...the thought of another man having her made me want to shatter the glass wall beside me. So I held her close and decided she was right. We could have each other right now, and that would be enough. It would have to be.

Then Nikki got a wicked light in her eyes, and she lowered herself to her knees in front of me—and for the next little while, the only thing I thought about was her mouth.

TWENTY-FOUR
NIKKI

BREAKFAST WAS DELICIOUS AND RELAXED. I ended up sitting next to Raphael's partner, Matt, discussing how Raphael had started his brand. We found a mutual connection in Marcus, Penny's husband, which was delightful. Penny had actually gotten a tour of Raphael's studio in the Garment District a few years ago, which proved that Marcus did, indeed, have at least one romantic bone in his body.

Rome stayed beside me, his arm around my shoulders, his gaze occasionally drifting to meet mine. It felt like we had an illicit secret, even though to everyone else, our sleeping together would be expected. But now, as I performed my job duties and socialized for all I was worth, I felt a little thrill every time his thumb stroked the side of my neck, or whenever his knee touched mine.

Lawn games took up most of the morning, and then guests were served a light lunch. After that, reports of the weather turning began to come in, so it was decided that the weekend would be cut short. Rome's helicopter was the fourth to leave, and I watched Garcia's estate shrink in the distance as we flew west toward the city.

Rome slid his hand over my knee. I turned to meet his gaze, arching my brows.

"Come home with me."

My heart thundered. "Is that wise?"

"Why wouldn't it be?"

"We haven't exactly defined what's going on here."

"What's going on is that I want you in my bed."

My lips twitched. "Do you have some of that delicious Belgian chocolate at your place?"

His fingers made slow strokes on the inside of my knee. "Of course."

"What about chocolate chip cookies?"

"Those can be arranged."

I turned to look out the window. "I'll think about it."

I sucked in a breath as his hand moved up my thigh to press the space where I needed it most. My head fell back against the seat as my gaze flew to the pilot, who could glance over his shoulder and see us at any minute.

"Think harder," Rome said, his eyes full of wickedness as his fingers stroked through my clothes.

I panted, then dipped my chin. Rome gave me one last stroke, then took his hand away. For the rest of the ride, my body felt keyed up and a little too hot. And despite my fears about the future, I knew there was nowhere I'd rather be tonight than in Rome's bed.

The helicopter flew over Manhattan and didn't deposit us on the Blakely office building. We landed on a tall tower studded with balconies, where Rome threaded his fingers through mine to lead me across the roof and into the building. We descended a set of stairs and emerged into a glorious penthouse apartment that was bigger than anything I'd ever seen. The top floor of it was dominated by windows surrounding a living space, with a dramatic balcony taking up three sides. The decor was modern, if a little impersonal.

Rome crossed to a bar and pulled out a bottle of wine and two glasses. I watched him, then drifted around the room to admire the modular couches, the unique, sculptural side tables, and the huge art canvasses on the walls. It was a little bare for my taste; I preferred a maximalist approach to design. Rich fabrics, a riot of color, too many pillows. This looked like it belonged in the pages of a magazine. It was beautiful, but it wasn't for me.

"Nice place," I said.

He poured the wine and took a seat on the couch, watching me inspect his space. "Thank you."

"Must take ages to clean," I mused, looking at all the hard surfaces that needed to be dusted and polished.

"I wouldn't know."

I snorted and drifted toward him. Sitting on the sofa with about a foot of space between us, I reached for the glass he'd poured for me. Before I could grab it, Rome's arm snaked around my waist and pulled me tight to his side.

"That's where you belong," he said, nuzzling at my neck.

A shiver went through me, but I resisted the urge to give in. I leaned forward and grasped my wine, then met his gaze over the rim. "I want to lay some ground rules," I told him.

He leaned back and laid his arm across the back of the sofa

before dipping his chin. His expression was half guarded, half amused. "Okay."

After my lust had abated slightly in the helicopter, I'd forced myself to think about what we were doing. And I decided that if life kept shoving me in the role of the place-holder, then that's what I should be. This man was a billionaire, the CEO of a corporation of his own making, a man who could twitch his fingers and get something delivered within moments.

He was my boss. The man who'd found my next apartment. The man who signed my paychecks.

He would always have more power than me.

The best thing to do would be to not indulge in the physical with him, but those horses had bolted, and I didn't particularly want to close the barn door in the first place. So I'd decided that if I wanted to keep this job—with the great bonuses, the health insurance, the salary—while also indulging in more nights like last night, then I'd have to put walls up within myself.

Yes, there was more to Rome than I'd originally thought. We connected on a level that I hadn't expected. I understood his history, even if it was very different from my own. But we could never be together. Not for real.

I was a placeholder—but I'd own it.

"This is temporary," I said.

Rome blinked.

I went on: "I'm not looking for anything serious," I told him. "At least not with—" I clamped my lips shut.

"At least not with me," he finished for me. He took a sip of his wine and set the glass down on a side table, then turned his eyes to meet mine. His gaze was dark, his emotions unreadable. "May I ask why?"

"A relationship should be built on mutual respect and some level of equality. I can't be in a relationship with a man who can take my job away if we get in a fight."

"You think I would do that?" The skin around his eyes tightened.

"I don't know," I said honestly. "We've spent time together these past weeks, but I honestly don't know. I'd rather not take the risk."

"So what do you propose?"

"Professionally, things stay the same. Personally, we have fun with each other."

"You want me to be your friend with benefits."

"Boss with benefits," I corrected.

"And what if I say I don't want that?"

I shrugged. "Then we leave it. I'm prepared to put this weekend aside and continue working as we have been. I know you need me for Monk."

A sardonic smile twisted his lips. "You're not entirely powerless, then."

"Maybe not."

His shoulders softened, and he reached over to tuck a strand of hair behind my ear. "I also have rules."

"Oh?"

"We're exclusive. I'm the only man in your life from this moment onward."

He'd been the only man in my life for a lot longer than that, but I wasn't going to tell him that. I nodded. "Fine. As long as that goes both ways."

Rome nodded, then stood and extended a hand toward me. I slipped my palm into his and let him pull me up to my feet. He took my glass of wine and set it next to his, then faced me. His hands slid over my waist, and his gaze was steady on mine.

"So. You agree," he said softly. "You're mine, for as long as you decide you want to be."

My heart rattled. I wasn't sure that was exactly what we'd negotiated, but his body was warm and his hands were drifting over my hips, so all I could do was dip my chin. "Yes."

A fierce, victorious smile stole over his lips. "Good," he said —and crushed his lips to mine.

TWENTY-FIVE
ROME

I'D NEVER BEEN the possessive type. A long time ago, I'd learned not to let people in. When you invited people into your inner sanctum, they had power over you. They could hurt you, reject you. They could leave. They could die. As a result, I kept people at arm's length.

I'd always been stronger on my own. It was a lesson I'd learned time and time again, and at the tender age of forty-two, it wasn't something I'd thought to change.

But holding Nikki in my arms and tasting her lips made me forget myself. I'd kept my expression calm while she told me what she wanted from me, even though I raged inside. I didn't want casual fun with her; I wanted all of her.

Still, I couldn't deny that she was right to put bumper rails on our situation. We'd lost control at some point, and now we needed to wrench the wheel so this speeding car was at least traveling between the lines.

I could bend my own rules for her—for this. I could indulge

this need to have her for my own without having to change the core of me. It was a win-win.

She was mine, for as long as she agreed to be. And I intended to make that last a long, long time.

Nikki let out a cute yelp when I lifted her legs and wrapped them around my waist. She clawed at my shoulders and dug her fingers into my hair, evidence that she wasn't in as much control as she thought. I smiled against her lips and inhaled the scent of her.

I'd lost my mind, and I didn't care.

Stumbling across the room, I made it to the internal elevator and mashed the button next to her hip. The door opened a moment later and I walked in as Nikki began clawing at the buttons on my shirt, tearing at it to get her hands on my skin. We both groaned when she ripped the shirt apart and slid her hands down my back. Her hips bucked, her hair falling out of the knot she'd tied it in earlier.

She wore lip gloss that tasted like strawberries. Her perfume was delicate and heady all at once. Her touch was insistent and gentle in turn. She was made of contradictions, and I was drunk off the unpredictability of it all. When I shoved my hand in her hair and felt the silken strands fall down, I let out a low moan. I fisted my hand in her locks and relished the small gasp that left her lips.

The elevator door opened, and Nikki slid down to her feet. She toddled on her heels but let me tow her along down the wide hallway toward my bedroom.

I locked us in. She cast one long glance around the room, then turned to look at me through her lashes. Her lips curled into a sinful smile, and she went to work undoing the buttons of her blouse. My chest heaved with every breath as I watched, intent on the slivers of skin that revealed themselves to me. My own hands were busy tearing at my shirt, pulling it out of my pants, and letting it drop to the floor.

I closed the distance between us and ran a finger over the edge of her bra. "I like this," I said, admiring the black lace and white underlay. Everything about her was considered, beautiful, intentional. I'd never met anyone who seemed at once so effortless while very clearly making an effort.

I liked that she didn't try to hide herself. I liked that her desire to drape herself in nice fabrics and expertly applied cosmetics wasn't hidden behind false modesty. She was a high-maintenance woman, and not ashamed of it.

The zipper on her pencil skirt gave me little resistance. She shimmied her hips as I pushed the fabric down, then grinned as I sucked in a breath.

My fingers coasted over the thigh-high stockings, the garters, the matching underwear. "You aren't real," I said.

Laughing, Nikki reached for my belt. I let her unlatch it and groaned as she reached inside to grip me. Blown-out pupils stared at me as she stroked me, her breaths ragged, her skin flushed.

I took her hand away then grabbed her around the waist and tossed her onto my bed. She bounced once, laughing, then toyed with the waistband of her underwear while I shucked off the rest of my clothing. I reached into my nightstand and pulled out a condom, setting it on top of the piece of furniture before kneeling between her spread legs.

My pulse was a steady drumbeat. It felt like I was marching toward the point of no return. Something was changing between us—within me. Nikki's dark hair spread out on my white pillows, her lingerie-clad body spread before me, and I wasn't sure I'd be able to let her go.

The thought blazed through me, and my control snapped. I tugged her panties aside and shoved my finger inside the wet warmth of her. She arched, her hands moving to grip my bedding as a soft cry escaped her lips. I added another finger, watching her lashes flutter, ignoring the insistent throbbing happening between my legs.

I liked seeing her undone. I liked mussing up all her careful hair, makeup, and clothing. I liked seeing lust cloud her eyes so that all that existed in her face was raw desire.

Raw desire—for me.

Her body undulated as I fingered her, knees pressing against my biceps. She clawed at the nightstand and found the condom, tearing the packet open with trembling fingers before thrusting it at me.

I hummed and leaned back on my heels. My cock jutted out and we both looked at it.

"You want it?" I asked.

"Shut up and fuck me, Rome."

I grinned and nodded at the condom. "Put it on, then."

She huffed like the insolent brat she was, then did as she was told. I groaned at the feel of her slim fingers around my shaft, the grip of her fist at its base. She flopped back on the pillows and looked at me expectantly.

I *tsked* and shook my head. "You want my cock, you'll come here and fuck it for yourself."

Her glare made blood rush down to the member in question. And when Nikki bit her lip before arranging herself on her hands and knees before me, I bit back a groan. She held her panties aside and positioned me at her entrance, then backed herself onto my shaft in a slow, torturous movement.

"Good," I said. "Keep going."

"You're such an asshole, Rome."

My palm cracked against her ass cheek. She bucked, then slammed backward. We both groaned. Her head fell down between her shoulders as her fists curled against the pillows, and I almost gave in. It was the sight of her bare spine, the dark lace of her undergarments, the sight of my red, swollen cock inside the woman I'd been craving for weeks.

But with a whine, Nikki began to rock herself against me, and I let out a long sigh. "Work yourself over my cock," I told her, unable to tear my gaze away from her sensuous movements. She picked up the pace, her movements almost jagged, a frustrated moan slipping through her clenched teeth.

"Rome," she complained.

"Yes, baby?"

"Please."

"Please, what?"

She slammed back into me, and it took all my self-control not to meet her thrust for thrust. But this was a woman who needed to be cracked open. She didn't just give herself up to anyone. The fact that she made those rules for us—that she thought she could keep herself from giving herself to me fully— made me want to take her to the edge and keep her there.

So I guessed she was right. I was an asshole.

"Fuck me," she whined, backing herself onto my cock as hard as she could.

I hummed, then gripped her underwear and tugged it aside

so I could get a better view. She moaned at the touch of my fingertips against her skin, her fists clenching into the pillows, so I met her next thrust with a hard one of my own.

Her answering moan nearly undid me. I held onto her by her underwear and gave her what she wanted, tugging her into my thrusts with my grip on that scrap of fabric. The unintelligible moans that slipped from her lips made my own curl into a smile. I ran my hands over her body and lost myself in the feel of her. The wetness. The tightness. The heat.

She was so perfect, it made my head spin.

Not wanting the moment to end, I pulled out of her and fit myself between the globes of her ass. When I heard her sharp inhalation, my gaze sharpened. I held her ass, guiding my cock in her cleft as her shoulders and chest fell onto the bed.

I'd never seen anything so good in my life.

"Do you want my cock in your ass?" I asked, and my voice was so dark I barely recognized it.

"I—I've never..." She turned her head to the side, and I could see her eyes were closed, her mouth open.

I smoothed my hands over her ass and waist, feeling the tremors that ran through her body. I pulled my hips away from her and looked down. The most violent wave of possession I'd ever felt took me over. This woman was mine, now and forever. She'd give herself to me completely. Maybe not tonight. Maybe not soon. But I'd die before I let her go.

I couldn't resist the urge to slide my finger in her wet opening, feeling the grip of her inner muscles around me. I angled my cock at her opening and eased myself inside as my hands spread her ass wide. Her skin glistened from where my cock had been, and I brought my index finger to her rear hole, the digit coated in her juices. She grunted and backed into me when I slipped it past the first tight ring. Her skin held a sheen of sweat, her hair plastered to her temples.

"You're going to come on my cock," I told her as I picked up the pace, "and you're going to scream my name while you do it."

"Yes," she moaned.

"And I'm going to keep this finger in your ass so you know how it feels to come with it there."

"Yes," was the desperate reply that came once more.

"When you're ready, princess, I'm going to take you here. Not tonight. Not until you're begging me for it."

Her breath gusted out. "Rome—yes. Yes, yes, yes."

"You belong to me, Nikki," I said, driving myself into her. "No matter how you try to deny it, I think you already know."

"Yours," she breathed.

"On your elbows, gorgeous. I want you to take all of me. Want you to feel how good it feels to have me filling you up like this. And when you come, you say my name. Got it?"

Something like a sob came from her, and then she was lifting herself onto her elbows once more. Words escaped me, and all that existed was the feel of this woman clenching around me, the darkness of my need for her consuming me. When she began to tremble and buck against me, I reached up to her shoulder with my free hand to pull myself deeper inside her, so she knew how it felt to take all of me. Her ass clenched around my finger as I drove it in and out of her ass, our bodies slapping together with wet, messy sounds.

My control was in tatters. I saw nothing but the color of her hair against the pillow, the glistening skin spread out beneath me. The shape of my handprint on her ass. She clenched and fluttered around me as she screamed my name—just like I told her to.

I groaned. "My perfect girl. Scream it, gorgeous. You take me so well. You feel so fucking good, Nikki. Perfect. Need. You're—" My own words were near gibberish as I panted them out, unable to think of anything except how good it felt to have this woman beneath me, giving me everything I'd ever wanted.

My release was moments behind hers. With my vision gone white and pleasure splintering through me, nothing existed but the feel of my woman around me.

I collapsed beside her as she fell to her side, her breaths jagged. I turned my head to take in the sight of her here, in my bed, well-fucked and panting.

And I knew it hadn't just been lust talking before. I wasn't going to let her go.

Her eyes opened, dark pools of brown gazing right to the core of me. Her makeup was smudged around her eyes, and her cheeks were red with the flush of her orgasm. We were beyond words. I curled my arm around her and tugged her to my side where she belonged.

TWENTY-SIX
NIKKI

I FELT LIKE A HYPOCRITE. A couple of short weeks earlier, I'd been warning Bonnie away from getting involved with her boss. And here I was, waking up in Rome Blakely's penthouse, every muscle in my body sore from what he'd put me through the night before.

Not that I was complaining.

I'd never had sex like that before. Not in a way that felt like I could let go of all my inhibitions, where letting go of control was as much of a release as the orgasm itself.

Rome slumbered next to me, his chest rising and falling in a steady rhythm. He'd been dominant in a way that I'd enjoyed last night. My cheeks warmed at the thought of the slight humiliation of having him tell me to ride him while he kneeled behind me unmoving, and I discovered I wasn't opposed to doing it again.

I liked the feeling of letting go of control. All I had to do when I was with him was exactly what he said, and he would shower me with praise. There were no worries about being the girl who's just the stepping stone on the way to someone better. No thoughts about being a placeholder. In his arms, I was *me*, and I was perfect. I'd never felt that way before. Especially not during sex.

And then there was the other thing. He'd slid his finger in my ass, and I'd been a moment away from telling him that I wanted more.

He shifted beside me, inhaling deeply before opening his eyes. In those few slumberous moments, the usual lines of his face were relaxed, and his smile was soft. He turned onto his side and threw an arm and leg over me, pulling me close to his body with a long groan.

"Morning," he said, sleep lacing his words.

"Good morning," I replied softly, giddiness sparkling through me.

He groaned, sliding his palm over my shoulder and down my arm. His touch was gentle but unhesitating. He wasn't asking permission to touch me like that, like it was normal to cuddle and stroke. I found myself enjoying the intimacy of it, my body sinking into the mattress. His fingers ran over my skin as his eyes remained closed, sliding down to my hip and over my ass. I loved the way he touched me. It made me feel safe and cherished and entirely present in this moment with him.

His eyes were closed. "You're wide awake, aren't you?"

I smiled at the plaintive note in his voice. For a man who presented himself as always in control, always slightly apart from everyone else, he sounded surprisingly unguarded. "Yes," I said. "Question. Do billionaires make their own coffee in the morning, or do you have minions to do that for you?"

"Minions," he answered, pulling me closer so I was draped over his chest.

I huffed, propping myself up so I could look down at him. He cracked his eyelids to meet my gaze, his palms sliding down to stroke either side of my spine. I shivered slightly, and his cock twitched where it was nestled between us.

Grinning, I said, "Since I'm one of your minions, maybe I should get us coffee."

"You should stay right here for at least another hour," he said as his hands slipped lower to trace the crease between my thighs and my ass cheeks, but he let me go when I slid to the other side of him to get off the bed. Curling an arm behind his head, he watched me as I put his button-down shirt on and found my underwear in a pile of discarded clothing. I held the black lacy panties up, frowning at them. They were a little worse for wear and I wasn't sure I wanted to put them on again.

"Is anyone else here?" I asked.

Rome groaned and checked the time on his phone on the nightstand. "Chef's downstairs in the kitchen, but no one should be on this floor for another few hours. Housekeeping comes by daily Monday through Saturday once I'm at work, but they don't come until midday on Sunday. There's a coffee bar through there."

He pointed to a pair of doors, and I dropped the panties, judging it safe to go commando under these conditions. I opened the doors to find a small living room. It smelled like leather and paper and him, and I was glad to see this place seemed a bit more lived-in than the vast space upstairs. A briefcase rested next to a desk, with a suit jacket hanging on a coat hanger slung on a doorknob to the left. There were books stacked on a side table and a pair of shoes that looked like they'd been kicked off at the end of the couch.

The coffee bar was fantastic. It had both a real espresso machine and a pod machine. I went for speed and ease of use and chose a pod, clicking it into place and pressing the appropriate buttons before investigating the mini fridge to figure out the milk situation.

Bent over and underwear-less as I was, I should have known danger approached. My only warning was a soft groan and the sound of Rome's footsteps on the plush rug, and then his hands were slipping beneath the rich cotton fabric of his button-down to stroke my hips.

Standing, I turned, but I wasn't prepared to be picked up and placed on the edge of the desk. I laughed as Rome buried his face in my neck, then my laughs turned to gasps as he reached between us. By the time my coffee was done brewing, Rome was positioning himself where I wanted him, his cock sheathed and steel hard.

With his hair mussed and a teasing smile on his lips, he looked deliciously undone. I liked this version of him. It felt like I was seeing a side of him that no one else got to know. Someone who wasn't perfectly put together. A man who didn't lock himself away behind a remote, difficult exterior.

He slid inside me slowly, his gaze holding mine. I was tight, but his touches this morning had been enough to spark arousal. Enough that the push of him against my inner muscles felt delicious. I leaned back on his desk and rocked against him as he unbuttoned the three or four buttons I'd managed to do up, spreading his shirt wide open so he could feast his eyes on my nakedness.

This morning's interlude was different from the frantic, intense sex we'd had last night. Rome held my legs wide and took me slowly there on his desk while the smell of fresh coffee permeated the air, the scent of his cologne draped over me from the fabric of his shirt.

His gaze held mine for a moment, then dropped it to my chest, to my stomach, then down to where we were joined. The way he looked at me was almost tender. I felt cared for as he watched me, his gaze full of some emotion I couldn't read. Admiration? Desire? Tenderness?

A warm hand stroked my sides, my breasts. His touch was reverent as it slipped down, pausing over my stomach. He stroked the skin below my belly button as his thrusts became deeper, soft groans rattling in his throat. I arched off the desk, needing friction, needing—I didn't know what I needed. I just knew the way he was looking at me and touching my body made me feel like my skin was on too tight.

I gasped when his hand slipped that little bit lower to the spot right where I wanted it. He used his fingers to get me over the edge, then held me through the resulting soft, gentle waves of my orgasm before taking his own release. I discovered I was trembling as he whispered sweet words in my ear, his broad palms smoothing down my spine. Rome's breaths were as ragged as mine. After a while, he placed a soft kiss on my temple, then pulled out of me and disposed of the condom. I caught my breath, legs dangling off the edge of his desk, then slithered down to put my feet on the floor and wobbled my way to the coffee machine.

His arms snaked around me as I put a drop of milk in my

cup, a low groan rumbling through his throat. His hands stroked my stomach, my hips, my thighs.

"Already?" I asked, laughing.

"It's the sight of you in my shirt," he said, huffing. A few strands of my hair fluttered in his breath, and despite the orgasm he'd just given me, arousal sparked low in my stomach. His fingers stroked the edge of my lower lips, and a fine trembling began in my thighs.

"Put your hands flat on the counter," he said against the skin of my throat.

I complied, and Rome pulled my hips back before kicking my legs apart. Then he knelt behind me and licked me from clit to opening, and all the way back to the cleft of my ass. My knuckles turned white as I gripped the edge of the counter, a gasp escaping my lips.

He hummed, sliding his tongue through my folds. "Want my breakfast," he groaned, then slid his tongue inside me while moving a finger to my bud.

By the time he was done with me, my coffee was cold and my legs trembled like a newborn fawn's. I collapsed on the floor and was scooped up in his arms and nestled against his chest as he carried me to the sofa on the other side of the room. I inhaled the scent of his skin, pleasure-drunk, dazed, thinking of nothing except how good it felt to be cuddled in his lap with my face mashed against his throat, his fingers drawing patterns on the outside of my thigh.

BY MONDAY, I was walking funny. I refused Rome's offer of a ride to the office, even though we had a midday meeting with

Clara and her team about the upcoming schedule of events. I made my way home to change and get ready, a silly smile plastered on my face.

Most of my stuff was packed—I was planning on moving things over to the new apartment this week once I knew what our schedule looked like—but I put on a simple wrap dress and made sure my hair and makeup were presentable. When I had my keys in hand and was ready to head out the door, my phone rang.

I blinked at the name on the screen, not having seen it there for a long time. After a brief hesitation, I answered. "Hi, Mom."

"Nikita," she said, voice brighter than I'd heard it in years. "How is my darling daughter?"

I bit back the snarky retort that wanted me to ask who her darling daughter might be, because it sure as hell wasn't me. But I wasn't going to get dragged down into bitterness if my mother was making an effort. I sat on the arm of my couch and said, "I'm good, Mom. How are you?"

"Oh, you know," she said, and I imagined her waving a hand. "It's all the same here. I miss you. How's work at the store? Did you finish your course?"

My brows jumped. It had been longer than I'd thought since we'd caught up. "Actually, I'm not working there anymore."

"Really?"

"Yeah. I got a new job, and it's been going really well."

"What about your promotion?"

There was a pinch in my heart. I grimaced. "That...fell through."

"I'm sorry to hear that," my mother said, and it felt disproportionately good to hear. It might have been the first time that my mother offered sympathy without immediately eclipsing it with her own woes and needs.

"Thanks. But it turned out great, actually," I said, glancing out the window at the waiting car. "I really like this new gig."

"What are you doing? We should do lunch! Catch up. A little bit of girl time."

Surprise wouldn't be the right word for what I felt. It was a mix of shock and tentative hope, tinged with bitterness. It felt like I was being offered a poisoned apple, but I couldn't help but reach out for it. "I'd like that," I said, "but I'll have to check my schedule. I'm really busy with the new job these days." And the man who'd given it to me.

"Great! We'll do something next week."

I rolled my eyes. Guess she could only truly listen so long. But maybe next week would work. "All right. Talk soon."

"Love you, Nikita."

I blinked, and the silence between us felt pregnant. Clearing my throat, I said, "Yeah. I...I love you too, Mom."

She huffed. "All right. See you next week!"

The phone clicked. I stared at the screen, frowning. My mother hadn't told me she loved me for years. Part of me wanted to believe she'd changed, that she was ready to see me for me instead of the vague, daughter-shaped presence in her life. But mostly, I felt wary.

I let out a breath, slipped my phone into my purse, and headed down to the waiting company car.

TWENTY-SEVEN
ROME

MY SKIN ITCHED with her absence. I focused on work as best I could for the morning, but my eyes kept drifting to the time, then to the door and the elevator beyond.

Cursing myself, I turned back to the screen in front of me and tried to focus on the latest numbers my finance team had sent through. But the numbers on the screen blurred as I thought of the way Nikki had looked wrapped in my shirt, splayed out on my desk yesterday morning.

Gritting my teeth, I pushed my glasses up to my forehead and rubbed my eyes. This was exactly why I never got involved with a woman—not truly. Not to the point where I was stroking her stomach while I fucked her, thinking that I wouldn't mind seeing it swollen with my child.

Wasn't that some kind of messed-up, lust-induced delusion? But it'd crossed my mind. More than just crossed it, actually. The thought of breeding her had made me come so hard I couldn't see straight for a full three minutes.

And I was hard now while I thought about it. What was wrong with me?

"Rome, I've got a message from Garrett. He wants to go over the schedule. I slotted him in for lunch—" Clara poked her head through the door and frowned at me. "Are you okay?"

"What?" I rolled forward, thankful my desk was solid oak. "I'm fine."

"You look—did the weekend go okay?"

"The weekend?" My voice sounded weird.

Clara stared at me for a beat. "With Garcia?"

"Oh! Right. Yeah, yeah, it was good."

"Are you sure you're okay?"

"I'm fine. What's that about Garrett?"

"I emailed you the details. Do you want me to get you a coffee or something? Sparkling water? Aspirin?"

"I'm fine, Clara. That'll be all."

She was still frowning when she closed the door, and I let out a soft curse. This had gone too far. I needed to get rid of Nikki, because she was intruding on my ability to do my job. And how could I be surprised about that? Letting people in meant weakening yourself. If I wanted to continue being successful, I needed to stay sharp. I needed to stay *alone*.

Anger burned off the remnants of my lust. Anger at myself, at Nikki, at Clara for noticing something was off. I glared at my computer screen and sent my notes back to the finance department, then attended to the email Clara had sent about Dean Garrett, grimacing. The man was a time-waster, but I couldn't afford to turn him away right now. I'd have to meet with him to go over details that we'd already clarified.

I scowled at the full schedule of events she'd dropped on my desk this morning for approval.

Pulling the paper closer, I uncapped a red pen and slashed two-thirds of the events. I needed to start cutting down the amount of time I spent with Nikki. She was distracting me from what truly mattered. She was making me think about things that would never be mine. A relationship. A child.

Who was I to think I was capable of caring for a child? What would I do with a kid? The best thing for it would be to be far away from me, in the care of someone who would take care of it properly.

And why was I thinking about this again?

Squinting at the sheet, I narrowed my eyes at the Thanksgiving dinner I had to attend at my parents' estate. Could I get away with going alone, or would that cause too many problems? The following week was—the Nutcracker ballet?

Was Clara out of her mind?

"Clara!"

She poked her head back in. "Yes?"

"Why am I going to the ballet?"

"Wilbur Monk gifted you his private box. Apparently at that luncheon a couple of weeks ago, Nikki got in a conversation with Roseanne about doing ballet for a year as a child but never having the opportunity to go see professionals. They sent over the tickets last week." She pushed the door open a little wider, leaning against the frame as she frowned at me. "If you don't want to go, I can come up with an excuse, but it was a thoughtful gift, and I think—"

"I have to go, otherwise they might take offense."

Clara pinched her lips and nodded.

"Fine," I said. "Thank you."

The door closed gently behind her, and my heart thumped uncomfortably. A few of these upcoming events I could reasonably attend alone. But if I went to too many on my own, people would begin to notice, especially with how many of them had taken to Nikki.

Why did she have to be so damn likable? Why did she have to be so perfect for me—for the job?

"Knock, knock," a voice said, and my anger evaporated. Nikki smiled at me in the doorway, then lifted a familiar white bakery bag, dangling it between nails painted a fresh, bright red. "I made a pit stop on the way here," she said.

She'd brought me cookies. I sat here and cursed her existence, and she'd gone and done something thoughtful for me.

This woman would be the death of me, and I wouldn't even complain about it. How could I push her away when she was so damn perfect?

I leaned back in my chair and watched her approach. Her hips swayed with every step, her camel-colored dress peeking through from between the lapels of her wool pea coat. Her shoes were impractical red heels that matched her nails and lips to perfection.

She propped herself on the edge of my desk and I didn't have the strength of will to tell her to get down. Instead, I watched the way her dress lifted to reveal a delicious length of leg while she put the bakery bag down on top of my red-marked schedule, digging inside for a warm chocolate-chip cookie.

My mouth watered, and it wasn't because of the cookie. Nikki broke off a piece, chocolate dripping over her finger, and brought it to my lips. I kept my mouth closed as I watched her, wanting to kiss that impertinent smile off her red lips.

She rubbed the melted chocolate edge of the cookie on my lip and sing-songed, "You know you want it."

I did want it, and I wanted her. I wanted a whole lot of things I couldn't have, and apparently I was weak, because I opened my lips and accepted the bite. When Nikki went to pull away, I wrapped my hand around her wrist and pulled her fingers into my mouth.

A soft moan sounded through her closed lips as I ran my tongue over her fingers.

Every thought I'd had before she walked in was forgotten. It was easy to think about distancing myself from her when she wasn't here, dark-haired, intoxicating, moaning at the pull of my mouth on her skin. How could I resist a woman like this? How could I go back to the infrequent, impersonal trysts I'd had before? How could I possibly give her up? Why would I?

"Delicious," I said, relishing the rise and fall of her chest. "Thank you."

"Welcome," she replied, breathless.

I glanced at the bag, then at her. My brows arched meaningfully.

Her teeth dug into that plush lower lip I loved so much, eyes darting to my office door.

"Worried someone will walk in?" I said, my fingers dancing up her calf.

"Rome..."

"I'll have the rest of that cookie now," I said, noticing the way she squirmed ever so slightly on my desk, the way her fingers trembled as she reached into the bag.

My girl loved being told what to do. She loved the risk of this moment. Hell, I loved it too. Being with her was the only time I felt alive.

Another piece of cookie appeared at my lips, and I frowned at her. "Bite-size pieces, Nikki," I chastised.

A gust of breath escaped her as she broke the piece in two before presenting it to me again. I caught her fingers in my mouth once more. Her breaths became ragged. I smiled at the way she squeezed her thighs together while I watched.

No, I wasn't going to let her go. And I wasn't attending these boring events on my own. And I also wasn't going to deny her the chance to attend the ballet if that's what she wanted to do. Hell, I was mostly mad at myself that I hadn't thought of it first—that I hadn't even known she'd want to.

This girl was mine to cherish. Mine to spoil. Mine to keep.

It was easy to remember that when a flush was draped across her cheeks from the simple brush of my tongue on her fingertips.

We finished the cookie. I stood, and she spread her knees to give me space between them. Perfect, willing woman. Her gaze was heavy-lidded as she watched me, chin tilted up like she needed my kiss.

She needed something else too. I slid my hand up under her skirt, cupping the warm, wet heat of her. When I squeezed, she let out a whimper. "Is this what you want?" I asked, and the gravel in my voice made it almost unrecognizable. "You want me to make you come?"

She nodded. "Yes."

"That's why you came in here teasing me with cookies, with that dress and those shoes?"

Her lips kicked, a sassy arch lifting her brow. "Maybe. Or maybe I just wanted to make you feel good. Thank you for a nice weekend."

I massaged her core and let out a huff. "I bet you did."

When I pulled my hand away, she moved her hips to chase me. Greedy woman. I smacked her lightly on the gusset of her wet panties, and her lips fell open on a breath, hips rolling to meet my hand. My cock was so hard it ached.

"We have a meeting to go to," I told her, and I twitched her skirt back into place. Her pout made me laugh, and I brushed my lips against hers. I pulled her off the desk and steadied her as she stood. "And Nikki," I said, "you're not allowed to touch yourself until I say so. Not allowed to ease that ache between your legs until I do it for you."

She glared at me. "This is the last time I'm ever doing something nice for you."

I grinned. "I doubt that very much."

TWENTY-EIGHT
NIKKI

THE INKLING that I might be in over my head entered my mind as I sat in that boardroom, as horny as I'd ever been, trying to focus on the schedule projected on the far wall. The rasp of my underwear against my tender flesh was almost too much, especially when I glanced across the long table and found Rome's gaze on me.

"...and Raphael Garcia has approved our initial storyboards, and he wants to take you out to dinner to talk through the new plan," Clara explained. "He specifically asked for Nikki to be there. I've slotted that in for Thursday evening."

Rome's gaze left mine, and I felt like I could breathe. He nodded at Clara. "Good. Send me the names of the team members that got that over the line this weekend and I'll head down to thank them in person."

"Will do," Clara said, fingers flying over her tablet. A chime sounded from Rome's phone a moment later.

The woman was an efficiency machine. I tried to uncross my eyes to focus on what was going on. The perfume commercial. My idea. Right.

Minor tweaks were made to the schedule, and I jotted down some notes about events. I'd have to research some of the upcoming projects and clients and make sure I had the appropriate clothing to wear to a few of these formal events. There was one white-tie gala that would require a new dress, but I thought I could manage the rest on what I already had.

"That's it, then," Clara said. "Thanks for your time."

Rome stood, straightening his tie. His gaze landed on me as I busied myself writing notes, and, fine, maybe avoiding his gaze.

"Jordan," he said, voice sharp.

I looked up. "Yes?"

"Are you coming?"

I frowned, glancing at the page. "Coming where? I thought today was clear."

"Down to thank the people who are going to make your idea for Garcia's commercial a reality."

"Oh," I said softly, straightening. "Really?"

"You should see what they came up with," he said. "You're the one who understands what Garcia really wants."

I couldn't help the smile that spread over my mouth. I slammed my notebook shut and tucked it into my purse. My heart thumped as Rome came closer, opening the conference room door for me. I followed in his wake as we cut to the elevators, my gaze tracing the broad line of his shoulders, his trim waist, his long legs.

It felt like I was floating. I couldn't believe that one of my ideas would actually be useful, that I could be part of something bigger than myself. And when the elevator doors closed on the two of us, I knew there was something else that gave me that floaty, delicious feeling.

Rome watched me from the other side of the space, his gaze dark. One look was enough for lust to spark in my veins. I was desperate for him to touch me, to make good on his promises. But he just let one side of his lips kick up, then glanced at the changing numbers above the door. When the elevator slowed, he moved closer, his hand sliding across my lower back.

I shivered, tendrils of heat wrapping through my abdomen.

We stepped out of the elevator, and I wondered if my face was very red. It certainly felt flushed. But no one gave me any weird looks until we entered a section of the office that held a few cubicles and group-working desks. A few heads popped up above the cubicles to stare like meerkats looking out for danger.

On the other side of the room, a few people clustered around a white table. I recognized Ophelia when she glanced up from the papers they were poring over. She straightened at the sight of Rome, her wide-eyed expression turning slightly confused when it landed on me.

Rome's shoulder brushed mine. He greeted most of the people around the table with a nod, then said, "Ophelia."

She blinked away from me and beamed at him. "Hi, Mr. Blakely."

"The client is pleased with the work you've done so far. Thank you for turning it around so quickly."

"Oh, it's no problem at all," she said, then turned to me, frowning slightly. "I thought you were fired."

Now, one thing about me is that I'm a staunch member of

the Women Supporting Women club. But the way her eyes sharpened on me made my hackles rise. I gave her a toothy smile. "I was," I said.

Her brow wrinkled.

Rome's hand slipped down the back of my arm to my elbow, and I resisted the urge to shiver. "Nikki's the one who came up with the idea for the revised commercial," Rome explained. "She's the one who pitched it to Garcia."

"Was she," Ophelia said, and it sounded more like a statement than a question. "How wonderful."

"Show us what you've got so far," Rome said, and we were herded through to a conference room. Rome pulled out a chair for me, which Ophelia noted with a glance in our direction.

I wanted to give her the benefit of the doubt, but she was making it pretty hard. Maybe she had a crush on Rome, or she didn't like the fact that I'd popped up somewhere she hadn't expected. Either way, it seemed I didn't have a friend in her. It probably didn't help that neither Rome nor I had really explained the nature of our relationship. How could we, when we didn't know ourselves?

I sat down on the creaky, faux leather chair, and Rome took a seat kitty-corner from me, rolling the chair back slightly so he could rest his elbows on his thighs. The lights were dimmed as Ophelia fired up the projector to take us through the work they'd done so far.

She was halfway through the storyboard when the touch of Rome's bare hand on my knee nearly made me jump out of my chair. He squeezed, and I forced myself to relax.

I glared at him, and he didn't even meet my gaze—but the edge of his lip twitched.

His fingers made tiny circles on the inside of my knee, and I forced myself to keep my breathing steady. On the other side of the table from me, Ophelia clicked through the slides to show what models they'd already booked for the shoot.

"Two of the models we used for the original shoot aren't available, but we should still be able to use some of the footage we got with them if we need it," she said.

Rome's finger moved up an inch, drawing a complicated pattern on the inside of my thigh. He was barely above my knee, and my pulse pounded between my legs. This was torture and so, so inappropriate.

And for some insane reason, I loved it. I spread my legs the slightest bit, and Rome's hand slid up another inch. As he stroked my skin, my chair creaked, making me jump.

"The only other thing is that the studio is booked out for the next month," Ophelia said, glancing up.

Rome didn't remove his hand from my leg as he studied the screen and said, "Delay the East Coast Candles shoot and slot this in at the end of the week. We want to get it over the line as soon as possible." His voice was businesslike as his fingers were gentle, teasing the tender flesh miles away from where I wanted them.

Ophelia dropped her gaze to the screen with a nod. "Got it."

Rome's hand slipped higher up my leg, and I squeezed my thighs shut, glaring at him. He still didn't meet my gaze—or move his hand.

I doubted Ophelia could see anything happening under the table. And even if she did, I found myself not caring. She was quick to throw me under the bus because of an honest accident that could have been prevented if I hadn't been locked in a supply room for two hours.

"Done," she said with a nod. "I've scheduled that in and will coordinate everything with the studio team."

Rome nodded and stood, smoothly taking his hand away from my leg. Ophelia bundled her computer up, turned the lights on, and led us out into the main office. It took all my focus to keep my legs steady as we made our way back to the elevators, neither of us saying a word until the doors closed and locked us inside.

Rome crowded me against the wall, his hand pressing between my legs over my dress. I let out a whimper as he ground the heel of his hand against my clit.

"Are you wet?" he asked, voice a bare rasp.

I glared at him. "Find out for yourself."

His smile was quick and blazing, made of pure delight. "I intend to."

The doors opened, and he swept his arm—and the hand that moments ago had been pressed to my aching core—toward the open space beyond. I realized with a start that we weren't on the top floor, but the lobby. I'd been so focused on the feel of his palm between my legs I hadn't realized we were going down, and not up.

I needed to get my head checked. This was so bad. This was out of control. This was going to bite me in the ass.

Unfortunately, there was also a possibility that Rome would bite me in the ass—literally—and that possibility held more sway in my lust-addled, logic-abandoned mind. I followed him out of the lobby to the waiting car. The driver nodded to us as I slid inside, followed by Rome, and then closed the door.

The privacy screen was up. My heart rattled.

"Where are we going?" I asked as the car began to move.

"You're coming right here," he said, and wrapped his hands around my waist to pull me on top of him so I was straddling his thigh, my knees hanging in the air off the edge of the seat. I crossed my legs on top of his calf for balance, gripping his shoulders as I gasped at the pressure on my clit.

"Grab the seat behind my head," he said in a dark voice, the one I was powerless to resist. "Good. Now make yourself come on my thigh like the good girl I know you are."

The glare I gave him would wither leaves, and for some reason it made one of those delighted smiles bloom over his lips. He bounced his knee the tiniest bit, making me bite back a groan, and said, "You have"—he checked his watch and tilted his head from side to side—"about ten minutes."

I think it was the sparkling look in his eyes that did me in. The expression on his face that was light and fizzy and just—just *happy*. That's what made my heart swell in my chest. That's what made me want to take this man's hand and follow him wherever he led me.

I rocked my hips and heat immediately began to spiral through my core. Rome kept his hands off me, but he leaned forward to nuzzle at my neck, to lay soft kisses on my jaw and neck. "You're doing so well, gorgeous," he said, and I bit back a whimper. "You look so perfect when you're about to come for me."

"Rome—I—" I gasped and rocked harder. "This feels so good."

"You like riding my thigh? Like making my pant leg wet so everyone will know what you did?"

No. But also *yes*. I whimpered and ground myself against him, using my arms for leverage as I rode his leg while he watched. He nibbled on my jaw and huffed when my movements became more frantic. The rasp of my panties against my core was too much and not enough. I felt so empty.

The car turned and I had to clamp my thighs around his to stay upright. Rome didn't move a muscle to keep me there, but he did groan appreciatively, sending more sparks shooting through my veins.

I didn't know how I'd gotten here. A few days ago, I was perfectly content to not have sex for long periods of time. Now one look, one touch, and this man had me rocking my core against his leg to get myself off.

I never should have bought him those cookies. Never should have started this.

"Need you," I panted. With every rock of my hips, my nipples rasped against the fabric of my bra. I wanted him to wrench my dress off and suck my nipple into his mouth, and the fact that I knew he wouldn't made them almost painfully sensitive.

"Keep going," he replied softly, leaning his head back to watch me. "Keep rubbing that wet pussy on my leg like I told you to."

"Please. Please, please. Touch me, Rome. Please." My knuckles were striped white and red on the seat on either side of his head.

His smile turned a little wicked. "Love hearing you beg, gorgeous. Now come for me."

I buried my face in his neck to muffle my cry. Pleasure detonated in my core, and my hands flew off the seat to wrap around his neck. When I came back to myself, Rome had his arms around me as he whispered sweet words of encouragement in my ear, peppering the sides of my face with kisses. He brought me back down to earth with soft strokes and murmured words, until I climbed off his lap and collapsed beside him.

We both stared at the little patch of wet on his thigh. His pants were a dark charcoal so it wasn't too obvious, but it was plain to see once you knew it was there. My cheeks burned. Rome stroked the spot with his thumb, humming. "Good," he said simply.

Then the car slowed, and Rome glanced at me. "We're meeting Dean Garrett for lunch. The scuba diver, remember? He wants to go over a few details about the schedule for his project."

I blinked. "What?" That wasn't on the schedule.

"I know," Rome said, eyes dark, "it could have been a phone call, but he insisted. I think he just wanted to see you again." His lips curled in a satisfied smirk as he ran his finger down the center of my chest, where a thin sheen of moisture had coated my skin.

The glower I gave him was one of my best, and it made him throw his head back and laugh. I straightened my clothes and huffed. "Tell me you didn't just make me ride your thigh as some alpha posturing bullshit with one of your business buddies. Tell me you're not that much of an asshole, Rome."

Rome leaned in and kissed my lips with more tenderness than I would have expected. "I made you ride my thigh because I've been desperate to make you come since the moment you walked into my office, Nikki. The fact that it might make Garrett wonder what put that pretty flush on your cheeks is just a bonus."

The feminist in me should have been upset, but I found myself liking the fact that Rome wanted to stake his claim on me. I wasn't just his plus-one today. I was just plain his.

TWENTY-NINE
NIKKI

THE DAYS MELTED into each other, and I drifted along as if on a cloud. I moved into a new apartment in Manhattan. It was part of a block of apartments owned by Blakely's corporation, and it was huge. My teal velvet couch looked a bit tired against all the gleaming new fixtures, but it was all I had.

It had a huge closet, which was a luxury I hadn't anticipated. I signed a year lease and let out a long breath. At least I had somewhere to live, and I could afford it.

Even if most of the time I spent my nights at Rome's place.

Two weeks after the thigh-riding incident—which Rome and I might or might not have repeated a time or two—I found myself in a cafe with my hands wrapped around a steaming mug of coffee. Eleanor sat across from me, regaling me with the gossip from the lower floors. We were finally getting around to meeting up for that drink she'd suggested over a month ago.

"Ophelia has been on a tear for weeks," she said, clicking

her tongue. "She's insufferable. She made two interns cry yesterday."

I grimaced. "Is it bad to say I never liked her?"

"She thinks very highly of herself," Eleanor agreed with a nod. But her eyes took on an interested gleam as she set her mug down on the table between us. "I overheard her on the phone saying that you and Rome had something going on."

I hid my reaction to the words with a sip of scalding coffee, taking my time to set my mug down before answering. There was an official line, of course. For all intents and purposes, Rome and I were an item. Before we started sleeping together, I'd had no problem saying so.

But now that we kind of *were* an item, it felt strange to have to lie about it. Except the lie was the truth. But the truth was a lie.

I shook my head. Whatever it was, it was confusing. Rome and I were...together. But there was a contract between us, complete with benefits and perks and a fat paycheck, and that made things murky.

Would he still want to be with me if the contract didn't exist? Did he actually want me for me, or was I just a convenient lay?

"We're seeing each other," I confirmed.

Eleanor's eyes went wide. She leaned back in her chair, staring at me. "What? Since when?"

"Well...you know he picked me up from the hospital when I hurt myself."

"I was sure he was just covering himself," Eleanor said, amazed. "Especially with them offering everyone a permanent contract right after that happened."

My lips twisted with a tinge of bitterness. "Maybe he was, and I won him over with my charm."

She laughed and shook her head. "Unbelievable. You know he hasn't dated anyone in years? People were saying he was some sort of sexual deviant and that's why he could never maintain a relationship."

I huffed. Rome Blakely absolutely was a sexual deviant. An insatiable, unbelievable, beautiful one.

"Does Ophelia have a crush on him, or something?"

Eleanor shrugged. "I think she's just angling for a promotion. That's the only thing that makes sense."

I hummed, nodding. I hoped it was professional interest. Not because I was threatened by her, but because I didn't want anyone asking any uncomfortable questions. Only a handful of people knew about the companion contract, but if word got out...

"We're going to Thanksgiving dinner at his parents' place," I told Eleanor to fill the silence.

She blew a raspberry and picked up her mug. "Good luck."

"Hopefully Joanne takes it easier on me than she did the first time."

Eleanor gave me a flat look and repeated, "Good luck."

I laughed and turned the conversation to Eleanor's beloved cat. She brightened and showed me a few pictures, and the subject of me and Rome was set aside.

As I left the coffee shop, though, I turned it over in my mind. I didn't like deceiving my friend, and Eleanor *was* a friend. We'd already made plans to meet again later in the week. She loved her job running around the studio, and she was happy to be scratching a life out for herself just like the rest of us.

She had a bubbly kind of energy, but it was underlaid with total calm. She talked about her retirement investments and her financial goals, about her plans for her life. She'd be the perfect person to talk to about my situation—if I were able to break the NDA and actually tell her the truth.

I left our coffee date feeling a little empty for not being able to share the truth with her. A little...alone.

Because no matter how crazy Rome made me in bed, and no matter how much he made my heart rattle when he gave me one of his rare, brilliant smiles, there was still a gulf between us. That contract bridged it, but it was just a stack of papers.

At the end of the day, he was a wealthy, well-connected man who could have his pick of women. And I was just me. I was the broke chick who spent way too much money on clothes. The girl who was stupid enough to get herself into a financial mess because she was too naive to know different. The girl who was always dropped when something better came along.

How long would it take for Rome to realize that he could do better? That he *should* do better?

Why in the world would he ever choose me, other than the convenience of the fact that I'd literally signed up for the job?

I was halfway to the subway station when my phone rang. As soon as I swiped to answer and heard Rome's deep rumble on the other side of the line, my thoughts quieted.

And that was the issue. When we were apart, I told myself it was a bad idea to fall for him. Then he crooked his finger at me, and I was all too eager to crawl to him.

"Hello, gorgeous," he said in my ear. "How do you feel about dinner out tonight?"

I shuffled off to the side to let people walk past, frowning at the overcast sky. "I thought tonight was free. Has something come up with one of your clients?"

He huffed. "I'm trying to ask you out on a date, Nikki."

My heart tumbled, and the jumble of thoughts that had been clouding my mind a minute ago cleared. I bit back my smile and said, "I'd like that. What should I wear?"

"My preference would be nothing," he said, which made a familiar heat twist through my abdomen, "but I guess, something nice. A dress."

"Done," I said.

"Pick you up at seven."

"See you then."

My smile lingered for a long time, and that evening, we had a candlelit meal in a restaurant that was too fancy for me to ever get a table without the Blakely name on the reservation. We went back to his place and made love, and I didn't think about my worries for the future once.

This pattern replicated itself the next day, and the next, and the next. We attended luncheons and dinners and galas and balls. Rome took me out, just the two of us, and made me feel like this romance between us was real. He took me to the ballet and fingered me to orgasm in a private box, whispering praise in my ear while I worked to stifle my gasps. He spread me out on his dining room table and ate me like I was his favorite dessert. He smiled every time I entered his office and curled his arms around me every morning we woke up in the same bed.

I was living a fantasy. A dream. There was no way this was real, with the fancy events and the fabulous clothes and the decadent food, but it *was*. And the way his eyes darkened was real. The way his hands clasped and claimed me—that was real. The way he nuzzled me and touched me at every opportunity. All of it made me forget about that flimsy paper bridge over the gulf of our differing circumstances.

THIRTY
ROME

NIKKI FROWNED at her phone screen as she waited for me on the couch in my office. I took my glasses off and pushed away from my desk and asked, "Is something wrong?"

She glanced up, brows arched. "Oh! No. Well, yes. It's my friend. She's going through a breakup, and I'm worried about her."

I nodded. My own friend Arlo was torn up about his former nanny, a willowy blonde with whom he'd become entangled. As I watched Nikki stand and turn to me, her hands smoothing down her clothes to straighten them, I felt a pang of sympathy. If Nikki walked away from me, I'd be a wreck too.

I crossed the space between us and indulged my urge to wrap Nikki in my arms. She sank into me, resting her head against my shoulder with a sigh.

"Is your friend okay?"

She shrugged. "She's pregnant, and the guy is a jerk." She pulled away, eyes narrowing on me. "He was her boss."

I took her chin in a gentle hold, brushing my lips against hers. "Are you worried about us?"

"Sometimes," she admitted.

"Why? I'm taking you to my family Thanksgiving, after all."

She gave me a flat look, and it made me want to push her down to the couch and spread those thighs apart so I could watch her expression transform to something softer. "That's my job, Rome."

"Ouch."

She rolled her eyes and grinned at me. "I'm sure your ego will recover."

My nose brushed the side of hers as I said, "Maybe you should make it up to me." I let my hand slip down to squeeze the curve of her ass and was rewarded with the slight catch in Nikki's breath.

"Do you ever worry about what happens to us after?"

"After what?"

She pulled away, her hands on my shoulders as she frowned at me. "We can't go on like this forever, Rome. You must know that."

My throat was tight when I said, "I try not to think too far ahead."

She pursed her lips, and I nipped at them to make them soften. I couldn't stop touching her. If she was in the same room as me, I wanted my arms around her. If there was a frown on her forehead, I wanted to kiss it away. If she gave me any kind of sass, I fought the urge to fuck her until she smiled for me.

I pulled her onto the couch on top of me so she straddled me, her skirt falling around us in a flutter of fabric. She sat back on my thighs and plucked at a stray thread on my collar, a deep fold between her brows. I touched the spot, and she smoothed it.

"When I'm with you, I can't think straight," she admitted, lifting her gaze to meet mine.

I huffed, my hands on her hips. "I know the feeling."

That made her lips kick, and a tightness in my chest eased.

"What do you want, Nikki? Do you"—I cleared my throat—"want to stop..."

"Having sex with you?" She arched a brow.

I jerked my chin down in a rough movement.

"No," she admitted, "and that's the problem."

My hands slid up her thighs, relishing the warmth of her skin. She closed her eyes briefly, and I rumbled in satisfaction. "Good," I answered. "Because neither do I. And I don't think it's a problem."

"What are we, Rome?" Nikki asked, eyes wide. "What is this between us?"

"You need a label?" My hands found the line of her panties where they cut into her hips. I dipped my thumbs under the elastic, stroking softly. "What's that going to change, Nikki?"

Her lids fluttered at my touch. "It would make this make sense," she whispered. "And then maybe I wouldn't be so scared."

"Scared of me?" My voice was rough. I was struggling to understand what she needed, and I didn't like the pinch in my chest at the thought that she wanted to end this. But she was on top of me, and it didn't feel like she wanted to pull away. Did she want to be my girlfriend? She basically *was*. Did she want to stop working for my company? Quit?

That made the pinch in my chest turn painful. She was here because she worked for me, but if she wanted to walk away...

How would I be sure she would stay by my side? How could I ever be sure she wouldn't abandon me entirely? She was employed by my company, and that meant she'd be here. That was all that mattered. That was what I wanted—what I was sure she wanted too.

"I'm not scared of you," she said softly, brushing her lips over mine. "I'm scared of my feelings for you. Scared that you'll wake up and realize you don't want me, and you'll just shake me off like a stray piece of lint."

A long breath eased out of me. She wasn't leaving. She didn't *want* to leave. And she...she cared about me. The thought of her having feelings for me made it hard to breathe, and I didn't quite know how to deal with the emotion it called up inside me. I didn't even know what that emotion *was*.

A few months ago, I would have scoffed at myself. I knew I was better on my own, and I knew that being vulnerable only opened you up to getting hurt. Those were deep, undeniable truths.

But Nikki was vulnerable, and I found myself feeling closer to her than I ever had before. With slight pressure on her hips, I pulled her forward, tilting my face to hers. She followed my lead, tangling her fingers in my hair to press a kiss on my lips. I tongued at her bottom lip and groaned at the taste of her.

"Clara could walk in any minute," Nikki whispered against my lips, but she didn't pull away.

"Better be quick, then," I said, sliding my hand under her panties to get at the wet warmth of her. I groaned as my fingers slid through her slickness, entering her opening with ease. She whimpered and rode my hand until her breaths were pants.

"This is so bad," she said, voice fracturing on the last word. Her breath was hot on my neck as her head fell forward.

I huffed a laugh, adding a second finger while my thumb found her clit. "Better be a good little girl and come for me then."

I wondered if this was always how it would be between us. I'd never felt this kind of insatiable desire with anyone before. I'd never been so desperate for a woman in my life, but somehow I couldn't get enough of Nikki. The only way we knew how to communicate was with sex. She was worried about something, but I didn't know how to ease those worries in any other way.

Her hips rolled over my hand until I slid my fingers out of her, replacing them with my other hand. There was a frantic, hungry need inside me. A need to claim her, to make sure she knew she was mine. All her fears were unfounded. They had to be. There was no way this connection between us could falter.

Sure, our arrangement was unconventional. And I knew, logically, that it had to end someday. But I couldn't see the shape of our relationship in any other way. I wasn't the type of man who could have a wife and kids and a normal life. I wasn't built that way. I didn't have the required neural connections in my brain that would give her all she needed in a partner. All she deserved.

But I'd be damned if that meant I'd let her go.

I wrapped my arm around her hip and found her ass with the tip of my finger coated in her arousal. I teased her there, loving the way she ground down on me. She gasped, pupils blown out as she lifted her head, her hands curling into my shoulders as she rode both my hands to a shuddering release.

We were both breathing heavily by the time the trembling in her limbs abated, and I pulled my fingers from her, wishing I could replace them with something else.

Nikki shifted, sliding to her knees on the floor before me. Her hands were at my belt in an instant, eyes darting to the door before meeting mine with a wicked glint.

"You don't have to—"

"I know," she said, and she pulled me free from the confines of my pants before taking me into her mouth in one long suck.

My hips bucked off the couch and my hand flew to the back of her head. She hummed, and my eyes rolled back. The silk of her hair tightened between my fingers as I fisted into it, feeling the sharp daggers of her pointed nails in my thighs as she sucked me off like she was desperate for the taste of me.

When I came, she drank down my release in greedy gulps, and three little words rose to my lips, bursting to come out. She lifted her head and smiled at me, dazed, running a finger along the edge of her lip while her tongue darted out to lick it.

My breath heaved. I stared at this woman, this goddess, at a loss.

"I'd better go fix my makeup," she said, and she rose to her feet like she hadn't just shattered something inside me without even trying. I watched her disappear behind the door to my office's ensuite then stuffed my softening cock back into my underwear before zipping myself up.

A while later, we took the helicopter to my parents' estate and sat through an excruciating dinner where no one gave thanks for anything. Nikki responded to their chilly formality with a kind of stubborn cheerfulness, smiling at veiled insults and complimenting the food as if my mother had cooked it herself.

At the sight of my mother's disapproving glare, my lips curled into an unrepentant smile. I found Nikki's fingers and threaded them through my own, then brought her hand up to my mouth so I could place a kiss on the back of it.

She arched her brows at me, eyes glimmering, and I wished I had the courage to name the feeling trying to burst out of my chest.

THIRTY-ONE
NIKKI

OUR WEEKEND AT THE MONKS' private island was fast approaching. It was the last weekend of December before the holidays started, and lots had happened. Bonnie had made up with Arlo in a dramatic stand-off that, coincidentally, happened on the ground floor of the Blakely building. I missed the whole thing because I was in the bathroom when everything went down, which was becoming a more frequent occurrence. I told myself I was drinking more water on account of all the energy I expended during sex, but I was still mad to have missed Arlo engaging in a bout of fisticuffs with a ghost from Bonnie's past. Besides that drama, things were good. Work ramped up, and I'd gotten to know most of Blakely's most important clients.

With some careful spending, I was inching closer to repaying my debts. Blasphemous as it might be, I eyed my closet full of beautiful clothes and wondered if I could sell some of the more valuable pieces to be rid of my mistake.

Because I was a new woman. One who was chosen, who

was worthy. Someone who wasn't just a placeholder or a stand-in while the main character waited for a better thing to come along. I was *me*, and that felt great.

I was a woman who'd get her first ride in a private jet. I whistled as our car slid to a stop at the bottom of the stairs on the tarmac, and Rome grinned at me.

"I'm glad I can still give you a few novel experiences," he said.

"You've given me more than a few." I laughed at the twinkle in his eye and turned toward the door that Keith opened for me.

"Enjoy your weekend away," the driver told me quietly, and I smiled at him and squeezed his arm in response. Beyond Keith was the airplane crew including a number of hostesses waiting for us at the top of the stairs. I had a moment of near panic at the sight of the jet, suddenly feeling like an impostor who didn't belong here at all, but Rome's presence at my back steadied me. We climbed the steps and entered the jet, and I delighted in the welcome drinks, the snacks, and the gigantic seats and lounge area.

Rome watched my reaction to everything, his lips kicking at the corners. I arched my brows at him, and he shrugged in response. I settled in my seat, and happiness spread through me like warm honey on a slice of toast. It was rare that I was able to read someone else's expression that way, that I could have whole conversations without uttering a word. But with Rome, it was possible. Sometimes, I could tell the moment he woke up beside me just by the cadence of his breath over my skin.

On the side table beside my seat waited a glass of champagne, some fresh fruit, and a couple of truffles the air crew had brought over. The snacks looked delicious when they set them down, and they were fabulous, but the longer I looked at them, the less I wanted to eat them.

"Still queasy?" Rome asked quietly, his knee nudging mine.

"A little."

I hadn't eaten breakfast this morning—or yesterday, come to think of it. It wasn't entirely rare. I sometimes skipped breakfast and had huge lunches. Or skipped dinner and woke up ravenous. I'd never been set in my routines.

I tried a tiny sip of champagne and grimaced before setting the glass down.

"That bad, huh," Rome asked sardonically, watching me. "That's not poor-quality stuff, you know."

"No, it's not that," I said, then tilted my head. "Well, maybe a little. I don't know."

Rome's hand landed on my leg, and he stroked softly. "Try to have some fruit, at least."

The warmth and worry in his voice made my insides melt to goo. I nodded and nibbled on a strawberry and was glad when it didn't upset my stomach. Then our glasses and dishes were being whisked away, and we were getting ready for takeoff.

"I'll tell you what, this is a whole lot better than cattle class," I said as we reached a cruising altitude, and the cabin crew came through with more menus and snacks. There was a full-size TV across from us, and I discovered my seat had massage features.

Rome grinned at me and nodded at a few items on the menu that the flight attendant hurried to bring to us. I found myself snuggled into his side while he fed me little bits of food, feeling cherished and warm and safe.

"I wish I could tell my girlfriends about this," I said,

wiggling my toes. "Not that it would be anything new for them at this point, but at least I could share it with them."

Rome went still beside me, then his fingers began to make shapes over my waist and hip. "What have you told them about us?"

"Nothing," I said. "I've signed an NDA, remember?"

"You haven't even told them we're seeing each other?"

I sat up and frowned at him. "I wasn't going to lie to them. They're my friends!"

He answered my frown with one of his own. "But it's not a lie."

"Not *now*. But it would have been before. And now... How would I explain?"

"You'd tell them you work for me and are also sleeping with me, and you're deliriously happy about it all."

I pursed my lips and gave him a flat look, which made him grin.

"Is that a lie?"

"Not technically, no."

"What about untechnically?"

"Then yes, it is a lie. Because there's still... I still am your companion, Rome. Officially."

"Unofficially too," he noted.

I nodded. This whole thing was confusing. "I just haven't spoken to them about it yet, is all."

"Are you embarrassed of me?" There was a note in Rome's voice—a hesitation I'd never heard before. An edge of vulnerability that was completely at odds with the confident man he was.

"What? No!" I cupped his cheek and kissed him. "Not

once. How could I be? It would make more sense for you to be embarrassed of me."

His gaze flicked between my eyes for a long moment, then his shoulders softened. "Never, Nikki."

I smiled and leaned my head against his shoulder. "Good."

His soft touch returned to my hip and waist, and drowsiness overtook me. By the time we landed just under five hours later, my stomach was settled and my heart was happy. A few times during the flight, I caught Rome frowning as he stared off into the middle distance, but his expression always cleared when he caught me watching him. He kissed me gently as the cabin crew prepared the doors, leaning his forehead against mine in a tender touch.

Then bright light streamed in through the open hatch, and we both stood up to go meet the Caribbean sun. I breathed in the salt-scented air and descended the steps, a smile stretching over my lips. Winter in the city had been dreary and slushy, with intermittent bouts of snow. I was glad to see the sun, at least for a weekend.

From the airport, we were driven to a jetty where we boarded a sleek white yacht. The captain greeted us, dressed in a crisp uniform and a bright smile. He ushered us on board, where we were plied with more snacks and drinks. I stood near the bow of the boat as we left the jetty and cut through the turquoise water, the sounds of the engine drowning out the delicate rush of the sea.

"What do you think?" Rome asked, leaning against the railing beside me.

I smiled. "Not bad."

His grin made my heart turn over. The wind ruffled his hair, and there were fewer lines around his eyes. His shoulders were relaxed as he gazed out at the horizon. I watched white sand pass us, palm trees waving in the wind. Sea birds circled overhead.

It was easy to forget that this was work. I tried to remind myself of it, but Rome caged me against the railing, nuzzling at my neck as we made a sweeping turn toward a little patch of land that was quickly growing in size. Curiosity burrowed into me as the island grew; I'd never been to a private island before.

Roseanne had called it small, but it looked big enough as the captain brought the yacht to bump gently against the dock. Staff members called out to each other and worked with an easy kind of confidence, most of them barefoot as they tied the yacht off to the dock. A walkway was set up, and Rome guided me onto solid land.

White sand stretched in both directions, with lush greenery lining it. Once on land, the dock met a paved road where two golf carts waited.

Wilbur and Roseanne exited from one of them, greeting us with wide smiles. I thanked the man who carried my bag to the other golf cart, then turned to our hosts with a smile. Roseanne greeted me warmly, with kisses on both cheeks and a squeeze of my shoulders. She wore a gauzy white outfit with loose white pants and a fabulous wide-brimmed hat. I felt like a sweaty, travel-weary mess next to her, even though I was wearing my favorite wrap dress and cute sandals.

Her voice was warm when she asked, "How was the trip? Not too choppy, I hope?"

"It was fantastic. I love your yacht."

"One of Wil's toys," she replied with an indulgent smile.

Wilbur pumped my hand and smacked a kiss on my cheek. "Welcome! We're so glad to have you. Do you trust your man to drive a cart, or do you want to take the wheel?"

I grinned. "I trust him."

The older man winked at me, then waved us onto the golf carts and we were away. Birds flitted from tree to tree as we wound along the paved path. The air smelled fresh and clean, but it felt dense and humid on my skin. Rome kept one arm on the golf cart wheel and the other along the back of the seat behind me, his fingers stroking the back of my arm.

I'd entered another universe. I'd taken vacations before, including a week-long stay at an all-inclusive in Mexico in my twenties, but nothing compared to this. Everything was so *easy*. There were no long lineups. No waiting. No inconvenience. Rome and I were whisked along to our destination with an army of people there to make every step of it as easy as possible.

"Relax," Rome said quietly, cheeks creasing as he smiled at me. "Just enjoy yourself, Nikki. You've already won them over. The hard work is done."

"Everything is so beautiful," I said, which was a bit preemptive because I hadn't even seen the house yet. And once it came into view, I was proven right.

"House" was probably the wrong word for it. The place was huge. The sprawling building revealed itself to us as we turned the final corner, its terracotta roof a beautiful contrast against the lush greenery. The walls were painted a buttery yellow, and it would have been cute if it'd been about a tenth of the size. Balconies lined both stories, with another building poking through the trees to the left. An infinity pool gurgled over its edge and cascaded into a water feature on the ground floor. We drove around the side, where more staff members were waiting to help us disembark. They wore pastel-blue uniforms and presented us with trays of refreshments.

"We'll show you to your room, and then you can meet us on the balcony once you've freshened up," Roseanne announced.

The interior was homier than I expected, with comfortable-looking furniture interspersed with antiques. It was welcoming while also giving off the impression of extreme wealth, with beautiful finishes and tasteful artwork. We were led along wide hallways to a gigantic suite. It was the Garcia house all over again, but with huge sliding glass doors that opened onto a private patio.

Roseanne left us with more words of welcome, and as soon as the door was closed, I threw myself on the bed and sank into the comforter with a satisfied groan. The bed dipped as Rome crawled over me, his lips curled into a smile.

"I see I should have taken you on vacation earlier."

"I don't know how I'll ever go back to my regular life after all this," I said.

"You won't have to." He planted a kiss on my forehead then got up and moved to the bathroom. I heard the shower turn on and busied myself unpacking the small bag I'd brought for our weekend. There was a little welcome tray with more chocolates and goodies on the nightstand, and I had one while I waited for Rome to finish. Once I'd showered and changed into a loose sundress, we went off in search of our hosts.

We found them on the balcony they'd pointed out before, relaxing on lounge chairs as they watched the sun dip closer to the horizon. Wilbur smiled at the two of us and offered us drinks, and Roseanne jumped up to uncover plates of chopped vegetables and other finger foods.

Rome sank into a two-seater couch and brought me down along with him, and I couldn't resist the urge to rest my head against his shoulder.

"Your home—your *island*—is unbelievably beautiful."

"That's all Roseanne," Wilbur said affectionately.

"If it were up to Wil, we'd be living in some box in New York City."

I laughed awkwardly, thinking of my own box back home. The one that had felt like impossible luxury compared to my older, dingier box.

"I know enough to listen to you when you insist," Wilbur said, smiling, "and you insisted on this place."

"When we bought it, there was just the guest house." Roseanne waved a hand toward the roof that poked out through the trees, the one I'd spotted on the way up. "Building the main house, the docks, and the landscaping has been the work of a decade."

"Looks like it's worth it," I said, smiling.

"Watch out, Blakely," Wilbur warned. "You'll be buying an island next door before the weekend is out."

Rome glanced at me, grinning. "Maybe that wouldn't be so bad."

I laughed, giddy. Who casually talked about buying islands and building lavish residences on them? How was this real life?

But I was here, and all I could do was enjoy the weekend. My brief for this trip was to be myself, and to make sure the Monks couldn't find fault in myself or Rome. Rome would work on closing the deal with Wilbur and finally secure the older man's business.

Over the weeks I'd been working at Blakely, I learned this deal was important. A lot of the huge clients had cut their advertising budgets and moved to smaller campaigns for social media. The Blakely Advertising Agency could offer those services, but landing a huge, multi-year, multi-campaign client like Wilbur Monk, whose company had many subsidiaries, would sustain the business through the next half decade.

It was a huge deal. But as I watched the sun go down and chatted with the other couple, it didn't feel like we were here to close a deal worth nine figures. It felt like we were visiting old friends.

After a delicious dinner of grilled fish, Rome and I retired to bed. He wrapped me in his arms and tugged me close, smiling at me in the darkness of the bedroom.

"They love you," he said quietly.

"I think they love you too." I brushed my lips against his. "Thank you for bringing me here."

His chest rumbled in agreement, and he returned my gentle kiss with a more demanding one of his own. We didn't talk for a while after that, other than whispered praise and desperate urgings. Later, just before falling asleep, I felt him stroke my hair to push it off my temple. His touch was gentle—loving. I never would've guessed that my gruff, arrogant boss could be so tender, or that I'd be the woman who brought it out in him.

This was shaping up to be the best weekend ever.

THIRTY-TWO
NIKKI

IT WAS NOT the best weekend ever. The next morning
started out pretty good, with a morning kayak on glass-still
waters and only a bit of queasiness when I sat down for breakfast. Our hosts were gracious, and we ended up going on a
nature walk with them after our food, where they pointed out
the natural rock formations on the other side of the island.

Lunch was lovely.

In the afternoon, Roseanne stole me away while Wilbur and
Rome disappeared in the older man's study to talk business, and
I found myself watching her press her fingerprint into a scanner
to unlock her closet vault.

It was my own personal utopia. The woman had *taste*.
Every designer was represented, even some that I'd never heard
of. She'd been collecting clothes her entire life and excitedly
showed me her favorite pieces from decades gone by.

We started pulling clothes from hangers and creating
outfits. I felt like I was back in my old job, helping a client find

the perfect gem they didn't know they wanted. I couldn't stop smiling. When I paired a black-and-white houndstooth blazer with a silky green jumpsuit, Roseanne tilted her head and considered it, her finger tapping her chin.

"I think you might be a genius, Nikki. I've never thought of putting those pieces together."

I laughed. "I wouldn't say genius. Maybe obsessive."

She showed me a few outfits she'd created herself, and I suggested a few simple tweaks to style them, like rolling the sleeves of an oversized blazer a few times, forgoing a belt that had come with a pair of pants in a matching fabric for something that coordinated in a slightly different way, tweaking and manipulating clothes to create more flattering silhouettes.

Roseanne's eyes sparkled as she snapped photos of the outfits we put together. "I feel like I have a whole new set of clothes!" she exclaimed.

There were a few pieces that belonged in a museum. A vintage Alexander McQueen dress covered in thousands of hand-sewn fabric flowers, for example, was worthy of its own display mannequin. I didn't even dare touch the fabric but clasped my hands at my breast in appreciation.

Her wall of shoes was a gorgeous, perfectly organized shelving unit with strategically placed lighting along every shelf. She had them split up by color and occasion, so they were almost an art installation instead of wearable garments.

It was *fun*. We were two grown women—me in my thirties, her in her sixties—and we were acting like little girls who got to play dress-up. Her jewelry collection was a mix of costume and fine jewelry. The woman loved rings that were just shy of gaudy and earrings that dangled all the way to her shoulders. I wanted to be her when I grew up.

Things went wrong when I let out a breath and sat down on the round ottoman in the middle of the room as a wave of fatigue hit me. It had been sunny this morning, and I thought I was feeling the effects of being outdoors for longer than I was used to.

"And these are what I wore to my wedding," Roseanne said, a soft smile on her face when she showed me a pair of white satin pumps with a simple gold buckle. "They cost me twelve dollars, and I love them best of all."

I leaned back on my palms and smiled. "They're beautiful, Roseanne."

She gave me a strange look then and asked, "Have you and Rome talked about marriage?"

I coughed, caught out by her question. "I—um—no. Not... Not yet."

She hummed. "And have you told him?"

Blinking, I tried to make sense of her question. "Told him what?" That I wanted to marry him? That would be a resounding *hell no*, I hadn't told him I wanted to marry him. He was still paying me for my presence, after all.

Roseanne gave me a look that was almost chiding, edged with fondness. She placed her wedding shoes back on the shelf in their place of honor and said, "About the baby, of course."

The world tilted. My vision went wonky. Roseanne turned to look at me, and her face looked like a distorted caricature of what it had been moments ago. Somehow, I found my voice. "The what, now?"

She laughed and came to sit next to me. "Darling, you don't have to pretend with me. I fell pregnant within a few months of being married to Wilbur, and I remember feeling all out of sorts. But you'd better tell him soon; otherwise, he's in for a shock. Rome doesn't seem like the kind of man who takes unexpected news very well."

I let out the most awkward, half-assed laugh of my life. "I think you might be mistaken, Roseanne. I'm not pregnant."

She arched her brows. "No? I could have sworn..." Her gaze narrowed on me. "I felt just like you do when I was early in my pregnancy. Exhausted beyond belief, a little queasy, having to use the bathroom seventy-three thousand times a day..."

"No," I blurted. "No, that's not it." I shook my head and leaped to my feet. "Nope."

Roseanne didn't push it. She just inclined her head and said, "I'm so sorry to have presumed, darling. That's my big mouth getting in the way again. Come on. Let's go out to the patio and have a nice refreshing drink, just us girls. The chef makes fresh juice from the fruit from our orchards, and it's to die for."

She swept out of the room, and I had no choice but to follow her. I felt dizzy and nauseous and terrified.

What if...

No. There was no way. With every step, my horror grew. I hadn't gotten my period in...a while. But my cycle was irregular, and I never tracked it. Maybe it hadn't been that long? I rewound the weeks in my head and couldn't remember ever having to wrestle with my period while wearing a designer gown or attending a fancy event. That was over two months without my cycle showing up.

I'd gone without my period for two months before. It didn't mean I was pregnant.

We'd used condoms every time. We were feral for each other, but we hadn't...

Horror dawned. The first time—the first time we hadn't used a condom, because we hadn't had one. At Garcia's anniversary weekend getaway in the Hamptons, there were bodily fluids all over us. That was about six weeks ago.

But that was *crazy*. I couldn't get pregnant from that.

...Could I?

Roseanne settled me onto a lounge chair and called for fruit juice. I'm sure it was delicious, but I tasted none of it. I sat there, slurping down my juice made from the fruit belonging to a disgustingly wealthy couple, staring at the azure Caribbean water all around their private island, and felt like I wanted to crawl out of my skin.

"You have a real talent with styling," Roseanne said in the silence, making me jump. Her eyes slid over to study me, and I felt like she could read my panic like words flashing across my face. "Have you ever considered making a career of it?"

"A career?" My voice sounded flat.

"Many of my friends would pay you for what you just did down there. Not to mention having you at our side when we go shopping."

"I don't..."

She took a sip of juice and set it down on the side table before glancing at me curiously. "What is it you do for work at Blakely, again?"

The world was pressing in on me. I couldn't think straight. Roseanne's gaze was on me, and I felt like she'd be able to tell if

I trotted out the tired old lie that I was a consultant for Rome. What did a consultant even do? All she had to do was ask me a few questions and the whole charade would fall apart, because I sure as hell wasn't able to dodge any incisive questions in my current state of mind.

The thoughts in my head were basically going around in a loop that went like this: *I'm not pregnant. No way. But what if I am? But I can't be. Oh, God, she's looking at me. Try to look normal. But looking normal made her think I was pregnant. There's no way. But what if I am...*

And on and on and on. And we were on a stupid private island so it wasn't like I could dart to a pharmacy when no one was paying attention to get a pregnancy test. I'd have to wait.

Hands landed on my shoulders, and I nearly jumped out of my seat. Rome chuckled, looking at me curiously. "Are you okay?"

"You gave me a fright," I said.

"We've had a big day," Roseanne cut in, watching me. "What if you head to your room for a rest?"

"Rest," I repeated dumbly. "Yeah."

"I'll take you," Rome said, and he had such sweet concern written on his face that I didn't know what to do. I couldn't blurt out what Roseanne had said, because what if I *wasn't* pregnant? Which obviously I wasn't. Rome took my arm and led me away from the couple, cradling me against his side as we walked through the house. "Are you okay?"

"I think the sun got to me," I mumbled. "I'm used to being a vampire."

He huffed a laugh and squeezed me closer. When we got to our room, Rome picked me up in his arms and settled me on the bed before drawing the blinds. He got me a glass of water and helped me strip down to my underwear, handing me one of his T-shirts to wear to sleep.

I wanted to refuse, because I was panicking and wearing his clothes while he took such sweet care of me would just make this whole thing that much worse. But the shirt smelled like him which settled my stomach somewhat, and I couldn't resist the temptation. I snuggled into it and fell into the lush pillows. The adrenaline that had left me feeling so panicked just moments ago drained away. Exhaustion slammed into me, and I was asleep in an instant.

THIRTY-THREE
ROME

I CLOSED the door as gently as I could, not wanting to wake Nikki from her nap. Worry squirmed through me—it wasn't like her to react like that to anything. Maybe she'd gotten a bit of heat stroke? We hadn't been out in full sun for a long time, but it was possible.

All I wanted to do was stay in the room beside her and make sure she was okay, but I couldn't ignore the fact that I was here to close the biggest deal my company had seen in years. Wilbur and I had ironed out some specifics, but he had yet to sign on to anything.

Torn between staying with Nikki and making sure he wasn't getting talked out of anything by his wife, I chose my professional obligations. We were leaving tomorrow morning; time was running out.

I found the older couple on the balcony, talking softly to each other. Roseanne glanced up when I walked out through the sliding glass doors, her brows arched above her sunglasses. "How is she?" she asked.

"Asleep."

"Poor darling."

"Did something happen?"

"She started feeling ill when we were down in my closet," Roseanne said, and I got the sense she was holding something back. Frowning at her didn't draw any more information, though, so I settled on a seat across from them.

"I was just telling Rosie about the agreement we came to," Wilbur said. "We're both very grateful you were able to make the trip down to see us, especially so close to the holidays."

I hummed. "To be honest, I think Nikki would have killed me if I'd canceled. She's been wanting to see your clothing collection since she first met you," I said, nodding at Roseanne.

The older woman smiled and took a sip of her drink.

"First thing tomorrow morning, I'll send a revised contract off to my lawyers," Wilbur announced. "I think it's time we put some of this in writing, don't you?"

My heart thumped. "Absolutely."

Wilbur nodded, satisfied. The momentary silence lulled me, and I wasn't ready for the sharp change in subject Wilbur made when he said, "When are you going to marry that girl?"

I'd been taking a sip of my own drink, delivered by one of the members of their army of staff, and found myself coughing the liquid up after inhaling it. "Excuse me?" I asked when I was able to speak.

"She's good for you," Wilbur said.

My throat burned. I cleared it, but it didn't help. "She's...

She's great," I agreed. "We haven't talked about marriage yet. We're taking things slow. We're not in any rush."

Wilbur and Roseanne exchanged a loaded look. It was Wilbur who said, "You might want to get in a rush."

I frowned. "What's that supposed to mean?"

The older man shrugged and leaned back in his chair, kicking his legs up on a footstool. "When I met Rosie, I knew that was it. I see the same thing with the two of you. No point in wasting time."

I nodded but said nothing. I felt out of depth in this conversation, and half my mind was still in the bedroom next to Nikki. Marriage...no. We barely knew each other.

She knows me better than anyone else, I argued with myself, then batted the thought away. It was too soon to get married. Way, way too soon. We'd known each other, what, a couple months? Two and a half? The old man was just obsessed with committed relationships, and he was entitled to his opinions. It didn't mean I had to marry the girl just because I liked her.

Still...I itched to get back to the room and check on her. I set my drink aside and stood. "Excuse me. I'll go make sure Nikki doesn't need anything."

"Of course," Roseanne replied with a regal nod. "We'll send word about dinner, but don't feel like you have to come out and keep the two of us old farts company if Nikki needs you more."

I gave her a jerky nod, then made my way back to the room. I found Nikki awake and curled on her side, reading something on her phone. She put it down when I walked in and gave me a soft smile.

"How are you feeling?"

"Better," she said, but I didn't quite believe her.

"Can I get you anything?"

A small head shake, and Nikki extended her arms toward me. I climbed into bed behind her and tucked her against my chest, curling my knees behind hers. She let out a soft sigh, and the unease that had pounded through me settled.

We stayed like that for a long time—long enough that the light coming in around the edges of the curtains changed to a darker gold. I intermittently stroked her hair and let my hands drift over her arm and side. My thoughts circled around and around, always coming back to the same thing.

Marriage.

I'd never thought of myself as someone who would have a wife. When I thought of my future, I always imagined myself standing on my own. That was the safest way to be. That was how I'd made my fortune, how I'd built my empire.

But Wilbur's words wriggled into my mind and made a home there. I thought about waking up next to Nikki every morning. Being able to take her to events and introduce her as my wife, not just my guest. Having her as a sounding board and a second opinion for the rest of my life.

She'd helped me over the past couple of months; business had improved with her by my side. She wasn't just a beautiful woman that charmed the people we met. She was observant and forward-thinking. She did more research than some of my own marketing teams in order to prepare for the various events. She dressed impeccably, which I was learning was less about style and more about sending the right message.

With Nikki by my side, I wasn't just the captain of a meaningless ship. My future wasn't simply the pursuit of more. If we were to make this real, I could see a life that was fulfilling, maybe even happy.

But I'd known her two and a half months. Even the thought of marriage was crazy, let alone speaking it out loud. Besides, our agreement was working. She got paid for all her efforts, and I got to spend as much time with her as possible.

There was another benefit to keeping things as they were. I didn't have to face my biggest fear: Nikki leaving. I knew that if I really let her in, if I told her just how much I wanted her and just how much I imagined a future with her, I'd be signing my own death warrant. I couldn't do it.

The fact of the matter was that she was here because I paid her. Sure, we were involved now, but what if the promise of a steady paycheck and a big clothing budget was worth more to her than a commitment to me? What if all the tender moments we'd had didn't mean as much to her as they meant to me?

What if I peeled off my armor and put a target on the most vulnerable part of me, handed her the knife, and told her she could drive it into my heart if she chose?

"We should get up," she said in a soft voice, turning her head slightly.

I inhaled the scent of her hair and placed a kiss on her shoulder. "Only if you're feeling better."

"I am. I don't want to leave Wilbur and Roseanne alone when they've been such great hosts. There's a lot riding on this."

"Don't worry about it," I told her, heart pinching. "You don't have to think about work right now."

She turned around fully, expression soft. Her fingers slid over my jaw and pushed into my hair, and I groaned at the feel of her nails against my scalp. Her touch dragged my eyelids down, making my whole body feel heavy. She massaged my temple, my crown, the nape of my neck. Her hand softened and slid to the side of my throat a moment before she shifted to brush her lips against mine.

Her kiss was soft and sweet, and it almost gave me the courage to strip that armor off and hand her a knife. How could this be fake when it felt so real? How could she possibly not want exactly what I wanted when she touched me like the feel of my skin beneath her palm was the only medicine she ever needed?

Pulling away, Nikki met my gaze. "We should get up."

I exhaled and nodded. "We should."

Her eyes sparkled as a teasing grin tugged at her lips, but she slipped out of my grasp before I could pull her on top of me. Laughing, Nikki shuffled to the bathroom and left me on the bed alone, embers of desire heating my blood.

But she was right. We needed to go find our hosts and make an appearance for dinner. We'd be heading out the next morning, so there wasn't much time to close this deal.

As I stretched my spine and let my feet fall to the floor, a deep sigh slipped through my lips. The last thing I wanted to do was go schmooze with a client right now—and that was possibly the scariest thing of all.

This woman had turned my life upside down. Business didn't hold my attention. All I cared about was her.

THIRTY-FOUR
NIKKI

THE TWENTY-FOUR HOURS that followed were excruciating. I put on my best happy face, drawing on the practice I'd had over the last two and a half months of attending dozens of events at Rome's side. I made pleasant conversation and made sure that my expression was either neutral or happy, because anything else drew a frown to Rome's brow.

He held me close all through the night, and barely left my side the next day. He asked me if I was feeling all right so many times I finally had to ask him if he was stuck on repeat. He gave me a flat look and pressed a hard kiss to my forehead in what felt like an act of affectionate defiance.

The biggest surprise happened an hour before our departure from the island, when Roseanne pulled me aside. I was desperate to get out of there, to get away from everyone, to find out if there actually was a baby growing inside me. It made me itchy and impatient, but I did my best to put on a pleasant expression.

She saw right through it. She gave me a little half-smile and squeezed my arm. "I'm so glad we got to spend this time together. And I know a lot of Wil's worries about working with Rome have been put to rest because of it."

My shoulders relaxed, and I nodded. I got the sense that Wilbur placed a lot of importance on his wife's opinion and that I'd passed some test this weekend without realizing it. "I'm glad to hear it," I told her.

"We'll be back in the city in the spring, and I'd like you to get in touch." She pulled out a business card and handed it to me. "The timing might not be...ideal," she said, only hesitating on the word for a brief moment. I knew she was talking about my maybe-not-so-hypothetical pregnancy, but neither of us acknowledged it. "If you're interested in working as my stylist, I think we'd be able to come to a suitable arrangement. I'm not sure how much the folks at Blakely are paying you for your consultancy work, but if you're interested..."

I ran my finger along the edge of the thick card, nodding. "Thank you. I'll think about it."

Her smile brightened. "Great! I'll be in touch. Take care of yourself—and that man of yours."

My own smile felt a little brittle, but Roseanne didn't seem to mind. She led me back out to the lobby, and we climbed into the golf carts and headed to the jetty. The trip back up north was uneventful, but I found myself feeling stifled by the luxury. There were so many staff members around, so many people waiting to serve us hand and foot.

I felt like an ungrateful brat, but all I wanted to do was be alone.

"I can have dinner arranged at the house," Rome said when we were finally in the car driving away from the airport, the weather outside blustery and snowy. "What do you feel like eating?"

I swallowed. "Actually, I was hoping to head back to my own place tonight."

He froze, then seemed to force himself to relax. "Of course. Whatever you prefer."

"It's not that I don't want to spend time with you," I hurried to add. "I just feel a bit... I just need some time on my own for a night."

Rome studied me for a moment, then let his fingers drift over my cheek. He pulled my chin over and pressed a kiss to my lips before pulling away. "You don't need to justify it to me," he said softly. "I'm the selfish one for wanting you to myself."

Tension drained out of me. I gave him a tremulous smile, more relieved than I expected to find that he wasn't upset. "Thank you."

His broad hand swallowed mine as he threaded his fingers between my own. When he brought my hand up to his lips to press a kiss on the back of my palm, I let out one more sigh and let go of most of my stress. This man was so kind and tender and perceptive. Being around him made me dizzy—made me forget how to think through my problems logically.

But I needed to sort through everything that had happened. I needed to find out if I was carrying his child.

He left me with a lingering kiss and watched me enter my building, not leaving until the elevator dinged open and I waved through the lobby doors at him. When I made it up to my place, with most of my stuff still in boxes and the unfamiliar apartment greeting me with a hollow echo, it didn't feel like home, but at least I could be alone.

I dropped my bag by the door and sank into the couch, leaning back on the seat as I closed my eyes. I stayed like that for a few long breaths, then I got a snack from the kitchen, changed my clothes, and headed right back out the door. I bought a value pack of three pregnancy tests, the weight of the box feeling heavier than it ought to in my purse on the way back to my place. I didn't waste any time unwrapping the first one and putting it to use.

My heart rattled. I didn't want a baby. I didn't want the complication of a child. Not when things were finally looking up, when I felt like my future was bright for the first time in many, many years. I was so close to paying off my loan. I might have an amazing opportunity to work for Roseanne. I had a man who treated me like a queen.

How would he react if...

I stared at the test, blinking rapidly. It didn't even take the required three minutes for two solid lines to appear in the window. Panting, I ripped open the second test, then the third.

But I couldn't deny the truth.

I was pregnant with Rome Blakely's child...

And I had no idea what I was going to do about it.

I SLEPT FITFULLY. Rome texted me to wish me a good night before he went to bed, but that did nothing to ease my mind. Around three o'clock in the morning, when I'd twisted myself in my sheets for the umpteenth time, I finally decided to get up and fix myself a cup of tea in the hope of getting drowsy.

I curled on my couch, ignoring the unpacked boxes around me, and sipped my steaming chamomile tea while I scrolled mindlessly on my phone. When I flicked to a messaging app, I was surprised to see Penny online. I sent her a message: *Can you not sleep either?*

Three or four seconds later, she'd read the message and was typing a response: *I'm in Paris! Something wrong? Want to chat?*

A strange feeling went through me. It wasn't jealousy, exactly. My friend could go to Europe anytime she chose. But it was a very stark reminder that she'd found her Prince Charming and married him. When she'd been unexpectedly pregnant early in her relationship with Marcus, things had worked out just fine.

I felt the chasm between us crack just a little bit wider, because what were the chances of that happening to me? Rome didn't even want to talk about dating for real, let alone tying our lives together forever through a child.

So yeah, maybe there was a bit of envy that pinched at my heart. But it was mostly despair.

I shimmied up to a seated position and swiped to answer Penny's call. "Hey."

"What time is it there?" she asked. "Three-ish? Why are you up? Is everything okay?"

I bit my lip. I could tell her about the pregnancy, of course. But...then what? She was in France, and she hadn't mentioned the trip to me before, so it must have been a last-minute thing. I didn't want to ruin her trip with my own worries.

And there was the other fear lurking at the back of my

mind: What if we just weren't that close? What if our friendship didn't go as deep as I thought it did? What if I filled a friend-shaped hole in her life, but if I got too difficult, she'd drop me?

Being single and pregnant with a messy relationship and maybe no job was difficult. In the dead of night, with the sounds of the city beyond my window deadened by the snow and the night, I didn't want to take the risk.

"Everything's fine," I said. "Just twisting and turning a lot tonight."

"Something on your mind?"

"Work," I lied.

She hummed. "How's that going?"

"Pretty well, all things considered," I said, which was the truth. I didn't say that it was all going to change once I told Rome he was going to be a father, though. I leaned my head against the back of the sofa and curled my knees up toward my chest. "What are you doing in France?"

"Marcus surprised me with a shopping trip, which he apparently planned with Emil and Leif as a surprise to the three of us for Christmas," she said in a warm voice, naming the husbands of our friends Dani and Layla. I imagined her glancing over at him. "We're having a coffee and a pastry right now. And get this! We ran into Bonnie at the Chanel flagship store yesterday! What are the chances?"

I let out a strangled laugh, but really I was trying to hide the sound of that gulf between us creaking and groaning as it widened. All of my friends had the means to take surprise trips across the Atlantic to go shopping the week before Christmas. They were part of the world that I'd dipped my toes in by virtue of hanging off of Rome's arm. That's where they belonged now.

And I was on the outside.

"That's crazy," I finally croaked. "What's Bonnie doing there?"

"Oh, just a getaway with Arlo and his kid. They're celebrating their new little family. They're disgustingly in love," she said fondly. "It's amazing."

My heart twisted. "I'm glad," I lied. In reality, I didn't feel glad. I felt like an outsider. Someone who was fun to have around in college, who was okay to invite over for a charcuterie board or a hangout but would never *truly* be part of the inner circle.

I was, and always would be, a placeholder for people to use while they were waiting for someone better.

"We should catch up when I'm back!" Penny exclaimed. "Although, we've been talking about extending our stay, so it might not be until the new year."

"That sounds great." My voice was dull, and I pretended to yawn. "I'd better try to sleep. Have fun shopping."

"Will do. Happy holidays!"

"You too," I mumbled, and I hung up the phone. Tears began to fall before I could stop them, my hand trembling as I forced myself to pick up my mug of tea. I could barely swallow the gulp of chamomile-scented water because of the lump lodged halfway down my throat, so I gave up and put the mug down. My cheeks were wet.

It was silly and selfish of me to be upset. My friends could take trips without telling me about it. They'd done nothing wrong.

Logically, I knew that. I knew I was being unreasonable.

But it still hurt. I was all alone in my echoing apartment, feeling like a transplant in a building where I didn't belong, clinging onto a stable life by my fingernails while other people floated by without any apparent effort. I felt invisible and small and lonely, and then felt stupid for feeling those things in the first place. I cried until my face ached, and then fell asleep on the couch, exhausted.

THIRTY-FIVE
ROME

NIKKI CALLED in sick the next day, which was a first. Clara informed me with a message that popped up at the bottom corner of my screen, and Nikki sent me a text a few minutes later. I sat at my desk and clenched my hands into fists, resisting the urge to jump in a car and head to her apartment to make sure she was okay. Instead, I ordered some chicken soup and a bunch of flowers to be delivered to her, and I turned to the contract with Monk to start ironing out the details.

Our weekend in Grenada had been fruitful, and I had to make sure we capitalized on it. I couldn't let myself be tugged toward the woman who dominated my thoughts while neglecting my duties.

Even if I wanted to.

I had the niggling feeling that something had happened, a splinter under my skin that I wasn't quite able to dig out. She'd felt ill; she was probably just sick. But she'd turned away from me. Ever since we'd known each other, she'd always turned toward. The change made me uncomfortable.

When my phone buzzed with a message from her thanking me for the delivery, some of the tension in my shoulders drained away. I liked caring for her. I liked being the one she could rely on, and I wanted her to turn to me for comfort and security. I wished I'd insisted on her sleeping at my place last night so I could nurse her back to health the way I wanted to.

As soon as the day was over, I'd be at her place to check on her.

I was interrupted from my rumination in the early afternoon when Cole knocked on my office door and poked his head in. "You busy?" he asked, which was strange. Typically he'd just waltz in without caring if he was disturbing me.

I rolled back from my desk and gestured for him to take a seat. Instead, Cole stood on the other side of my desk holding a manila folder. He cleared his throat but said nothing.

Arching my brows, I said, "Yes?"

Not one to beat around the bush, Cole lifted his gaze to mine and replied, "I've been headhunted. I've been offered a position as the director of a small company."

I blinked.

"Not a competitor," he rushed to add. "It's a software company."

"I see," I said, even though I didn't. "What do you know about software?"

"Not much," Cole admitted, "but I know about sales. They're in the finance industry, which is..."

"Your area of expertise."

He let out a long sigh and pulled a sheet of paper from the folder in his hand. "My letter of resignation."

A flurry of emotions ran through me, and it took all my self-control to keep them off my face. I wasn't sure if I succeeded when Cole shifted his weight from foot to foot, as if he were preparing to run.

I wasn't surprised; Cole was talented. He'd have recruiters pestering him on a daily basis. But although this wasn't unexpected, the loss of my second still felt like a betrayal.

After everything we'd been through together, all the opportunities I'd given him, he was just going to *leave*?

I took the letter from him but was unable to read past the first line. It landed with a soft scrape on my desk, and I lined it up perfectly with the edge of my keyboard before saying, "Will you sit down, at least?"

"I wasn't sure if you'd want me to stay," Cole said, taking a seat. "Rome, I just want to tell you, working here has been a great experience. I appreciate everything you've done for me. I don't want to leave on a sour note."

I nodded. "Neither do I." The words were gritted out, but I meant them. Or I wanted to mean them. At that exact moment, there was a sort of howling in my head, a little boy's voice crying out into his boarding school bed's pillow while a thunderstorm raged outside, the evidence of his bedwetting soaked into his pajamas, shame and fear and loneliness his only companion. That little boy wanted to cut Cole to size and tell him to leave my office and never speak to me again. He wanted to get on the phone and sully the other man's name so his precious opportunity at the fancy financial software company crumbled to dust.

But I wasn't that kid anymore. Hell, I wasn't even the man

I'd been three months ago. I didn't think of life as a game to win, or a stone from which I was meant to squeeze out every drop of blood. I enjoyed myself, on occasion. I looked forward to the future.

Could I really begrudge Cole for wanting a bright future of his own?

I met my friend's gaze. He stared back at me, arching his brows, waiting for me to bite his head off. The lump in my throat stopped me from being able to say much, but I did manage a croaked, "Why now?"

Cole braided his fingers together, then opened them up and stared at his palms as if the answer were written there. He let out a long sigh. "Ever since we found out about the exposure from hiring so many independent contractors," he admitted.

"You fixed that," I said. "You're not leaving because you think I'm mad about that, are you? I'm not."

"It's not that," he said, lifting his gaze to mine. "I realized I've been coasting. I should have caught that years ago, Rome. I should have *known*. But I've been..." He cringed, and finally finished his sentence with, "bored. I've been bored, Rome. I need a new challenge. Something I can't do on autopilot. And I'm sorry to do this right before the holidays, but I wanted to tell you as soon as I was sure."

It hurt. It hurt that he called my company boring, that he wanted to move on, that he was nervous about my reaction in the first place. It hurt that I'd have to keep running this company without my good friend at my side. It hurt that he was just another person who turned his back on me when I needed them most.

But I rallied myself together and stood, extending my hand across the desk to him. "You'll do great," I told him.

"I'll stay until the Monk contract is settled," he promised, pumping my arm.

I gulped through a tight throat and nodded. "Thanks, Cole."

He nodded, then slipped out the door again. An email pinged, reminding me of my responsibilities, and I threw myself into work to distract myself until I could go see Nikki and feel her arms wrap me in their warmth. I'd feel better once I was next to her. This wouldn't hurt so much once her fingers were running through my hair, her lips dropping soft kisses on my jaw.

Everything would be okay once we were together, which was just a few hours away.

Except those few hours stretched when I got a call from my mother, who needed me to stop by their place as soon as possible. When I told her I couldn't make it tonight, she pulled out her top-shelf guilt trip and convinced me. I'm not even sure how she did it. She barely said anything but, "I really need to talk to you *tonight*." But there was a flavor to her silences, a weight to the emphasis of her words. She twisted a particular screw that tightened just the right bands around my heart, and I heard myself agreeing to meet her at five o'clock.

I'd resisted becoming that little boy in his boarding school bed when Cole was in front of me, but apparently I wasn't strong enough to resist my mother beckoning me to the estate on Long Island. There was still a part of me that wanted my mother's approval, even though I hated myself for it.

When the helicopter landed, I checked my phone for the hundredth time. Nikki hadn't responded to the text I'd sent telling her I'd be over after I visited my parents, but it didn't look like she'd seen the message. She was probably sleeping off whatever illness she'd caught during our trip.

A staff member met me at the back steps, which I took two at a time. I was led through the ornate hallways to my mother's favorite sitting room, where she sat on an overstuffed couch with a laptop on the coffee table in front of her, papers strewn all around, and glasses perched on the edge of her nose. Beside her lounged my brother, who barely looked up from the phone screen he was staring at when I walked in.

"Good," my mother said when she saw me. "I was worried you'd try to play the rebel tonight. Come here."

Her words rankled. Play the rebel? Just because I didn't like being summoned? Even though I was *here*. I'd come running when she'd snapped her fingers, and I felt weak and stupid for it. Instead of having my arms wrapped around the woman I lo—the woman I wanted to see, I was miles away gritting my teeth and clenching my fists at being chastised like an errant child.

But just as I always did, I stuffed the discomfort down and took a seat next to her on the couch. Upon closer inspection, I saw that the papers on the coffee table were seating charts for a wedding. My brother's wedding to Natasha. I frowned. "What was so important that you needed me to rush over?"

My mother pulled her glasses off her nose and folded them carefully. "We've been completing the seating charts, darling. I'm sorry, but there's just no room for your plus-one." Her face was utterly calm. Serene, even. She met my gaze with her icy blue eyes and didn't even blink.

"There are three hundred and twenty-five guests at the

wedding, Mother," I said through clenched teeth. "What difference does one more or less make?"

"It makes a world of difference," she clipped.

"The girl can't come," Will said, finally looking away from his phone. He arched his brows at me. "Got it?"

"Why not?"

"Because it's my wedding and I said so."

I narrowed my eyes at my brother and then shifted to look at my mother. She was busy straightening the pages on the coffee table, tapping them together as if the discussion was over and we could all pack up and leave.

"No," I said, standing.

She paused and glanced up at me. "Excuse me?"

"I said no. I'm dating Nikki. She's...important to me. I want her beside me at family events."

My mother let out a long sigh and stood up to face me. She smoothed her hands down her tweed skirt, then held her hands at her stomach and met my gaze. "I understand why a man would be attracted to a woman like her, Rome, but the fact of the matter is that just isn't done."

"What the hell is that supposed to mean?"

"Don't speak to me like that," my mother snapped. "You know precisely what it means. Every one of those three hundred and twenty-five guests will be dignitaries, businesspeople, connections, and family members. What would they think when they found out that you hired her to be at your side?"

I blinked, rearing back. "What are you talking about?"

My mother pursed her lips and arched her brows. Her silence said, *Really?*

"I don't know what you're talking about."

"It's impressive that you kept it under wraps for as long as you did, darling, but the truth will come out eventually. We can't have an escort sitting at the head table."

"She's not an escort," I bit off.

My mother made a soft hum, her disagreement more than clear.

"Forget about me coming as well, then," I said, mind racing. "Rome!"

I stomped away, waving off the butler who tried to accost me and direct me to the dining room. I cut through the backyard to the helipad, blood boiling, wanting only one thing.

To see Nikki.

I needed to hold her in my arms, because my world felt like it was crumbling around me. My best friend had found a new job. My family... I was seeing my family for who they really were. Callous, cold people who cared more about appearances than they did about their own people.

And how did my mother know? How could she possibly have found out? Did she have a spy on my legal team? Cole?

No, not Cole. He wouldn't. Would he?

I'd figure this out, and I'd fix it. I wouldn't let my mother's callousness ruin the biggest business deal my company had ever made. I wanted to believe she wouldn't do that, but how could I be sure?

She and my father had shipped me off to a top-rated boarding school because they didn't have time for me. My brother was treated completely differently, the little prince of the family who could do no wrong. Those people didn't love me. They didn't care about me. None of them did.

The only person in my life who did was Nikki. She had the

ability to make me soften with nothing more than a look. She made me feel like I wasn't raging against the storm on my own. She was my shelter. My woman. My rock.

And she'd finally sent me a text message. *I'm beat,* she wrote. *Going to bed. Can I get a rain check on the snuggles?*

Clipped into the helicopter as it took off, I read and reread the message a dozen or so times. Then I dropped my hands between my knees and let my head sink down, defeated.

THIRTY-SIX
NIKKI

IT WAS A LIE, of course. I wasn't going to bed. I was pacing my apartment, staring at boxes, looking at my bed, opening the fridge, and trying to distract my mind from running circles around me.

Five minutes after telling Rome not to come over, I stared at another text message I'd typed out telling him to come over anyway. But my finger hovered over the "send" button, and I couldn't make myself press down.

What was I *doing*?

Me, the placeholder, the stepping stone, the woman that no one *really* wanted. Did I honestly think that a handsome, successful, wealthy, charismatic man would choose *me*? Did I really think this was anything more than convenience?

I was a special kind of delusional.

Frustrated with myself, I stripped my shirt off and looked at myself in the mirror. I knew it was weeks and weeks too early to see a bump, but I still studied my reflection from all angles.

Maybe I'd made the whole pregnancy thing up. Maybe the tests I'd taken were faulty. And yes, I'd bought a new pack of three and taken them all today, and all of them proclaimed me well and truly pregnant.

There were probably things I should be doing—doctors' appointments, vitamins, ultrasounds, and whatnot. I didn't even know.

But doing them would require admitting to myself that I was pregnant. And it still didn't feel quite real.

Or maybe it felt a little *too* real. Every little twinge, every slight wave of nausea that I normally would have dismissed as a strange quirk of my body was a reminder that there was an embryo inside me, and it was growing with every minute that passed.

And a little niggling thought made itself at home in my brain. If I was so replaceable, what would happen when Rome found out about the baby? Would I just be an incubator? Someone to carry his child, who was then tossed aside?

I put a hand against my bare stomach, a rejection screaming through me. I wouldn't let him do that. I *couldn't.*

Meeting my own gaze in the mirror, I realized what that meant.

I *wanted* this child.

But—that was crazy. I couldn't—

Points of pain peppered my scalp as I pulled at my hair, letting out a noise of frustration. It was better that I'd told Rome not to come; I didn't want anyone seeing me like this.

My phone ringing made me jump. I turned it over to look at the screen, heart sinking at the sight of my mother's name.

Two deep breaths later, I was reasonably sure my voice would come out okay. "Hi, Mom."

"Honey! How's my favorite girl?"

I leaned a hip against the bathroom vanity, arching my brows. Typically we sent each other holiday and birthday texts, and then let the guilt push us into a bi-yearly phone call that both of us hated. There was no favorite about it.

"I'm good," I lied. "What's up? Is everything okay?" I didn't add, *because it's weird that you're calling me*, but based on my mother's answering snort, I guessed she heard it anyway.

"Everything is great. I just made plans with the Williamses for the holidays. We're going on a cruise!"

"Oh," I said, surprised. "Right."

"I assumed you'd be doing something fancy with those girl-friends of yours, which is why I didn't ask if you were coming home for the holidays this year."

"Yeah," I said noncommittally. My girlfriends were all shopping 'til they dropped in Paris without me, so I most definitely was *not* spending the holidays with them.

And Rome...

God. I needed to tell him about the baby. Would he be able to tell something was wrong with me if I delayed?

"Listen, honey, I wanted to ask you something."

I blinked, shifting my attention back to the call. "Okay..."

"Do you think you could talk to Penny about talking to her husband about a job? The Williamses' son is graduating college, and he's looking to start his career, so..."

My bathroom walls were painted a soft shade of blue. I stared at the paint, frowning, as my mother's words sank in. "Is *that* why you've been calling me lately?"

"What? I can't call my daughter? I need a reason?"

"Well, based on the fact that we barely speak to each other, yes," I snapped.

"You have a lot of nerve speaking to me like that, Nikita. After everything I did for you. After everything your *father* did! All I ask is a tiny favor for a friend's son, and this is how you react?"

Her tirade continued, and I pulled the phone away from my ear.

It shouldn't have hurt so much. It shouldn't even have been a surprise. I barely had a relationship with my mother, and I *knew* her calling me wasn't just because she wanted to chat. We had nothing in common. Our bond had been severed when my father died, when she'd drowned in grief and left me to fend for myself.

But...

God, I wanted my mom. I wanted *someone* to turn to right now. Someone I could ask about what the hell I was supposed to do.

My mother was more concerned with impressing her neighbors and helping their kid get ahead. She would've never dreamed to ask anyone for a job on *my* behalf, her actual biological child. I was a reminder of the husband she'd lost. I was tainted.

But now I was a useful stepping stone for her to impress her friends. I wasn't a daughter or even an actual person with feelings. I was just someone who knew Marcus Walsh. Someone who might make her look good when she went on that cruise with the neighbors.

My name echoed through the phone speakers, and I just

tapped the screen to hang up the call. Then I set my phone down, turned on the shower, and stripped off the rest of my clothes. I sat on the shower floor and cried until the tears stopped, then dried myself off and went to bed. Alone.

I AWOKE with a sense of clarity.

Things had come to a head, and I could no longer deny it. Working for Rome while pregnant with his baby was untenable. I had to make a decision, and I had to make it now.

Roseanne Monk hadn't officially offered me a job, and I didn't know if I was comfortable working for her when Rome and I hadn't been entirely honest with her about our relationship. But she *had* shown me that I had options. I didn't need to stay at Blakely. I had a small savings account now, and I had a lease on an apartment for the next year. I wasn't on the brink of destitution.

I had time.

Time to figure out how I'd care for a child. Time to figure out how to tell Rome about the baby. Time to face my fears and take responsibility for my part in this.

In all my relationships, I'd been happy to be put in a box that other people defined. In some cases, like my current employment, it was spelled out in black and white. I was the companion.

But if I really was pregnant, and if I really did end up with a baby sometime next summer—to be confirmed whenever I worked up the courage to go to the doctor—then I had to start sorting my life out.

I would be a *mother*. And no matter what life threw at me, I wouldn't put my kid in the same position my mother put me in. I wouldn't let my own hang-ups cloud my judgment. I wouldn't blame my child for my own mistakes and weaknesses.

I'd been hurt by so many people. I'd felt pushed aside. But no one could push me aside from this most important responsibility.

And the way I saw it, the first thing I had to do was extricate myself from my job at Blakely. My relationship with Rome was developing quickly, but it was still clouded by the fact that he paid me to stand at his side. I didn't want that murkiness anymore. I wanted him to want me for *me*. I wanted him to choose *me*.

For that to happen, I couldn't work for him. There was no way of having my paycheck be contingent on my performance as his sidekick if I were to believe that he truly cared about me.

I had to quit—or at least broach the subject with him. I wouldn't march in there and tell him I didn't want to work for him anymore, but I *would* say that in order for us to continue as a couple, I couldn't be his employee.

It was the only logical way forward.

Then, once that was settled, I could make the doctor's appointment and figure out if I did have a baby growing in my womb. Once I confirmed it, I'd tell Rome.

First, I had to make sure that he felt the same way I did—that what was growing between us went beyond the bounds of our contract. That I was more than a companion to him. That this was real.

Only then could I face the pregnancy.

So, I dressed in my favorite navy dress with the peplum and the white piping and big cloth-covered buttons. I curled my hair and applied my makeup with deliberate care. With each swipe of my mascara brush and dab of foundation, a sense of calm settled over me.

I could do this. I might have been passed over for promotions and taken advantage of by friends and family, but I wouldn't let myself be shunted off to the side now. If Rome truly cared about me, he'd choose me.

The company car was already waiting downstairs, as confirmed by Rome himself this morning. I nodded to Keith and got in the back seat, taking a few deep breaths to settle my nerves before heading into the office. The whole ride, I rehearsed what I'd tell Rome. I tried to play out his reaction, to predict what he'd say.

He wouldn't be happy, but he'd come around. He'd want me to keep working for him because it was convenient to have me close, to order me around.

But he'd understand why I couldn't keep doing that. Why I wanted more.

I had to trust in that. Had to believe it.

Otherwise, I was on my way to blowing up my entire life.

THIRTY-SEVEN
ROME

MY KNEE BOUNCED as I sat at my desk reviewing emails. The little clock in the corner of my screen kept drawing my eye despite my best efforts to ignore it.

Nikki would show up today. She said she would, so she would. I had no need to doubt that.

But Cole was leaving, and my mother and brother were backing me into a corner. I'd been on edge since yesterday, and I didn't know how to shake this sense of impending doom.

Something was wrong, and I didn't know what.

I needed to figure out how my mother had found out about the contract. Was it Nikki? Had she broken her NDA? Was there someone in my organization telling secrets? I'd set Arthur on the hunt for the leak, but I hadn't told Cole. What if he quit because he'd betrayed me?

People were turning their backs on me, and I needed Nikki here to look at me, to touch me with those gentle hands, to tell me that she wanted *me*.

I just needed one touch. Just one stroke of her hand against my cheek, and everything would be okay. One single person to see me for me, and nothing else would matter.

Finally, I heard her voice greeting Clara on the other side of the door. I leaned back in my chair and a moment later, Nikki was poking her head through the door.

"Clara said you were expecting me," she said in way of greeting.

"Come in," I told her, pushing up from my chair. I crossed the space between us and wrapped her in my arms, inhaling the scent of her hair like it was the only thing keeping me tethered to sanity.

She melted into my arms but didn't turn her face up for a kiss. I stroked her back with my palm and asked, "How are you feeling?"

"Better," she said, and it sounded like the truth, even though I got the sense she was holding back.

"But?"

Nikki pulled away from me, her brown eyes wide as she stared up at me. "I want to talk to you about something."

The words made me freeze. Dread left a dirty, acrid taste on the back of my throat as I tried to read her expression. My arms were still around her waist, but she dropped her gaze to stare at my chin. When I spoke, my voice was rough. "About what?"

Her breath skated along my jaw. Nikki pulled back until I dropped my arms, her teeth biting into her lower lip. She finally met my gaze again, brows arched. "Can we sit down?"

She was breaking up with me. She was going to stand there, looking like that, and tell me that she didn't want to be with me. That she was turning her back on me, just like everyone else did. She'd tell me that I wasn't worth the effort, that I wasn't good enough. Not in those words, but I'd be able to read it clear enough in her gaze.

At least my mother would be happy. I'd be able to attend my brother's wedding solo, just the way she wanted. This little secret would be kept under wraps—or maybe my mother would wrap it around my neck like a leash to forever keep me controlled.

My molars ground together. "No. Say what you need to say."

Her shoulders softened, brows drawing together. "Rome—"

"Just spit it out, Jordan."

She stiffened in front of me, confusion flitting in her gaze. "I just wanted to talk about us. This—this relationship. You... I..."

"It's not working for you."

She inhaled deeply, and that hesitation was all I needed to hear. I spun around to lean my knuckles on my desk, throat so thick I could barely breathe.

"Rome, I think you're misunderstanding. I want to be with you. I've loved this... I've loved what we have. That's exactly what I want to talk about. I want to keep seeing you."

The wobbling beneath my feet steadied slightly. I turned my head toward her and asked, "But?"

She wrung her hands in front of her, squeezing one hand so hard with the other that the tips of her fingers went red. "But I don't think I can keep working for you. I want—"

I scoffed. "Right. I see. I offer you the world and you throw it back in my face."

"Rome, that's not what I said at all."

"That's exactly what you said." The words came out as a

hiss. I straightened and faced her. "You're all too happy to take the paycheck and the nice clothes and private flights, and then you throw it back in my face the minute you think you don't need me anymore. How's your closet looking these days, Jordan? And your bank account?"

She'd used me. Milked me for all I was worth. I'd been right from the start.

Her spine straightened, twin spots of red appearing on her cheeks. "I'm trying to build a *relationship* with you, Rome."

"Oh, right." I snorted.

"What's the alternative?" She dropped her arms to the sides, spreading them slightly. "I just keep working here, we keep fucking behind closed doors, and when someone finds out, we just play it off? When a client gets wind that you're paying me to stand at your side, we keep pretending I'm a consultant? When it hits the press, we just deny it?"

My vision went red. "Is that a threat?"

"What?" Nikki put her hands to her head and let out an incredulous laugh. "Wait. Stop. This isn't happening. Everything is going wrong." She took a deep breath and let it out slowly, then lifted her gaze to mine.

She *looked* sincere.

But how could I trust her sincerity? How could I trust that she'd stay by my side when no one else did? The only reason she was here was because I was paying her. If we removed that... If she wasn't actually employed by me and required to be here...

Then what would actually make her stay?

"Rome," she said softly, "I want to be with you. Really, truly be with you."

We stared at each other as the silence thickened. My throat felt raw. My chest ached. I *wanted* to believe her. I wanted to take that sincerity written on her face and have it be everything I needed.

But it wasn't.

No one wanted me. Not without an ulterior motive. Not without an exit plan.

Cole was my best friend, and he was turning his back on me. He was pursuing his career, and I couldn't begrudge him that, but I fucking *did*. And my family treated me like an inconvenience that could be summoned and dismissed at will. The only person that had ever cared about me was Reggie, and he died when I needed him most. Would he have stuck around if I hadn't made the effort after high school? Or would he have turned his back on me once I was out of sight the way everyone else did?

So yeah, I wanted to believe Nikki. But I didn't.

"What brought this on?" I asked, my voice like crushed gravel.

She licked her lips and gulped, eyes sliding to the side. I could see her marshaling her thoughts, figuring out the best way to let me down gently. She shouldn't have bothered. I already knew what was coming. She'd tell me that she just cared about me so much, but we needed to have more time to ourselves. She'd back away slowly like I was a wounded animal who would attack if she turned around and ran. And then she'd cut me out of her life the way everyone else did.

That's what I thought would happen, which was probably why the words she said shocked me so much.

"Roseanne Monk offered me a job," she said, lifting her eyes to mine. "And it's not that I was interested—well, I mean, I *was* —but it just made me realize that our—"

"She *what?*"

Nikki blinked. "I haven't accepted."

"You're damn right you haven't. You're soliciting work from my clients? Is that what this has been about the whole time?"

Nikki took a step back, and I realized I'd lurched toward her. She put her hands up. "Rome, it just got me thinking, is all. It was a casual offer. It just made me realize that maybe—maybe it would be best if you and I... If we did this the regular way?"

I had no idea what the hell she was talking about. All I knew was that Nikki had leveraged her position as my plus-one to advance her own career. She was clever, I'd give her that. I didn't even see the betrayal coming. To use the one thing I was proud of, the company I'd built from the ground up—

"Get out."

"Rome—"

"*Get out!*"

She jumped, scrambling for the door. I heard the clip-clop of her heels as they headed for the elevator, and Clara's voice as she called out to ask if Nikki was okay. All I could do was drag in deep breaths as I shoved my fingers through my hair, pulling at my scalp until my vision righted itself.

I heard the shuffle of a foot on the floor and turned to see Clara in the doorway, frowning at me.

"Start Ms. Jordan's exit paperwork. She's no longer employed at Blakely, effective immediately."

Clara stared at me for a beat, then dipped her chin. "Right away."

The door snicked shut, and I was alone. I almost started

laughing. Of course I was alone. How else would I be? Did I really think Nikki would swan in here and wrap her arms around me and make everything all right? Did I think she was *different?*

I was a fucking fool. The worst kind of fool, because I should have known better. Not one single person in my life had stuck by my side. Not unless they had a fat paycheck or used me as a rung up the ladder. My acquaintances were clients. My friends were nonexistent.

Nikki had read me properly from the very start. She probably never cared about me at all. She saw the pathetic, lonely, business-obsessed loser that I was, and she decided to work me for everything she could.

But she could have done it for longer, my brain reminded me. *She came in here to tell you she wanted to be with you. She wanted a relationship.*

I snorted and dismissed the thought. She didn't want me. She probably saw the precarious position she was in, and she wanted to secure her spot by my side. Get all the perks and no risks. She'd have another job with one of my biggest clients, so she'd have me over a barrel personally *and* professionally.

Very neatly done. Clever woman.

I should have known.

THIRTY-EIGHT
NIKKI

I MUST HAVE BEEN a special kind of stupid. I really thought I could walk in there, tell Rome Blakely—*Rome freaking Blakely*—that I wanted a relationship with him, and then we'd skip off into the sunset together.

The tears didn't hit until I was nearly home. Actually, I didn't start crying until I walked in and saw my teal couch in my unfamiliar apartment, with all my boxes of junk yet to be unpacked.

This wasn't home. It never would be home, because I couldn't afford to stay here unless I found a steady job with a decent paycheck. Even then, did I really want to stay somewhere that Rome's people procured for me? Did I want that constant reminder?

I stood with my back to the door, and the whole crushing wave of emotion bore down on me. I was broken under the weight of it, pulled out into the open ocean by its undertow. Sliding along the door, I fell until my butt hit the ground, and realized tears were soaking my cheeks and dripping down onto my dress.

What a ridiculous idea—to think I could *actually* get everything I wanted! To think I could ask for a man to choose me and be delusional enough to believe he would.

I'd never been good enough to be chosen. Not for a promotion, not for a friendship, not for a shopping spree, and certainly not for a loving relationship. What was there to love in a placeholder? There was nothing to me except an empty vessel, a vague shape of a woman that people could use when they had nothing better lined up.

And Rome had no qualms in showing me exactly what he thought of me.

I *tried* to explain. I tried to tell him that I wanted him—and he didn't care. He didn't reject me because of a misunderstanding. He rejected me because I simply wasn't good enough.

And why would I be? Did I really think this was some kind of Cinderella story? I'd be swept off my feet, and land in the lap of luxury ensconced by the strong arms of a gorgeous, wealthy man?

Things like that didn't happen to people like me.

At some point, when the light changed and I realized I'd been on the floor for hours, I picked myself up and shuffled to the kitchen. I stared at the sink for a while, then went to the bathroom. A shower made me feel more human, but it barely helped.

I took out my phone and told myself to make a doctor's appointment. I needed to deal with the other issue—the one growing inside me. But making an appointment meant admitting that it was happening.

I was pregnant, and my baby's father wanted nothing to do with me.

As if to underscore that point, my phone chimed with an email from the Blakely HR department. I was officially terminated from Blakely, with full severance. I snorted when I saw that, even though I knew I couldn't turn my nose up at a chunk of money. Not when I was jobless and pregnant and alone.

But Rome was just buying me off, exactly the way he did in that conference room when he first presented me with the companion contract.

I *actually* thought he cared about me. I actually believed all this insatiable sex meant something more.

Like I said—special kind of stupid.

Two and a half months ago, I'd thought my life was on a downward spiral. I had no idea what was coming. This was so much worse. I'd actually had hope that life would get better, only for it to be snatched away.

I turned my phone off, buried myself in my duvet, and slept.

I slept for nearly three full days, shuffling up to use the bathroom and shovel food in my mouth when the grumbling in my stomach became too insistent. I turned my phone back on at some point and saw messages from my group chat with the girls, a few photos from Penny, a text from Eleanor. I answered none of them.

Did these people actually want to speak to me? Unlikely. I wasn't worth their time. They probably kept me around for pity, or because I filled some specific function in their lives. I made them feel better about their lives by comparison, probably.

My bed became my refuge. It was hard to do anything other than the necessities, and even those sometimes became too difficult. I showered as much as I could, ate whenever I could force a few bites down, and tried not to think of anything. I stared out my bedroom window a lot, at the fat snowflakes that fell down, the orange light from the streetlights, the concrete wall across the street. One morning, a cat jumped on my windowsill on its precarious journey somewhere else.

Christmas came and went. I forced myself to answer whatever messages came through, but I ignored the phone calls from Penny and Layla. My mother didn't call. Neither did Rome.

New Year's fireworks alerted me that another week had passed. I rolled onto my back and listened to them booming somewhere over the river, thinking about all the people reveling all over the city.

Was Rome kissing someone new already?

The thought made me puke. I nearly missed the toilet as I stumbled from my bed to the bathroom, nausea making my ears ring. Hugging the porcelain, I began to sob.

Something popped then. Some soap bubble that had been keeping my emotions muffled, my mind protected from the worst of it. I thought of Rome moving on within days of our fight, and I cried as I flushed the toilet, cried in the shower, and cried as I dried myself.

But when I stepped out in my living room, my hair wrapped in a towel turban and my body in a terrycloth robe, the tears dried up. Piles of boxes stared back at me, some of them flapping open, taunting me.

Was this really how I wanted to spend my days? Sick, in bed, throwing up and barely eating, ignoring the reality of my situation?

Everyone else could treat me as a non-person, but I *existed*.

I was real. I was flesh and bone, and I *mattered*. Maybe not to my family or friends or lovers. Maybe not to my bosses. But I mattered to *myself*.

Stomping across the room, I tore open the nearest box, yanking it so hard the flap ripped and took half the cardboard with it. Books came tumbling out, along with a random throw pillow.

The pillow was a soft pink crushed velvet with ridiculous tassels at each corner. I picked it up, feeling the softness of the fabric, the waterfall of the tassels' ends between my fingers. Stroking the pink pillow with my thumbs, I marched over to my couch and set the pillow in one corner, fluffing it slightly so it looked right. Then I stood back with my hands on my hips, and a painful twist in my chest smoothed out.

I mattered. My home mattered. My things mattered.

I deserved to unpack all the knickknacks and possessions, if only for myself. I deserved pink velvet pillows and bookcases with perfectly aligned and alphabetized spines. I deserved a new plant, damn it.

No one else was going to buy me one.

Gritting my teeth, I picked up the books that had spilled out from the ripped box and set them in a corner. I'd need a new bookcase. My vintage Turkish rug was rolled up behind the couch, so I pulled it out and spread it over the floor, tucking it under the front legs of my couch. My coffee table was nudged under the window, buried under half a dozen boxes. I set the boxes aside and put the coffee table where it was meant to be.

I had a beautiful quartz tray that I used as ornamentation, and I knew I'd packed it in a small box...there! Triumphant, I pulled the tray out of the box, as well as a pretty little jewelry jar that was too small to fit anything in it but looked pretty on the tray.

Bit by bit, with a kind of zeal I hadn't felt in a long time, I unpacked my things and found homes for every useless little trinket, every book, every bauble. No one could accuse me of being a minimalist, but that wasn't a club I wanted to belong to. As I arranged my living room then moved on to the kitchen and bedroom, my shoulders straightened and my mood lightened.

This wouldn't be my home forever, but it was my home *now*. It was the new year, and I'd be damned if I spent it wallowing in self-pity, wrapped in a duvet surrounded by bare walls.

I'd wallow in self-pity wrapped in a duvet surrounded by fabulous artwork I'd bought at a dozen different flea markets over the course of a decade, thank you very much.

Chuffing to myself, I worked through the night. By the time the sky outside lightened, I collapsed onto my favorite teal couch, surrounded by all my beautiful things, and I smiled.

That was better.

I was still wearing my robe. My hair had mostly dried in my turban, and it would be a disaster when I finally decided to deal with it, but that was a problem for Future Nikki. For now, all I could do was rest my head on my soft pink pillow of crushed velvet—and sleep.

THIRTY-NINE

ROME

HOLIDAY PARTIES WERE TORTURE. I hadn't realized how much Nikki's presence softened the sting of networking events, how much easier it was to talk to people when she was there to facilitate the conversation. How much I enjoyed being able to put my hand on her lower back and feel the heat of her body through her clothes.

Two weeks passed in a slow torture, and after the third soiree where I was asked incessantly where my dutiful plus-one had disappeared to, I decided that was enough for me. I closed myself off from all social activity and threw myself into closing the Monk deal.

We signed the contract on New Year's Day.

I'd secured my company's future. I'd paved the way for the next few years of financial success. I'd done exactly what I'd set out to do.

And the victory was hollow.

Employees celebrated around me. Clara even wrapped an

arm around my shoulders and patted me with her palm in congratulations, and I mustered a curt nod in response. My legal team toasted to a successful negotiation, and Cole lifted his glass with the rest of them.

I bit back the urge to tell them all to get out. I'd done that once before, and it'd only made me feel worse in the end.

You could call her, temptation whispered. *You could apologize.*

For what? What could I possibly say to her after what had transpired between us?

She'd been hired to do a job, and she'd done it skillfully. Then, just like everyone else, she turned her back on me. The fact that she'd wrapped her abandonment in pretty words and honeyed promises meant nothing. If she wanted to be by my side, she would've stayed. End of story.

Cole found me in my office, where I'd gone to hide from the revelry. He dropped onto one of my sofas and gave me a long look. "You think she'll be vindictive?"

I poured myself a drink and didn't meet his gaze. "Who?"

A soft scoff was the only immediate response, until Cole said, "You know who."

He was right, of course. Nikki. Who else? "No," I answered. "What would she have to be vindictive about?"

"The fact that you threw her out of here."

I glared over my shoulder at him. "She marched in here and basically quit. What was I supposed to do?"

Cole put his hands up, and I took a deep breath. He'd marched in here and quit too, and it wouldn't be long until these chats were a thing of the past. Who would talk sense into me when Cole was gone? I set a drink down on a coaster in front of him and took a seat on the opposite couch with my own. The alcohol burned on the way down, and I relished the pain of it as I swirled the liquid in my glass.

"Is she going to be working for Roseanne?"

Sighing, I looked at my second-in-command, soon to be former second-in-command. "Probably. Roseanne would be smart to hire her."

"They could get close. The truth could come out."

I grimaced. The truth could come out regardless, unless I figured out how my mother had found out about the companion contract.

It was a problem.

We'd lied to Wilbur. We'd pretended to be a couple, closed the deal on false pretenses. It was a gaping hole of exposure, and it scared me a hell of a lot less than the pain in my chest that splintered through me every time I thought about Nikki.

"It's in her best interests not to tell Roseanne the truth." I couldn't even say Nikki's name out loud. It was pathetic.

"Right," Cole said. "Makes sense."

"You think I should reiterate that fact to her so she understands."

Cole shrugged. "I could do it for you if you don't want to speak to her."

I sighed. It was tempting to have Cole do my dirty work for me. He could find Nikki, tell her to keep her mouth shut, and we could live our separate lives like nothing at all had changed in the past few months.

But that would be cowardly, and I'd learned long ago that if I wanted something done right, I had to do it myself. I should have kept that in mind before hiring Nikki as a companion in the first place.

"I'll do it," I told him, resigned.

That's how I found myself at her building the next day, pressing the buzzer between the two sets of glass doors to see if she'd let me up.

"Hello?"

Even the sound of her voice through the terrible intercom speaker sent a spear through my chest.

"It's me," I said, then cleared my throat. "Rome."

There was a long pause. Or at least, it felt long. The seconds dragged by, one after the other, and I wondered if she'd leave me here without even a word.

Then a buzz sounded, and the click of the inner doors told me she'd unlocked it for me. I stepped through, throat tight, the thumping of my heartbeat echoing in my ears.

I stared at my own reflection on the way up in the elevator, fixing a few stray strands of hair like a vain asshole, because apparently I still wanted to look good for her when she opened the door.

Still, when it swung open and Nikki stood before me in all her dark-haired, dark-eyed glory, I didn't feel like fixing a few flyaway pieces of hair had helped me prepare for the sight of her before me.

She was barefoot, wearing soft, loose pants and a shirt that hung off one shoulder. Her hair was up in a clip and she wore no makeup, but her cheeks were flushed. She looked amazing. I hated it.

"Um, come in," she said, stepping aside. "Can I get you a drink?"

"No," I answered, gruff, "I won't be here long."

Was that disappointment on her face? I couldn't tell, and Nikki turned away from me slightly. She crossed the space and took a seat on her couch, tucking her feet under her as she lifted her chin to meet my gaze, waiting patiently for me to speak.

Not wanting to sit on the same piece of furniture as her—being that close would be dangerous—I pulled a rickety-looking dining chair and spun it around so I could sit and face her. All her things were just this side of shabby, but they went together in a way that gave her place an easy, homey feel. She'd made herself at home in her new apartment, and for some reason it made me feel sad. Maybe because there was no room here for me.

"You said Roseanne offered you a job," I started, not wanting to waste time here. The place smelled like her. Her personality was baked into every inch of it. It drove me to the brink of insanity just to sit in her space and not be able to touch her.

Nikki blinked at me, tilting her head slightly. "Yes."

"You understand that if you divulge the details of our"—I cleared my throat—"relationship, there could be issues for both of us."

Nikki's shoulders dropped, but the expression on her face didn't change. "Did you come here to warn me about keeping my mouth shut, Rome?"

Her words were soft, but they hit me like blows. I could hardly get my response out through the gravel that had taken residence in my throat. "Yes."

She dropped her bare feet back onto the floor, and I noticed her toenails were painted a soft shade of pink. "Understood," she said, standing to cross the room to stand at the door. She opened it and glanced at me meaningfully. "In the future, a text or an email will suffice. There's no need to bother yourself with a personal visit when you need to threaten me."

"It's not a threat," I said, joining her at the door. "It's the truth."

As Nikki met my gaze, her back was straight and there was no moisture in her eyes. A door had been shut between us, and I had the awful, sinking realization that I was the one who'd done it. Maybe I hadn't even done it when I'd kicked her out of my office. Maybe there'd been a sliver of light still coming through the opening, but I'd walked in here and slammed it shut.

"Goodbye, Rome," she said, and there was steel in her voice.

I tore my gaze away from the line of her neck, the shape of her body in those loose, shapeless clothes. She was just a former employee. A former lover. She didn't mean anything to me, and I meant nothing to her. Now we were on the same page, and we could both move on.

"Good luck with the new job," I told her, then walked out of her apartment.

The worst part of the whole visit, I realized when I got back to the car downstairs, wasn't the widening gulf between us. It wasn't the stilted conversation. It wasn't the dead look in her eyes when she said goodbye, or the scent of her all around.

No, the worst part was that despite how horrible the visit had been, it was better than not seeing her at all.

FORTY
NIKKI

ROSEANNE WAS in Grenada until the beginning of March, so we set a meeting for the fourth of the month when she'd be in the city. I spent the first two months of the year getting my life in order. I had enough savings to pay off my debts, but I had to sell most of the designer clothes and accessories I'd acquired during my employment at Blakely in order to sustain me until I could get an income.

So for all the fun I'd had during those two months, I was left with none of the luxuries that had pushed me to sign the contract in the first place. It seemed fitting, but I did hate letting go of my Judith Leiber bow purse.

As the days turned to weeks, I found the courage to go to the doctor. I booked the scans and read the pamphlets. I lay in bed at night, overheated and unable to sleep, imagining a newborn baby at my breast, wondering how soft their skin would be, if they'd have any hair when they came out.

Rome's visit had been awful, of course, but oddly, it had

given me more strength. It was clear he wanted nothing to do with me, and all I could do in response was move on. I'd tell him about the baby eventually, I promised myself, but it was so early. No sense opening that can of worms until I knew for sure that everything would be okay.

It was a convenient excuse for my cowardice.

In the weeks leading up to my meeting with Roseanne, I kept busy, but I avoided my friends. My newfound strength was brittle, and I knew that one nail driven at just the right angle would shatter me. If I were to feel like a sad little wretch, watching them jet set off to Europe for shopping sprees without me, I'd lose my courage.

So I went through a couple months of self-imposed isolation. When I was feeling gracious toward myself, I called it nesting. My new apartment was my cocoon, and I the chrysalis undergoing a transformation.

But when the fourth of March came around, my transformation didn't feel quite complete. I was just over twenty weeks into my pregnancy and my bump was beginning to show. I'd learned a few days ago that I was having a girl, and it was starting to feel real. I dressed in a tunic dress with comfortable shoes, taking extra time with my hair and makeup.

Roseanne met me at a cute café in Midtown. She sat in a tall, winged armchair like a queen, her loose pants draped artfully over her crossed legs, a mug steaming in her delicate grasp. When she looked up at me, the diamonds dangling from her ears twinkled in the coffee shop lights.

"Nikki!" she exclaimed, setting her cup down to stand. She hugged me tightly and planted a kiss on my cheek. "You look fabulous. I've paid for your drink already, so just dash up there and tell them what you want," she said, nodding to the barista.

To her credit, though her gaze drifted down to my midsection, she didn't ask any indelicate questions. I smiled at her and did as she said, ordering myself a peppermint tea before joining her at the table with my drink.

"How was your winter?" I asked, wrapping my hands around the hot mug.

"It was wonderful, but it's good to be back in the city."

I hummed in agreement. My heart was beating rapidly, all my carefully planned speeches fluttering out of my brain as the woman across from me read me like a book.

"You're not going to work for me," she guessed—correctly, "and you're here to let me down easy."

I let out a long breath that ended on a weak laugh. "No wonder Wilbur takes you along to all your social engagements."

Roseanne laughed, then looked at me with such kindness that I nearly changed my mind.

But I'd had two months to think about this, and there was only one way forward. I liked Roseanne and Wilbur. I liked them a lot.

I couldn't lie to them.

If I were to accept the job as Roseanne's stylist, I'd have to come clean about my contract with Rome. And if I did that, I'd be breaking my NDA. Worse, though...

I'd be hurting Rome.

No matter what happened between us, our time together had been intense and full of so much joy that I was hardly able to contain it all. He was a complicated man who closed himself off when I wanted him to open.

But at the end of the day, I loved him. I loved him so much that thinking about him felt like a hundred daggers quivering in my chest. I loved him enough to give up my dream job, to sit here and politely turn down a future that would provide stability and growth for the price of hurting the man I loved. I couldn't do it.

"I can't tell you how much I appreciate your offer, Roseanne," I started, "but I have to refuse for personal reasons."

"May I ask why?"

I took a deep breath. "Rome and I have gone our separate ways," I admitted. "I think it's best for my own sanity that I try to avoid the circles where he spends his time."

"I didn't take you for a coward." Her gaze was sharp. She saw right through me.

I shrugged. "I guess you were wrong."

"There's something you're not telling me, but I'm going to let it go for now. How's the baby?"

I jerked back, and Roseanne laughed.

"Don't look so shocked. I could tell when you came down to visit us before the holidays, darling. It's more than obvious now." She gave me a loaded look, and I leaned back in my chair, laughing.

"The baby is a gift," I said simply. "I can't wait to meet her."

Roseanne smiled at me. We finished our drinks while we talked about fashion, and then she left me sitting there, feeling exhausted and wrung out.

I'd turned down the opportunity of a lifetime, and that was okay. The last opportunity of a lifetime had landed me pregnant and on my own, so I was happy to play it safe for a while.

"You!" a voice cut through the noise of my thoughts and

drew my gaze to the café entrance. Penny stood there, red-haired and freckle-faced, a little boy on her hip, a furious expression on her face. "You've been avoiding us! I thought we talked about this when Layla was playing the ostrich with her head in the sand." She stomped over to me and loomed over my table, as much as someone so short could. She pulled her phone out of her purse and, one-handed, tapped on it and put it to her ear. "Bonnie? I just found Nikki. Hurry up and get to the coffee shop, because I'm not letting her out of my sight, and I don't know if she's going to make a run for it."

"There's no need to be dramatic," I said, trying to make it sound like a joke—but there was a weight in my chest that I didn't want to look at too closely.

Penny stood beside my chair, boxing me in, while her boy wriggled his way out of her grasp and crawled onto the seat across from me.

"Hello, Tim," I said to him.

"Hi." He pulled a toy car out of his pocket and started making engine noises, driving the car along the strip of pale beige that ran along the edge of the table.

"Where have you been?" Penny accused. "We stopped by your place and heard you'd moved! And you've barely been answering our texts."

"Well...I've been in hibernation," I admitted. "Some might say I've been nesting." I ran my hand down the front of my loose tunic dress, letting the fabric trace the outline of my tiny bump.

Penny's eyes grew huge. Her jaw dropped. She widened her stance like she'd bodily block me if I tried to make a run for it and got her phone out once more. "Bonnie! Hurry! There's an emergency here!"

As if to underscore the point, little Timmy began making siren noises as he drove his toy car over and back along the table.

And I couldn't help it. I began to laugh. It wasn't really funny. This whole situation was tragic, really. All my girlfriends had gotten their happily-ever-afters, and I was looking at a life as a single mom. I still hadn't told Rome about the baby. I was jobless, and I had about four months' worth of cash to sustain me through however long it would take to find a job as a heavily pregnant lady.

In short, my life was in shambles.

But Penny was here, and Bonnie came in, her bump a little more obvious than mine on her thin frame, blond hair wind-blown and glossy. The two of them got on their phones and called reinforcements, namely Dani and Layla, our other two girlfriends.

They sat me down and I told them the whole sordid tale, NDA be damned. They laughed and cried and hugged me, and I realized I'd been wrong about these women.

They saw me. They *loved* me. I wasn't a placeholder or a stepping stone to them. I wasn't a vague, woman-shaped entity in their lives that they picked up and put down whenever it was convenient.

I was a friend. A friend who had hurt them by keeping myself apart.

But, oddly, I felt like I'd needed my months of isolation. I'd needed that time to remind myself that I mattered; otherwise, no matter how many times one of them wrapped me in a hug or held my hand or told me they'd help me through the next year, there was no way the old me would have believed them.

I would have thought they were telling me pretty lies, and I would have gone home to lock myself away on my own.

Now, as they rallied around me, I was ready to accept their support.

"You'll need baby things," Dani said. She had two of her own. "Don't worry. We'll figure that out for you. Won't we?"

"Damn straight," Penny said, and Tim looked up with wide eyes. Penny kissed his head and said, "I know I said a bad word. I'm allowed. You're not."

The mischievous glint in the little boy's eyes told me he didn't quite believe his mother. I laughed, knowing I had that to look forward to in a few years.

The future wasn't quite as bleak as it had been an hour before. I was still jobless and broke, but I realized that I mattered to these women. And I mattered to myself.

The only thorn in my side was the little detail of telling Rome about the baby. Now that the first trimester had well and truly passed, my list of excuses was dwindling down to nothing. Roseanne had said it to me straight: I was acting like a coward.

It was time to face the man that had broken my heart and nearly broken me in the process. I just didn't know if the newly transformed me would be strong enough to deal with the consequences of his reaction.

FORTY-ONE
ROME

WILL and Natasha were lucky with the weather for their wedding day. It rained in Lake Como for a week straight leading up to the big day, and the morning of the big event, the skies cleared and revealed a beautiful, mirror-still lake surrounded with rolling hills. The trees were only just starting to bud, so the hills weren't as lush and green as they would be a month or two from now, but it was still a beautiful sight. As it was only early March, it was the off-season, so we had the whole place to ourselves. My family had rented out the entire luxury hotel on the bank of the lake, and the whole place was abuzz.

Nikki would have loved this view of the lake, with the early morning sun glinting off the water and the surrounding slopes. She'd worn a dress the exact color of the water on one of our first nights out together.

I turned away from the sight, grimacing. I had to stop thinking things like that. We'd been apart for longer than we'd been together; it was getting ridiculous.

"Rome!" My mother walked down the cobblestones leading to the lookout where I stood. I leaned against the hip-high stone banister and waited for her approach. She surveyed my tuxedo with a critical eye, plucking a piece of lint off the lapel. "I need you to go see your brother. He's already drunk and making a fool of himself. I want him standing on his own feet in his wedding photos."

"I wonder if Will wants the same."

She gave me a withering look and clip-clopped back up the path. Halfway up, she turned to give me an exasperated look. "Well?"

I pushed off the balustrade and followed her. Doing my mother's bidding once again. Some things never changed. She hadn't mentioned Nikki or the contract, but it hung between us. She knew, and she knew I knew she knew.

My brother was well on his way to being plastered when I found him in his suite, his tie askew, his nose red. I took the glass of alcohol out of his grasp and replaced it with water.

"You're no fun," he complained.

"I have strict orders to get you to your own wedding without you falling flat on your face."

Will snorted. "Try-hard," he mumbled under his breath. "Always have to be the perfect son, don't you?"

I frowned as I dumped his drink down the sink, grabbing another water for myself. "What the hell is that supposed to mean?"

"*I'm* the one who's marrying the perfect girl, the one they wanted me to. And still, she thinks I need *you* to make sure I do it properly."

"I have no idea what you're talking about."

"Oh, fuck you, Rome."

"I'm making you a coffee. You need to sober up."

"Perfect Rome with his perfect business and his perfect schooling. When are you going to let me have a win, for once?"

I whirled. "Are you serious right now? You're the golden child who can do no wrong, Will. You're the one they love. I'm the reject who gets the scraps."

"Boo-hoo, poor little Rome who just wants to be loved by Mommy and Daddy." Will snorted, stumbling back and sitting down abruptly on a long, low seat at the foot of the big king bed. His head lolled. "When are you going to take that stick out of your ass and realize that they judged everything I do based on *you*?"

Standing across from my sneering brother, it was hard for me to make sense of his words. My hands shook as rage shot through me, so I turned my back on him and busied myself with the coffee machine. It was one of those pod ones, which reminded me of the machine in my apartment, which reminded me of Nikki splayed out on top of my desk when I woke up with an insatiable need to have her again that first morning we woke up together in my apartment.

I slammed the machine closed and mashed the button. "You need to sober up, and then you'll go downstairs and get married."

"I just want to be treated like something other than an idiot," Will said quietly. "I would have liked to have been sent away to school."

"You would have *liked* it?" I roared. "Liked the isolation? Liked being left there for holidays because our parents were off doing their own thing? You would have liked feeling like no one cared about you because the truth was, no one did?"

Will slumped, his back arching at a weird angle as he lay on the foot of the bed. "I would've liked the choice. I had to stay there and be treated like an invalid. 'Wear this. Stand here. Be quiet. Study here. Major in that.' You have no idea how good you had it, Rome. No fucking idea."

The machine behind me stopped humming, but I didn't move. The scent of coffee filled the room. I stared at my brother's sprawled limbs, his untucked shirt, his stubbled jaw. "Do you want to marry Natasha, Will?" I asked quietly. "It's not too late to back out."

Will let out a dry husk of a laugh. "It's about two years too late to back out, Rome. I'm stuck with her now. A mini-Mom."

I shuddered, turning to grab his coffee. My brother groaned as he pushed himself up to a mostly seated position, nodding his thanks as he took the hot drink.

I fixed my own coffee and took a seat on a chair across from him. My whole world had turned on its ear in a single conversation with my brother. He was jealous of me? Of the way I'd grown up?

How could he possibly think that I had it better out of the two of us? I was shunted off to boarding school, ignored, and told to keep quiet. The only thing I got from my family was a trust fund and a last name, which, admittedly, had set me up for a successful life.

A successful, empty life.

But Will...he had the affection and the attention of two people who might not be capable of caring for their children the way we'd needed them. Maybe receiving our parents' attention had been more toxic than lacking it. For the first time in my life, I considered the pressure Will must have been under for the entirety of his life. I knew the expectations our parents put on us; I'd always fallen short.

Based on Will's half-drunk ramblings, it sounded like he felt the same. Neither of us had gotten what we needed, and we'd been pitted against each other in the process. The whole thing made me feel tired and sad.

I stared at my brother as he stared into his cup. As gently as I could manage, I said, "You don't have to go through with this, Will. I'll back you up if you want to call it off."

Will snorted, then downed the coffee in one shot. "No," he said, wiping his mouth on the back of his hand. "It's too late for that."

The wedding seemed more tragic after that. Will made it downstairs, looking presentable enough that I avoided getting an earful from my mother. He put on his most engaging smile and laughed with all the uncles and aunts and family friends, all the business associates and important personages in our parents' various circles. He kissed his bride and grinned as the guests threw rice, and even managed a passable impression of a man in love as he spun his bride around the dance floor for their first dance.

But for the first time, I saw the tightness around his eyes, the slight grimace at the start of his widest smiles.

He was miserable. We both were.

"Rome," my mother said behind me. "I want you to meet someone."

I turned to see my mother standing beside a couple and a

younger woman. She was shortish, blonde...and familiar. "Ophelia? What are you doing here?"

My mother smiled. "Rome, you remember the Gerbers, don't you?"

Shock splashed through me. I looked at the older couple, recognizing acquaintances of my parents.

The family resemblance between them and my employee was striking.

"Our daughter was determined to make her way in the world without our influence," Ophelia's father said indulgently, smiling at his progeny. "We're so very proud of her."

My own mother cut in with a sharp smile, "I understand Ophelia has been performing very well at Blakely. Hasn't she, Rome?"

I frowned at my mother, then at the other three. "What's going on here?"

"We just wanted to introduce you two properly," my mother said, giving me a significant look. "I'll let you and Ophelia catch up. I'm sure you have *lots* to talk about."

She ushered the parents away, and I was left with my employee. She blinked up at me, a coy smile on her lips. "We met before I started working at Blakely, actually. A gout charity four years ago. I was there with my mother."

"I see." My mind raced as I tried to understand what was going on. Ophelia knew my parents, but she'd never mentioned it. My mother knew Ophelia worked for me and didn't tell me.

Was this a setup? My heart thumped. Was this the mole? This was the woman who'd fed information back to my mother?

"You mother mentioned you'd be here on your own," Ophelia

said, touching my sleeve. She took a step closer to me so I could smell her overly sweet perfume. I jerked back, and her expression hardened. She dropped her hand from my arm but didn't back up.

I glanced across the room and saw my mom staring at us intently, watching if her snare had closed around me as she'd planned.

I was supposed to choose Ophelia the way Will had chosen Natasha. I was supposed to go along with what was expected of me, chasing the carrot of my parents' affection while they wielded the stick of their disapproval.

And suddenly, in this beautiful resort, surrounded by people wearing designer gowns, dripping in jewels, eating the best food and drinking the best wine, I realized just how empty my life really was.

I took a step back, studying Ophelia. "How much has my mother pumped you for information about my company?"

Ophelia lifted a shoulder in a subtle shrug. "Only as much as I wanted to tell her."

"What did she promise you in return?" I sneered. "A ring on your finger?"

Ophelia watched me, then lifted her chin. "I see you're still hung up on a woman that's so far below you. She'll ruin your life, Rome. She already has. Did you know she refused to work for the Monks? So not only is she a social climber, but she's also an idiot to boot."

Rage momentarily blanketed over me, but one thing Ophelia said stuck out. "She refused to work for the Monks?"

A touch of victory entered Ophelia's gaze. She sighed and said, "Crazy, right? Trying to sabotage your biggest deal because you broke up with her. It's pathetic. She should have kept her legs shut and stayed in her place."

Ice descended over me. I blinked slowly, tamping down the urge to throttle the woman sneering at me. I lifted my chin. "You're fired, Ophelia. HR will be in touch by the end of the day."

She arched a brow. "On what grounds?"

I turned on my heels and stalked away.

"On what grounds!"

Her words chased me out of the room, but I didn't turn.

Because I knew the truth.

Nikki hadn't refused to work for Roseanne Monk because she was trying to sabotage my deal. She did it because she was trying to *save* it. Even after everything I said to her, the way I treated her—she still put me first.

A woman with that much integrity wouldn't be able to lie to Roseanne about me, so she gave up the opportunity of a lifetime for the sake of my company. My reputation.

For me.

It was just like her standing up for me at the gala honoring my parents. Just like the hours of research and preparation she did for events where she could have just as easily stood beside me and said nothing.

Nikki *cared*. She'd cared about me, about my company, about her work. And I'd thrown it back in her face the moment she tried to ask for something honest for herself.

I was a colossal asshole.

I cut across the room toward the exit, but my mother accosted me just outside the door.

"What do you think you're doing, Rome?" she hissed, her nails digging into my elbow as she dragged me out of the room.

I tore my arm away. "You've been spying on me," I told her, my voice oddly flat.

"Don't be dramatic. She wanted to play the rebel for a few years, but Ophelia is a good girl and she's ready to come back into the fold. I think you'd be good together. Her parents—"

"I don't give a shit who her parents are or what they can do for you if I date their daughter."

My mother's jaw hardened. "If this is about that girl—"

"This is about *me*, Mother. I'm done."

The words came out of me before I really understood what I was saying, but once I spoke them out loud, the clarity they provided put my entire life into sharp relief. I'd spent so many years being torn between resentment and desperation for affection. I hated my parents for their rejection, yet I jumped at every phone call, answered every demand.

I was so desperate for a scrap of love that I really thought it was okay to be treated like an accessory in their lives.

Maybe it was the sight of Will vowing to love and cherish a woman he had no interest in marrying that did it. Or the realization that my parents would go as far as to plant someone in my own organization to get information on me. And then, the cherry on top of the shit sundae—to try to set me up with her! As if a bit of family espionage was just par for the course when the eldest son decided to build his own company instead of dancing exactly to the family tune.

I was done. Utterly and completely. I no longer cared if these people approved. I no longer craved their attention, their affection, their time.

Truthfully, I hadn't even realized I *had* craved it—not until that need was gone.

Or maybe, I realized how empty my familial relationships were when even at a distance, Nikki gave me something that meant so much more.

"She isn't good enough for you, Rome," my mother hissed, accurately reading the direction of my thoughts. "You think a girl who came from nothing can stand at your side? You think she can actually help you get to the next level?"

"What level is that, Joanne?"

"Don't you call me by my first name. I am your *mother*—"

"You aren't. You haven't been that for a long time."

"What's that supposed to mean?" Her voice jumped up an octave as her arms fell to her sides.

"It means exactly what it sounds like. I'm not rushing over every time I get a summons. I'm not entertaining your opinions or your judgments. I'm not answering your calls. As far as I'm concerned, my family is dead."

Her face went white. "Rome—"

"Goodbye, Joanne." I began to walk away.

"People will find out about that contract, Rome. Your company won't survive the bad press."

I paused and turned. "Is that a threat?"

"It's the truth."

"I don't think anyone will find out, actually," I said, coldness creeping into the edges of my words.

My mother scoffed. "How do you figure?"

"How embarrassing would it be for you if everyone found out the lengths you'd go to set me up with a woman? You'd be laughingstock, especially because there's no way I'll ever date the Gerbers' daughter. And all those businesses you've invested in—how many of them would be happy to find out about your little spy? Everyone would be suspicious of you. No one would trust you. The whole house of cards might just fall apart."

Eyes that shot flames bore into mine. I withstood her glare for a few long seconds, then turned around and walked away.

In the lobby, an elevator opened as I pressed the button, and a few moments later I was in my room, phone at my ear, my suitcase open and on the bed.

"Clara," I said, "I'm coming back. I need the jet to be ready as soon as possible."

"On it," she said, and I hung up the phone.

An hour later, I was on my way to beg forgiveness from the only person in my life that truly mattered. The only woman who had defended me, even when she had no power. The only woman who kissed me like she cared about *me*, and not what I could do for her.

The one who told me, clear as day, that she couldn't work for me because she wanted a real relationship. She wanted me.

I'd been too wrapped up in my own hurt to realize she'd been offering me the world. I just hoped it wasn't too late to make amends.

FORTY-TWO
NIKKI

WHEN THE BUZZER SOUNDED, I was in the middle of a reality TV binge, wearing my comfiest pair of sweats while curled up on my sofa with a giant bowl of popcorn. I'd spent the day journaling, walking, and spending time with the girls to try to figure out how I was going to talk to Rome about the baby.

I thought I was ready. I had it all planned out. I'd tell him that he didn't have to be involved and I didn't need anything from him, but I wouldn't keep the baby from him if he wanted to be a father.

I didn't want to open the door to a relationship with him, because I knew he couldn't offer me what I really wanted. The past few months had taught me that I was no longer happy to accept life as the placeholder. That had become a self-fulfilling prophecy; I thought it was all I deserved, so it was all I asked for.

In reality, I deserved so much more.

Rome couldn't offer me the kind of love that lasts decades and only gets stronger, and I didn't want to settle for scraps.

I'd pour all my love into my child, and that would be enough. It would have to be.

I was calm. I was at peace. I was ready.

Then the buzzer rang.

Putting the bowl of popcorn on the coffee table, I groaned as I sat up. I hit the pause button then rubbed my eyes and hauled myself up to my feet. The nausea from the first trimester had passed and I was feeling more energetic, but it was late.

"Hello?" I croaked, pressing the button on the intercom.

"Nikki—"

I took my finger off and the line went dead. Wide-eyed, I stared at the speaker as my heart took off at a gallop. That couldn't be—

A buzz interrupted my thoughts. I answered, my finger trembling as it pressed the button. "H-hello?"

"Don't hang up," Rome said, breathless. "Please. I need to talk to you."

The thumping in my breast was so violent I put my palm to my chest as if I feared my heart would jump right out. Suddenly, my throat was dry.

He knew about the baby. He was here to confront me about it.

Roseanne? She might have told her husband, and he would have congratulated Rome. Of course. I never should have met with her. I should have sent her a polite rejection email and avoided her completely.

But then I wouldn't have reconnected with the girls, and I wouldn't have realized just how wrong I'd been about my place in the group.

"Come on up," I said, resignation sinking into my pores. I

pressed the button to unlock the front door, then quickly tidied my front room. I fluffed some pillows and shoved the bowl of popcorn in the kitchen. I folded the throw blanket that had been wrapped around me and stacked some books on the shelves in the corner.

He knocked.

I stared at the door like it might jump over and smack me, then took a deep breath. I was being ridiculous. This wasn't going exactly to plan, but that didn't mean it was a disaster. Rome was here in person, wasn't he? He hadn't sicced his team of hotshot lawyers on me. That boded well.

I hoped.

The lock felt stiff as I opened it, the door heavier than usual.

And Rome was there on the other side. I hadn't quite believed it until I saw him. His eyes were bloodshot, and his hair was a mess. He looked like he was wearing a tuxedo, which was strange. Had he come straight from an event? Was he drunk...?

"Can I come in?" His voice was raspy, but he didn't slur, and he didn't smell like alcohol.

I nodded, opening the door. "Sure. Can I get you something? Water? Uh—actually, I only have water." I let out an awkward laugh that died on my lips when I saw the look on Rome's face.

He looked...distraught.

"Nikki," he said, stretching his hands out toward me and quickly pulling them back. "I—I wanted to apologize. The way I treated you... You deserve so much better. I'm sorry."

I blinked. "Oh. I—thank you."

"I've realized a lot of things over the past twenty-four hours, and one of them is how precious you are to me. Is there any way

—could you ever forgive me? I'd like..." He shoved a hand through his hair and released a sharp breath. "I'd like to just erase everything I said to you and tell you that yes, I want everything you offered, but I know I messed up."

His gaze skimmed down my body and back up again, and I felt a strange sense of detachment. Here was a man that I'd loved, standing in front of me telling me everything I'd wanted to hear.

But if he knew about the baby, then he was only doing this because of his future child. Not because of me. He'd left me wallowing on my own, humiliated, broke, and isolated. He'd turned his back on me when I told him I wanted a real relationship with him. That hadn't been enough. All the time we'd spent together, the secrets we'd shared, the promises we'd made —they meant nothing. They weren't enough.

Now that I was carrying his baby, I was enough?

My jaw hardened. "You did mess up, Rome. I'm not sure I can give you what you're asking."

His shoulders slumped, despair entering his gaze. "I—I understand. I thought..."

"I know," I said, when he didn't continue. "Listen, I appreciate you coming here. I was planning on calling you this week. I'm sure we can come up with a coparenting arrangement that works for both of us. I'll be looking for full custody, especially when the baby is an infant, but—"

I clamped my lips shut at the look Rome gave me. His frown had deepened with every word, and now he was staring at my stomach like he'd suddenly turned into a human ultrasound machine.

His gaze lifted up to meet my own. "You're *pregnant?*"

I blinked. Frowned. "Isn't that why you're here?"

"You're pregnant?" He repeated the question as a whisper.

Suddenly, I realized that I might have made a mistake in my assumptions. I opened my mouth then closed it again. All my carefully planned speeches vanished. I forgot everything I'd written in the journal and everything my girlfriends had encouraged me to say.

Because the look on Rome's face transformed from shock to joy to...to *agony*. He dropped his gaze to the ground and covered his face with his hands, drawing in a long, shuddering breath. My own emotions were running riot through me. My eyes watered and my heart still hadn't returned to its normal rhythm. It was hard to breathe.

"You didn't know?" I croaked.

He shook his head, swallowing thickly. "No."

I blinked back my tears. "So everything you just said...you said it because you really want me? Not just because I'm pregnant with your baby?"

The silence that stretched between us was taut. It vibrated with the tension of all our unsaid words. It held us apart and kept us together, so we were both frozen a few feet apart, trembling, watching each other for the slightest sign.

Rome was the first to move. He stumbled forward, and then I was closing the distance and our arms were around each other. His lips dragged over my jaw as he placed kisses over every bit of skin he could find. When he finally reached my lips, Rome kissed me like a man starved. He held my face with both hands and kissed me until we both had to stop for breath.

One of his hands slid down my side and came to rest on the side of my stomach. His eyes were full of unshed tears when he met my gaze, his lips glistening from our kiss. "Is this real?" he whispered. "Is this happening?"

"I'm not sure."

His gaze flicked between my eyes, and that sharp agony returned to his expression. "You thought I was only here because I wanted the baby. You thought I was apologizing because I found out you were pregnant."

A boulder had lodged itself in my throat, so all I could do was nod.

Rome closed his eyes and rested his forehead against mine. He kept a hand on the side of my bump as his body trembled, our breaths mingling near our lips.

When Rome pulled away, he didn't go far—only a couple of inches, far enough that he could meet my gaze. "I love you, Nikki. I didn't even know what love was until you came into my life. Maybe that's why it took me so long to realize the bone-deep fear I felt was just one facet of my love for you. I'm nothing without you. I *have* nothing without you. I came here ready to get on my knees and beg you to forgive me, because the way I treated you was selfish and wrong and cruel. You are the light of my life, Nikki. You're the one who makes me want to wake up in the morning, who makes me reach for the other side of the bed before I've even opened my eyes."

"Rome—"

"Let me finish," he interrupted softly. "Let me apologize properly, because I know you were offering me the kind of relationship that I didn't even know existed, and I threw it back in your face. I'm sorry I pushed you away. I'm sorry I let my fears of abandonment and rejection get in the way. I'm sorry I let you stand in my office and strip off your armor to show me your vulnerability without doing the same thing. I'm doing it now. You're the air that I breathe and the food that I eat. You're what I need to live, Nikki, and I'm sorry I ever made you feel differently. I know—" He took in a shuddering breath, a tear escaping from the corner of his eye. "I know it's a lot to ask for you to accept my apology, especially because I haven't even been here for this"—he stroked my side—"but please. Please, I'm begging you, baby—"

"Shut up and kiss me, Rome," I said, because I couldn't take the pain in his eyes, and I felt like I was dying from the few inches of distance between us.

He didn't have to be told twice. Rome crushed his lips to mine and wrapped me in his arms. I parted my lips on a sigh and his tongue slid against mine, sending a shiver coursing down my spine. He tasted like home, like love, like happiness.

And he'd come here for *me*.

"You're not mad I didn't tell you right away?" I asked, breathless, between kisses.

"I didn't deserve to know," he said, dropping to his knees in front of me. He pulled my shirt up over my bump to kiss the slight swelling, framing my stomach with his broad hands. "I didn't deserve that courage from you. Not after I already pushed you away."

I combed my fingers through his hair, only realizing tears were falling from my eyes when one landed on the back of my palm. His hair was cool and silky, a contrast to the rasp of his stubble against my stomach. He pressed his cheek to my skin and sighed before glancing up at me.

"Never again, Nikki," he said, solemn. "I'll never put you

second. I'll never make you feel small. I'll never make you question whether I'm here for you, and you above all others."

My breath caught, vision blurring with tears. But there was one thing I had to ask, even though the answer was obvious. "And you want the baby?"

Rome let out a soft breath and stood. He put his thumb on my chin and tilted it up to capture my gaze, his other hand wiping the tears from my cheek. "Nikki, I've wanted to put a baby inside you since the first time we slept together." His grin was rueful. "It scared the shit out of me, but it's true. I'm in love with you," he added simply, "and I'll do anything for you and our child. Yes, I want the baby. But I want you more."

I softened against him, hooking my arms around his shoulders. "I'm in love with you too," I told him, a tremulous smile on my lips. "That feels good to say."

"Damn right it does," he growled. I yelped as he picked me up, striding across the apartment to the bedroom. "I love you, Nikita Jordan. And I'm never letting you go."

I laughed as he placed me down on the bed, propping himself up above me before laying a soft kiss on my lips. "I like the sound of that," I told him, then curled my hands into his lapels and brought him down to my mouth once more.

The groan that came from Rome undid me. Heat curled deep in my core, and I spread my knees to let him nestle between them, loving the weight of his hips against mine.

He lifted his torso off, brows drawn. "I don't want to crush the baby."

I grinned. "Guess I'll be on top."

Rome huffed, then shuffled down, dragging my sweatpants with him. "First, this," he said as he put his mouth to my core.

I arched on the bed, a gasp escaping my lips. I shoved my fingers through his hair and ground on his lips as Rome groaned, spreading my legs wide so he could feast on me properly.

I came just a few moments after he put his fingers inside me, a bright, intense orgasm that left me panting. Then a frantic energy captured us both, and articles of clothing were flying across the room as we rushed to get naked. I straddled Rome's hips and placed my palms on his bare chest, unable to stop smiling down at him.

Happiness fizzed in my veins, ramping my need for him higher. His hands bracketed my hips, thumbs stroking the edge of my bump.

"You are so beautiful," he said, eyes on mine for a moment before they dropped to my breasts, my stomach. His hands stroked up my sides, exploring the new curves of my body, and I believed him. I felt beautiful in my changing body. I loved the way he stroked the new contours of it, the shape of my stomach, my swollen breasts.

Impatience nipped at me, even though I could tell Rome would be happy to stroke my skin for an eternity. I lifted myself up and reached between us, stroking the hard length of him. He groaned, hands squeezing on my breasts as I lined his cock up with my entrance.

"Nikki—"

I dropped myself down onto him and rocked. Rome gasped, eyes flying open, hands dropping to my hips. Pleasure splintered through me at the feel of him inside me, skin to skin, the length of him stretching me deliciously.

"You feel so fucking good," he groaned, one hand clamping on my hip while the other slid to my stomach. I expected him to reach for my clit, but he kept his hand on my bump, stroking softly while his hips rolled into mine. Our movements became deeper, more languid, and I leaned forward to prop my hands on his chest.

"I love you," he said, happiness suffusing his features. "I love you so much. Love your body. Love the baby you're growing for us. Love the life we'll have together." With every sentence, he thrust up from under me a little deeper, until I whined and gasped atop him, clinging to his shoulders as heat wound deep in my core.

"Rome," I gasped, grinding my hips into his.

"Ride my cock, gorgeous," he commanded. "Let me feel you squeeze me."

Powerless to resist the order, I rode him until pleasure drenched me from head to toe, until I trembled with the need to come, until his sweet words of love and praise ran together in my head and all I heard was my own thundering heart.

Then Rome's hand reached between us, and he found that bundle of nerves so desperate for his touch. I came with a cry, riding the man I loved, while he told me how amazing I felt and how beautiful I looked doing it. He groaned, and I opened my eyes to see a desperation enter his eyes. I was still coming down from my orgasm as another wave of lust crashed through me.

It was the look on his face that did it. The craving—for me. His hands moved over my hips to stroke my ass, then he was lifting me off his hips and placing me down on my hands and knees. His movements were rough, but he supported me until I was steady.

"Need you," he said, kneeling behind me, his hand dipping between my legs to feel me. I whined as I backed into his touch, shivering as he let his fingers slide up higher to tease my rear. "I want your ass, Nikki. I want all of you. Want you to be mine."

It wasn't what I expected, but it sent a dart of excitement through me. We'd hinted at this. It had excited me before, in the heat of the moment. And now...

My heart thundered, and I pointed to the nightstand. "Lube."

His breaths were harsh as he tore the top drawer open, pulling out a squeeze tube of lube. He coated his fingers and brought them to my crack, and I jumped at the coldness of them. His other hand made soothing strokes over my hip and flank, and he slid a finger inside me.

"You look so good like this, Nikki," he said, voice a bare rasp. His finger stroked me, in and out, and I grunted, fingers curling into my sheets. "Relax, baby. We won't do anything you don't want to do."

I nodded. "Okay," I whispered.

"You still good?"

"Yes."

He added more lube—and another finger. His free hand dipped between my legs to tease my clit, and my thighs began to tremble. I let out an unfamiliar, keening noise, hips backing into his touch as my body craved more. I wanted to share this with him. Wanted to know what it was like. Wanted to break every barrier that could exist between us, tie us together forever.

His fingers scissored and stretched until I begged him for more. Then he was there, his cock covered in lubricant, the head of it intruding against me.

"Okay, gorgeous?" he said, his voice quiet—belying the tension I could feel emanating from him.

"Yes," I replied on a pant.

Then he was there, pushing into me, and the stretch became intense. But Rome was slow, soothing me when I tensed up, praising me when I took him deeper. Our bodies were slick with lube and sweat and my own arousal. With every inch of his cock that entered me, I felt a little more tension release. It felt *good*. Pleasure began to fizzle in my veins, dark and intense. When he finally seated himself inside me, I let out a huff of breath and glanced over my shoulder.

His eyes were dark as they met mine. The muscles of his neck were stark as he held my hips, stroking me gently, moving his hips a fraction of an inch to get me used to the movement.

Then, despite the intensity of the moment, his lips split into a wide smile. "I love you so much," he told me, and he began to move in earnest.

Maybe it was his words that started me flying over the edge, or the way he reached around to play with my clit. Or maybe it was the intrusion in my ass, the stretch and pleasure of feeling him there. Whatever it was, it didn't take long for me to bury my face in my pillow to muffle my screams, body trembling as I received him. I came harder than I thought possible, pleasure blinding me as it splintered through me. Distantly, I heard Rome let out a rough grunt, his movements becoming jagged. When he joined me at the peak, his release hot inside me, another wave of pleasure ran through me.

It was the single most erotic, intense experience of my life. I collapsed on my side as he eased out of me, and the bed dipped for a moment as he disappeared. I heard the shower run for a few moments, and then Rome returned with a washcloth. He wiped the mess between my legs with gentle strokes, meeting my gaze when he was done. His eyes were bright, his cheeks red.

What undid me, though—what made it all finally feel real—was the gentle, feather-light touch of Rome's lips to my forehead. He set the washcloth aside, and I closed my eyes and snuggled into him with a smile on my lips and hope anchoring itself in my heart.

There'd be more time for talking later, when my heartbeat was back to normal. For now, I pressed my skin against Rome's and let myself settle into the knowledge that I belonged to him, and he belonged to me. This was the real deal. True love. The two of us together—forever.

FORTY-THREE
ROME

I'D REALIZED something when I woke up next to Nikki the following morning: begging her for forgiveness had only been the beginning. There were so many areas of my life where I'd pushed myself to be better, to be more, to make more money, to grow the business...all because there was something lacking within myself.

That's how I ended up meeting Wilbur Monk for lunch that day.

He shook my hand with a violent pump of his arm. "What's the emergency, Blakely? It's not often you ask for a same-day meeting. Is everything okay with our first campaign?"

We'd started working on a campaign for one of Wilbur's subsidiary companies that had expanded into health foods.

"The campaign is fine," I told him, taking a seat at the two-seater table in the corner of the restaurant. I smoothed my tie and touched the edge of the white tablecloth, dreading this conversation.

But it had to be done.

"I have something to tell you," I started, "about me and Nikki."

Wilbur's brows arched. "Okay."

Before I could go on, we were interrupted by the waiter. We put our orders in and waited for him to pour glasses of water, and I used that time to try to get my heart rate back to normal levels. I wasn't entirely successful.

"You're looking a bit green, Rome," Wilbur said, shaking his napkin out to place it on his lap. "What's going on?"

"I wasn't entirely honest with you," I said, deciding to rip the Band-Aid off.

Wilbur's thick eyebrows twitched together. "Go on."

"Nikki and I did meet at work, and we are together now. I intend to take your good advice and marry her as soon as possible."

Wilbur hummed. "So what's the problem?"

"She was hired as an assistant for the production team, and I met her when there was an accident on set. I ended up hiring her to be my plus-one for the various events on my calendar. That's what she was doing as a consultant for the company. I hired her to be my date, and I never expected it to turn into something real, but here we are. I lied to you, Wilbur. Never directly, but I made you believe she and I were an item for much longer than we actually were, all because I was desperate to win your business. I'm sorry. I understand if you want to rethink our business arrangement, but I felt it better to come clean now, because I respect you as a man and as a business owner, and—"

I stopped when Wilbur gave me a strange look. His face had gone slightly red, and his eyes were bulging. Then, like an explosion, laughter burst out of him loud enough for the other restaurant's patrons to turn and stare. He threw his head back and guffawed until tears rolled down his cheeks.

"Uh... I..." I stared at him, at a loss.

"That's a new one," he said, dabbing his napkin at his eyes. "You're telling the truth, aren't you?"

"Yes."

"Oh, Roseanne is going to love this. She knew something was funny between the two of you, but she thought it was the baby—"

"You knew about the baby?"

Wilbur waved a hand. "She guessed it when Nikki was sick when you came down to visit. How's Nikki doing?"

I couldn't help the smile that curled my lips. "Good. Great. We're having a girl."

Wilbur's gaze softened. "Congratulations, Rome."

"So you're not mad?"

"Oh, I'm furious," he admitted. "You made a fool out of me."

I gulped. "Right. And—"

"But I think falling in love is a good enough comeuppance for anyone, and especially you, under the circumstances."

I clamped my mouth shut for a second, then dipped my chin. "So you still want to work together?"

"I hired you because you're the best at what you do. Now, I'm guessing Nikki refused the job with Roseanne because she was afraid of this secret coming out?"

"She didn't want to lie to you, and she didn't want to compromise my business."

"Roseanne will be happy. Should I let her know to call Nikki?"

My heart thumped, and I nodded. "Sure. I haven't spoken to Nikki about it, but if she's interested…"

"Good. Now, I've got ideas about a few of these proposals we've sent through. While we're here, we might as well get some work done."

My mind was still spinning, but I forced myself to focus on Wilbur's comments, noting them down so I could bring them back to the team. By the time my lunch was done, I felt like I'd narrowly escaped being hit by a train. Wilbur shook my hand once more, then got into his waiting vehicle and was driven off while I watched him go.

My phone buzzed. Nikki. She wrote, *How'd the lunch go?*

I smiled. *Good. On my way back.*

There was work to do. I had to make sure Ophelia was let go and Wilbur's comments were sent to the right people. I had quarterly reports to review and a meeting with my executive team.

But all that could wait. There was only one place I wanted to be.

I nodded to my driver and got in the back seat, and he took me home to the woman I loved.

EPILOGUE

NIKKI

OUR BABY GIRL, Cleo, was born pink and screaming after only four hours of labor. Holding her for the first time was an indescribable experience. I knew that from that moment forward, everything had changed. As I looked up at Rome and saw the moisture in his eyes, I saw the same thought reflected back at me.

He kissed my sweaty forehead and ran a finger down our girl's arm, his hand trembling as he did. "You were amazing," he told me.

"Thank you for being here."

"Of course."

He'd rushed from work to the hospital when I called him. I was two days past my due date, so it was no great surprise, but it still felt like a shock to feel contractions coming on, and an even greater shock to be told to push.

Over the past five months, I'd moved in with Rome and taken the job with Roseanne. We'd talked about marriage, but

I'd wanted to wait until after the baby was born to tie the knot. Rome seemed impatient to put a ring on my finger, which made me feel giddy and loved.

Not long after he met with Wilbur Monk, he told me that Ophelia had been let go. She'd made threats, but after discussing it with me, Rome decided to be open about how he and I met. To anyone who asked, he told the whole story: the accident with the perfume bottle, the fear of litigation, the tense negotiations between us. Somehow, he made me look like a shark who deserved to be at his side, and our story was just one of many. Once it was all out in the open, there wasn't much Ophelia—or anyone else—could threaten us with.

I was glad not to have any secrets. I liked being able to stand at his side and be myself—and have that be exactly enough.

We brought our baby home and spent three weeks cooped up at home, learning how to be new parents. I felt worn out, exhausted, and happy. Rome was right there beside me to rub my feet and fluff my pillow, and I fell in love with him all over again.

After our self-imposed isolation, we received visitors. Our friends came by to meet the new baby and offer their congratulations, but we both fielded phone calls from our parents. Neither of us wanted to invite their judgment into our little bubble of love.

It was the beginning of a distancing, and it was necessary. I kept the line of communication open with my mother, because although she hadn't been there for me the way I'd needed, I didn't think she was a bad person. Rome, on the other hand, decided he needed space. There were no more monthly dinners, no more summons, no more helicopter rides to the estate on Long Island.

As the weeks went by, I watched him become a more relaxed, confident version of himself, and I wondered how much those monthly dinners ground him down. I was glad to see him thrive—and even gladder that he was doing it with me and our child.

She was a gorgeous baby with her father's eyes and the cutest laugh I'd ever heard. I snuggled her for about twenty hours a day, and somehow it still didn't feel like enough.

One evening, after we shared cake for Cleo's two-month birthday, I propped the baby monitor on the coffee table and leaned my head against Rome's shoulder. He wrapped an arm around my shoulders and let out a long sigh before pressing a kiss to the top of my head.

"You still want to marry me?" I asked as we stared out into the night sky.

"I will marry you tomorrow if you let me," he told me.

I smiled, tilting my head to meet his gaze. "Let's set a date, then."

Rome kissed the tip of my nose and said, "Yes. But first..." He shifted, sliding off the couch so he was kneeling on the ground in front of me. He pulled a small ring box out of his pocket and flipped it open, turning it to show me the most beautiful solitaire diamond ring I'd ever seen.

I gaped at the grape-sized stone. "Have you been carrying that around in your pocket all this time?"

"I was waiting for the right moment," he said, grinning at me, then sobered. "Nikki, will you make me the happiest man alive and tell me you'll be my wife?"

I was a blubbery, hormonal mess. Tears were already wetting my cheeks as I croaked out a "Yes!" and threw my arms around his neck, tackling him to the ground between the sofa and coffee table. He landed with a low grunt as I peppered his face with kisses. I sat up and wiped my eyes before extending my left hand. "Put it on."

His fingers shook as he plucked the ring from its velvet embrace and slid it onto my finger. It felt heavy, and it threw sparks of color all over my hand. I sighed, admiring it, then slid my gaze to meet his.

Rome's hands stroked my thighs, a soft smile tugging at his lips. "I love you, Nikki."

"I love you more."

He shook his head. "Impossible."

I smiled, then leaned forward and pressed a soft kiss to his lips. When I felt a twitch between us from behind Rome's pants, I arched my brows.

"Don't worry about that," he said. "I don't want to hurt you."

The doctor had cleared me for sex two weeks ago, so I smiled. "You won't," I promised, and I knew all the way to the depths of my heart that it was the truth.

EXTENDED EPILOGUE
NIKKI

THE SMELL IS what hit me first. Rich, decadent chocolate wafted over me as soon as I stepped through the tinted glass door. My shoulders dropped and I inhaled deeply.

"Wow," I breathed.

Rome's hand drifted over the small of my back, his other palm cradling the baby carrier strapped to his front. He grinned at me. "Good, right?"

"Mr. Blakely! Ms. Jordan!" a man exclaimed in slightly accented English, coming around a display case to greet us. "Welcome. We've been expecting you."

"Thank you for opening for us, Jules."

Jules beamed at us. "When we heard you were coming to visit, I was delighted to hear you wanted to stop by. And this must be little Cleo." He smiled at the little sleeping bundle strapped to Rome's chest, then winked at me. "My daughter just had her second. Being a grandfather has been the best gift of my life."

"I'm sure your grandchildren appreciate all the sweet treats you're able to give them as well," I said, smiling as I shook his outstretched hand. "I know your chocolates have been keeping me going for months since Cleo was born."

Jules laughed. "One of the great pleasures of being both a chocolatier and a grandfather. Now, come! Follow me."

We did just that, stepping through a curtained opening into an intimate dining room. A small, round table had been set. Jules pulled out my chair while Rome sat across from me. While my fiancé gently unstrapped Cleo from the carrier, another worker wheeled over a bassinet for us to use.

That was one thing I hadn't quite gotten used to since Rome and I had officially been together. Life was so much *easier*. It was his money, of course, but also his influence. It was the way people treated us, making sure every need was met and then some before we had the chance to realize we needed something.

I leaned over Cleo and touched he soft cheek, then smiled at Rome. "Thank you for this."

"I'm just getting started," he said with a twinkle in his eyes.

I leaned back when Jules appeared to put gold-rimmed plates in front of us. Then the other worker came back with a platter of tiny, intricate chocolates.

"From left to right, we have our classic ganache truffle. Next is a delicate hazelnut praline with arabica coffee notes. Beside that is, I believe, Mrs. Blakely's favorite—"

"Caramel," I said, and it was almost a moan.

"Caramel," Jules confirmed with a smile. "Our specialty caramel with a layer of praline, enrobed in our finest dark choco-late." He must have been able to tell my mouth was watering, because he motioned to the chocolates in front of us. "Please."

I went straight for the caramel, bit into it, and let out an inelegant grunt.

Rome smiled at me and bit into the classic cocoa-covered ganache truffle. He reached across the small table to lay his hand over mine, and we enjoyed our chocolates in silence for a few moments.

"You know," Rome said when he'd swallowed, "When you ate that truffle in my boardroom right after turning the screw on me to extract every penny you could from that contract—"

"Hey! I had no idea what was going on!"

He let out a laugh and squeezed my hand. "Right. I'm still not sure I believe you, Nikki, but you should know that that was the moment that I knew I couldn't let you go. Red lipstick, flashing eyes, and the pure attitude of biting into that chocolate. It was all over from then on."

A thrill went through me. "To be fair," I hedged, "you're the one who brought that bowl of chocolates into the room. You couldn't expect me *not* to indulge."

His thumb coasted over my knuckles, and his eyes softened. "Maybe I wanted you to."

Jules brought out more trays of chocolate, along with delicious coffee to cut the richness. We tasted wild honey-flavored chocolate. He told us about the provenance of the cacao beans, about the process of making chocolate, about how many years it had taken him to perfect his praline recipe.

Cleo woke up fussing, and I took a break from chocolate to nurse her. Then we ate more chocolate, and left the shop with bags of specialty truffles, two perfect, glossy chocolate mousse cakes, and one fruit tart that I must have stared at longingly for a few seconds too long, because Jules added it to our bulging bags despite my protests.

We walked out into the cobbled Antwerp street, but I was surprised to see our driver had disappeared. Rome didn't seem alarmed, so I gave him a sideways glance.

"What's going on here?" I asked.

"Let's walk this way," he said.

Willing to play along, I ran my hand over Cleo's downy head where it was nestled in the carrier against Rome's chest—her favorite place to be—then fell into step beside him. We walked for a few minutes, admiring the architecture and the tree-lined streets, the copper statues and the wide stone boulevards, and finally turned down a side street.

We stopped in front of a door. Rome pressed a buzzer, and the latch clicked. He opened the door for me, his hand sliding down my spine as he guided me inside.

"Where are you taking me?"

"You'll see," he said mysteriously.

Glancing over my shoulder, I frowned at him, but all Rome did was motion for me to walk up the narrow staircase that dominated the tiled lobby. Knowing I wouldn't get anything out of him, I made my way up the steps. He guided me to the left, where light spilled out from one of the doorways.

My heart thumped as we approached. I was full of chocolate and happiness. How could this trip get any better? Two days ago, Rome had simply told me that he wanted to take me somewhere special, and we'd left the following day. When we landed in Belgium, I'd thought we were just here for a weekend getaway to visit his favorite chocolatier.

But now I knew there was more to this trip than I'd anticipated.

We turned the corner and stepped through the door—and I gasped.

Garment racks lined the far wall, filled with a froth of white lace and silk and tulle. Wedding dresses. Directly in front of me was a tri-fold mirror in front of a small round platform, with plush, velvet couches in a semi-circle around it.

And on the couches were my best friends. Penny was the first one to jump up, followed by Bonnie, Dani, and Layla. In a flutter of enthusiasm, they all hugged me as they cooed and cheered at our arrival.

"Finally!" Layla exclaimed. "We've gone through all the dresses and have a bet going for which one you'll pick."

"Dresses?" I said, pulling away from my hug with Bonnie.

Penny laughed and hooked her arm around Rome's. "Yes, dresses! Mr. Romantic here wanted to hurry things along a bit."

I looked at my future husband and arched a brow.

He looked not the least repentant. "You need a dress, Nikki."

"Did you really just trick me into wedding dress shopping?"

"I flew you and your friends halfway around the world to come to this very salon so that Lina could find the perfect dress for you."

"The perfect—" I inhaled sharply, then turned to see a short woman emerge from the side room. Her hair was blond and utterly straight, cut in a blunt bob that fell to her jaw. She was dressed in all black clothing that had simple lines but obviously masterful construction. Her eyes were sharp and assessing as she took me in, then turned to Rome. "Thank you, Mr. Blakely. I'll take it from here."

"But—" I shook my head, turning to face Rome. "We haven't even picked a venue! How can I choose a dress when I don't know what kind of wedding we're having."

His smile was soft as he used a finger to tilt up my chin. When he pressed a kiss to my forehead, all the fight left me. Then he pulled away and said, "Pick the dress first, and we'll have the wedding to match. Pick five dresses and marry me five times over. I don't care, as long as I get to call you my wife."

How could I fight with that? I shook my head, then smiled as my husband-to-be leaned over to press a kiss to my lips. Then he said his goodbyes and left me in the capable hands of Lina and my four best girlfriends.

Lina clapped her hands. "Good. We've got a lot to do. Let's get started."

The next three hours were a whirlwind. I tried on every dress Lina had arranged. I drank champagne that went straight to my head. I watched Penny and Bonnie shed a tear when I emerged in an over-the-top princess dress that was way too much for the kind of wedding I wanted.

...Or was it?

"I think you should take Rome up on that five weddings idea," Layla said, lifting her champagne flute. "I can't pick a winner."

"Or one ceremony dress, one reception dress, and then something shorter for the dancing portion of the evening," Dani suggested.

Lina nodded. "Very wise."

"Wise?" I protested, laughing, but my eyes were already trailing over the dresses I'd tried on.

"I think she's already picked which ones she wants," Penny said, "but she's too afraid to say it out loud."

I bit my lip. Bonnie laughed, pointing her own glass at me. "She definitely has."

"Let me try the strapless one on again," I said to Lina.

The short woman's lips curled into a tiny, pleased smile. "Excellent choice."

Once I had the dress on, I stepped up onto the round dais and looked at myself in the trifold mirror. The dress was simple and elegant, with a removable organza shawl that added a touch of refinement. Delicate buttons lined the back of the dress, and the smallest train swept on the ground behind me.

I turned to my girlfriends and said, "This one for the ceremony."

Penny was crying. She nodded vigorously. "Yes!"

For the reception, I chose a figure-hugging gown with a deep plunge and ivory lace. It was a touch retro, with dramatic bell sleeves and clean lines. I loved it.

And then I decided I couldn't live without a short, fringed dress with a high neckline and the type of flounce that was made for dancing.

It was ridiculously over-the-top. It was too much. But later, when I was giddy and full of champagne and I blurted out to Rome that he was in fact buying me three wedding dresses, his lips curled into a satisfied smile.

"Good," he said, and all his love and attention and care was wrapped up in that single word. Then, with his fingers tangled in mine, he led me through to the bedroom of our lavish hotel suite, laid me down on the downy comforter, and reminded me of a few of the reasons I loved him quite as much as I did. Then I did the same for him.

It was a great trip.

Four months later, I got to wear all three dresses when we tied the knot. Lina surprised us with matching outfits for Cleo, who slept through the entire ceremony and most of the reception.

My favorite frock ended up being the short, flouncy number; that's the dress Rome helped me take off at the end of the night—which, incidentally, he only did after he bent me over the side of the bed and showed me just how much he loved it when I called him "husband."

It was the best day—and night—of my life. But the best part was that I knew things would only get better.

THE WRONG BOSS

AN EXCLUSIVE PREVIEW OF
COLE AND CARRIE'S STORY

BEFORE

ONE

CARRIE

THE BRIDE LET out an ear-splitting shriek mere moments before wrapping me in a viselike hug. "Carrie!" my cousin and best friend Hailey exclaimed, breathless. "You're saying you finally did it?"

I pulled away and arched a brow. "Hold on a minute. You're making it sound like you've been waiting for me to break up with Derek for ages."

"Longer than ages. Eons. An eternity." She squeezed my arms, her fresh manicure digging into my triceps. "I've been waiting for you to drop that jerk from your life since that night in undergrad when he told you your sequined handkerchief top was trashy."

I held back my wince at the memory. The shame that had burned through me that night was still the beginning of a campaign to chip away at my self-esteem. Derek's words—those and many more like them—were etched on my psyche, and it had happened so long ago. I never did wear that top again. That had only been the beginning of Derek's snide, razor-sharp comments. I concealed the remnants of humiliation behind a grin. "That was six years ago."

My cousin nodded. "Exactly." She wore a satiny white dressing gown, and her hair was sectioned and wrapped around Velcro rollers. A makeup artist laid out her tools in the corner of the room, but Hailey paid her no mind. My cousin's liquid brown eyes were on me as she said, "Please don't go back to him, Carrie. Please. I'm begging you."

"Isn't today supposed to be about love and commitment?" I tried to shrug her hands away and gave her a sardonic smile. "You're getting married in just a few hours and you're telling me to stay single."

She lifted her index finger and pointed it at me, her beautiful fresh nails ready to be photographed alongside the new wedding band that would soon join her engagement ring. "Don't do that. We're not deflecting right now."

"Fine. But can we please talk about something else?"

"Sure. Just as soon as you promise that Derek will never again stink up your life with his foul, dirty socks."

I bit my lip to hide my smile, and Hailey's sparkling eyes told me she knew she'd won the argument. "I hated finding his socks everywhere," I admitted.

"I hated that you gave up and started picking up after him instead of laying down the law like you usually do."

"He broke my spirit," I said, meaning for it to sound like a joke. It came out slightly wobbly, though, and Hailey saw right through me.

"Never again," she intoned.

"Never again," I echoed.

Then my cousin smiled at me, squeezed me in another bone-crushing hug, and turned to the other bridesmaids in the room to announce, "We need more champagne!"

I was swept up into the chatter, laughter, and chaos of wedding preparations. The maid of honor was Hailey's sister and my elder cousin, Julie. She made sure my glass was topped up with bubbles as the hairstylist tackled my mane of thick brown hair.

"I'm happy for you," Julie told me for the millionth time.

I laughed. "Did *anyone* like Derek?"

Julie gave me a flat look, which made me laugh harder. The lightness that had filled me as I drove away from Derek's and my shared apartment in Philadelphia, my old car bursting with all my worldly possessions, swept through me again. Never again would I have to listen to Derek judge my outfits, or my hair, or the way I cut my steak. Never again would I have to pretend to enjoy bitter, overly hoppy IPAs when all I wanted was a sweet, fruity cocktail with an umbrella and a maraschino cherry in it. Never again would I have to cancel plans with girlfriends because Derek moped about being left alone at home.

The anchor chain around my waist was gone.

I could finally pursue my career. I could move to New York City, just like I'd dreamed since my freshman year of undergrad. I could have *sex* again! Real, hot sex with a man who listened to my needs—assuming I could find one. Did men like that exist anywhere outside of the romance novels I'd hidden from Derek's prying eyes? I met my own gaze in the mirror as the hairstylist smoothed my hair into a bouncy blowout. In my new reality, men like that existed, and I would find one. Eventually. When I was ready.

Because I was *free*. I could do *anything*.

"I really wasted all those years of my life with him, didn't I?"

"They won't be wasted if you learned from them," Julie said, a moment before being called away to use her extra-dexterous fingers to help with the thousand buttons marching up the back of Hailey's dress.

I smiled at the stylist in the mirror as she sprayed my hair into submission. Bubbles of champagne burst on my tongue as I sipped my drink. My shoulders relaxed, and I let a smile curl my lips.

Freedom tasted *good*, and the champagne wasn't bad either.

"All done!" the stylist told me, using her fingers to position the front pieces of my hair just so. She squeezed my shoulders and moved on to the next bridesmaid, and I set my glass down while one of the makeup artists approached. Hailey's brides-maids chattered and laughed. The door opened and closed, and I heard my aunt Jackie's scratchy voice behind me just a moment before she appeared in the mirror.

"Heard you finally did it," she said, grinning at me. Her makeup and hair were already done, and she wore a gorgeous dark-blue mother-of-the-bride dress with a boat neck and a perfect bias cut. "Saw all that junk in your car and Hailey told me you finally left that useless lump of meat. I think I'm prouder than the day you graduated college."

"All right, all right, I get it," I replied, huffing. "Derek was no good. Can we please move on?"

"We just want to make sure you know we approve," Hailey called out from her chair.

The makeup artist smiled at us as she waited for Hailey to

face forward again so she could glue false eyelashes on. "Sounds like there's a story here," the artist said.

I watched her place the lashes with expert care, but it was Julie who cut in and said: "There are a hundred stories. None of them are good."

I met my own makeup artist's gaze as she approached with a clean sponge and a bottle of foundation. "You know, I really could have used this pep talk earlier. Why didn't any of you tell me what you really thought of Derek?"

"You've got your mother's stubborn streak," Aunt Jackie said. "No use telling you anything before you come to it on your own."

A chorus of agreement sounded from all corners of the room, and I tilted my head in reluctant agreement. There were a few times, after bad fights, when I'd called Hailey to vent my frustrations. She'd tried to gently suggest that the relationship might not be working, and I'd shut down. After all, I'd spent most of my twenties with Derek; wasn't I in too deep to turn back? I wanted a family, and what if I never found someone to have it with? Wasn't it better to stick with the imperfect relationship I knew?

Now, with the benefit of hindsight—fresh as it might have been—I realized I'd been wrong. It felt too good to be free of my ex's judgmental presence to think that breaking up with him had been anything but the right decision. Time would tell whether it would work out in the long run. Maybe my fears would come true. Maybe I'd never meet anyone who wanted to start a family with me. Maybe having kids and a husband and a quiet, simple, happy life wasn't in the cards for me. Maybe hot men who truly cared about their partner's pleasure only existed in books.

But I'd deal with that later. It was my favorite cousin's wedding, I was single, I was free, and I wouldn't let myself get bogged down with thoughts of the future. Breaking up with my ex had been the hardest thing I'd ever done—but it *was* done.

The makeup artist dusted a tiny bit of powder under my eyes, then stepped back and smiled. "Gorgeous."

I stared at myself in the mirror, straightening my spine. Ducking behind a screen to put on the dress Hailey had chosen for us, I was careful not to disturb my hair or makeup as the slinky, silky peach dress slipped over my skin. The straps were spaghetti-thin. It was a backless dress, with the straps criss-crossing all the way down to nearly the base of my spine, and I was grateful that my small breasts didn't require any kind of support.

Derek's voice popped into my head as I adjusted the fabric over my chest: *"You should get a boob job. I'll pay for it,"* he'd told me just moments after rolling off me the last time we'd slept together, which had been nearly five months ago. He'd pawed at my chest, gathering up the small amount of flesh in his palm before catching the horrified expression on my face, immediately rearing back. *"What?"* he'd protested. *"You know how flat you are. You'd look way better with bigger tits. You can't look at me like that and tell me I'm wrong. Your saving grace is your ass, Carrie. You know it's true."*

Instead of breaking up with him right then and there, I'd researched breast augmentations with a sick feeling in the pit of my stomach. Not because I judged anyone for their cosmetic surgery choices, but because deep down, I didn't want to go under the knife because my boyfriend found me lacking.

I shook off the memory and the shame that still accompanied my reaction to his words. I'd been so twisted up by our relationship, by him, that I'd lost sight of who I was.

No more. I would learn to love myself again, small breasts and all.

A wolf whistle greeted me as I walked out from behind the screen. Hailey beamed at me and announced, "I think we should find someone for Carrie to hook up with tonight."

"Hailey Jane Benson," Aunt Jackie snapped. "Today is your wedding day."

"Yeah, *my* wedding," Hailey quipped, grinning. "It's also the first day of the rest of Carrie's life."

"Let's just focus on getting you down the aisle on time," I said, checking my hair in one of the many mirrors in the room before finding and slipping on the pair of cream heeled sandals to finish the outfit. The back strap of the shoe hit a fresh blister on my heel, and I frowned down at it. That would be sore by the end of the night.

"We can focus on more than one thing," Hailey pointed out.

"Aren't a couple of Seth's groomsmen single?" Julie asked, naming Hailey's college sweetheart and husband-to-be.

"They are," Hailey replied, wiggling her eyebrows at me.

I rolled my eyes, but I was smiling. My cousins always managed to cheer me up, and today was no exception. It's not that I wanted to sleep with someone else right away. It's that I *could*. If I wanted to. Which I wasn't sure I did. But the thought was a dangling thread of possibility just waiting to be tugged. What would unravel if I gave in to temptation?

The smart thing to do would be to take some time to heal. I knew I wasn't ready for a relationship. I probably wasn't even ready for a rebound. I needed to get to know myself, to figure out why I'd let myself be treated like crap for so many years. Derek had found every crack in my confidence and wriggled his way into the very heart of my insecurities. He'd made me feel weak.

What if I fell for a charming, cruel man again? What if I learned nothing from the first serious relationship of my life?

Suddenly the chatter and noise in the bridal suite felt oppressive. I needed some air—needed to get away from all the well-meaning comments. "I'm going to go check on preparations downstairs," I announced to the room at large.

"Come back with a few bottles of champagne!" Julie called out.

Nodding, I pulled open the door, stepped into the hotel hallway, and let the noise of the wedding preparations go silent behind me with the snicking of the latch.

A long sigh slipped through my lips. I was lighter, yes. I was happy to be free of my ex. I was ecstatic for Hailey and grateful to be able to celebrate her wedding.

But it was a whirlwind, and I needed to get my feet back on the ground.

Inhaling deeply, I called the elevator. Once I was downstairs, I poked my head into the ballroom that would house the reception, watching the caterers and DJ set up under the watchful eye of Hailey's wedding planner. My heel's strap rubbed against the wound on my foot as I made my way across the hall to the ceremony space, and I leaned a hand against the wall to adjust it. Once my shoe stopped rubbing at my worsening blister, I glanced at the ceremony space and smiled at my uncle Greg, who was helping one of the workers adjust the lights that would illuminate Hailey and Seth.

Hailey would have a gorgeous wedding. My shoulders relaxed, but I only made it a few steps before the pain of my blister had me clicking my tongue. Glancing down at the wound, I huffed a sigh at the red skin. That's what I got for shoving my feet into the uncomfortable flats I hadn't yet broken in when I was in a rush to pack and get out of my apartment. Then I drove all the way to New Jersey in them, exacerbating the issue.

Small price to pay to escape the relationship, I told myself.

"Hey, kiddo," my uncle said, curling an arm around my shoulders. "Jackie told me you finally dumped the dead weight."

I gave him a half-smile. "Not you too. I had to escape the bridal suite to get away from everyone's comments about my breakup."

He squeezed my shoulder and let his arm drop, having reached the extent of his brand of physical closeness. Uncle Greg wasn't a touchy-feely man, but he'd always been there when I needed him. When my mom passed, Jackie had been a mess, and it was Greg who stepped up and kept us all afloat. They were like surrogate parents to me—as much as anyone could be. My father had left when I was young, and my mother had passed right before I graduated high school. I don't know what I would have done without my aunt and uncle—and without Hailey and Julie. I probably never would have worked up the strength to leave Derek without having them to fall back on.

Smoothing his hand over his white mustache, Greg winked at me. "Always thought you could do better than him."

"You and everyone else, apparently. And yet no one seemed to want to tell me what they really thought at some point over the past six-odd years."

"We had to let you come to your own conclusions," he said. "You've always been your mother's daughter."

A pinch in my heart was a familiar remnant of my grief, but I managed to smile through it. "You calling me stubborn?"

"Muleheaded as all heck," he confirmed shamelessly, laughing. "When Jackie introduced me to her sister, I was relieved I got the nice one."

"Aunt Jackie's the nice one?" I quipped back, skeptical.

Greg chucked my chin. "You're all cut from the same cloth," he said. "Same as my daughters. Wouldn't have it any other way." His eyes were soft as he added, "You girls have everything you need up there? Planner's getting on my case about starting on time. She said we've got less than an hour to get everyone seated."

"I'm getting some more champagne for the room," I told him. "But maybe I'll just wrangle everyone and get them downstairs instead."

"Smart," Uncle Greg replied. The wedding planner appeared in the reception doorway and called his name, and I waved him off with a smile.

I took a step toward the elevator, then winced. I wouldn't be able to walk down the aisle with this blister, let alone dance the afternoon and evening away. Changing directions, I headed for the lobby. The front desk would probably have bandages, but I knew I had special blister bandages in the box of toiletries I'd hastily packed and stuffed into the back of my car. That and medical tape would mean that I wouldn't have to worry about slicing my wound open when all I wanted to do was dance and let loose.

Plan made, I hobbled toward the revolving glass doors and made my way toward the parking lot. The air outside was thick as soup, with summer hanging heavy in the air. Not wanting to be outside in the muggy heat too long, I hurried around the corner—and froze.

Someone was standing next to my car.

No. Not standing.

Someone was *breaking into* my car.

Just. My. Luck.

Moving faster, I stumbled over some loose gravel in time to hear the tinkling of broken glass against asphalt as whoever-it-was smashed my back window.

Of all the days for something like this to happen. Wasn't this just *great*? A breakup followed by a night spent hastily packing all my things while dodging Derek's vitriol, and then a frantic drive from Philly to Newark to make it to the wedding on time, and now this.

I looked at the ragged creature hunched behind my vehicle, and I felt the keen edge of my freedom, my *life*, trying to slice me open one last time. After all the years of emotional and verbal abuse. All the ways I'd made myself smaller to fit into the box Derek made for me. All the dreams I'd set aside.

Now some jerk was going to rob me? On my favorite cousin's wedding day?

I just—couldn't let it happen. I was so *sick* of being taken advantage of. Sick of being beaten down. No one was going to break into my car and steal my stuff.

I wasn't small, or weak, or scared.

For the first time in a long, long time, I was *angry*. Furious at myself for allowing Derek to treat me the way he had. Enraged that it had taken me so long to leave him. Incensed that some asshole saw all my belongings and decided he'd help himself.

"Hey!" I yelled.

The man looked up. He wore a dingy gray hoodie and a black baseball cap. I couldn't see much of his features at this distance except for a scraggly beard and hollow cheeks, but he saw me hobble-sprinting in his direction, and I could tell there was a calculation happening behind his eyes.

There was no way I'd win in a fight between the two of us. I was downright scrawny, and he looked street-hardened and mean.

But that was *my* car he was breaking into. *My* worldly possessions he was trying to steal.

Hell. No.

His arm reached in through the broken back window.

"Put it back!" I yelled, arms pumping as I ran toward him. My heels clacked against the asphalt, but it didn't matter that my footwear wasn't appropriate for a street fight. "Put that back right now!"

He glanced up at me again—and smiled. He *smiled*. Brown, broken teeth cut a jagged line across his mouth, and the first inkling of fear trickled through me. My anger burned it away.

Momentum still propelled me forward, and I was too far gone to stop. Too enraged by the sight of him trying to steal from me. Too tired of people walking all over me when all I wanted was a good, modest life.

I'd never asked for much. All I wanted was a decent relationship, a steady job, and eventually a couple of kids and the quiet sort of happiness that came from a life of simple pleasures. I wanted contentment. I didn't need money or glamour or fame.

And yet.

And yet at every turn, life drop-kicked me in the ass. I was *over it*.

I'd fight him. I'd fight a drug-addicted, desperate person for whatever he'd stolen while I wore a beautiful bridesmaid's dress, because it was *wrong*. It might ruin my cousin's wedding. It might delay the strict start time. It might land me in the hospital.

But I was so fucking *sick* of feeling powerless that I couldn't stop. Good sense fled my mind and was replaced with white-hot rage.

Rage that exploded into something bigger when I saw what the thief held in his fist. My hand-carved teak memory box dangled from his hand. Broken, dirty fingernails clutched the intricate carvings on the lid, and horror swept through me.

Not that box. He couldn't take it. Anything but that box. It didn't even have anything valuable in it, other than a single earring missing its twin.

But it was valuable to me. It had the ticket stubs from my monthly movie dates with Mom. A card from my thirteenth birthday when she'd written me a note that never failed to make me cry. A photo of her holding me in the hospital, minutes after I'd been born.

That box held everything I cared about. It carried the last

remnants of my mother's relationship with me. It was everything I had left of her.

"Put it back!" I repeated, voice breaking.

The man set his shoulders. His smile widened, and now I was close enough to see the devil in his eyes. He stuffed the box in his hoodie pocket and widened his stance. His beard was greasy, and his cheeks were sunken and pale. Whoever he was, he was deep in the mire of an addiction.

I couldn't fight him. If I did, I would lose.

But I couldn't *not* fight him. I couldn't let him get away with the only scraps I had left of my mother.

"It doesn't even have anything worth taking in it," I said, slowing to a stop near the hood of my car. The length of the vehicle separated us.

"Pretty box full of pretty things," he replied.

"Please."

"Come closer and ask me nicely." He reached into his pocket and took out the box, waving it back and forth. Taunting me.

Vision blurring with tears, I curled my hands into fists. I was wearing sandals with a four-inch heel and a satin dress, and my hair and makeup had been perfected by professionals. I didn't know how to fight—let alone fight someone who looked like they ate desperation for breakfast, lunch, and dinner.

But the wooden box waved back and forth, and the addict's taunting, broken smile pierced me like the tip of a poisoned lance.

The pain of it shook my bones, and I knew what I had to do. That box meant more to me than anything. I'd put myself in the hospital if I had to. I'd get on my knees and beg for forgiveness if I ended up ruining Hailey's wedding, as long as I got that box back.

I wasn't going to let this man walk away with it. Not when this was supposed to be my fresh start, when I had nowhere to live after this weekend, no one to lean on, nowhere to go. Not when my past was a graveyard of mistakes, when everyone took great glee in telling me that they'd known my only long-term relationship was terrible right from the start.

I didn't care about anything in that car. Not really. Nothing except that hand-carved teak box containing scraps of paper and a single little earring.

Calm descended over me. I let my knees go soft, and I prepared myself to go into battle. The man holding my memory box smiled wider, slipping my most treasured possession back into his pocket. Then he made a little flick with his fingers, a "come at me" gesture that told me he was enjoying himself, and I knew this was it.

I exploded into movement. It would only take a second to reach him, and then he'd know that he underestimated me.

Just like Derek. Just like my aunt and uncle and cousins who didn't think I could handle the truth. Like the bosses who had passed me over for promotions, the colleagues who had dismissed my ideas because I was just a silly little administrator in their big, fancy company.

I would *not* let this dirty, drug-addled thief underestimate me too.

But just as I started running at him, the man's gaze shifted to look over my shoulder. His eyes widened, and by the time I reached my back bumper, he'd spun on his dirty sneakers and was sprinting halfway across the parking lot, my box of treasures gripped in his grimy fist.

A wordless, rage-filled yell tore through my throat. Then I heard the pounding footsteps.

A moment after that, a man dressed all in black went sprinting past me, chasing the degenerate who'd stolen the last pieces of my mother. Startled, I stared at the sharp line of his jaw as he sprinted past, his dark hair fluttering off his forehead. Then all I could see was the back of him, spine straight, arms pumping, shiny black shoes pounding the pavement as he chased the thief.

"Who the hell are *you*?" I yelled, even though it didn't matter. Hopping as pain lanced through the back of my heel—stupid blister—I set my jaw and redoubled my pace.

Whoever he was, he'd scared away the thief and lost me my chance at getting my memory box back. So either he would help me get it back, or he'd get a piece of my mind. Wisps of anger fluttered around me as I attempted to follow the two men. With every step, I fell behind.

Despair caught me in its grip. The thief was turning a corner and moving out of sight, and the man in black didn't seem to be gaining any ground. I had to catch them. *Had to.*

But fate had other ideas. As I put on a burst of speed—the final bit of energy I had left—my spike heel got stuck in a storm drain, my ankle rolled, and I face-planted in the middle of the hotel parking lot.

He's her knight in a black suit. And neither of them is happy about it.

Get it here: https://geni.us/TheWrongBoss

ABOUT THE AUTHOR

Lilian Monroe adores writing swoonworthy heroes and the women who bring them to their knees. She loves making people laugh and is eternally grateful to have found people who share her sense of humor.

When she's not writing, she's reading (or rereading) a book, walking, lifting weights, or attempting to play the guitar with very limited success.

She grew up in Canada but now lives in Australia with her Irish husband. He frequently asks to be used as a cover model for her books, and she's not quite sure whether or not he's joking.

ALSO BY LILIAN MONROE

For all books, visit:

www.lilianmonroe.com

Manhattan Billionaires

Big Bossy Mistake

Big Bossy Trouble

Big Bossy Problem

Big Bossy Surprise

Forbidden Boss

The Wrong Boss

Dirty Boss

Tempting Boss

More surprise babies!

Knocked Up by the CEO

Knocked Up by the Single Dad

Knocked Up...Again!

Knocked Up by the Billionaire's Son

Yours for Christmas

Bad Prince

Heartless Prince

Cruel Prince

Broken Prince

Wicked Prince

Wrong Prince

Lone Prince

Ice Queen

Rogue Prince

Small Towns are the best towns

Four Steps to the Perfect Revenge

Four Steps to the Perfect Fake Date

Working with the Enemy

Faking It with the Firefighter

Conquest

Craving

Combat

Calamity

Small Town + Later-in-Life Romance

Dirty Little Midlife Crisis

Dirty Little Midlife Mess

Dirty Little Midlife Mistake

Dirty Little Midlife Disaster

Dirty Little Midlife Debacle

Dirty Little Midlife Secret

Dirty Little Midlife Dilemma

Dirty Little Midlife Drama

Dirty Little Midlife (fake) Date

Filthy Little Midlife Fling

Merry Little Midlife Matchmaker

Forty and Fighting Dirty

Brother's Best Friend Romance

Shouldn't Want You

Can't Have You

Don't Need You

Won't Miss You

He'll do anything to protect his woman

His Vow

His Oath

His Word

Enemies to Lovers/Workplace Romance

Hate at First Sight

Loathe at First Sight

Despise at First Sight

Fake Engagement Romance

Engaged to Mr. Right

Engaged to Mr. Wrong

Engaged to Mr. Perfect

<u>**Mountain Man Romance**</u>

Lie to Me

Swear to Me

Run to Me

<u>**Doctor's Orders**</u>

Doctor O

Doctor D

Doctor L